Devil's Divide

Also by Jeffrey M. Anderson
Little God Blues
Black Widow Blues

JEFFREY M. ANDERSON
Devil's Divide

IKEN PRESS

Published by Iken Press
www.ikenpress.com

First published 2017

All rights reserved. No part of this work may be reproduced or stored in an information retrieval system (other than for purposes of review) without the express permission of the publisher in writing.

The right of Jeffrey M. Anderson to be identified as author of this work has been asserted by him in accordance with the Copyright, Designs and Patents Act 1988.

This is a work of fiction. Names, characters, businesses, places, events and incidents are either the products of the author's imagination or used in a fictitious manner. Any resemblance to actual persons, living or dead, or actual events is purely coincidental.

Text © 2017 Jeffrey M. Anderson
www.jeffreymanderson.com

ISBN 13: 978-0-9909795-4-8

Designed and typeset by Mousemat Design Limited
www.mousematdesign.com

Printed and bound by Createspace
www.createspace.com

For Robert and Tanya Anderson

PART ONE

Chapter 1

"If money isn't loosened up, this sucker could go down..."
President Bush declared Thursday as he watched the $700 billion bailout package fall apart before his eyes..."
President George W Bush, as quoted in the New York Times,
25 Sep 2008

Play the game with all your heart, but only if you invented it. Clay Holloway wrote that in *The Coin Age*, his mostly-forgotten book about the Void, a time when the sucker really did go down – when, on Red Tuesday, the invisible hand reached for the invisible switch and billions were compelled to live in candlelight.

Four years before the publication of his book, and seven months after that bloody Tuesday, Clay sat in a paint-encrusted rowboat, his bike tilted against his lap, being ferried across the upper reaches of the San Francisco Bay. His rower was a gruff woman with an overlarge head, red-framed glasses and short-cropped gray hair.

"You row folks all the time?"

She paused, her oars in the air, and scowled as if at a bad pick-up line. She returned to her rhythm, her monumental face rocking back and forth to the pulling of her oars. "Two Jacks, right?" she called out, in sea captain mode.

"Don't worry, I have them."

"And that's a bargain. Crowbarring a big lug like you across."

"They won't be waiting for me on the other side?"

"You think I'm selling you down the river?" She pulled up her oars and glared at him; her smile broke like a street opening up in an earthquake.

The creaking of her oarlocks resumed, the frowning block of her forehead coming at him, going away, at him, away, no sign of effort. "They'll be waiting for you all right," she said, "waiting for you to come to them. Like spiders with their webs. That's how they'll catch you."

Clay surveyed the Carquinez Bridge that spanned the strait of that name. It was the first checkpoint on I-80 east. There were many; he knew that. The USG insisted its citizens stayed put; they didn't want hundreds of thousands of Bay Area residents descending on the Central Valley breadbasket like a storm of locusts. In its contract with its constituents, the US Government, known as USG, often as useless G, was a non-negotiable dictum: we will feed you; you will stay put.

There were two militiamen up on the bridge having a smoke, admiring the view. One of them made a windshield wiper motion with his right hand. Good luck, you'll need it, that ironical waving seemed to say.

"You think we'll lift ourselves out of this mess?" he asked, more to watch that scowl break than for any kind of answer.

Her face turned soft, beatific. "I like it the way it is."

"How's that?"

"You ever been poor? Stood outside a restaurant watching the fancy folks snapping their soft fingers at the waiters?" She left it there for several strokes. "So now they can snap all they want. Snap. Snap. Snap. Finally, we've got some equality in this country."

Beads of sweat appeared on her forehead. Clay, half-hypnotized by the closer/further away rocking action of her face, searched the opposite shore for an obvious landing spot.

"Where're you headed?"

"Sacramento. See my Mom. Haven't heard from her."

"Uh huh."

"Gotta try." He didn't owe her any explanation, regretted giving one.

"Fat tires, huh. Now there's an original idea! Go off-road and outflank those webs."

He glanced at his mountain bike. Her pudgy bare feet rested under the back wheel, next to his knapsack. Her little toe was on a higher level than the others and flexed, almost like a wink, in a rhythm counter to her strokes. They were approaching the point, a dilapidated jetty fifty yards away. She shipped her oars and let the boat drift. As a businessman, he knew all about squeezes. Stop short and renegotiate.

"Let's see the two Jacks." Her upturned hand became a turtle on its back.

He picked them out of his shirt pocket, unfolded them, snapped them taut, handed them over.

"I told you two Jacks."

It had taken the USG desperate months of bickering about the new ten and twenty dollar bills until finally Congress compromised with the Dual Mug solution. The GOP insisted Reagan should be on the twenty because he was worth more. The Democrats insisted on Kennedy because he was there first. Worth more/there first, worth more/there first – the debate raged on while the nation sank further into the mire. Finally, they reached a compromise: equal runs of each mug on both denominations. The nation now had the New Dollar, consisting of the Gipper and the Kendy (aka Jacks). There were stores that only accepted one or the other. In liberal San Francisco, you led with your Gips in the hope some sucker would take them.

"They're both legal tender," Clay said, taking his Gippers back, handing over the Kendies.

She rocked up on one cheek and put the money in the back pocket of her jeans. "Tender? Like a slab of meat that's been pounded and pounded 'til all its muscle fibers are broken? Hah." She started rowing again. It was low tide and the acrid, rotting smell of the approaching mud flats stung his nostrils. The jetty just about reached the water line, some of its walkway boards hanging down from its beams.

"Careful out of the boat. I'll hand you your bike once you're on the ladder. Cross to the other side. Walk along the beam, far left okay. Whatever you do, stay away from the middle."

"Thanks."

"Tell you what," she called up to him on his rickety perch on the jetty, "when you get turned back, when you slink on home, I'll take your Gips on the return trip."

That first night he spent just off the appropriately-named Refugio Valley Road, and had a late breakfast at a USG food bank in Vallejo. The next checkpoint was just short of the coastal range, and only truck convoys were being allowed through. Cars made angry U-turns, dipping down through the dirt median and back west from where they came. Where did these folks get their gas? Even doctors were on bikes these days.

Rumor was you could do a private deal at the checkpoint. Accidentally drop a wad of New Dollars and sashay on by as the guard bent over to inspect the cash. Not here though. There were too many people, too many militiamen for a deal to be anything other than public. Besides, was the New-D still worth stooping for?

He'd have to outflank the checkpoint, climb into the warm brown hills of the Coastal Range, and bump down the far side into the Central Valley. If it took him, say, two days to reach civilization he could survive on his current provisions, two water bottles and a fistful of standard-issue government g-bars, confections of rolled oats, sunflower seeds, protein powder, nuts, honey or corn syrup, and, if the gossip were true, saltpeter – potassium nitrate – supposedly put in army chow for decades to dampen the libido. Already the idle populace had created a noticeable bump in pregnancies.

In the failing light and on into the night he climbed to the higher reaches of the western side of the Coastal Range. He unrolled his sleeping bag in a fold high up in the hills, and managed a few hours' sleep before the sun took the chill out of the morning and he could press on toward the final summit.

Two "final summits" later he was walking his bike up a steep ascent, surely the final final one, when he ran straight into two privates on patrol toting M16's.

"Where're you headed, friend?"

"My mother. Down in the valley. She's not doing too well."

"How do you know that?"

He didn't. "USGmail." This government-run email system had been operational for two months, too short a time to take hold, but the privates might not know that.

"You should have told them that at I-80. What you're doing up here's illegal."

"Used to be a free country."

All three took time out for rueful smiles.

"You got a mother?" Clay asked.

"Nah, I crawled outta the swamp." The kid was early twenties. His crew cut and government-issue glasses made him look like the star of a 50's science class. He relied on a wry smile, everything an interesting game, everything with an angle.

"And what about you?" Clay asked the quiet one, a freckle-faced redhead with rubbery lips and bulbous bloodshot eyes, even younger, late teens, half Clay's age.

Red turned to Crew Cut for an answer.

"Well, I don't know about you fellas, but I come from a time when mothers meant something." Which was rich – he'd been ignoring his mom for years – well, that's the way it felt. Susan handled all the day-to-day stuff. Clay just sent the right cards at the right times, when his sister told him to, and showed up on the standard occasions.

The kids studied the ground.

Crew Cut said, "I've gotta tell you, if you try to head thataway," he nodded towards the valley to the east, "our orders are to shoot. Take you down with our chimerical bullets." He had the erect posture of a career soldier, drilled to follow orders. "Howie, you remember training? Thighs or lower for US citizens? Got that?"

"On a bike?" Howie said. "Jeez." He shook his head, a little too vigorously, "Them chimericals hurt bad. Real bad."

"I imagine they do," Clay said. He had struggled to get this far. His legs ached, his stomach had had just about enough of oat bars, and his eyes were scratchy from lack of sleep. Here he stood on the verge of a downhill plunge that, in a few hours, could empty him out into the valley. So close.

"Well, God bless you boys."

"Hey!" Howie called.

Clay ran his bike toward the crown of the summit and hopped on. Chimerical meant pretend, right? Crew Cut knew that, but what about Red? Now he was moving, working up the gears as the Central Valley came into view, the warming air tickling his sunburnt his face, his stiff legs knotting up from the sudden unprepared exertion.

A rock fragment kicked up and nipped at his calf, followed a split second later by the crack/zing of rifle fire. God damn, privates shooting at their own citizens was just about believable, but ones not getting paid?

He pumped furiously to get over the approaching rise, plunged over it, too steep, way too steep, bike wavering, wobbling. Rocks all around, baring their fangs. Shit.

Down and down, faster, weaving and wobbling, rocks all around, unavoidable. Just there a boulder, angled like a ski jump. He hit the jump, braked hard but still too fast, pivoted at a small crack at the top, a 180 so sharp it almost sent him backwards, shot along the side of the boulder, just below a chasm. If he could get more speed down the boulder to a nose-like outcrop he might ski jump clear of the yawning gap and make that flat top rock down there. Now! Straight down the boulder, out and out, silently screaming as he plummeted seven feet. Bang – front tire hit the flat top rock, back tire short and into its side. He flew superman style, bikeless, feet coming up over his head, towards a dull horn of a rock. Hurtling in slow motion toward impact, he rolled his shoulder, while desperately trying to keep his feet from pulling his body upside down. He hit the rock hard, knapsack first, a hard stab into his back, bounced off the rock in a three quarter roll along the hillside.

He lay there stunned, alive and mostly pain-free. He could move his legs, his arms, heart rate still at hummingbird speed. Besides a stinging pain from his skinned palms, and a dull deep throb in his back, he seemed okay. No blood or broken bones.

"All right!"

Cowboy whoops.

Three privates sat smoking in the shade of a large boulder up above.

Clay took his time standing up and re-assembling himself. The smokers pulled on their smokes and ambled down.

"Brother, you must be in one hell of a hurry."

"That's some pretty fancy riding. When you hit the top of the big rock? Well, I thought you were going to hit the valley the hard way."

Willfully ignoring the dull throb in his back and the burning in his lacerated hands, Clay scanned the lower reaches for his bike. He'd have to hope it had been as lucky.

"One of your eager beaver pals took a few pops at me."

"Friend, no disrespect, but you ain't worth a bullet. Those're for terrorists and foreigners."

The privates helped him find his bike just on the other side of a gentle fold. The back fender, a thin fiberglass awning, was twisted out of all use, the basket welded to his rack badly skewed. The handlebars were crooked. The front rim had taken the impact of the boulder. It resembled a lazy lasso.

"You ride up here for recreation?" one of the privates said.

"Recreation? That might not be the right word."

"You're based where, Green Valley?"

The senior private – he was wearing an army uniform unlike his comrades in tee shirts with US Army printed on them – scanned the wide hazy expanse of the Central Valley as if searching for Clay's house.

"Closer to…" Damn, all he needed to say was, Yes, Green Valley. He needed the name of another town on the eastern side, one he'd pretend to be returning to. "Er… I think the fall's done my head in. Fairfield."

Get-with-the-program, said the lead private's look.

"What's the bedroll for?" asked one of the juniors.

"Ballast," he nodded, straight-faced.

They let him go. The front wheel just about turned after he unclasped the brake calipers and stomped on the rim to get it in some kind of true. He humped banged-up body and bike, east toward civilization, testy from lack of sleep, the wearing-away of adrenalin, and a hunger intolerant of oat bars.

Snarled at by the ferrywoman, patronized by boy/men, shot at, smashed by rocks – in the first forty miles? He had an equal distance to go to reach his mother. If he ever got there.

Chapter 2

The family in front of Clay were listening to a transistor radio, an analysis of the President's speech urging Congress to approve a return to the gold-backed dollar. He sounded more angry than optimistic. This had been less than a month after the Meltdown, and the food lines had continued to grow. The disaster retained its B-movie values: the strange faces, more Felliniesque than famous, the cliché dialog, and a plot that strained credulity. Citizens shuffling forward to be fed, confused and accepting, like steers unaware of their meat pie futures.

It had been such a quick fall. The knockdown blow, the world-wide stock market Meltdown. The US economy back up on one knee, like a boxer gathering his wits, and finding he had none. Not out cold, just too scrambled and lethargic to challenge gravity any more.

A woman in line behind him said to her companion, "You know what this whole thing reminds me of? My divorce. That time before you give up, when you close your eyes and squeeze your hands into fists and will yourself to fall in love all over again."

Did that sound familiar? Madeline had left him nearly four months ago, even though she claimed she still loved him. Two months after that she'd gone back home to Boston. She needed time, she said, time to get back in touch with a period in her life when "everything worked". Now everyone had nothing but time, a dull limbo, and no action, unless you counted the endless shifting forward of the food line.

Forty-five minutes later he arrived at the food. The transistor radio had been turned off, either to conserve batteries or in disgust. Now came the part where you had to confirm your status as shiftless mendicant, and the government's as hard-boiled benefactor. Meals were bought with your best government smile. A combination of "yes I hardly deserve this but one must subsist" and "I sure do appreciate your work here, unpaid as it is". You had to state your choice. The stern volunteers did not allow for generalities, none of your "that one there" or "the yellow one". No, you must state your choice clearly.

"The Coolidge, please."

To underline its beneficence all USG soups, casseroles and stews, ladled out of huge pots, were named after Presidents. A fish stew was called The Nixon; chili, the Coolidge; macaroni and cheese, The Hoover, but in California also The Dam; goulash (paprika but no lamb, only chicken) was The Garfield. The least popular by far was the Carter, a bland vegetarian stew. On a day they were rumored to be serving the Carter you had to arrive early before the USG ran out of the other slop.

For a time, life wound on as if a dull holiday, the vacationers forced indoors by the harsh economic weather. In real life however, vacations must end and one must re-engage with purpose, dedication, direction. Meaning. This interlude was not sustainable. Something had to give, as it had in other cities, where rumors swirled of violent gangs, assaults and abductions. Who knew if they were true? The USG radio played down any disturbances.

Winter arrived. Standing in torrential rain in San Francisco was an ordeal, but how were they coping in snow-bound Boston? Madeline's last emails, sent just before the internet crashed for good, contained any number of conflicting signals: she missed him; she was sleeping better; she had reconnected with school friends; there was no one like him she could *talk* to; she missed California; she didn't miss her friends there as much as she would have thought. Tortured by her indecision, maybe there still was a chance. He had a wife in the same way that he had a job – Executive Director of a non-profit called Childlift – on hold, pending developments.

Once every few weeks he cycled down the deserted freeway to Susan. His sister was campaigning for him to visit Mom over the Coastal Range in the valley. "If you can cycle down to me," she'd nag, "a round trip of fifty miles, how hard can Sacramento be?" Sue handled all of Mom's affairs, employing Mrs. Hernandez to go in twice a day to cook meals, take care of the house, and keep an eye on Mom's increasingly addled wits. "Clay, it's only eighty miles, and I haven't heard from Mrs. H. in months."

"No surprise there. What's she going to do, dial on a landline for hours when she's busy looking after Mom?" Communication was nearly impossible. With millions of idle people wanting to call, to surf, to tweet, to poke, the internet groaned and gasped and sputtered. Less than a month after the Meltdown, late-October, the internet died. Cell phones crashed even earlier. Landlines still worked if you were prepared to dial for hours. Getting a connection was like winning the lottery. Over the first four months the USG tried to get the internet functional twice, pleading for limited use, but the hundreds of millions of idle surfers, all on the beach with their boards waiting for the same wave, made that untenable.

"Sue, we've been through this. The roads are closed. They've got the army patrolling the highways, roads and hills. They say it's dangerous beyond the Bay Area."

Here it came, that disappointed frown, the you're-better-than-that face. He finally reached the stage, six months into the Void, where he had resigned himself to his mission, but he made her work for it first. Big brother genes. An aversion to being bossed around.

It was a trap though. If by some miracle Mrs. Hernandez, out of a sense of obligation and a gullible belief in Sue's IOUs, was still taking care of Mom, why she'd clap her hands on his arrival, hang up her apron, kiss Elaine good-bye and that would be the end of her. And that's assuming she was still around. Either way what could he do, with no credible exit line, no wife or job to go back to? To ride to Sacramento was to move there.

Chapter 3

"Actually, I haven't seen Elaine recently," Pastor Purley said. He was a large floppy man with an overheated face and a shaggy mop of white hair, a veritable dandruff factory. He had a way of sharing his respiratory challenges, punctuating his talk with wheezing, heaving breaths. Discreetly, Clay wiped his hand on the back of his cargo shorts, the pastor's handshake as clammy as August on Bourbon Street.

"These other people living in Mom's house, who are they?"

"This can happen."

"They wouldn't talk. Or didn't understand English."

"The police, what's left of them, can barely cope with your basic murders, let alone fun and games with houses."

"If the police can't be bothered, I'll – "

"Don't. Don't go back there. These people move in packs. They take over neighborhoods as a unit; they are prepared to defend them as one. Elaine probably lived in a nice house, three, maybe four bedrooms? That's more than she needs, so it is taken away from her. I know you're angry, but anything you do will be futile... and dangerous."

"What is this, communism? Each according to his need?"

"I think you'd call it anarchy."

He hit his hand against his thigh in frustration. What kind of new world was this? Where riding eighty miles to see Mom became a life-risking enterprise? What chance did he have taking on an organized gang? "Where is my mother?"

The Reverend performed a consummate Christian shrug, such matters small compared to God's ultimate rewards. "She's probably over in Rancho Duro." He smiled religiously, tiny before his God, big in his mission. "It's on the other side of 99." *The wrong side of 99.*

"So, these folks that have appropriated Mom's house, I should turn the other cheek?"

The good Reverend smiled. "Some would take comfort that the Day of Judgment will weigh heavily upon those who stole Elaine's house from her. Yes, I know, you are not prepared to wait that long. You are a man of action. My advice is to focus on your mother. She will need your help. That should be your action plan."

"I'm not going to forgive those bastards, if that's what you're aiming for."

The Reverend rolled out his Tolerant Smile. He had made the sign of the cross at enough christenings, weddings and funerals to be acquainted with the long game – that each of God's children has but one turn through this world, and one chance to do a deal for their souls. Time was on his side. "Sacramento has its rough areas. We are on the border of one of them. So your decision on whether to forgive or not? You may not have to make it here, in this world. These people have guns."

Rancho Duro had started in the early Noughties as a homeless encampment on the hardscrabble ground of a demolished grain elevator. It expanded, partially contracted, expanded more as the nation's economy fizzled and sparked. By the time Clay arrived it had swelled to twelve acres of tents, plywood huts, and camper shells only a mile and half west of his mother's house.

He approached a woman sitting on a hard chair unraveling a sweater.

"Your mother? She'll be an OBG," the lady said, examining his bike. "So I'd start over at Pacheco."

He removed his sunglasses, met her eyes. "I'm not sure I follow you."

"Pacheco's so-called because it's near to the elementary school of that name. It's over in that direction." She pointed. "They got better facilities there for folks like your mom."

"Like my mom?"

"No offense, but, what are you, sir? Pushing forty? So your mom, she's gonna be an OBG."

He took a deep breath. He couldn't blame the grim reality of Rancho Duro on this woman. He'd just have to hope that Mom didn't live here. But where did that leave him, and more crucially, her? "An OBG?"

"OBG's your Oldie But Goodie. Now, if you jog left of the camper over there and try to weave your way straight, when you get to the mare turn left, keep asking for Pacheco."

"The mare?"

"Yeah, the mare."

"What's a horse doing in the middle of… this?" His arm swept across a swath of the plywood, canvas and tin can city.

The woman laughed so hard she dropped her half-undone sweater. He waited to find out what was so funny. Finally, the last few spasms subsided and she said, "Not clip clop mare, speech-making mayor."

"The Mayor of Sacramento lives here?" Why did he feel dizzy?

"No, Mayor of RD. Once upon a time she ran for Big Mayor, you know, Sacramento itself. That was some time ago."

"What's with the sweater?" he said, after a long sigh; something about her busy hands, the sweater disappearing, got on his nerves.

She shook her head "No yarn now so I just keep knitting and unknitting. Kinda sums it all up, doesn't it?"

He made his way in and out of the make-shift alleys. OBG's, young families, teenagers hanging out, sullen prime of life unemployed men and women, all engaged in keep-busy activities, cards, knitting, darts, guitar picking, scavenging projects, rock tossing games. In no time he had perfected the Rancho Duro nod, curt, sympathetic, with echoes of "can you believe this?" and "we'll get there".

He had no trouble finding the Mayor's tent. It attracted a flow of people to the end of an orderly line. The Mayor was a large black woman. She sat in a deckchair in the shade, listening, nodding, but taking in the scene. He returned her vague bow. Hers said, You'll be in this line before it's over.

After nearly an hour a card player escorted him to a cart man whose job was to deliver USG meals to the sedentary OBGs.

"I know an Elaine," the cart man said. "She's in a camper over in WTF. You're her son?"

He grunted and nodded at the same time. So, Mom actually lived here, unless it was a different Elaine, living in the California equivalent of a South African township.

"Her house has been taken from her."

"Mine too. We tried to fight it, Hetty and me, but…"

The walk took forever. Abruptly his guide rolled out his hand and stepped back. That lady sitting right there was Mom? No, it couldn't be? His mother, always a stylish dresser, wearing a shiny blue track suit? He could imagine one of her wry comments. *I'm too old to go out for the Olympics.* She sat in a fold-up chair in a strip of sunlight between her camper shell and the tent next door, her right arm resting along the chair, hand dangling, her lapis lazuli ring catching the light. At least the locusts hadn't stripped her of that.

"Mom." She wasn't asleep but didn't respond. A blue tarp threw a bouncy submarine light over the dirt area in front of the camper and a picnic table, on top of which sat a bony-faced youth, late teens, with quick jittery eyes and long brown hair that fell lankly from a haphazard central part.

"Mom," he said again.

She rubbed her forehead as if a rash was there. The young man hopped down and ambled over to her. "I think you've had enough sun, Elaine. Let's get you some shade."

"Where've you been, Bruce?"

"Been right here."

The kid got her to her feet. The way he handled her, the contact familiar, gentle. "Elaine?" he said, after he'd relocated her under the dancing blue tarp world. "Elaine? This man just called you Mom."

Bruce disappeared into the camper, left Clay alone with her.

"Remember me, Mom?"

"'Course I do." She squinted at him uncertainly.

"I've cycled all the way from San Francisco to see you," he said to fill the silence.

Bruce came back out of the camper with a fold-out chair, handed it over.

"And who exactly are you, Bruce?"

Bruce raised his hands in mock arrest. "Just a neighbor comes by from time to time."

"Bruce here looks after my interests." A sudden burst of clarity, which took her more focused eyes to her son. "C'mon son, give your mother a peck or two."

Already she was fading, her eyes clouding over. A rank and musky odor as he kissed her, no trace of her normal perfume. The knees of her track suit were stiffly accordioned, her zip-up top stained with food.

"Are you getting enough to eat, Mom?"

"Uh huh."

"What happened to Mrs. Hernandez?"

"Does she live around here?" she asked Bruce.

"She's probably back in Mexico," Bruce said. He sat on the picnic table, body hunched, throwing his face forward, gaunt in the tarp's blue light.

"Mexico's better than here?"

"Just as fu... messed up, only they've had like two hundred years to know how to deal with it."

Clay looked up into the clear sky, trying to come up with more questions, trying to convince himself they were worth asking. A low chatter from the tent next door, the sound of cards being shuffled, and from somewhere a baby starting to cry with the loud insistent whine of a being that has figured out that what it needs is not on offer.

"What about medication?" he asked Bruce. "She needs that thyroid drug."

"Levothyroxine. Only factory that's making it is over in India. There's some boat supposed to be on its way. I check every week. Don't I Elaine?"

Elaine followed a starling as it coasted to a perch on a tent line next door, her eyes clouding over again.

"But what about now?"

"We're doing every other day until the ship comes in." Bruce glanced at him, met his eyes. "Don't worry, Mrs. Muller approved it. She's the retired nurse that covers WTF."

"WTF?"

"This part of RD is called that 'cause its next to the Waste-to-Fuel plant."

"And the boat's on the water? You know that?" He sighed. Why was he giving Bruce such an inquisition? This overgrown gamer had obviously done a lot more for Mom than he had. "I can't believe it's the third world that's coming to our rescue."

"Yeah…"

After the first world collapsed, the lesser countries coped best. Now the USA depended on Indian medicines, Philippine medical supplies, Turkish cigarettes (military only), Brazilian bullets, Bangladeshi clothes, Mexican shoes, and the Greek ships that carried them.

"Why's he around here all the time?" he asked Mom after Bruce had ambled off the set.

"It's his camper." Another flash of clarity. Her eyes sharpened for a second, almost as if an actor aware of her part.

"Where does he live?"

She gave him a sly look, eyes searching hesitantly, back to guessing. "Here?" More question than answer.

"As in sleeps here?"

"Sleeps?" She looked into his eyes, suspecting a trick question. Maybe deep down, somewhere, she understood her addled state, one in which he could ask the same questions, talk about people they'd just talked about, ask the same questions a third time and for her it was all new.

"Sue sends her love, Mom," he said for the second time, hoping for some form of recognition.

She frowned tightly, sensing someone important, telegraphing that. "Your daughter? Sue?"

"I know my darn daughter," she said with dull eyes.

"And Mrs. Hernandez – don't you remember her?"

The question must have triggered an association with her former house.

"It's better here," she muttered. "People are so friendly." That last sentence recited as if from a tag line.

Running out of questions, even third-time-around ones, he got up and paced around the blue sub-tarp world with the trance-like surrender to unseen forces that you get at a long airport delay. An interminable time later the light softened, a chill crowding into the pleasant afternoon. She used to be so sharp. Any time she said "that's interesting" or "oh, really" it signaled something witty or trenchant. If he brought a new girlfriend home, Elaine had a way of half-paying attention, leafing through a magazine, and making the judgment in minutes. "I wouldn't want you to think it is all about making a lot of money," one girlfriend said, a would-be corporate lawyer. "And what is it you would want me to think, dear?"

From the camper door came a stale sweet fruity smell – vomit? He dived in and opened the camper windows, put the cover back on the slop bucket, came out for air, plunged back in to do more cleaning. Her bed was up high, over the truckless truck cab. The sheets! It shouldn't have been surprising that they hadn't been washed in months. Still, it was.

Mom wasn't hungry, swatted irritably at his spoon, dignity insulted, when he tried to feed her. He stayed with her even as his stomach tightened in hunger. A middle-aged woman in a clean track suit and a weight-of-the-world smile arrived. "I'm Mrs. Flaherty," she said to him.

"Clay Holloway, Elaine's son."

She nodded, all business now, sitting down across from Mom. "Now Elaine I just finished that stew. You know what? It's a lot better than yesterday's. I liked it, that I did. Give it a try, why don't you. Just a bite. I'd be interested in what you think."

A next-door neighbor, Karen, noticing that Clay had missed the dinner call, escorted him to a USG food substation. "That way we can have a little chinwag." On the way he grilled her on all manner of basic questions about RD. Sanitation, toilets, medicine. "Think of a hobo camp and you'd not be far wrong," she said, in the hoarse rasp of an ex-smoker, as they threaded their way out of WTF and over toward Pacheco.

"Oh lord I miss 'em," she said of her cigarettes, a woman who felt that all silences needed filling. "This here Void will be the life of me." Her gravelly laugh tipped over into a cough.

On the way back from the substation – it served only snacks and you'd better have a compelling reason for wanting them – they talked about what people did at RD to occupy the time.

"For me and Merv it's cards. RD's got musicians who'll stroll through. We got plays and concerts over at Pacheco. Bingo there, too. A lot of people with a lot of time, best to be productive. Mainly though the old folks need help. They get cold. They got their challenges, their aches and pains. Your Ma's lucky with that camper."

"And with Bruce?"

"Lives with his folks over in Loma Linda Estates, just on the other side of 99 there. I guess this place's exciting compared to Double L. Not that I've ever been there. Ol' Bruce can get your Mom going. They'll be howling with laughter. Cheers the place up. We all need that."

"How long have you lived here?" he asked, munching a mealy USG apple.

"Don't know that you can call it living." Another rasping laugh that broke into a full-scale cough. "I've known Merv for years. Poor man. He used to work for the Alfaflux Corporation. One fine day some New York snakes bought it. Made him a private contractor. He was looking for a more honorable company when Luanne, that's his wife, came down with cancer of her privates. Merv lost the house paying for her treatment, then lost Luanne anyway." She itched the back of her neck. "I tell ya, this whole Void thing? I'm kinda glad it's happened. If it's that effed up I say 'tear it down'."

He left that comment to echo into the failing light as they made their way to WTF.

"I visited Merv here, just to see how he was doing. Kinda eased my way into his tent. Probably would've lost my house sooner or later anyway."

The next morning, grouchy from a noisy night on the ground, he sat at the picnic table shaking his head. The Trap. He knew it when he left San Francisco, and now its steel claws had snapped shut, a trap worse than he could have imagined: stuck, not at a comfortable three-bedroom house, but at a homeless encampment. For the next three days, sitting by Mom as she lolled, half-awake, wrapped up in her own thoughts, to the extent she still had them, he started to rationalize. What could he do here that wasn't already being done? Not only did Mom have Bruce, there was Mrs. Flaherty, other volunteers. And Mrs. Muller, the nurse. Besides Mom seemed happy enough in her partial obliviousness, as happy as he could expect in such diminished circumstances. His depression, already starting, would only drag her down. Bottom line, she didn't know who he was anyway.

Over at Pacheco they had seven laptops hooked up to the USG network, powered by stationary bikes taken from an old gym. Four hours queuing, fifteen minutes on the bike followed by an equal amount of time on the computer.

Are you there yet? Sue, not Madeline. *How's Mom? How was the ride? Speak to me.*

He typed his answer, reluctantly. *Mom's been kicked out of her house. She's in a homeless encampment. It's awful yet it's good too. She has a lot of friends here. I can't see my way to a solution.*

He hit "send" and instantly regretted it. Who said the truth shall set you free? He sat slumped and frozen before the computer. A boyish tech guy who had been overseeing several older users, came over. "Having problems?"

"Not technical ones."

"Some folks don't know about the Matrix yet." He explained that the USG had just set up a simple system that correlated old email addresses to your new USGmail one. All Clay had to do was hit the small red "M" at the top of his home screen, and, once the Matrix was activated, type in his old email address. Clay shivered. He could contact Madeline this way. Sure the chances of her figuring out the red M (when he hadn't) and registering her old email address were miniscule. But just the possibility brought her closer. He hadn't heard from her in over six months. No doubt she'd want to let him know how she was doing, find out about him, commiserate about the Void and its hardships.

That evening, the dutiful son taking Mom's slop bucket down to the closed gas station, he couldn't get that red M out of his mind; it burned there like a brand. M for Madeline. There it was, his excuse, his mission, his quest. Boston. A flood of longing engulfed him. Was it real, something willfully ignored now fully exposed? Or was he just good at rationalizing his actions? It brought back that bipolar world again, where love and wanting could turn instantly into a wearisome, corrosive dread. But wasn't it good to love and to want, even if only for a scrap of the day? Without a doubt he would prefer it to his current idle nothingness. He would knock, her door would sweep open, and all would be redeemed by her smile. It would work again, the way everything about her pulled at him like an errant puppy, her smell, her hair, that smile. Sure it would work. Until it didn't.

Next day, for something to do, he paid a visit to the Mayor. She sure did attract a line, like a big planet pulling in minor rocks.

Belle Brown had a theatrical way of mopping her forehead with a handkerchief. She squinted at him, maybe recognizing him from before. Maybe not. "How can I help you?"

"I figure where there's a line there's hope."

"I unnerstand from our Latino friends they got to share one word for both hope and wait. They may be on to something."

"How did you become Mayor of this place?"

"Certainly didn't choose to, that's a fact. I ran for Big Mayor a few elections back and that turned out to be good enough for enough folks here. They started coming with their problems." She shook her head, telegraphing her disbelief. "Now, you are a visitor here. I'm no seer or nothing, but I seen you with your bike. The water bottle holders, basket, plus you got that lean and burnt face – so you pedaled some distance. You do that for one of two people. Your Ma or your love interest." She dropped down an octave over that last phrase. "An' you're looking more guilty than satisfied so I'm guessing Ma."

He hung his head.

"You, sir, are worried. She is sick, senile, lost without her meds. How can such a thing happen? What can you do? How can you hightail it out of here with the cleanest conscience possible?"

He pursed his lips, met her eyes. "You're not much of a politician…with that kind of talk."

"I never pretended to be electable. And I apologize for bein' so… direct. But you're not the first, second or fifth person coming here with these concerns."

"That means you must have a ready answer."

"I do. Thing is, you know the answer just as well as I do. You just don't happen to accept it. So you come to me, hoping for one closer to your liking. Do you want that kinda answer?" She gave him a serious, leveling look. "Now, don't you worry none, we'll take good care of your Ma, if necessary to the exclusion of all the other oldsters in need of help. Why we'll – "

"Okay. Okay. It's a miracle anyone comes to you with their problems."

"No, brother, the true miracle is that they come back for seconds." She shook her head. "Now," she said with a kind of fist-into-palm change of pace, "What you say to helping us? We got ourselves a Survival Fund, helps buy medicines and basics for those in need." She held up her hand. "Yes, I know, there's not much to buy these days. Trust me, there's still enough."

"Why, you *are* a politician."

She shrugged. She wasn't the subject; he was. What kind of man was he? Just another in a long line of disappointments? "Your Mammy, you say she's Elaine in the camper over in WTF."

He couldn't help smiling. The subtle way her needle worked at the swollen abscess of his guilt. He'd left San Francisco with a hundred and forty New D's, spent fifty in Fairfield buying new bike rims from an annoying teenage boy who saw a man with no options and exploited that. How much to donate of his remaining seventy? And why did the donation feel like he was buying his freedom?

"Do you take checks?" He didn't wait for her response. "I give the cash to you?"

"You wanna receipt?"

"It'll have to be a mixed salad of Jacks and Gips." He counted out and handed over fifty New D's. Didn't buy much of value these days, anyway. Excepting, of course, his freedom.

Bruce was the one person at Rancho Duro who knew he had arrived with no intention of going any further east. He needed to depart in a way that didn't leave the boy feeling taken advantage of, dumped on with Clay's problems, stuck watching him trade the idle squalor here for the sparkling invitation of the open road. A way, too, that suggested a replacement mission rather than gratuitous abandonment – a cycling to, rather than a cycling away.

"I hear this is your camper."

"Kinda is, yeah. The previous, uh, resident said I could have it…before he died. Poor old Mr. Betheny, I guess he couldn't think of anyone else. There's no will or nothing if that's what you're getting at."

He waved that away. "Thanks for letting Elaine use it."

Bruce flitted his restless eyes on Clay's face, not locking on his eyes. "So you're outta here, right?"

"What!" A knee-jerk response. Maybe it was for the best. It saved him from a tortuous explanation of his New Mission. "I have been thinking about it, truth be told."

"Tomorrow?" The boy sounded hopeful, wanting him gone. What was this?

"I haven't decided anything."

"Uh huh."

Those last two days at Rancho Duro he kept trying the idea on for size, the epic cross-country ride, Boston, 3,000 miles, mountain ranges, scorching deserts – the chivalrous quest of winning back his woman. A mission that rang true. Noble, romantic, active, all the opposites to his current life. Sure, it was impossible. Look at what he'd gone through for eighty miles from San Francisco. Why, the chances of pumping over the Sierras were so small that he'd simply let reality do the turning back for him. In that light he wasn't abandoning Mom as much as going on a week's mountain diversion.

He kissed Mom good-bye. To her he could have been going off to the store. Bruce shook hands; Karen waved from the next site with a self-satisfied smile.

Bruce said, "That woman always wins. It's unreal."

"Wins what?"

"She put her money on today." Reading his frown, he added, "You cutting out."

Chapter 4

"Would you be interested in our loyalty card?" The woman behind the register caught him with her alert brown eyes, held him for a penetrating instant, then glanced to the long line of lunch hour book purchasers.

"I'm not a very loyal person. Sooner or later I'd wind up sneaking off to one of your competitors." Clay's first words to Madeline, seven years before the Void. Something about her eyes, she hadn't been evaluating him as such, yet he found himself wanting a longer hearing – fairer?

"I think that's okay. What I mean is, we wouldn't see that as a betrayal."

"So, I have cards for all the major bookstores – where's the loyalty in that?"

She gave him his receipt, her eyes already signaling the next customer as he handed her his business card.

"I'd love to continue this conversation. It's intriguing to talk to a complete stranger about betrayal."

She gave him a "nice try" smile, her eyes going to the next customer. Her angular face, brown hair pulled back in a tight ponytail. Her rich caramel eyes, a light dancing quality there, the kind of dance that, right now, wasn't seeking a partner. The next customer, duly summoned, had lumbered up to make a threesome.

"Send me an email. We'll meet for coffee. Just give me the time and place," he said, ever the businessman – leave nothing nebulous, outline the next steps, avoid the difficulty of her having to call. Still, this was a small deal, more about sailing on a lunchtime thermal, one of those mischievous perfect day ones. A close was a close, though.

Chapter 5

After a fitful night under the bushes in Roseville, the Sierras were starting to build. He started to find his cycling rhythm. Everyone should live hemmed in by mountains. They protect you from invaders, but also from your delusions of escape. Was it the incline of the road or his guilt about his mother that pulled him back down towards the valley? And another weight pulling at him, less powerful for being further away, pulling him east toward the one person in the world who understood him – used to, anyway. Just one hug, one long and intoxicating infusion of her hair would wash over him like forgiveness. He was coming to Madeline from so far away that it was the trek itself, its magnitude, that provoked his imagination, the reality of arrival lost in that glare.

"Fancy bike you got there."

He was taking a break, sitting with his back against the Post Office that said Weimar – its facade resembled a child's drawing of a house, a triangle on stilts. Out of the glare he made out a stout figure, too bright yet to know whether flab or muscle. He stood up, blinking, sizing up the situation. Muscle, mainly.

"Glad you like it."

"Pretty light." The man hefted it high with one hand. "Light means expensive."

"What does expensive mean… these days?"

"Country'll get a new dollar. The bike'll weigh the same."

A pale and fleshy face above a bulky body, average height – someone who spends a lot of time indoors, lifting weights. A caterpillar of a mustache sat below an almost dainty pug nose, no malice or emotion in his expression. "I'm taking it. Unless you want to challenge that."

"Bit too hot for a fight," Clay tried. What had he hit recently except a budget target?

"I reckon it won't last all that long."

Pug squared up to him, put his dukes up, but only as far as his chest, daring Clay to take a shot. Clay crouched, circling, out of range.

"You gonna fight in your bike helmet. Shit."

With a guttural bellow, Pug attacked. Clay crumbled under a fast tattoo of blows, stomach and right arm, this fury the prelude to the knockout punch. He circled waiting for it. A right from far back, here it came – at the last instant he swayed and came up under it with a right that had his body behind it. Crack! They fell back, both startled by such a resounding pop. Pug tested his nose, found blood on his hand. Stared at his hand in wonder. "Blood gets on this shirt and I will kill you," he said, leaning forward to keep the blood and snot off his Guns N' Roses tee shirt.

Leaning forward to protect his shirt from any blood, Pug walked over to the bike, lifted it, looked at Clay with no emotion, and walked away.

"Hey! Bring back my bike," he called with the bravado of a winner, but the fading authority of someone who could barely lift his right arm. A second round, fighting with one arm immobilized would be foolhardy, but there was his self-respect to consider. He followed Pug at a distance, but Pug ran into one of his buddies, whose glare tipped that "foolhardy" into "suicidal".

He rested up in the shade of a brick-fronted café, boarded up, having trudged six miles up from Weimar. One of the news racks out front still held a yellowing local paper: *Funds for Rec Room Slashed*, complained the headline. Across the street the sign above the three-bay building said Colfax ire and Brake, the missing "T" oddly appropriate. He looked East. West. Nowhere. He should find a cop, report his bike stolen, describe the perp. Rally a posse that would show up at Pug's door, wherever that was, with torches and a rope. Something. Anything was better than this abject listlessness. But he slumped further down against the café's brick wall, warm from the heat. Why contest divine retribution for the shameless abandonment of Mom? He had struggled, clawed and bled to win a little over a hundred miles. The next three thousand had to be impossible now.

The light honk of a car horn – he did a double take; there were no car horns any longer. A patrol car. Placer County Sheriff. He got up and walked over as the window whirred down.

"New to these parts?"

"That a crime?"

"Some folks might see it that way. Where'd you walk from, if you don't mind my asking?"

"From the valley. Lost my bike in Weimar." He described his assailant.

The sheriff barely listened. He had a pock-marked face, hawk-like nose and a stiff manner contradicted by a pleasant smile. "Okay, here's the deal," he cut in. "There's a Chevron station up there a quarter mile. Wait for me there, okay?"

Citizens were waving and hollering at the patrol car, a big event in their lives, a new event. The sheriff checked his rear-view mirror and headed out before Clay had time to step back from the car. Wow, first a real car and now hot pursuit.

He walked up to the gas station, its pumps coated with grime. A window washing squeegee still sat in a dry pocket of the central island. A light breeze, moderating the heat that was starting to take spring seriously. Across the street, just before an on-ramp to I-80, a ragged billboard showed a faded model holding a smartphone. *Because you need it all. Now.*

He sat down, back against a pump, and stared down the main street, Canyon Way, from where he had come. It wasn't long before distant shouts heralded the patrol car cruising up the long street, folks waving, hollering, trying to flag it down. It came right at him, made a crisp right, swung left putting the passenger door in front of him. The sheriff motioned him to get in. The back seat was taken up with his blue bike.

"Thanks," Clay said, getting in. "You sure do fast work."

"One of these days I'm gonna lose my patience with that doofus." The sheriff glanced at him, his sharp eyes never quite connecting. "Now, I've gone ahead and assumed that you won't be pressing charges. We've got no way of following through on them. In return I've obtained Garth's sincere apology. Good enough?"

"I'm in your capable hands, sheriff." He sat in the front seat, a rifle rising like a handbrake between them. The sheriff pulled out of the gas station, took the freeway on-ramp, and headed east on I-80.

"Am I being arrested?"

"What would I be arresting you for?"

"Running out on my mother."

"Prisons would be pretty darn full if we prosecuted that one. Right now prisons are emptying. Folsom's only thirty miles from here. They're letting most of the cons out. Drug offenses, robberies, GBH, even some murders. Gotta be the devil himself to be kept back." He glanced over at Clay, his sharp eyes at an angle to dilute the power in them. "Most of them head west, but we get our share."

"They head up into the High Sierras?"

"Some of them like the idea of Reno."

He fought back the urge to ask the sheriff about their destination. He wasn't certain why. Now a check point, a few cars backed before it. Cars! Where could they have come from? The sheriff passed them on the shoulder and breezed through the checkpoint, saluting the Army guys as he did so, continuing east. He pulled into one of those dirt strips that cops use to cut between east and westbound lanes.

"It's illegal to ride a bike on the interstate." He held that for a moment, deadpan. "There's another checkpoint just west of Donner Lake. I don't know what you do about that one, it's mainly granite and cliffs around there."

"Thanks, sheriff."

"There's this small part of me that still believes that in a free country people should be left to screw up in their own individual ways. Good luck."

"You too," he answered, extracting his bike.

"The bag's for you," the sheriff said – an old paper shopping bag with Fourth of July fireworks on it, the bottom moist and oily. Food!

He pumped up the freeway, over-geared to keep the torque off his legs. The cool, pine-infused mountain air. The open road, that limitless feeling of inventing your destination as you move through the scenery. This was the life, pure improvisation – until the gods started improvising too. Seven miles in and the low shuddering growl of trucks tightened his thoughts, louder and closer, higher pitched, bearing down on him. Up here there was none of the frontage roads he had taken from Sacramento. No escape. He worked up the gears, sprinting to outstrip the wall of rock on his right. He came over a rise, moving fast, now flying down a short descent. The first truck popped and growled as it hit the descent just after him. Now the highway ramped up again, quickly robbing him of speed. As if copying him the semis used their downhill speed to climb up again, thunderous horns sounding. The first semi passed him in a pall of diesel fumes, nudging him toward the steel guardrail that protected errant cars from a steep incline. The second semi passed even closer, forcing him into the rough stuff near the barrier. The third he could have reached out and touched. Each truck slower than the last as the incline slowed the lead trucks. Would they really crush him? He unclipped and hopped over the barrier, swinging his bike after him. The semis were chugging up the grade so slowly that he exchanged looks with every passenger. Kids with rifles, grins, and a range of gestures: mock salutes, over-friendly waves, an Arabic salaam. Two index fingers formed the barrel of a pistol and shot him twice. A line came back to him from what seemed the distant past. "You're not worth a bullet."

Chapter 6

Five years before his encounter with the bookstore siren, Clay walked out of grad school clutching his MBA and, after a two-year stint with a second-tier New York investment bank, jumped ship for a management job back in California at Steel Umbrella Inc., Jack Lenahan's new insurance vehicle. Lenahan, accomplished at building insurance empires the old way through purchasing, merging, growing and selling, was trying a new route, building from the ground up – new people, a new attitude to insurance, a sales machine with the latest CRM technology, well-trained account execs, and healthy bonuses for accomplished closers. Win the contract was the mantra. Win. Win. Win.

Clay had heard enough sermons on sales success. The great closers were risk takers who dared to think outside the box, who understood that a corporation is not a monolithic structure that acts in its own best interest, but an amalgamation of rival fiefdoms, petty interests and above all job-protection strategies. Inspired by all the rah-rah talk, Clay chased the ballsiest, juiciest contract he could find. EvDev Inc. was one of the country's largest property development and office rental companies. Buildings and content insurance for EvDev's vast holdings would mean millions in premiums. Nail that and Clay would be a hero. And with the inevitable bonus he could pay off a large chunk of his student loans, over $100k. After that he could get down to finding a more stimulating job.

All EvDev's employees were wary of making a decision, lest it was questioned by EvDev's owner and Chairman, the ship's captain whose booming voice was designed to reach the forecastle in a howling gale. Mr. Otakar Dubkhadze was an impetuous, unpredictable character given to random bouts of generosity and cruelty. EvDev's building and contents insurance portfolio was handled via one of Dubkhadze's Georgian pals so Clay would have to bypass his normal contact, the Director of Facilities, and hit it at the top. Dubkhadze direct. That meant schmoozing with Dubkhadze's PA, Phyllis, a woman whose humanity had been pounded out of her by years of her boss's ranting and raving. Her agreement to forward his message, he suspected, had a strong element of lamb-to-the-lion perversity to it. "Okay, I'll mention it to him," she said in a "you'll be sorry" tone.

On the flight down to Burbank, Clay memorized the phonetic pronunciation of a Georgian song that one of his staff had printed from the internet.

"Sorry about the accent," he said, having recited it as he stood before the great man in his large office.

"A noble attempt," Dubkhadze said doubtfully. "I shall tell you about that song. First, tell me why I should do business with you."

"Steel Umbrella is a new kind – "

"No. You personally. You are young and ambitious. Within two years you will move to a better job for more pay. You will do anything now because you will be gone and someone else can Pick Up the Pieces." Dubkhadze liked to talk in headlines.

Clay nodded. Dubkhadze's swept-back hair, black as the leather chair he was tilted back in, highlighted the prominent nose, a porous strawberry-textured blob that had been broken and poorly set decades ago. That damaged nose, combined with a glare in the eyes that came and went like an erratic lighthouse beam, radiated a streetfighter aura.

"There's another angle here," Clay said.

"And what angle is that?"

"It could be EvDev that hires me."

"Aha, then you could fix things with your former employer?" His eyes glinted.

"Mr. Dubkhadze, there will be nothing that needs to be fixed."

Dubkhadze stood. "Let me have a copy of your proposal." He walked his guest to the door of his sizable top floor office, offered his hand.

"Thank you, sir. You were going to tell me about the song."

"Yes, the song. It used to be most popular in my native town. In actuality it is the favorite song of the second most famous man from there. You may have heard of him. Ioseph Vissarionovich Djugashvili. You know who that is?"

"No, I don't sir."

Dubkhadze clucked in disappointment, nodded good-bye.

On his way out he asked Dubkhadze's PA, "Who's this friend of his called Jug-ash something?"

She adjusted something about the frozen wave of her blond hair while shaking her head. "Djugashvili?" she said, correcting him like the strict school marm she could have been. "He changed his name when he left Georgia. You will know him as Josef Stalin."

Chapter 7

The Sierras were starting to build now, the air cooler, fewer signs of civilization. That first aching of his lungs from the higher elevation. A pulsing at his temples. As he pumped, two up from granny gear, he mulled over the fight with Pug. How, sitting at that gas pump, he'd nearly thrown in the towel. Yet now he was ratcheting up to the 7,200-foot summit. At what point had he decided this?

He had found a rhythm now, the constant incline and his low gear combining into a pace not much faster than walking. *Elevation 4,000 feet*, said a sign. Not far beyond it a man stood in the road ahead of him, in the shade, hard to make out, until, fifty feet away, it was too late.

"Off the bike. Slow and easy," The man said, motioning with his rifle. He was on the tall side of average, a certain insolence in his cocked hip, the rifle at a careless angle. Probably Latino: EC for easy.

"No shooting! No shooting!" This from a small and thin man, similar age, maybe late twenties. He stood on a large slab of rock. Was that a houndstooth cap he wore?

"Shock?" Rifleman called into the trees. This brought out a third, a middle-age man of average build, who stood on the road behind Clay.

"Your show, Aug," Shock said to Rifleman.

For a long moment Aug seemed an actor who'd forgotten his lines. "We'll be wanting your food."

"If I give you my food – "

"Hey boss, this is no place to be bargaining."

"No shooting! No stealing!" Houndstooth sat down on the slab and glared at the men down on the road. "Miss Pia said so."

"We let him go, he coasts down to the cops," Shock, the middle-aged man, said.

"We take his bike?" Aug said.

"He walks."

"Oh man, you mean we got to shoot him?" Aug said, as if his to-do list was already chock full. "We haven't even robbed him yet."

"No stealing," Houndstooth said again.

"Shut up, Billy," Aug said.

"Let her deal with it," Shock said. He surveyed Clay's knapsack and smirked. This was Aug's show, and Aug had apparently forgotten about the food.

After hiding his bike in a stand of pines, the three amigos escorted him up a steep path. They hiked along a forest contour for twenty minutes, pockets of snow among the pines, and arrived at a meadow, full of tall grass and liberally scattered with clusters of buttercups. At its top a lodge, its high glass aimed west. From their low angle the planes of glass were full of a high and aching blue. Smaller structures bracketed the lodge, with a few more running down the northern side of the meadow.

"I'll get Miss Pia," Aug said. He had only taken a few steps when he waved to a small blonde at the top of the wide stairs to the Big Lodge.

They watched her short but svelte frame as she descended quickly to them, her face pinned like a loose banner to high cheekbones, her small blue eyes a tad too far apart.

"Augustin, no guns, not here. Remember? You'll upset the guests."

"He'll upset *me*," Clay said.

Miss Pia considered him for the first time. She was all business, twenty-something, attractive, seemingly half his height. She said, "You're from inside?"

"Inside?"

"No way, Miss Pia," Aug said.

Miss Pia looked at Shock. He nodded gravely, dark, purposeful. He had a sputtering determined expression, a tank used to mowing down a tree rather than going around it, but a tank that had taken a hit, lost a tread maybe, condemned to circling. His broken eyes were full of her, dependence and desperation in his face.

"Mr. Shockley, why is he here?"

Shockley gestured toward Aug. *His show.*

Billy said, "No stealing. Please Miss Pia, tell him."

"It's not stealing," Aug said, "it's… remember when you explained to us about the greater good? How we lose because of all the guests, how there are a lot more of them, so we have to…"

"Be nice," Billy said. "Nice, right Miss Pia?"

"Yeah, nice," Aug said. "Isn't it better for fifty people to eat than this one dude here?"

"Did you ask this gentleman if perhaps he would be willing to share? No, I didn't think so," Miss Pia said.

Billy went over and stiffly patted Aug's shoulder.

"Listen, we are sorry," Miss Pia said, stressing words that weren't normally stressed, Scandinavian of some kind. "You are free to go. Billy, please see our visitor to the road. Mr. Shockley will come with me." She took Shock's hand and led him toward the Big Lodge. From behind, her walk had a feminine fragility to it, as if her propulsion system had been taken apart and put back together with one piece left on the table. The three tracked her sinuous exit.

"You folks are short of food?" Clay said.

"We are the hunters," Billy explained.

"This is what? Some kind of hotel?"

"Alta Alma," Billy said.

"Alma Alta," Aug corrected. "It is a Retreat."

"Retreat. Just what this country needs," Clay said, mostly to himself.

"No retreat. Not now. Advance," Billy said, understanding. "No talking here."

"If it's a silent retreat what about those folks over there?"

The lower, southern, part of the meadow held a miniature Stonehenge, ten flat rocks in a circle. There were people in bright flowing clothes sitting on nine of them. A woman stood in front of the tenth, talking. The scene resembled a gap-toothed smile.

"It's Tuesday," Aug said.

"They tell stories," Billy said. "They tell stories on Tuesday."

"And Fridays," Aug said.

"Stories? What about?"

Aug looked at Billy, "What do they talk about, Billy-o?"

"Food."

He turned so his knapsack was out of their direct view. Over at Stonehenge the speaker, a thin white-haired woman talked on, her slow and elegant gestures more likely outlining the collapse of civilizations than instructions for recipes. He tried to fit a commentary to the gestures. *Then you coat the lightly pounded veal with the aioli mixture. Now you drizzle it with grated parmesan.* But why torture himself?

Billy had drifted closer to Stonehenge. He stood at the eight o'clock position behind a pale strawberry blonde in a pastel green robe. None of the ten took any notice of him.

Aug said, "Billy don't understand all this talking. Usually the guests they sit in their cells or they sit together in the big hall. Billy thinks they are in prison. He thinks we are all in prison. He doesn't understand how women can be here. It is like a miracle. And... Billy likes women."

"How'd you come to be here?"

"We all been released from Folsom, three months back. Shock sold us on Reno. Only problem, it was winter. We got this far." He stopped as if he'd just remembered something. "At least we have a purpose here, to hunt and to guard against the psychos. It's only a matter of time before they release the nasty *cabrones*."

"Hunting? Shouldn't these people be vegetarians?"

"A lot are. Just as well since Shock's been on a dry spell. Shock don't like killing no more. He done filled up his quota with his family."

"He killed his family? They let him out?"

"Pretty lucky, eh. The USG don't discriminate between cops."

"I don't understand." He turned to keep his knapsack out of Aug's sight.

"Not people, cops. Cops, your crimes of passion?"

"Seriously, they're letting out murderers?"

"They're letting out most everyone. Drugs? White crime? It's see you later, man. Your murders are more complicated. USG reckons if you kill your ol' lady, it's like a one-off. Who else you gonna kill? So, you kill your whole family, it's even better. I mean, now there really is no one left to kill." As an afterthought, he added, "Besides, Shock didn't mean to do it. Well, he did at the time, but no more than a minute, then he didn't mean to do it again. But it was kinda too late."

"He's got that kind of temper," Clay said, "he could kill just about anyone."

Billy wandered back, bored with the talk on cooking.

"USG don't look at it like that. Family stuff's family stuff, right? Within the walls of your house. Now your armed robbery, icing someone, that's out in public, outside of those walls."

"Family stuff!" Billy added, eager to help.

"Family?" Aug said, "What family you talking about Bill-bo? You thinking of starting one with Mrs. Waggoner down there?"

"What were you in for Billy?"

"Mrs. Wag. Mrs. Wag." His voice filled with urgency.

"Billy, he likes women, no doubt about that. Dude's an orphan. He don't understand why he can't have a momma. All the man wants is some warmth from a woman. 'Cept with the ones that might give it to him he...well as Miss Pia says it, *he lacks subtlety*. So he winds up with the harder ones. All they do is orphan him all over again."

"So it wasn't women he got sent in for?"

"Nah, women is a whole 'nother kind of prison. He got to Folsom for following the wrong people. When the shooting finished he was holding a fired gun. I mean, look at him, won't even shoot a Bambi..."

Billy was still tracking the strawberry blonde, lacking all subtlety. A hunting dog pointing.

"Pia's his momma now. Never seen him so calm. She's good with Shock, too. Problem is, Shock's our only good hunter, but he can't kill no more. The baby deer he got two weeks ago? Only the last coupla days he's come around. Billy? Well, if it was a Mamma deer he just might hug it to death. Me? I don't have no patience to find the damn things, get close enough for a sure kill. We only got so much ammo."

"What does Pia do for you?"

"We talk..." He studied the tree tops for a long moment. "This here Void has opened up a lot of second chances." He notched up his voice in Billy's direction, "Ain't that right, Billy? We deserve a second chance?"

Billy still ogled, a parody of lust, the strawberry blonde. "Second chance," Billy said. "Third chance."

Pia came down to them, wearing a light smile that had trouble behind it, like wallpaper slapped on a crumbling wall. "You boys have to help Mr. Shockley. He's having his doubts again."

"Killing a deer's different to killing your family," Aug said. "I keep telling him that."

Pia shook her head. "Please, Augie, only positives. Tell him how helpful it is, how he keeps us alive with his skill. Nothing about his family."

"Family. Nothing." Billy said.

"Billy, come here."

Billy shuffled over to Pia, bashful. She hugged him lightly, comfortably, familiarly. "Don't say 'family' around Mr. Shockley. Is that a promise?"

"Hey," Aug said, "What about Billy? He don't have no family neither."

Pia threw a "we've talked about this" frown at Aug. "I must go back to him." She turned to Clay, "I'm sorry, we have an emergency now. Billy? The road? Remember?" She gave Clay the full force of her eyes, nodded good-bye. She and Aug headed away, Aug to the Big Lodge.

The ten in the meadow were all on their feet now, stretching. A gong sounded up at the Big Lodge and residents started materializing from most of the structures, and from other directions. They somnambulated to the lodge in silence. Billy joined them, forgetting all about his charge.

The Big Lodge's windows were open to the mild day. The first diners sat at refectory tables, spooning from bowls. The others waited in line. He might be a new face, but no one remarked on that. Billy took his plate of mush and sat beside his Stonehenge quarry and across from Aug.

Clay slipped outside with his bowl, walked down the slope away from the silence and sat on one of the Stonehenge stones. Two o'clock if west was noon. The yellowy paste had a cloying grassy taste. Yams, saffron, some herbs, bulked up with what tasted like lawn cuttings. At least it was seasoned! Everything the USG doled out was a bland mush. That's how the USG controlled distribution, the firsts stifling any thoughts of seconds – so the joke went.

Time to climb higher into the Sierras. He left his bowl and spoon on a bench outside the big building. Fifty diners sat forty feet away, and through the open door only the occasional clinking of forks on plates interrupted the peaceful day.

"Hey, dude, you still here?" Aug said, coming down the steps. Already it was a refreshing miracle to hear a normal voice.

"Just leaving."

"I hate you! Hate you. Hate you. Hate you." Shock's voice, drifting out over the quiet day.

Aug said, "Shock's having a rough time. He's in love with Miss Pia."

"Sounds like he's at the hard part already."

"Hey, Billy, you in love with Pia?" Aug said to Billy just emerging from the silent hall. "Dude, I know you love Pia but you're unfaithful to her, always drooling over Mrs. Waggoner."

Clay said, "What does she do in there?"

"Talks mainly. Calms him down." Aug took a second for some personal reflection.

"Shock doesn't sound all that serene to me," Clay said.

"No. Ever since he shot that deer. We had to make him, didn't we Billy?" Aug looked down, embarrassed. "These folks need to eat. Thems that's not vegetaranians. Billy don't eat meat on the idea you shouldn't eat someone more intelligent than yourself. Ain't that right, Billy? Shock's the only hunter, but he's lost his heart."

"To Pia!" Billy yelled.

By now six retreatists had assembled around them, as if the meadow equivalent of street theater. They regarded with calm intensity these three complicated conflicted beings on display.

Miss Pia came down the slope to them.

Aug said, "Shock okay?"

Pia shrugged. "At least he hates me. This is good."

"How can that be good?" Clay asked.

"He is too busy hating me to hate himself."

Clay had to leave for the highway, get out before unknowable tentacles started wrapping him into an untenable embrace. The food in his pack was for the road, not to share. Hard and unfair but survival meant the equivalent of putting his oxygen mask on first.

In contrast to the pleasant meadow and the alien rituals of the Retreat, he'd soon be facing the steep inclines of the High Sierras, an elevator shaft in which he'd strain every leg sinew hoisting himself up to the fortieth floor. Ding! High mountain vistas, glacier-sculpted granite, snow, as much water as there was lack of food. From there he could coast down to the trackless wastes, first of Reno, then the Great Basin Desert.

"How's Shockley?" he asked Pia, who ended up escorting him to the road herself.

"What you want to know is why I work with a man who has done what he has done."

"Guess so." Her lithe frame led him to the road.

"I tell you this in all sincerity. He loves his family. One moment the blood rises. It is so quick and so complete. I want to understand this because something similar happened in my life. Not as bad, but… Anyway, I try to help him. And the other two." She turned and gave him a small smile.

"You trust him with a gun with that kind of temper?"

"He needs me."

"He probably needed his family."

Now she turned, hands on hips. "What do you suggest I do? The snow has melted. If they let out the worst prisoners, and they come this way…"

Better not point out Shock's limited enthusiasm for shooting anything. "What I don't understand, how did they find this place?"

She chuckled. "Billy. Somehow he knew we were here. No one understands how he knows this."

"Aug says Billy thinks he's in prison what with the cells and communal meals and all."

Miss Pia gave a scoffing snort, and smiled, slow-breaking. "Maybe he is not so simple after all."

Chapter 8

The clerk at his lunchtime bookstore had sent him an email. "Dear Mr. Vice President, if you can be loyal to a just cause please drop by this Saturday and sign our petition." She gave the time and location details. "Take care, Madeline", she closed, lower case.

A bright breezy Saturday in early June. "Finally," she had said when he sauntered up to her card table near the main entrance to the grocery store. "I finish in forty minutes." She looked at her partner, a small and compact Asian lady, and smiled. They'd talked about him.

"Where do I sign?"

"Don't you want to know what you're signing?"

He pointed to the poster taped to the table and flapping in the fog-bearing breeze: Fight Cappuccino Capitalism. "Cappuccino is total exploitation of the Capuchin brotherhood," he said. "Blatant monkism. It's not right."

The Asian woman laughed. "I hadn't thought of it like that. Do you know if those monks are still around?"

"No, I don't."

"Our petition is to protest all these chain coffee places in the Haight that are squeezing out the local cafes."

"Doesn't that mean they're already here? The horses have bolted?"

"It's the principle," Madeline said. "And it's an indirect way of telling people they should support their local cafes."

"Fair enough," he said, appending his signature uneasily. The signature two up from his was in lavender. "Listen, I don't want to get in the way. But if either of you would like to warm up with a hot chocolate or something I'll be over at Black Cow Books."

In the book shop Clay hunted down the Economics section. His eye caught a blood red title on a thick tome, *Corporate Seduction, Ethical Rape*. He leafed through a random middle section, page after page of dense text.

"Having second thoughts?"

He turned around. How long had Madeline been standing there?

"You mean about signing your petition?" He lifted the book in her direction. "Listen: *'Money is a narcotic. If you don't have it, you must substitute for it with other drugs. If we could all wake up from these vapid and manufactured dreams we could change the world.'*"

"Don't you think there's some truth in that?"

"It's an interesting viewpoint. Way oversimplified, but interesting."

"Let me show you something," she said. She took the book, leafed nimbly through it, pointed to a sentence with a thin index finger that tapered into an unpainted, trimmed nail.

"*'Like any successful rapist,'*" he recited, "*'the corporate imperative is to ensure that the victims don't press charges.'* He shut the book to seal in such radioactivity. "That's pretty strong."

"I do volunteer work for the Charger, full name Daily Press Charger. It's an online paper. You can guess what it's about."

"Really? What do you do for them?"

"A business summary. If your Wall Street Journal is a photograph, the Charger is the negative. I synthesize reports from all over the country, reports of corporate wrongdoing and wickedness. It's called The Rap Sheet. I'm not crazy about that name. I also write articles on Big Pharma."

"Oh. Has – "

"No." She gave him a prim smile. "No, your outfit hasn't starred. Yet. It could have, the story about the lady you shafted in San Leandro. The one who – "

"I'm familiar with the story. It wasn't our finest hour." Something of an understatement. Steel Um, as they were now calling his company, would be paying an order of magnitude more money than the actual claim to counter that chunk of bad PR. But the lawyers and actuaries were chanting "precedent" like priests at a sacred rite.

"You lucked out. It wasn't important enough. No, that's wrong. It *is* important – it's all important to someone – but on the scale of corporate malfeasance it's too far down the list. It's rather a long one."

He slotted *Corporate Seduction, Ethical Rape* back onto the shelf.

"You're not going to buy it?" she said, not serious. "Or do you feel threatened by such views?"

"No. No, I don't. If you had written about the Louro case, the San Leandro one, I would have stood there and taken your slap like a man. Anyway, the local papers did a pretty good job on us. We certainly didn't get off lightly. I guess it's good I don't work for a drug company."

"Don't get me started or I'll go all preachy. I can't help it. Shall I cut to the last line?" She frowned her way into a narrative voice, "Thousands of people are dying because of the aggressive pricing policies that put profit over…" She slapped her hand against her thigh. "Humanity? Compassion?"

"People – that would complete your inside straight of P's."

She smiled, nodding. "That's our tag line. It's just that it sounds too PR-ish when said conversationally. Or perhaps I'm just tired of saying it."

Or tired of talking about it. "Can I buy you a coffee or something?" It was nearly five, a beer should have been a possibility, but maybe not with Miss Organic here.

She smiled, disappointed. "It's a nice day. Golden Gate Park is a few blocks from here. You need to break free of the narcotic and change the world."

"Meaning?"

"Meaning you don't have to buy me anything just so…No, let's just leave it that I don't want you to buy me anything."

Chapter 9

He spent one last day in California, a rest day in Truckee. He caught up on calories at the USG there. Visited the Bartmart – every town had at least one area given over to trade, barter, deals of all kinds. He was hoping for bike paniers, saddlebags to take weight from his knapsack, using his New Dollars while they still had some credibility. Beware of Reno, they all said. Buy here, stay here. If you insist on heading east try a night run, quick, avoid downtown.

He followed the local advice and hit Reno in the dead of night, a flanking run to the north. From a dark sidewalk a young lady waved him down, her arms semaphoring a vague distress. He slowed down, on his guard. Out of the shadows her confederate lunged for him.

"Let's have your bike. Now." He was a Big Guy with the authoritative manner of a cop, a flat-footed former one. The waning wedge of moon chose this time to hide behind clouds.

"What have you got in trade for it?"

"Hah!" the girl snorted, her guffaw as physical as a sneeze. She was a sleek dark-haired number with a provocative posture that led with her hips.

"Just give me the fucking bike," Big Guy said with some force as he stood casually, off balance, not ready for action. Clay nodded, and swung off his bike on Big Guy's side, scything the front wheel straight into his crotch, and fell from the early lunge. Big Guy – with his sad why'd-you-have-to-do-that look, a this-woman's-already-been-breaking-my-balls one – moaned. Now this. The scene jumped and he was off, swinging his bike into line. The girlfriend, running along with him, sank her talons into his back, more interested in blood than bike, working into the flesh with excessive vindictiveness. "Get over here. Now!" she screeched at Big Guy.

Big Guy was almost upon them, massaging his crotch with a squint of wounded disbelief as he performed a credible hobble/trot. The talons on either side of the knapsack continued their painful grasping. Her left hand sensed the bruise from his bike accident two weeks ago, probed toward it.

He turned and yelled at his raptor-like antagonist, "Ma'am, careful, I'm HIV positive." His bike jumped forward as he pedaled free. Glancing over his shoulder Big Guy was hobbling up to his snarling girlfriend who stood slumped examining her claws for blood.

This wasn't working, this night run with a flanking loop north of downtown. Reno teemed with former dealers, croupiers, floor walkers and security men used to being up and about in the dead of night. So… no stopping, no slowing, a medium fast push even through intersections.

Three bikes emerged from the shadows. He hopped a curb and shot through a vacant lot, dodging the beer bottles and garbage. His pursuers would know the area. One dead end and it was all over. He turned counterintuitively left, back the way he'd come, darted up a driveway and lay flat behind a car. Damn, what were the chances that the tires were still inflated, jacked up as if to reveal his panting, pathetic hide. He waited as long as he dared, got ready to head east, but one of his pursuers was doing exploratory loops just down the street.

He tried the garage door behind him. It turned. He swung it up enough to crawl under it, dragging his bike after him. So, like many visitors to Reno, his first night had more morning than night to it.

He woke to voices just outside the garage door. "Come on, Henrietta, before the line gets too long." Food! He walked his bike, following his unwitting hosts to the local USG, his toes hanging over the ends of his hiking sandals, a purchase at the Truckee Bartmart.

The queuing citizens were restless, the servers surly. Two glum scanners stood, surveying the hungry and undeserving supplicants before them. Based on their stony glares, you didn't want to stand out. The folks around him ignored them in a way that didn't ignore them.

"What's that line over there for?" he asked a middle-aged lady in front of him. It was shorter, moving quickly.

"You new in town, huh? Didn't know that was still possible."

The man behind them said, "Food here is based on the old internet model. The basics are free but you definitely want to upgrade to premium."

"The USG here has subcontracted to one of our casino operators," the lady explained.

"How do you go about upgrading?"

"Trade in your bike. Why not? You're gonna lose it no matter what," the man said. "See that table over there? They'll tell you how many stars they'll give you. I'm guessing five. That's five decent dinners. The other way you get this shit and no bike."

"In other towns it's not like this. You folks should fight the system."

"You ever heard of Tommy "the Corpse" Novotny? You're more than welcome to go share your concerns with him."

Internet model or not, the USG food bank was serving Presidents, same as California. Just like voting, you chose the one you hoped you could stomach. He got a decent ladleful of Old Bush. The USG surprise, if not the chef's. In California it was mostly a cross between spaghetti and lasagna. Here it was tube noodles, tomato sauce and pellet-like balls of something you hoped was meat, and thinking more about it, hoped it wasn't.

"Soak that roll up good, otherwise you might break a tooth."

After brunch he rode quickly, glancing back every minute or so. Even in daylight every shadow had a crouch in it. He charged through intersections in a push to get through the town, ready to turn right to avoid a collision with other bikes, and unusually, a few large cars, invariably with tinted windows and fancy wheels. Almost on the edge of town he hit an intersection at the same time as a gold Cadillac, coming north to his east. The car squealed to a stop and a large man sprang out of the back. "Get over here, now!" Clay was halfway down the block when a buzzing disturbed the air near his left ear. A muted pop sounded an instant later. He turned hard right over a lawn, through a side garden and to a back yard where two young boys were playing with building blocks. Around the back – was that a mother yelling at him? – and out the other side, back the way he'd come. The gold Caddie passed slowly by and he hopped off his bike, nailed. But the car kept on down the road and didn't return. Finally, some luck.

He pumped out of Reno on the south side of the Truckee River as it flowed south of I-80, out to the east, eventually swinging north to empty into Pyramid Lake. Rivers in Nevada worked the same way as piss off a wall, running down and away until it pooled somewhere. He cycled on the wrong side of the river and of the I-80 roadblock. Nothing about escaping from Reno was going to be easy. Either that, or it was merely a fitting introduction to the endless desert ahead.

Chapter 10

They walked from Black Cow Books to Golden Gate Park. She wore a brown and yellow dress with a light-yellow cardigan loosely buttoned halfway, and a brown tweed jacket thrown cape-like over her shoulders. Quite different to the trend-conscious women in his circle. Somehow Madeline's narcotic jibe made him bristle with – with what? Not anger as much as frustration.

"A successful economy has to have a high degree of constancy," he started, in one of those intent monologues that fit with a late afternoon stroll. "And there is nothing more constant than good old greed. Most everyone wants more. Right? And if they don't, even better. Your altruists don't threaten the system at all. And sure it has its ugly side. Corporations are under huge pressure to sell more, make more, grow grow, grow. So yes there is some truth in that 'press charges' comment. But who is it that's putting the corporations under such brutal pressure? Why, the shareholders. People who want the corporation to make more so they can make more." He became aware of his surroundings at a stop light. The nostril tinge of eucalyptus trees and Pacific brine. Bicyclists, skateboarders, roller skaters heading to the park. The percussive beat from a car stereo. He hadn't had this kind of discussion since his freshman year at UCLA. "Have you ever sailed?" He tried out a sage nod, having sailed about five times in his life. "The one thing you want is a constant wind. With that you can adjust and move in any direction."

"It's such a nice day," she said. "Look, they've made a pattern in that flower bed." Red, white and blue flowers were arrayed to suggest the flag.

During his monologue they had walked all the way to the enormous white glasshouse of the Conservatory of Flowers, and he hadn't actually noticed it. Here he was arguing the case for corporate America and she fought back with flowers and sunshine.

Sitting on a grassy bank, they watched the in-line skaters scissor backwards through pegs spaced equidistantly over a thirty-yard run.

"Shouldn't it be a metaphor for something?" he said.

She smiled. "It doesn't feel right, does it?"

"What, going backwards?"

"Not spending any money, just sitting on the grass. Being an observer of life."

The fog had retreated, the breeze had died away, and their bank now had the full benefit of the sun. When was the last time he just sat and closed his eyes? Lately, pleasant weather was what he rode his bike in or jogged through. "You're right. I should stop and smell the roses."

"Yes, and not buy any."

"What's that supposed to mean?"

"That you want to buy me something so you can own me – just a little bit."

"A hot chocolate and you're going to come back to my place?" She sat so primly, knees folded up to her inclined face. A world of amazement out there before her. "And anyway, didn't I buy you even more of you with my signature?"

"I was afraid you were going to say that."

"Is that why you're doing this? A sense of obligation?"

She broke into a sigh of a smile, as if she felt sorry for him. A black man, tall, massively built, glided backward as smoothly as ripped silk, knifing through the pegs. It was hypnotic, such size and such liquid grace.

"Could you do that?" she asked.

"What, go backward? Never. Our family motto is Ever Forward. Or should have been."

"It still could be, right?"

To fill a lengthening silence, he said, "I like to work for it, grind up a mountain so I can coast down."

"All that energy, I wonder where it comes from?"

They stood up.

"I know I shouldn't say this but you remind me of my father. Just a little." She laughed, her eyes playing on him. Somehow the whole effect enabled her to get away with such a comment. Still, it was a cheap shot.

"Privileged male?"

"Hmmm." She turned to him, her eyes sharpening. "My Dad, it was so easy to make him incandescent with anger. Poor man."

"He's gone?"

"Yes gone." She smiled, one that turned into a grimace. "Oh no, not that gone. Only Florida."

"What does he do for a living?"

"Insurance." She burst out laughing. "Your face just then. I'm only joking. Dad owned a chain of hardware stores. Yes, I know, chain, chain, chain. What he does in Florida? Well, we haven't talked in a while."

They walked back to Haight Street along winding paths through the Eucalyptus trees and acres of grass, not talking. His life needed shaking up, he knew that much. He'd worked hard all his life. Always they scared you into working because the next stage, they claimed, was an order of magnitude more challenging. In elementary school you were threatened with the rigors of Junior High, in Junior High it was High School, in High School it was College, and throughout they wielded the granddaddy of all threats, The Real World. But now, at twenty-eight, there were no more threats. He was thriving nicely in the Impossibly Difficult Real World, all whips and spurs in the past. He had made it and he was bored. He needed a change, something different in his life. He had thought career; it hadn't occurred to him that change could come from a partner. Before, with his girlfriends, it has always been about compatibility. Before, he was the sole agent of any change, anything else would have been too passive. Was it possible that Madeline could shake up his life and still prove compatible? He doubted it. And yet, what did he have to lose by finding out?

Chapter 11

Just short of Lovelock, Nevada. Brown desiccated hills, a rolling plane. The entire scene as dry, as prehistoric as lizard's skin, as blank as the sun. He stood on the empty freeway, straddling his bike. Day Nineteen of his eastward trek. In a hard eight hours' riding, pushed along by a gusting tailwind that gritted up his eyes, he had come all the way from Fernley, conquered the notorious forty-mile desert, a flat alkali wasteland between the eastward-flowing Truckee River and the Humboldt flowing west, the two turning north and south respectively as if to avoid each other. It was the most dreaded part of the California Trail that had brought the Forty Niners and other immigrants out from the East.

Weeds were wedging through cracks in the fast lane. There it was again, the crack/thud of a shotgun. Hunting meant meat. When it came to fresh meat it didn't hurt to beg. Or offer his assistance with the skinning, the portage. The eating. The oat bars were driving him crazy. He may as well have been putting his muzzle in a feed bag – and much of that was over the Sierras.

At the third crack/thud, the sound reverberating from nowhere and everywhere, he remounted, clipped his free right shoe back into the pedal and headed down the highway. A glint to his right, off to the southeast, so he walked his bike through the sagebrush and bunchgrass, to a frontage road more weed garden than road. He continued toward the glint, some white structure out there, and toward a fourth shot, more boom than thud, until he reached a series of looping roads and culs-de-sac, pristinely sidewalked, ready for the American Dream to be stamped all over it. A few foundations showed the footprint of these future houses.

Hopping a curb and riding closer – the white gleaming shape turned out to be RV's, self-powered homes, tin cans on wheels. They were parked in a tight circle. Even closer now, five or six kids were pedaling madly on BMXs, beating on the aluminum arc's flanks, trying to get to the windows with their baseball bats. Old men were leaning out of the vehicles, fending off the riders with fishing poles. A man with a leathery and overlarge bald head shouted, "Get out of here or I'll shoot."

An older teen stood back from the action, a shotgun over his thin shoulder at a jaunty angle, four green shells at his feet, his legs spread. Mr. Macho, crowing over the RV he'd just peppered with shot.

Clay glided up from directly behind. Shotgun was a scrawny kid, with a tattoo on his neck. Some kind of serpent.

"What're you hunting?"

The kid wheeled around, his eyes widened with surprise. Recovering, he said, "Guy with the gun gets to ask the questions."

"This a stick up?"

"Buncha old farts don't wanna share." He had the indoor pallor and the addled squint of a pothead and the twitchiness of a pothead out of pot.

"When you get their stuff you gonna share it back with them?"

"Huh! We'll take our share and call that sharing."

"Sounds to me like stealing."

"Don't make me laugh, dude. Cops don't come out 'cept for murders. Real bad murders. And that's only if they can find themselves some gas." He gave a lop-sided smile, savoring the implied lawlessness of that tableau.

Another gunshot, like a small dog's yap, high and sharp. One of the cyclers twisted on the ground howling, his hands clutching at his thigh. As Shotgun shifted his weight, Clay grabbed the weapon off him.

"What the…that's my personal property. Give it back." Gunless, Shotgun's voice climbed an octave as the defiance leaked out of his face. "Why the hell did they have to go and plug Dwayne for?" Just now his world sounded a cold and unforgiving place.

"You talk with bullets, you gotta expect to be answered in kind."

Shotgun squared to him, his weight balanced, his fists clenched, ready for violence, not ready for it with his larger antagonist.

"Your friend needs a hospital. That means, what, Winnemucca?"

"You gonna help carry him? It's like fifty miles."

"You need to do a deal with the settlers."

"The what?"

"The Old Farts with their wagons in a circle. All I'm saying is they might have enough gas to get to Winnemucca."

"You shittin' me. I ain't dealing with those murderers."

"I'll deal with them. Just don't run off."

"I ain't going nowhere." His baleful look at his shotgun told why.

The pain had come on and his partner-in-crime was yowling in a way that got into your gut and stirred up the acid there. What had had aspects of a game gone wrong was no longer a game at all. The boy was seriously hurt.

Clay wheeled his bike towards the nearest truck window, holding the gun, breach cracked open, high over his head.

The other kids had split, leaving Shotgun, the victim, and a younger rider whose idea of trouble was to ride around faster than the others, but in a farther orbit.

Two men in the windows didn't want conversation, they were too busy protesting. Destruction of property. Terrorizing their womenfolk. They were going to take care of these Huns and didn't need an interloper to talk them down.

"Gentlemen, you just shot a boy..."

"Scram! Now! He deserved it." One of the fishing rod bearers said. Then in a more resigned tone, "Self-defense, anyhow."

"You got a wife in there? Someone intelligent enough to play this thing more than half a move in advance?"

"Martha's staying outta this."

"Earl, now who is this man?" An elderly lady with the face of a prune, if prunes were bronze, popped her head in the window. This was getting to be a regular puppet show.

"Ma'am, have you got someone who can tend to the boy?"

"Just hold your horses. Riley's on his way."

A man came around from the northern arc of the circle, striding in a bent-forward stoop, his square jaw and gray buzz cut framing a serious frown. Twenty years earlier he might have been formidable. Now his head weighed too much: it tilted his body forward so that he glared up from a downturned face. He held a walkie talkie. "Okay, I'm there. Copy." A pause. "I said copy." He stared at the device in disbelief. "I said…"

"We can hear you Riley," said Martha from the truck window.

Riley gave her an annoyed swat, wound the crank furiously. "I'm here. Copy."

A flurry of static. Riley held the device as if about to dash it into the ground.

"Call in your first aid," Clay called out to Martha.

"You stay out of this," Riley said. "Vince, come in. Come in Vince."

Martha wouldn't meet Clay's eyes. This thing had to go through proper protocol, through Riley.

The injured boy's howling was a harsh reminder that they needed to hurry.

"Hey," Clay said to the young orbiter, "Come here and take this." He held out the walkie talkie.

"That's stealing," Riley said. "God-damned Chinese crap."

"You can go back to playing spies when the boy's been seen to. He's hurt bad. Where I come from that's GBH. The police need to know about it."

"Shit."

The truck door opened and old folk started edging out, two grandmas with a first aid kit, three men climbing out after them. One of the women cut off the victim's pant leg and applied a tourniquet as the men stood over the scene, hands on hips, just in case the threat wasn't over yet. Shotgun hung back, outnumbered, wanting out of there, except Clay had his shotgun, and his youngest recruit who, still holding the walkie talkie, had drifted over to the winning side. The grandmas were clucking and cooing and stroking the poor boy's dirty forehead. He held his leg with a muffled groan.

The deal was done. Shotgun agreed to cease and desist in return for a lift to the hospital with his fallen comrade. The oldsters surrendered the offending weapon – no doubt they had others. In return, Clay gave them the empty shotgun for later collection. One of the RV's headed out for Winnemucca with the victim and Shotgun.

After turning over the walkie talkie, the one remaining marauder, the orbiter, said, "We were just bored. I tol' Hulk the shotgun was a mistake. Boy, my uncle's gonna skin me alive."

"Good for him."

"Hulk shouldn't've fired at those RV's. It was s'posed to be one shot up in the air."

"Guess he got carried away."

"Guess that's what happened to Dwayne." The boy laughed at his joke, nervously.

Two of the Grandmas stood with him, holding up BMXs, the victim's and the orbiter's, that they'd agree to store. The boy tried not to smile – he had traded up to Shotgun's bigger, better bike.

The oldsters departed, leaving Clay with the orbiter, a small wiry boy with reddish brown hair and gloppy freckles. He looked about twelve, but the way he carried himself, talked, hung in there and didn't run off, might put a few more years on him.

"Where'd you come from?" the boy asked.

"80. Heard the shotgun."

"80's dangerous, isn't it? Robbers and wild trucks and escaped prisoners and stuff. We come from that way." The kid pointed to a dirt trail through the brush that led to Lovelock, well away from the freeway. After an awkward pause, he added, "Which way you goin' on 80? How far?"

"East. Boston."

"That's east all right."

"Yep." Clay executed a vague salute.

"You goin'?"

"I'm not gonna move on down the line standing here."

He stayed in Lovelock, off Broadway, in a park next to the courthouse. From a dry barren hill a lonely "L" presided over the town. He shook his head. One ninth of the Hollywood sign and a thousand times less glamorous.

A plaque gave Lovelock's history. 150 years ago it was called Big Meadow, a major resting stop on the California Trail, offering lush marshland to weary pioneers. A place for them to marshal their resources for the push across the parched forty-mile desert to the water of the Truckee River. The plaque, in need of updating, said "Lovelock, a barrel of fun for all".

In the early morning he left the town to its fun seekers, and was soon pumping past a prison, isolated out in the sagebrush, pinned up against the same barren range of hills that held the "L". Finding his rhythm for the day, he daydreamed about how many cons still remained locked up in there. Every sign he passed warned drivers not to pick up hitchhikers. It would take a hell of a lot of sangfroid to stand in front of the prison, newly escaped, and calmly thumb a ride.

At his first rest break, doing his knee bends and leg stretches, another cyclist hove into view on the road far back. He kept an eye on the follower, who doggedly matched his speed, never further away or closer no matter how vigorously he pedaled.

Absent the climb and with more desert experience he might have tried for the seventy-two miles to Winnemucca in one day. So, no hurry – a day of steady climbing would take him to a campground by a manmade lake, twenty-five miles east of Lovelock. He took a break in a strip of shade behind a shot-up van, a bullet hole in the windshield, the vehicle slued around and facing the non-existent oncoming traffic. No blood on the seats, though. Nothing else either, it had been stripped. There had been other abandoned cars east of Reno, some with the same bullet holes around their wheel cowlings, many with shredded tires, but none as violently assaulted as this one. Fifty yards out in the scrub the skeleton of a motorcycle.

"Hi."

Clay, reverie interrupted, jumped. It was the boy, the orbiter, from the RV circle.

"Didn't mean to spook you. Sorry," the boy said.

"Where're you headed?"

"East." Deciding this might be too laconic, the boy added, "Utah."

"What's your plan?"

The kid shrugged.

"Listen, I'm talking food, water. Bedding."

"There'll be a Bart in Winny." Another shrug. "I'll figure it out."

"I'm not sure how I'm gonna make it and I'm prepared. Kind of." The boy did a poor job of stifling a yawn. He must have been tracking him since the previous afternoon, and been up early to match the early start. "Are you running away or running to?"

"Both." The story came out, the boy's need for Clay's goodwill just about overcoming his reluctance to venture beyond five-word sentences. He had been staying with his uncle, got trapped there by the Void. He didn't get on with the uncle, wanted to be with his mother back in Utah.

"You haven't thought this through – how unforgiving the desert out here can be."

"I've lived in it for three months." Clay had to admit it trumped his two days.

Half an hour's riding later, the approaching whine of an eastbound truck convoy started to build. The first of the day out of California. "Follow me," Clay said. They walked their bikes off the road bed and out into the sagebrush.

"Watcha doing that for?"

"You'll see."

The first truck drove out on the verge kicking up dust and sending rock chips flying, tooting its horns as it did so. In the second cab a bored-looking GI just about managed to flip them off. In the next cab a young blonde hiked up her tee shirt showing off a fine pert pair. The cab after showed dual moons, male and female. After that: tits, finger, ass, finger, tits, tits, finger, ass/ass, nothing, finger, finger and the show was over. A few empty beer cans kicked down the highway in the convoy's wake.

"That was neat! How do you get a job like that?"

"See your Army recruiter. When you're old enough." *If we have an army by then.*

They were back on their bikes now.

"What're the girls for?"

"You'd have to ask them."

The boy swatted at him, playfully.

"What're you gonna do with the gun?"

"The Beretta? Keep it."

"Isn't that stealing?"

"No. Technically, I'm carrying off evidence of a crime – that's the illegal part."

"They gave it to you?" the boy asked.

"Gave it by way of not asking for it back."

He let the boy lead, assessing his endurance. After a mile the boy fell back level. "Why do the girls… really, what're they there for?"

"Haven't talked to any. Probably their version of riding around terrorizing poor old folks. You know, bored?"

"I reckon being an adult is just getting used to being bored."

"You might be on to something there. Really, it's just a lack of imagination. This world is always an interesting place. You don't even need to look that hard."

"Those trucks sure were interesting."

"That's just a passing fancy. You wanna know what's interesting? Survival. Things won't stay the same. They'll either get better or worse and it's best to be prepared for worse."

They were quiet for a time as they rode in tandem in the early afternoon heat off the blacktop. The rumble of another convoy loomed behind them.

"Oh boy!" said the boy.

This one was all horns. A few fingers.

"What's wrong with those guys?"

"No telling. Maybe they're busy."

"Wow! You mean like threesomes and stuff?"

Clay blinked. Jeez, at that age he was pretty shaky on twosomes.

"Why are they so…unfriendly?"

"It's against the law to ride a bike on the interstate. This is their pathetic way of reminding us of that sorry fact. Country's in the toilet and they're worried about not putting the seat down."

The plan was to climb towards Winnemucca and let reality talk the boy out of his ridiculous quest. One shivering night, if he made it that far, and the boy would be coasting back to Lovelock come the morning.

The camp ground of the Rye Patch Recreation Area overlooked a sizeable lake made from the dammed-up Humboldt River.

"Will Dwayne be okay?" the boy asked as they sat on the shore after a relaxing swim.

"Your buddy that was shot? He won't die. Trouble is, hospitals are running out of supplies. If the bone's shattered… Anyway, what was he doin' to get the Old Timers so riled up."

"Letting the air outta their tires."

"That's a low blow for sure. There's not being able to go anywhere, and then there's staring that sad fact in the face. What I don't understand is what those folks are doing off by themselves."

"There's a decal on most of their vehicles. An oval shape with SSA in red letters? Turns out it stands for Senior Survivalists of America."

"End of the world stuff?"

"Uh huh. My uncle Ezra, not that he's my real uncle, was one. I got shipped out to him for a couple a months. He talked about the end of the world like he wanted it to happen. He had years of food. Solar powered everything. Guns. Escape routes. Meeting points. Talked about how he'd keep hungry people from trying to muscle in on his stuff like, bring it on so he could take care of them."

Clay sat in a pleasant groove, the mild sun drying his lake-washed limbs.

"Yes sir. Meals at his place were worse than the USG, if you can believe that. Out of date cans of glop. Ravioli. Noodles. Small wieners."

A light breeze brought just the right amount of coolness. He could sit here forever.

"His main thing was sun storms. But also volcanoes. Asteroids. Earthquakes. Funny that we got hit by something invisible. Matter of fact I'm not sure what we got hit with."

In the morning the boy was shivering, pipe-cleaner arms wrapped around his thin chest for warmth. His eyes sagged and popped open.

Clay looked away from the struggling boy. All he had to do now was drive it home, no mercy. He couldn't do it, though. "Guess I should know your name."

"Jarome Hargreaves." He winced that away. "I go by Sonny."

"Your uncle will be worried about you."

"He doesn't give a, a hoot."

"Come on, he's responsible for you."

Sonny grimaced, stoically silent.

"So, you're going back to your parents?"

"My Mom. She's in Centerville, just north of Salt Lake City."

"What about your Dad?"

"I got an address."

"Your mother a Mormon."

"Yessir, she is."

"And your Dad?"

"Yeah. My step-dad too. He's a Mormon, but more to the point he's an asshole. That's all there is to say on that one."

"You don't get along with him?"

"No, sir, I don't. Never liked the set up. That's why my uncle... took me away. There's too many damn boys is what my new Pa says."

"And what, too many wives?"

"Yes, sir." It was the lonesomest "yes, sir" you'd ever want to hear.

Back on the road, more shot-up cars, one with three bullet holes in the windshield, blood on the seats. No mound out in the desert, though. At noon they rested at a shot-up Cadillac.

"Sleep in the back."

"It's okay."

"Go on. We've got plenty of time."

Three hours later Sonny was tough to rouse, a fierce kind of sleep that had a balled up fist, and sour mouth movement in it.

"Guess another half hour won't hurt," Clay said into the car. When time expired he stood out on the shoulder with his bike, baiting an approaching convoy. As a huge wall of radiator came hurling at him at 60 mph he stood his ground, like a matador standing in against a bull. The blast of horn from the enraged driver rattled his inner panes and had Sonny out of the car, rubbing his fists into his eyeballs.

"What are they doing?" Sonny yelled, angry at this sudden violent world.

"Life on the interstate. We've got another 400 miles of it before we hit SLC."

Chapter 12

Months after his first meeting with Dubkhadze he received an invitation on thick cream paper with even thicker gold embossing. Mr. Clay Holloway's presence was requested at An Evening of Song and Entertainment, the famous, the notorious, Dubkhadze Independence Day Celebration – only this was Georgian Independence in late May. "You've been invited to the Georgian Orgy?" EvDev's Director of Facilities said in a what-is-the-world-coming-to tone.

"There's got to be a catch, right?" Clay said, playing down the value of the invitation. He was already on shaky ground by going over the D of F's head.

"You're on your own there, pal. Nothing that man does would surprise me."

The party was held at Dubkhadze's "Ranch" up in the San Gabriel mountains north of LA. A fleet of limos ran guests from the parking lot of a hardware superstore in the flatlands to the stone-fronted three-story structure, as imposing as a prison. The arriving guest was guided by a dual string of torch lights, and by the subdued buzz of conversing partiers, to a large garden around the north side of the house. A wide terrace in the back served as refreshment central with a bar and tables sagging with food. A stage with sound system was set up at the northern edge of the lawn. Clay arrived to find over a hundred guests, all male, standing in clusters, many on the terrace but others spread out on the green expanse of lawn. An all-female, all-blonde team of champagne servers and catering staff circulated with wine and canapes.

"How'd *you* get this far?" one of the blond servers said familiarly. "Turn around."

He obeyed her with as much dignity as he could muster after such disparagement. Her breath tickled his neck and her breasts poked against his shoulder blades as she proceeded to loosen his tie and slip it noose-like over his head. "There, that's better isn't it?" she said. His tie now hung uncinched around her neck.

At 9pm the entertainment started, Circassian dancers whirling around in long robes and dresses cinched tight at the waist, followed by a sword-swallower, a belly dancer, a snake charmer. Backed up by a house band, Georgian friends took the mic and sang a song from the old country, introduced by Dubkhadze himself, full of easy flattery.

Talking to a licensing lawyer, Clay snacked on canapes and sipped champagne – his glass refilled so regularly it was impossible to track the consumption level. A blonde server slid into his lap. She threw her arms around his neck as if corralling a young steer.

"What is it you do that makes you so big?" she purred.

"Why, you're wearing someone else's tie," he said, slurring the "else's" slightly. When she had gone in search of friendlier perches the lawyer said, "You know what I've noticed after years of attending Otakar's parties? When you're standing you don't have a lap."

Blondes were distributed in laps like daisies in a field, their loosened ties making them look like sinful schoolgirls. There has to be a catch, Clay was thinking. I'm not Georgian; I'm not important. Would Dubkhadze, who had a reputation for brutal negotiations, resort to blackmail? Oh, the incriminating pictures his people could take! Even a shot of Miss Makes You So Big in some chump's lap might be enough of a threat to give Dubkhadze the leverage he needed.

At midnight he stood near the stage, making a show of appreciating the entertainment. As compere, Dubkhadze would see him, maybe remember him, and think about chasing up the Steel Umbrella proposal. Not that Dubkhadze appeared to notice him as a string of friends and flatterers filed up to pay their respects to the master of ceremonies.

"And now a special treat," Dubkhadze announced, taking the mic. "I would like to ask my good friend, Mr. Clay Holloway, to sing one of our old songs."

Clay eyed the line of pulsing torch flames that marked the exit to the street. He could run out and down the road, hitchhike back to the flatlands. Or sprint to the lower terrace and careen down the mountain side and lose himself in all those bleary lights.

Two of the female Circassian dancers were standing on either side of him, ready to escort him to the stage. As the violins hit the first bars of Stalin's favorite song, Suliko, every Georgian in the garden sat up and looked down.

He mounted the scaffold. Had Monica, one of his account execs, chosen that song out of spite. He had been tied up, needed to leave for his plane, but asking her to find and print out a phonetic version of a Georgian song was a small step up from asking for coffee. And now he was going to pay.

The band struck up and played the intro, a lilting melody that spanned an octave with a complicated rhythm. They played it again, and again, ratcheting the tension, as he kept missing that start. He gulped, and launched into the song with such cornered rat focus that only two things existed in the universe, his all-flats voice, and a cloud of humiliation so huge and dark that it threatened to wipe out all of humanity. It had been nearly three months since he'd memorized those phonetic syllables on a fifty-minute plane trip. Desperately he tried to dredge them up. The first lines might have been close. What he did with the next ones, well he certainly wasn't going to ask afterwards. He did okay in the short lines of the bridge. The musicians came around for the next verse and he froze. They came around again and one of his Circassian escorts leaned in to share the mic. They sang the next stanza as a lop-sided duet, except her words were different. She sang well, deeply sorrowful. Her eyes met his in the incomprehensible drama of the song's lament. She had striking eyes that flickered and flamed like the gas torches that encircled the terrace.

"Will you marry me?" he said as the polite applause died down.

"Sure," she said in a pure California accent. "Just get Mr. D's okay and we can set about getting his name lasered off my butt."

At the end of the evening, the first hints of light in the eastern sky, Clay sought out Dubkhadze and thanked him.

"I'm hoping all that champagne will erase any memories of my performance."

"What performance is this?"

It took Clay, still drunk-sounding, and wrong-footed by Dubkhadze's bright eyes and bushy tail, too long to get the joke. "You're right," he said, "you couldn't call it a performance. It's like sex, if you don't deliver you haven't performed."

The Georgian had his crude side, but not now. He frowned quizzically. "Mr. Holloway, if you sing a Georgian song it is best to sing it in Georgian. Not Russian."

It was so late it was early. Clay's head pounded from a potent mix of booze and humiliation. Dubkhadze looked impossibly fresh, his eyes alert, his bearing easy but erect. Ah, the twin brother trick.

"I almost forgot," his host said. "For you." He handed over a crisp envelope.

Clay didn't open it until he sat slumped on the plane back to San

Francisco. It contained the last page of the Steel Umbrella contract, signed by the great man himself, and a page with the words in English and in Georgian to Suliko. His eyes fell on the opening line on the English side. *I was looking for my sweetheart's grave.*

Chapter 13

He got tired of letting the boy lead, of matching his erratic speed – no rhythm there as they climbed towards Winnemucca, the desert so blank and unforgiving. Out here, time was fractal, minutes, hours, days, epochs were just different magnifications of the same thing. Money? The fall of a great nation? Just so much dust on a bleached horse skull.

They reached Winnemucca in the early evening. "What do you mean you don't have any money?"

"I'll, I'll do…okay." The boy was too tired to string a sentence together.

"You need blankets, a knapsack of some kind, a sweater. It'll have to be a kindness-of-strangers operation. Start with women, ones about your Mom's age. You ask them an innocent question – where's the USG? Or the Bart? – smile nicely, work those hound dog eyes. The secret is to underplay it." Yawning wouldn't hurt; Sonny was dead on his feet.

While Sonny went trawling for necessities, Clay spent two hours in line at the USGmail stations. The tiny chance of a message from Madeline had added some zip to his pedaling through the barren desert wastes. All he got for his effort was an all caps message from Sue. He didn't read it. Didn't need to.

"It's your deal Sonny, so you knock." The boy tottered, his eyes easing shut, snapping open, faltering again. The trailer door was answered by a tall thin woman with an elongated, vaguely bovine face. She assessed the pair with alarming directness. A compact, darker-skinned lady peered at them from behind her.

"Hi, boys." To Clay she said, "I'm Nora."

The three adults exchanged knowing looks over Sonny's gaping yawn.

"I'm Beatrice," her friend said. She pronounced it Bee-AT-trice.

Sonny said, "We come about the bedding, remember?"

Nora clapped her hands once, laughing and turning to Beatrice.

"The boy needs blankets or a sleeping bag," Clay said, figuring that would acknowledge the misunderstanding, and let them go on their way.

"Yes, we know. He was very specific." Nora said, not containing a wide smile.

The boy was just about falling down on his feet, didn't object to a spell on the floor of the trailer.

"What do you ladies do out here?" Clay said, as the three of them sat in the cooling evening air.

"We're what you'd call freelancers," Nora said.

"Lancers? What're you spearing?"

"We're more like the spear-ees. This town's always survived on one-nighters," Nora said. "People passing through. There's only so many hours you can hang on to that steering wheel."

"Lotsa big rigs used to park at the Chevron down there and the drivers walked up this hill. Two days alone and away from your old lady, and you're needing female company in all sorts of ways."

"Nowadays," Beatrice added, "the big rigs come with their own bed in back and company up front." She was a café-au-lait lady with dark brown eyes, heavy lashes, a shy excuse of a chin and a body that made you forget the chin.

"That's right, Trice. We're like a town with the shut down rail line. Cut off."

True to their profession the talk came around to money. "You know Beatrice still keeps a wad of old dollars. For like sennamental value."

"I told you, Nor, all those bills've got cocaine on them. Reminds me of happier times."

"And what do you do for money," Nora asked Clay. Down to business.

"Hardly matters does it? I got a few Kendies. Don't even know what they're good for anymore."

"You're in Gip country now, my friend. But we're prepared to be open-minded, isn't that right Trice?" Nora said lightheartedly yet sadly, for form. Clay was a browser not a buyer; he'd made that clear.

"I haven't told you this yet, Trice, but I've decided to become a virgin again. I reckon if the USG can declare themselves a new money I can declare myself a new pussy. And when this Void gets fixed, I can become a blonde again."

"The body changes all its cells, doesn't it?" Beatrice said. "Is it two years? So, stop doing it for that long and voila you got your cherry back." She smiled, something a little bit shy there.

"Nah, doll. I reckon it's like the US Dollar, what's popped is popped."

"So what do you do here, now that there are no truck drivers wanting your company?"

"I'm working on scraping enough New D's together," Beatrice said, "so I can head home. Back to Louisiana." She gazed out into the night. "You ever tasted café au lait? You got any Gips? I can make you happy. I'll even take Kendies."

"What difference does money make?" he said. "You book a flight that doesn't fly? A bus that's sitting on flat tires? How are you going anywhere?"

"The convoys? Hook up with those lonely GI drivers and…I can start back on my redemption when I hit Tallulah."

"Where's that?"

"Upstate Louisiana. It's got one foot in Mississippi."

"Coming or going?"

"You could try the corn jockeys, Trice," Nora butted in. "Find someone with enough fermented corn juice you could maybe make Denver or something."

"Those corn jockeys aren't capable of heading in one direction for more than ten minutes. Besides the Interstate's dangerous." She turned to him, "That's right, isn't it?"

"It's not that bad. Um…." Wait a minute, he'd been shot at, chased, sideswiped. He'd cycled by a wrecker's yard full of mangled and shot up cars. His bike had been grabbed at and fought over. "On second thought I guess I wouldn't advise it."

Beatrice went around the trailer, came back with an ax, handed it to Clay. "You chop up some kindling and I'll set up the fire. It's getting cold. Woods around there." She pointed to the back of the trailer. Nora excused herself. It wasn't exactly clear where to.

Beatrice sat next to him in a comfortable quiet, the fire taking hold, the stars pulsing. With Sonny collapsed in her trailer, there was a couple-after-the-kid's-gone-to-bed aspect to their small talk under the wheeling night sky.

"Maybe it's you who should consider a deal with a corn jockey," Beatrice said. "Just might buy you three hundred easy miles. Throw your bike in the back."

"Buy? With what?"

Beatrice smiled, talking just to fill up the night. "You're going to need help to make it all that way." A sudden shift in the tone, talking the way a wife would, discussing challenges, on his side, part of the team. That comfortable married feel, such a distant echo of his time with Madeline. That distance seemed irrecoverable, and yet here he was riding thousands of miles to recover it.

The night wore on, the stars arced, time to turn in.

"Y'all welcome in my bed, soldier."

"I'd be standing at attention all night."

"Watcha guarding?"

"My fidelity."

"I have ways of hollering 'at ease'."

"Look, I'm bone-tired, kinda married, and got nothing of value I can give you." He managed a well-timed yawn. "Save it for some younger buck."

In the trailer his resistance was low. She removed one of his main objections, his rank clothes, washed away his grime and sweat with a sponge. He melted in the warm luxury of cleanliness and her touch, cordial, not too intimate. As she massaged his back and his legs, he fought the deep pull of sleep. And lost.

A deep nourishing night in a real bed, a restorative sleep full of Technicolor dreams about easy pedaling over soft and manageable hills.

"Well cock-a-doodle-doo!" she said, her confirming hand down below.

"Beatrice?" His voice quivery, beseeching.

"Don't worry, I know what I'm doing."

She sat on the side of the bed brushing her hair and counting the strokes, her café au lait back sleek and endless as her other hand moved sinuously.

"One hundred twenty-six. One hundred and twenty-seven."

"Beatrice?"

"It's okay, hon. We have a saying, Doesn't count in Nevada."

"Uh huh."

"One hundred seventy-seven. One hundred seventy-eight."

"Beatrice?" He bleated her name like a lost lamb.

"Sush." She stopped. "You sure you're okay with this?" She asked with a teasing glint. She started on her brush strokes again, left him out of it for fifteen of them. Made his eyes beg, forgave him with a smile. Beatrice had the silkiest hair in Winnemucca.

"This wasn't supposed to happen," he said afterwards.

"Sometimes in life you just gotta roll with it."

Splayed, unable to move, he could hear Sonny stirring down in the kitchen area. For some reason he had heightened positional awareness.

Behind his head, three hundred miles to the west, his dimly-aware mother was fading into dementia. Beyond his feet, buttoned-up Boston sat nearly twenty-five hundred miles in the other direction. If Madeline could abandon him, what's the big deal if he fought his corner. It felt a small betrayal.

"So, tell me, what are you gonna do in this strip mall in the middle of nowhere," he said, packing up his things. To minimize the weight in his knapsack, he rolled the Beretta up in his bedroll, along all the other heavy items.

"What's anyone gonna do anywhere in this Void? Everyone's sitting around with a finger up their ass. At least here that costs extra."

Beatrice pulled him back from leaving her bedroom, took his hand and led him around the bed to a window which she slid open with a smile. "The boy," she said. "He thinks the world of you."

The two cycled down Winnemucca's main street, past an endless parade of sagging motels, boarded up chain restaurants and strip malls.

"You don't want to visit your shot-up pal at the hospital?"

"Nah, Hulk will be there. I'm going to try to forget about that jerk off."

"Hard to do when you're riding his bike."

At their first rest stop something made Clay count his money. He had hid his small wad under Beatrice's mattress, and had had to scoop it from under her nose while packing. Nine New D's when there should have been eleven. He'd go back in anger if she had left him with eight. Just the right touch, again. There was JFK on the top bill looking all bloated and horny. A man who understood all aspects of commerce.

Sonny pedaled more vigorously today, constant in the lead, if a trifle on the slow side. But slower was better, forcing a lower gear, less torque on his bad knee, enabling him to relax. His time with Beatrice felt like permission, to abandon his past, to enter a less constrained, improvised future, his life a boat that's slipped the last rope securing it, now free to be carried by unknown currents – out into the desolate seas of the Nevada desert.

Chapter 14

It would be nice to see you again…

Three weeks after their stroll in Golden Gate Park, and now she writes? She had been amiable but clear: they were from different worlds. Was it his contrariness, his savoring of a challenge, or his sales-closing impulse that had him saying he'd like to see her again? An invitation for her to change her mind. Three weeks, two messages ignored, and now an invitation to a dinner party? He thrashed around like a hooked fish. Over several days he worked that hook like a cracked tooth, something new, to be explored. No, he wouldn't accept, wouldn't even answer. Why condemn himself to such a doomed enterprise? No, definitely not. Even though, deep down, he knew he would accept, something to do with self-respect had to be dealt with first.

The address was a house out in Visitacion Valley. Not a great place to park his sleek German speedvagen. He arrived at the door with a bottle of carefully researched pinot noir.

"You must be the insurance guy," said the hostess, a curly blonde with a thin face that framed a sour smile. She seemed reluctant to relieve him of his bottle. In the living room he encountered an array of people in opium-den mode, spread out on the floor on pillows, slouched on the sofa, or perched on its arms. A few stood over by a large fish tank.

"Hi, I'm the insurance guy," he announced in his designer jeans, black crew neck, and cotton blazer in the latest blue.

"I'm Deborah," the hostess said, back with a glass of wine. "We'd just about given up on you."

Madeline's email had said 8pm-ish. It was twenty minutes after eight. "How do you know Madeline?" he asked, took a sip of wine, cloying, like fermented rotten fruit. Definitely not his.

"We're roommates, or house mates I guess you'd call it."

"Where is she?" His sour smile could have been about the wine.

"Somewhere." She held it there for a long moment, giving her terseness space to make its statement. "I bet she didn't explain about our dinner, did she?"

"Not really."

"There's a bunch of us who get together for…evenings like this. We have different topics on the agenda. Tonight, it's not a topic, it's a task. Each of us has to invite the most interesting person we've met in the last year, or whenever."

"Really?" He telegraphed a self-deprecating frown.

Madeline came down the hallway on the arm of an older man with pointed goatee and wild hair. "There you are," she said, and skipped up to him, kissed him on the cheek, so quick she was out of there before he knew what had happened. Her smell lingered though, some lightly fragrant flower. "Oh and this is Jorge." Hor-hay.

"And what interesting person have you invited?" Clay said to Jorge, after they'd nodded to each other.

"Jorge is so interesting he can get away with inviting himself," Madeline said.

Jorge cast a mock-puzzled look at her.

"Sorry I'm late," Clay said.

Madeline, picking up on his sarcasm, came closer and whispered in his ear. "That's just Deborah, she's, well, it sounds like you've figured that out already."

They ate dinner buffet style, there being too many guests for anything else. Vegetarian casseroles, brown rice with stuff in it, various dips with pita bread, a multi-hued salad. Jug wine. Banana bread and brownies for dessert.

Madeline balanced on a sofa arm to eat. The four guests on its cushions scrunched up to make room for Jorge. Clay found a place on the floor.

"Let's get started," Deborah said, when the assembled group were half way through dinner. Each inviter gave a short introduction of their choice of most interesting person. There was a civil war buff; an activist lawyer representing abused women; a city official in charge of the methadone program; a husband and wife team of hydroponic farmers. What is this, he thought, the start of a game show?

"I invited Clay Holloway," Madeline said. "Clay?" He raised his hand, last and least interesting. "Well I guess you all know Clay is in insurance." Light laughter. "And I invited him because we're all the same. Month after month we sit around agreeing on everything. So I thought we should be open-minded enough to entertain another point of view. And I invited him because…" She held it there for a moment.

"Because he too is open-minded."

"What kind of insurance do you do?" someone asked him.

Do? It sounded like, What drugs do you take. "Mainly buildings and contents, some residential but mainly commercial."

"And what value does your product give to people like us?"

"Do you really want to go into this?"

"Madeline is right; we should be open-minded," Jorge said.

"Let's take homeowner insurance and let's say that in an average year ten houses will be largely destroyed by fire. We don't know which ten. Hopefully no one does. Let's say the average cost to replace one of those homes is $200,000. Remember that most of the value of a house is the land. You can have a system where each resident saves up that kind of money, just in case, or you can pool the risk, and say we're all in this risk business together we'll all pay a little so that no one loses a lot."

"Well explained," Jorge piped up. "But let's say we don't want to be *together with* a corporation. What if we want to pool the money ourselves?"

"In principle that should be okay."

"Listen to him, backing away already."

"Hear him out," Madeline said, loudly.

"Yes, tell us about your principles," Jorge said.

"Anyone who chooses to jump into your pool." he said, addressing Jorge, "is, by definition, a consumer. That brings all sorts of government protection into play."

"Exactly," one of the fish tank brigade said, "the government telling us what to do."

"Limiting our freedom."

"That's one argument. But look at Jorge's pool of money, let's say it's five million dollars. Where does he keep it? Under a mattress? In risky investments that may or may not play out? What if he absconds with the money, or borrows it, thinking he'll be able to pay it back? What if something happens to him? Who takes over."

"I know, we can insure against that happening."

"What do you do if someone doesn't pay?" he said.

"What do you do?"

"There's a tough line between being a friendly company and a financially responsible one."

"I know what comes next," Jorge said. "Economies of scale. A large pool can offer lower premiums than my pool. And that pool may be based in New Jersey so how do I know it is financially responsible? Oh,

I know, the government can regulate it. When a smaller local company wouldn't need that."

"The one thing to understand about insurance is that it's the most potentially dangerous financial invention of all time. Any business which takes in cash first and may pay some out later is a temptation that crooks can't resist. Take in cash, grow, play hard ball on claims, and you can amass a fortune quickly, a cash fortune. Quite honestly, it is an industry that needs to be regulated."

"I prefer my pool," Jorge said.

"And your corporation is more efficient than a small pool?" Deborah said. "How much do you make?"

Clay shrugged. "I'm guessing too much?"

"People in this city are going hungry, and fat cats like you are eating in five star restaurants paid from your off-shore accounts?"

"What is it you're advocating?"

"Making business more friendly. Truly on the side of the consumer. Admit it, you're not really on the side of the consumer."

"You're welcome to start up your own insurance company and prove it can be done better your way."

"Would you help?"

"I congratulate, you Madeline," Jorge said. "A most interesting guest!" He smiled at her warmly. "Now Clay – and I must say, you've been quite sporting to take all this – you must admit there is a vast and growing inequity in our society, the rich are getting richer and everyone else is sliding down the hill. How can people go hungry in a society like ours?"

Ours? Jorge was from South America somewhere. That's what Ernesto sitting next to Clay had said. "They've put him in jail twice," Ernesto had said, as if talking about badges of honor.

"Our system is far from perfect. I would argue that it has the means of becoming more perfect within it. Just because I work in the system and benefit from it doesn't necessarily mean I am against wholesale reform."

"What does 'doesn't necessarily mean' mean?" Deborah said.

"Yes, please be specific. This is interesting." Jorge practically winked at him.

"I would close out a lot of tax loopholes. Crack down on tax evasion and off-shore fun and games. Increase regulation of some aspects of the financial service industry. And definitely wipe out large scale government subsidies in many industries."

"But this has been going on too long," someone said. "Maybe

you're right that it *could* be changed from within – but that hasn't happened. Decade after decade. It's time for more drastic action."

Clay started to speak.

"There's only one way to get people's attention these days: burn it down," a young man in a red wool cap interrupted, out-voicing him. "Then we'll have the headlines we need. National hand-wringing. Why did these people do this?"

"Yeah, burn it down it and it grows back better."

"It's true," Deborah practically shouted. "Sad, but true. It's the only way to get people's attention."

"Can I ask you to avoid the properties we're insuring?" he said. He found and met Madeline's eyes and sent a thanks-a-lot look her way. She smiled and telegraphed a slight head shake: *it's just talk.*

"Shall we bore you with thousands of incidents in world history where active, angry, yes even violent protest has brought just demands to the table, and achieved real progress?" the activist lawyer demanded.

"Please," Jorge said, standing up, "let me clarify. Our friend here uses the word 'violent' too freely. We don't want violence. Of course not. And no burning down either. But perhaps we can turn up the volume of our peaceful protests just a little."

"Yes, exactly," said a short man in a Grateful Dead tee shirt. "Edgier demonstrations. Get the cops to react a bit. A fire in a dumpster rolled out into the street."

Clay tried to get Madeline's attention so he could nod good-bye. He couldn't risk his career by being present at such revolutionary talk. Maybe she'd show him to the door.

"Hey, what if Mr. State Farm here reports us to the cops."

"Even he wouldn't do that," Deborah said.

What a nightmare! If they started talking about him in the third person, he didn't need to be present. Madeline had disappeared somewhere in the back of the house. After ten minutes he gave up waiting.

"Tell Madeline good-bye, from me," he said to Jorge.

"I will confess to you," Jorge said, walking him to the door. "There are times when I too wish I could walk out of here. It's all talk, the same talk, always the same. Madeline was right to invite you." He smiled sympathetically. "Our little group needed your views. You have been most sporting."

At the door Jorge offered his hand, as if agreeing a deal. A deal, it seemed, that involved Madeline, and a deal that excluded him.

Chapter 15

Nevada is mainly flats and mountains, some three hundred of the latter, short yet substantial, placed like so many logs aligned north to south. The highway takes you north around this one, south around that. In between and all around is the flat thirsty desert, porous, dusty, dotted with cheatgrass, sagebrush, bunchgrass. The Great Basin Desert.

Sonny bore a light load in his new knapsack, the g-bars, other food, a haphazard first aid pouch, spare wheel spokes, inner tubes, and clothes. Clay, his heavier load evening out their speeds, let the boy lead, enjoying the barren grandeur of crumbling hills and rolling desert. Rested, unhinged, free, he tried to beat himself up over Beatrice's ministrations. In the nearly ten months he'd been separated from Madeline, he had given in to temptation only once, riding a light smile back to her apartment from their place next to each other in the USG line. She treated it as light sport, a pleasant passing of a breezy winter day. "That was nice," she said, after, meaning it. Yes, she had been off on her ride. He had pushed her like you would a baby in a swing, wee-hee-ing into the sky. While he stood glumly behind her, lost and pushing, lost and pushing. How could that be so bad, and last night okay?

The succession of shot-up cars had diminished as they had neared Winnemucca and were just as sparse after it. Clay was pumping along in daydream mode, matching his speed to Sonny's lead. All these sagebrush bushes so randomly placed, yet so all-pervasive. Like stars, they filled the desert with no obvious pattern, yet no obvious empty spaces either – something alien in their placement, in their multitude as if they were a plant world array searching the heavens for signs of plant life.

Out of nowhere the wind picked up. A dark brown wall appeared in the east. Clay could feel a pressure drop in his ears. A dust storm. He started pumping vigorously, came up level with Sonny, urged him on. They had to find an abandoned car. The wall grew nearer, the morning darkened. Now a sprint to a white van in the distance. Good news for stowing the bikes; bad news for the shot-up windshield. Five bullet holes. The driver's side window was down a few inches. With a dead battery it would stay that way.

Sonny covered three of the bullet holes with two hands and his sweatshirt, and a foot on the far wide hole. Clay used his left forearm and his sleeping bag to block out the cracked open window. His right hand blocked out the final hole. The dark menace was before them now, the wind rocking the van, the sand scouring it to a loud insistent growl. It got no darker though and in ten minutes the dark mass had passed by to the northwest.

"Must have been caught by the edge of the sucker," Clay said.

"That was enough for me."

They waited an hour for the sand to clear out of the air, and rode on with tee shirts over their mouths and noses until they were well clear of the storm zone.

Now, just east of Golconda, where the freeway started climbing toward the summit of that name, the shot-up cars started accumulating again, a veritable linear junkyard.

"Don't like the looks of this," Sonny said.

"Lotta cars up here."

"Notice how the shot tires are on the passenger side? Someone must be out there," Sonny gestured toward the thin strip of desert off to their right that ended in steep barren hills, "Picking them off."

He hadn't noticed. With the rhythm of his riding he had been off in his own world as they pumped up the incline.

"Bounty hunters," Clay said, preferring to stick to his daydream of his hometown, and like most of his daydreams it had food in it. A carnitas burrito garnished with sour cream and guacamole.

Nothing like imminent danger to interrupt an imaginary lunch. They both had the same question, so obvious it didn't need to be spoken: would the bounty hunter shoot at bikes? "Could be they're in it for the corn juice," Clay said. "These hot shots ride at night from what I've heard. Max of two hours. That's good enough for Elko from Winnemucca. These bounty hunters take the cars out near Golconda so it's a no brainer to leave your car and walk on down to the town. The good folks of G-town hike up the next morning and drain the fuel tanks. Like a cross between a speed trap and a death trap."

In their slow grind up the grade they searched in all directions for signs of trouble. Any shooter would have to be off to their right. There was no cover there. They came around a sweeping turn.

"What?" Clay said as he came up even with the boy who had slowed down to a crawl.

"Man on the road up ahead."

They cycled together as the man started to grow on them, trudging west down the eastbound side of the freeway. As they closed on each other the man showed them his open hands, a what-can-one-do gesture.

"Got shot up. Just short of the summit," the man muttered as they approached. "You friends spare any water?"

Clay offered up his water bottle – hard not to when it was on display, clipped to his bike. Their new friend didn't appear injured. He was a spare man, early thirties, with gold rim glasses and a thin-lipped smirk that kept trying to twist into something more amiable.

"There's a town back this way, isn't there?"

"Town? You could call Golconda a town, if you're feeling generous." Clay met the stranger's eyes, sensing some kind of plan.

Gold Rims backed away from them, ten feet, and said. "Put your bikes down and stand back from them." He had a long-barreled gun aimed in their general direction. "Further. That's right." He picked up the blue bike and looked it over in an angled way that kept Clay and Sonny in the frame. "I'll be needing your shoes," he said to Clay. "Take them off, slowly, and toss them underhand by the bike."

"This is highway robbery," Clay muttered for Sonny to hear. "Where's a convoy when you need one?" And to Gold Rims, "At least leave me my stuff."

Gold Rim's lips had given up on their amiability project, he smirked, walked the bike a safe distance away, gave them a long last look, swung up and on and coasted back down the highway to Golconda. They watched his frame swoop down, soon lost around the same sweeping turn that had first revealed him.

"I'm going after him," Sonny said, charging away on his bike before Clay could protest. Without shoes, the pavement was too hot to give chase.

He took off his cargo shorts and used them and his sun hat – he'd lost his helmet in Reno – to manufacture step after step toward the nearest car several hundred yards down the grade. True to form a convoy whined up the grade as he step/tossed, step/tossed his way to the car, a white station wagon. And true to form it turned out to be a carnival convoy. His semi-naked state brought out their exuberant and festive side. Horns, flesh and fingers.

At least the wagon's foot mats could serve as his stepping stones to Golconda. He decided to wait for a cooler time, less sun, less heat off the blacktop. The car's battery was dead. The glove compartment showed Gordon Watkins of Reno as the owner. A litter of small coins and a baggie with light blue pills took up a compartment in the central console.

"Taking a break?" Sonny said. With nothing to do, his mind in neutral, Clay dozed in the reclined passenger seat.

"Huh, what?"

"Here are your shoes. Or do you want your sandals?"

His eyes needed time to adjust. Was that his bike he could make out in the bleached wash of the bright day?

"You know," Sonny said, "I never thought I'd say this, but I don't need to see another Woohoo as long as I live."

"What's a Woohoo."

"Trucks all mooning and fingering and…stuff."

The day held three or four hours more bike riding in it but Sonny was tired from walking both bikes all the way up from Golconda. The two made camp in the station wagon.

"Sonny, you're the hero so you can drive."

They sat in drive-in movie mode as Sonny told his story, which being Sonny, didn't last all that long. "Turns out that most of these cars up here are owned by crooks on the run from Reno. There's a whole bunch of them hanging out at the schoolhouse in town. They get their cars shot out from under them up here and come rolling down into Golconda." This was a lot of sentences for Sonny. He paused to catch his narrative breath. "Two months ago one of the crooks shot at one of his pals. The citizens of Golconda went to the schoolhouse with their shotguns and rifles and took away their weapons. When I told one of the old timers about the arrival of another gun he sure took an interest. Him and his pals went over and took it. Ol' Gold Rims was busy talking to his friends, didn't check out your roll so we still got the gun." Sonny took another narrative rest. "Bike was the easy part. Took two shotguns to get our friend to give back your shoes."

The sound of yet another convoy grew from a vague background growl to something more urgent. They slumped in their seats until it passed.

"What's Golconda like?"

"Like a ghost town with people living in it."

"What do they do for food?"

"They got rifles. They got water from the Humboldt that flows behind the town. I think there's some kinda deal with the USG. They shoot up the cars; the USG swings by with g-bars and stuff."

They debated for a time about the bounty hunter, who could be setting up his sights a hundred yards from where they slept. It would be smarter to make the summit and coast down to wherever the highway bottomed out, far away from the shooters and shot up cars. But Sonny's legs ached, not used to walking.

"You know, Sonny, I'm getting tired of guns being pointed at me. It's such a cheap, no-questions-asked solution to any problem."

"Well, we got a gun ourselves. We should pack it in your bed roll so we can reach in and get it quick."

"It's no good unless you're prepared to use it."

"Oh, I don't know. Ol' Gold Rims did all right by it. Who's going to risk their life over a bike?"

They bedded down head to toe in the folded down wagon bed. Sonny nodded off quickly. Clay stayed awake listening for the sounds of hotshots gunning for Elko, and for shots aiming at stopping them. Eventually he drifted off. With all its windows up they had to keep the doors ajar for a cross breeze. In the middle of the night Clay surfaced to hear an animal scrabbling under the seats. Probably dining out on a ten-year-old French fry, he thought. And he's welcome to it. Desert life being so damn hard.

Chapter 16

"The Court calls Mr. Clay Holloway to the stand."

Sworn in, just like a movie. Federal court. The USA versus Jorge Ybarra Saavedra. Nothing good can come from this, he thought. Remember, straight answers, nothing flip or ironic.

The defense attorney, Flanagan, took his time, allowing the drama to work its spell. How could the young man in the expensive suit help the bearded revolutionary? Facing the packed court room, Clay searched for Madeline, hoped she wasn't here, yet found himself disappointed not to see her.

Sharply dressed yet somehow anonymous-looking, Flanagan played up Clay's respectable presence at the Visitacion Valley house, ran him through the exchanges that night about insurance, how Clay argued in favor of the corporation and in favor of government regulation.

"And is it true that some of those present argued in favor of anarchism, going so far as to advocate burning down buildings?"

"One person said 'burn it down'. I can't say if that amounts to advocating anarchism."

"Just one person?"

"Someone else agreed with him. There was talk of how violent demonstrations have succeeded in drawing attention to just causes."

"And what were your feelings on hearing that?"

"Objection."

After arguments at the bench the question was allowed.

"Uncomfortable. It seemed to be just talk, but how could I be certain?"

"Now, Mr. Holloway, is it true that the defendant stood up in your presence and in the face of active suggestions for violent demonstrations said that he did not want violence?"

"He said that…"

"Yes or no."

"Yes."

"Did he at any time that night advocate illegal activity of any kind?"

"To the extent that I am aware of illegal activity, I would say no."

"*To the extent that you are aware*...what do you mean by that?" Flanagan threw a lop-sided smile toward the jury.

Yes, Clay realized, it helps him that I'm a bit hostile: makes my testimony carry more weight. "It means that I am not conversant with every last article of the municipal, state and federal codes."

"Very well – let me rephrase the question. The defendant is charged with money laundering, tax evasion, wire fraud, and advocating the overthrow of the United States Government, all activities which I think we can agree are illegal. Did you hear the defendant talk about any of those activities?"

"No."

"Thank you, Mr. Holloway."

The prosecuting attorney, a willowy black woman bounced out of her seat, quickly approached him, then seemingly struggled to form the complicated events surrounding the witness into a first question.

"Now, Mr. Holloway, what were you doing at this party?"

"Doing?"

"Who invited you?"

"A woman called Madeline."

"Madeline. Does she have a last name?"

"You'd have to ask her."

The prosecutor shook her head, smiling. "Are you in the habit of accepting invitations from someone you hardly know?" she said in a raspy voice full of withering sarcasm.

Flanagan objected.

"I'm trying to establish the context of the invitation, your honor," the prosecutor explained. The judge allowed the question.

"The context is that she was a very attractive woman."

The courtroom laughed. The prosecutor turned to the jury to bask in the light relief she had delivered to them. Clay exchanged a look with Jorge Ybarra, awkward in his off-the-rack blue suit and conservative tie.

"Is it possible, Mr. Holloway, that the sole reason this *very attractive woman* invited you was so that you could be present at a scripted drama in which the defendant could stand up and deny his advocacy of violence of all kinds?"

"Objection!"

"I will withdraw the question."

Exiting the court, a light smack-smack echoed off the tiled floor behind him as he strode down the dark corridor. Madeline. She was jogging to him, her leather sandals slapping. She hugged him, then stood back to take him in.

"I looked for you," he said.

She shrugged. "I was there. I had to be."

"Stand by your man."

"He's not my man. But…he's a friend. A friend who could go to jail for a long time." She stepped back and studied the miracle of his presence. "I'm so glad to see you again. I owe you an explanation. Really, it feels like I owe you several. You must absolutely hate me."

"You can take comfort from the fact that I said under oath that you are very attractive." There was a bloom about her, a vitality, the kind a woman gets when pregnant after long months of hoping, the world spinning at exactly her speed.

"You said I *was*…."

"The past tense is because you are in my past. Or were in my past – now."

"Can we go somewhere? A coffee, maybe?"

"I think there's a Starbucks around here somewhere." He looked at his watch, didn't hide that. "It'll have to be quick."

The late February weather was gusty. It had stopped raining but the angry clouds weren't finished laying siege yet. He steered her through the low rent area of the Mission District, past the '50's cafes with bad coffee to a restaurant he knew.

"What would you like to drink?" he asked her. "I'm going to have a drink drink."

"I'll have what you're having, but… I want to pay."

"I was thinking of a Manhattan. Except – "

"Sir," she called to the bartender, interrupting, "two Manhattans, please." They stood at the empty bar. It wasn't noon yet.

"Perfect?" the bartender asked.

"Regular," Clay answered.

"So now you have *me* on the witness stand," she said. "You can ask me anything you want, under oath."

"Is it the cause of anarchy that you embrace or just Jorge Ybarra?"

"There's always both." She lightly swatted his forearm. "I'm in the middle, between him and you." She met his eyes, allowing him to drill into hers and search for the real person down there somewhere. "I would say that his advocacy of radical change is on the same scale as your complacency of a society in need of radical change. What I mean is you're both good people and the answer is in the middle somewhere."

Complacent? Him? He was a hard-working take-charge kind of guy. How could that translate into complacency? And didn't he write a sizeable check for Steel Umbrella's annual charity drive? But that was something he was supposed to do, and, more importantly, seen to do, waving that large check in front of the grateful volunteer. In all of thirty seconds he'd fashioned a get-out-of-jail card.

"You're not going to ask me why I treated you so badly?"

"No." No, he wasn't going to cite his large donation; that would only delay her victory. He didn't like losing; and yet in another way he did. It was different to be shaken up like this. He needed to look forward, where this annoyingly incisive person fit in his life. So no, he didn't care for history, for her tortuous explanation laced with self-justification and recrimination. Her dog got run over; her aunt was poisoned; her mother had run off with a tango dancer.

The Manhattans came. They clinked glasses.

"You certainly are bitter about the whole thing," she said. "Maybe that's good. You'd only be bitter if you liked me, or did once upon a time."

"I like you just fine. I don't need any explanation." She had his email address. If apologizing was so crucial, she had had the easiest way in the world of doing that. What was she going to do – apologize for not apologizing?

She sipped her drink, not looking at him. Perhaps adjusting to his soured mood.

"It's funny," he said. "You're right; I do sound bitter. I haven't thought about you in months. Nothing – good, bad or indifferent. At the time I think I wrote it off as one of those unpleasant things that was Probably For the Best."

"You're sitting there thinking, all she had to do was send me an email." She cocked her head, as if trying to coax a smile out of him. "I didn't do that because I too thought it was for the best. You know the expression 'cruel to be kind', well I'd already been cruel, so all I had to do was nothing and I could be kind. Kind of."

"What changed?"

"The trial. When I heard you'd be called as a witness. I put that down to fate. That we'd see each other again." She took a healthy sip of her drink. "Mmmm, not bad."

"It's pretty strong."

"Look at you, too much the gentleman to ask the question you want to ask. The answer, by the way," she said with just the slightest mushiness in "answer", "is yes. Yes, kind of. Jorge suggested I invite you. Maybe because he had that script. Although it's not like him to plan that far in advance. What I mean is he wasn't even indicted then. Okay, so why would he suggest I invite you otherwise?" She shrugged. "I'm trying to be honest with you here. God knows you deserve it. But, it's complicated. Because he is, Jorge. It could have been Jorge being playful, or mischievous, or bored. Or, his way of off-loading me."

"Off-loading you?"

"That doesn't sound right, does it? How can I explain? There's a part of Jorge that likes to play god of his little kingdom. Lurk above the stage pulling the strings. Why not set up little Maddy with this handsome insurance guy, this white, privileged, bourgeois guy. Let that develop some momentum and then the great Jorge can step in and reassert his claim on me. The great Jorge wins out over white America. I'm exaggerating big time, but the point is still valid."

"How is that an exaggeration?"

She smiled, looking down. "Jorge. If our little romance usurped his claim, he'd be fine with that. He's competitive, fiercely competitive. But not when it comes to women." She put her tumbler down a little too hard.

Clay gave her an assessing look. Everything about this woman seemed complicated, almost opaque. "What about Jorge?"

"Mr. Flannigan says the government's case is thin and that the prosecutors are doing something called grandstanding. He predicts the government will offer a deal: they'll drop the charges if Jorge agrees to go back to Uruguay never to return."

"What about Jorge and you?"

"Do you know that I'll be twenty-seven next month? You're older right? So, you know how you get to the point where you think, Was this my plan? To be here now, doing this? Was this what I went to four years of college for?" She took a sip of her Manhattan, smacked her lips approvingly, but looser, a hint of sloppiness.

"Why don't we sit at that table so I can see you?" He let her lead, taking a generous gulp of her drink behind her back. The last thing he wanted was a drooling and weaving drunk full of slobbery confessions.

"You were talking about being twenty-seven." She was lost in the table top so he added, "It sounds like you're not going to be seeing much of Jorge, unless, that is, you visit him in prison or in South America."

"Oh Jorge, he doesn't care about me, not personally."

"Personally, as in girlfriend?"

"He has good manners. I like that in a man. But, you know, good manners apply to, like, everyone."

The bar area of the restaurant was starting to fill with the lunch crowd. He motioned to the bartender for coffees by daintily holding a cup handle and tipping it.

"Jorge is only married to the cause. To him women...they are a sideline. A bit of fun when he has a free moment." She polished off her drink. "It makes me sick." She burped internally, as though her narrative were going over a small speed bump. "How woman run after him, only too happy to make him coffee, get him this, run out and buy him that. Feminists, hah. Except who am I to talk? I guess that means I'm sick of myself, huh?"

The coffees came. He slipped the barman some bills.

"We're not doing so hot, are we?" she said. "You know why? Societal expectations. We were both raised to look on this," she threw her eyes, a little too wildly, around the room, "as some kind of date. That rushes everything. It's all wrong."

"Listen," he said, glancing at his watch. "I have to run." Before you go off on a long jag about men, women, disappointments and heartache. "Let's get together sometime."

"Yeah, okay. Sometime."

Chapter 17

"We got three bullets and each one needs to have meat at the end of it. The time for shooting tin cans is over." Why did half his comments sound like lines from a b-movie? "We'll have to hope it doesn't *jam*," he said, starting to use food-related words as a poke at Sonny. They hadn't made Elko, forced to stop short and camp out in the sagebrush.

The boy grumbled as he took the proffered Beretta. He'd been pleading for a chance to hunt down one of the jackrabbits that were bounding around. Well, why not? Sonny couldn't have less experience than him.

"Two hands, one supporting the straight arm to take the recoil. Right?" He'd seen that on a cop show once. "Be patient. You gotta sit still out there. Rabbit's gotta come to you. Okay?" Why did he enjoy talking about something he knew nothing about? Maybe being a father was like this.

The boy wore a serious frown, meaning to pass this test of hunting competency. "My uncle wouldn't hunt 'em. He'd shoot them all right. Said touchin' them wasn't good, some disease. Gotta use gloves. Anyways don't see any. Maybe they got called in for dinner."

"Theirs or ours?" He liked the boy's confidence. "One shot," he called to him. "Then it'll be my turn."

"You won't need any turn."

What chance did Sonny have? Just when you thought the rabbits were stopped they bounded away; when you thought they were zigging this way, they zagged that. Or stopped smartly, sniffing danger on the breeze. All from at least thirty yards away.

He started disassembling Sonny's bike rack. Its strut would serve as a skewer. Maybe he should have waited, not wanting to set the boy up for failure.

The color had drained out of the sky. The mountains lost all definition. Finally, a shot echoed. It sounded like a polite cough, small and far away. He stood up. The first stars were threatening to come out;

the light so gloaming he couldn't see out to the boy. Long minutes later Sonny appeared, holding a rabbit, jerking mildly, the Beretta slid into the waist of his jeans like a Miami detective.

"Good shooting. You've got the safety on?"

"Nuh unh."

"My advice, speaking as the voice of experience, is that it's generally a good idea to hold on to your nuts."

"Two bullets, three kills. That'd be pretty good shooting."

"You might be receiving your award posthumously. That means it'd go in your coffin with you."

"They still makin' any of that stuff. Awards? Coffins?" He extracted the gun and engaged the safety.

Clay held the warm little corpse still while Sonny sliced its neck with his hunting knife.

"Sonny, any idea which way Mecca is."

"What, the Casino?"

"You have any trouble pulling the trigger?"

"Nuh unh."

They watched the life seep out of the bunny.

"My mom was a vegetarian," Sonny said, apropos of nothing.

"Was?"

"Her new husband made her stop." He looked down at the desert floor. "Here, I'll skin it."

"Guess these days you can't afford to be particular."

"Eldon's such a dickhead." He concentrated on skinning and gutting the rabbit, "Shootin' would be too merciful," he tried to laugh, didn't pull it off. "Nuts would be about the right place."

"Well you're fourteen. You'll be outta there in a few years."

"Mom won't though. I just wish I could get big enough to bump my chest 'gainst his."

Clay shook his head. Sonny's step-dad sounded like the type who would take that out on the mother. The boy read his mind, sharp as he was. "I wouldn't hit him or nothing; I'd just look him in the eye and…" He trailed off, lost in his vision. "When it comes down to it, he's your regular coward."

"Most tyrants are."

They were quiet while Clay tried to get the kindling to take.

"What do you think's gonna happen, with the country and all?" Sonny said, still busy with the rabbit.

"The New Dollar needs time. It'll get there." Once more with enthusiasm.

"Like this fire here?" Sonny worked the skinned rabbit onto the prong of his bike rack. The fire was having trouble organizing itself into any kind of conflagration. "I keep hearing the New D's not gonna make it. Did Kendy really say he was a German?"

"Yeah, from Berlin. Maybe I'd better spend them while they still have some buying power."

After Reno, the talk about the New D had been increasingly negative. And the talk before that wasn't exactly rosy. His nine remaining New D's, all Kendies, were his ace in the hole. Now they were looking a lot more hole than ace.

The fire took hold at last. They didn't say much as they waited for it to burn down to embers. Now the fire hissed and spat to the dripping rabbit fat.

Sonny said, "It's crazy that we can't get back to the old way. You know what it reminds me of? Time I fell out of an apple tree. Got the wind knocked out of me. I felt fine, just couldn't breathe. I kept telling my lungs to take in some air. Wasn't used to my body ignoring instructions."

"That's the best metaphor I've heard on the subject." Also an apt metaphor for his last year with Madeline. Before, their time together had been as easy as breathing.

"Ray says you take what you need."

"Who's Ray?"

"My Uncle back in Lovelock. He says you gotta understand the way Christianity is constructed. Sure, it's bible wrong. But since there's no law out there you do what you want and ask for forgiveness after."

"Everyone comes to that way of thinking, we'd have frontier justice, vigilantes, revenge feuds, anarchy. Take your little stunt with the oldsters, riding around terrorizing them. Look how that ended."

They listened to the fat hiss into the fire.

"Funny thing, it was my idea." Sonny stretched his lips into a pained smile. "I told Hulk how I'd seen this group not going to the USG. Meant they must have their own stash of goods. Guess I wanted to be a hero with ol' Hulk. Now? He's just this total loser."

"You won't find me disagreeing with you." He glanced at the boy. Sometimes he appeared to be growing up before his eyes. "You think your friends will go back after them?"

"Without a shotgun?"

Finally, the rabbit was ready, the hot juicy meat falling off the bone. "What was that you were saying about rabbits and disease?"

"Nothing."

As Sonny hunched up in his too-thin blankets off to his left, Clay lay fully awake, such a self-contained package of fires and fuels, buzzing like the stars. Connect the right dots and map your future – that's what some people still believed. But out in the black desert there seemed as much light as blackness as if your future was limitless. Maybe that meant Boston was possible. He caught a shooting star in his peripheral vision. Another one. How naïve he'd been - the Great Basin Desert was supposed to be barren and flat, like a drum skin with sand cast on it. But all these summits, Golconda, Emigrant, and now an imminent third, Pequop at nearly 7,000 feet?

How could all this possibly be real? This still new version of himself, camped out in the desert – just over there a fourteen-year-old companion. The United States of America, on its knees. Where had he left normality behind? San Francisco was from another era now. The crisp briny air. The sea smells, the kelp and eucalyptus. The bay, its sailboats. The high and coruscating light. It was bright as a dream, far away, condensed into a star-like point.

Now a light, moving across the sky. A plane! Out of the northeast. No, it was moving too fast. It must be a satellite. Up there, waiting for a signal. Waiting. Waiting.

Chapter 18

"Nice car," Madeline said when Clay picked her up. "Do you really need to go 160 miles an hour?" she peered at the speedometer.

"When you're in insurance sometimes you have to get out of town fast."

She was wearing a diaphanous sarong and button up red cotton blouse. The slit of her sarong opened to reveal the elegant swooping curve of her calf, the complicated architecture of her bare foot, her daintily-arrayed and unpainted toenails. Now up to her face, the silky chestnut hair, caramel eyes.

"I'll take the backpack," he said, once they were parked and got ready to set out.

"Thanks."

"Do you mind adjusting this?" He hefted her backpack.

He took in the citrus-like smell of her hair as she leaned in to loosen, then cinch up the straps. "Thanks for dealing with my…baggage," she said.

It was a bright sunny day, the light dancing off the bay, yet the westerly wind had the ever-looming fog's chill in it as they took the ferry over to Angel Island. The green hills of Belvedere fell away as the boat made its short run. A party-like atmosphere as passengers, the first of the day, filed off the vessel and onto the empty island, a National Park.

They hiked the long way, counter-clockwise around the perimeter road to her favorite spot, a sheltered beach that looked straight out at the Bay Bridge and over to Alcatraz and San Francisco. She spread out the picnic blanket.

"Oh, and here." A little too quickly, she handed him a beer, a Belgian lager he'd never heard of. "Jorge recommended it."

"Is he calling you to go to him in Paraguay?"

"Uruguay. He says he'll be back. He says he has nothing to worry about because to the government all Latinos look the same."

"That government is probably reading your mail."

"That's why he does it. Keeps them on their toes." She smiled. "Come on, I didn't invite you on this picnic to talk about Jorge. Or me."

"What should we talk about then?" It was just a meaningless question, but it came out sounding aggressive, a little bit hurt.

"We could just let the nice day do the talking."

He took in deep lungsful of air, breathed out slowly. "Relax, damn it!"

"There you go," she said, laughing. "We're on an island, right? Your very fast car is across the water."

He took a swig of beer and took in her slender frame, bent over the backpack retrieving food and setting up the picnic. What had changed? Why were they suddenly more comfortable together? "Are you concentrating hard on relaxing?" she asked, her back still toward him. That was it, she wasn't merely reacting to his moods, she was in there working them. Or maybe that had started in her email inviting him on this picnic. If you can just hang out with me, she had written, without analyzing, assessing and rationalizing me I'd like to invite you... But she had also written, If we can just be friends.

The previous weekend he had gone out with Sandy, Miss Reliable. Her law firm sponsored a Start-up of the Year awards dinner that nicely complemented their corporate law department and she needed a partner. She had returned the favor several times when Steel Umbrella held their Partner Dinners. Attractive, a thin blonde with bangs over her elfin face and impossibly full lips, she'd meshed so well with him at the dinners that a colleague asked him when he was going to do the honorable thing. He could talk easily with her. When they disagreed, it was almost always about degree and not kind. But what? There was something too businesslike about her. A dinner with Sandy was like a client dinner with lower lights and less ostentatious wine.

She was smart coastline to Madeline's steamy jungle. With Sandy you had a clear view of the headlands while enjoying a crisp white wine. With Madeline you checked your water bottle and your compass and searched for a way through the undergrowth.

"Can I have a sip?"

"Here."

A family had set up not far away. Their two children were yelling at the water's edge. The husband sitting watch; the mother lying down on their blanket, possibly asleep. The husband resembled someone he knew, a work colleague his age. At nearly thirty he could be that family man.

"Nice spot," he said. The mildly lapping waves, the bay full of sailboats parading before the city front. The shrieks of children at play.

"Thanks" she said, handing him his beer. "That's enough alcohol for Madeline." She stood up and unwrapped her sarong, slipped out of her running shorts, unbuttoned and took off her blouse. "Let's go in the water and cool off."

Just friends, he smirked, taking in her curves as revealed by her black one-piece swim suit. I can sail off to friendship island and leave my raging hormones parked across the water. Didn't she understand?

The bay was shallow here. A children's beach ball got caught in a gust and he swam out to rescue it, the ball leading him a cruel chase into deeper water.

"Thanks, mister," the little boy said, and kicked the beach ball back to him, wanting to play. Clay exchanged nods with the father, kicked the ball a few times with the boy, until a little sister ran in and took it away. Madeline sat on the picnic blanket, happy to wait for him to play with the boy.

"You're getting a bit red," Madeline said. "There's some shade over there."

They moved back further from the shore. Out in the bay a containership appeared certain to run over a sailboat, dwarfed by the sharply angled bow of the huge vessel. In the middle distance another island, Alcatraz, pointed its blunt bow at them. They ate in a comfortable silence.

"Have you forgotten all your cares now?" she asked.

"I block all that out on weekends."

"You can do that? Are there other large pieces of your life that you can block out at will, just like that?" She got up, dusted off her tightly sprung bottom, as if to say, Block this out. "What are you laughing at?"

"Nothing," he said, watching her wrap her sarong over her slender legs. You would almost think, he thought, that she didn't know what she was doing.

Chapter 19

A month in and the Great Trek East started to falter. Their steady climb to Pequop Summit through Elko and Wells was like the slow ratchet of a roller coaster, from the top of which they could go whooping and swooping all the way to Utah, leaving only a flat wind out to Sonny's home in Centerville. Sonny, though, had the glum look of a boy sent to detention.

They had taken a rest day in Elko to save up for the fifty-mile climb to Wells, fallen short nevertheless. Camping out in the scrub, they took another rest day at Wells, saving up for the final twenty-eight-mile climb to the summit, and the thirty-six mile downhill to Wendover on the Utah border.

"Hear from anybody?" Sonny asked, as they pedaled out of Wells. They had taken turns waiting in the USGmail line. The smaller the town, the fewer the USG terminals; it was always an ordeal. So much for their early start.

"Just my sister." USGmail was still new. It would take time for people to figure out new addresses, discover the Matrix. But with every passing day, there was that jackpot chance that Madeline might contact him.

"She still angry?" Sonny had heard a sanitized version of his Mom desertion story, one in which Rancho Duro was missing, and Mrs. Hernandez was not.

"Yep, she thinks I'm crazy to try for Boston. Women, they're so damn sensible."

"Sensible as in right?"

"We, my friend, are living on Planet Uncertain. There aren't a lot of good answers; probably fewer sensible ones. Look at you. Is it sensible for you to cycle four hundred miles with a stranger to be back with your Mom? Not when you started out, right? But with every mile it becomes more and more sensible. You reach Centerville, it's not only the sensible answer, it's the right one."

"I don't want to go back there."

"I know that." The first convoy of the day was heading westbound, probably out of Salt Lake City five or six hours earlier. Yes, they were closing in on Utah. "I'll let you in on a little secret. I'm not all that sure about Boston. It's like the least worst answer."

"Let me guess, we're living on Planet Least Worst."

They ground on for several hours, Sonny in the lead. He called a rest stop at the 233 turn-off. "I keep hearing the chances of getting across the Rockies on 80 aren't good. This road takes you north to Idaho, totally skips Utah." He met Clay's eyes, couldn't hold them.

"You know what? I've never met a man with seven wives."

"It's only five."

"Well he needs to add a couple more so the whole thing will scan right. I met a man with *seven* wives. It's from an old nursery rhyme."

"Nursery, huh. That man's always working on more babies."

They were late hitting the summit. Only the women's bathroom at the rest area offered shelter from the biting wind. Its steel door had been crowbarred open. "When you gotta go, you gotta go," Clay had said.

"I keep hearing it's a conspiracy. You know, the Void," Sonny said, too cold for sleep.

"You buy the super-hacker theory?"

"I'm not buying anything." Sonny said, chattering in his thin voice. "No money to do that anyway."

Clay drew his sleeping bag over their shoulders. He'd heard any number of theories at various USGs and Barts. Slavic hackers. Swiss gnomes. Russian oligarchs. Chinese military. US hedge funds. The inevitable cabal of Jews. Muslim extremists. "People would prefer it to be a hacker, or a bunch of conspirators. It's an explanation that wraps the whole thing up in a nice package. That way the Void is someone's fault, a bad guy you can point to, someone we can arrest and punish."

"It all happened pretty smooth and fast."

"Falling apart's like floating down stream. We live in a world where it all flows from order to chaos unless an outside force is constantly applied. The garden turns to weeds, the church falls to ruin, empires crumble into dust. There's no hacker in a garden full of weeds."

"Why is it like that?"

"For that, my friend, you'd have to ask God. If he'll take your call."

"You're just saying it 'is because it is'. That's not an explanation. Besides, every church I see is in good shape."

"Leave the church be for a hundred years and see what happens.

The universe runs from order to disorder. Every star will collapse. I'm not setting myself up as some guru, but here's how I see it. We think we've got the world all boxed up and under control. Our brains are powerful, and there's a ton of data out there to support just about any theory. That means there's always a reason. Usually there's several. But it's not like that. It's all a fudge. We do our best to take the randomness out of our lives, and we do such good job of it we convince ourselves the world's under our control. The randomness is still there, though, we've just covered it up with excuses is all. When in fact at the heart of any system there is an essential wildness."

Sonny shook his head. "Centerville must be outside of the universe. That sucker will never change. Not even for the worse."

Hunched together to beat the cold, they ran out of topics, and slept fitfully, sitting under the dead hand dryers.

The next morning, they glided down to Wendover like eagles down from their high aerie, down and down, fluttering to a perch on the Utah state line. The bracing dawn air soothed Clay's scratchy eyes. What a sweet release to coast like this, despite the beaten-up palms itching from the cold. Near to flying. They clocked ten miles in not much more than half an hour, stopped for breakfast, g-bars washed down with snowmelt, then swooped onwards.

Just beyond the second summit, his head down to minimize the cold wind causing his eyes to water, Clay caught motion. He snapped his head up to see Sonny in mid-air, sailing clear of his bike, then sailing some more, as his bike bounced down the road. The boy hit the asphalt shoulder first, his left arm breaking the fall, then he rolled and rolled down the slow lane until he came to a stop in an inert heap. *God damn, the sweetest part of the ride and he ruins it.* A thought like a blink at a piece of eye grit, then concern. A medical emergency in the precise middle of nowhere.

Sonny lay on the road moaning. Clay glanced behind him. No semis, but a faint deep roar from the west. He bent over the boy. "Can you talk?"

"Uh huh."

"Can you move your legs? Arms?"

"I think so, maybe. Just a minute, okay?"

The convoy growled over the summit, engines juddering as it picked up speed on this downhill grade. He got the boy under the arms, but no, there might something wrong with his spine.

He ran out for the bike, desperate to get the convoy away from the slow lane where Sonny lay. Without thinking he dragged the bike further into the road, out into the fast lane, and toward the rock wall on its margin. The lead 18-wheeler closing now, sounded its low horn like a bellow from a beast. He stood away from the rock wall, daring the lead truck to charge at him – and away from the boy. The truck sounded its horn again and moved over into half of the fast lane, so close now he could read the Peterbilt logo on its grill. It rushed by, missing him by ten feet. Then the next truck was on him, whooshing by closer, maybe eight feet, the convoy flexing snake-like, each truck closer to the wall. Until...

He sprinted up the road, toward the next truck, like leaning into a left hook. It whooshed by missing him by eight feet. More loud horns. He ran on, not looking, on and on as horn after horn sounded. The last truck blew by then flared out toward the wall, missing it by five feet. He closed his eyes, shaking, as the noise from the convoy dimmed into the distance, then jogged back to the boy, up on one elbow like a fighter taking a count.

"Don't know what happened," the boy said, rubbing his lacerated left arm with his right hand.

"Can you move okay?"

Sonny blinked slowly. "I'm gonna be sick."

Concussion. Countless miles from help. A few g-bars, two e-bombs – Sonny's phrase for hard boiled eggs – and three water bottles. Sonny needed to stay off his feet, rest, drink plenty of water, get out of the sun, all while the desert, parched and desolate, waited blankly.

He walked the boy down a small incline to be away from the convoys and fashioned a shelter by stretching a blanket over their bikes.

West Wendover was at least twenty miles away. Could he leave Sonny with most of the water, and go for it? No, the boy needed monitoring. At a minimum he needed to rouse him from time to time and confirm he was still functioning.

They had passed a shot-up Ford just east of the second summit. Windshield cleaner, radiator fluid might be good on the lacerated arm. When he got to it, the car, coated in dust, didn't seem promising. It had taken several shots in the radiator, and front wheel cowling. Nothing in the car's rear area though. He scrunched up under the trunk and examined the gas tank. No sign or smell of any leaks. The gas flap once pried open gave off the smell of gas. With the battery long dead, there was no telling how much if any corn juice remained down that black hole.

He jogged down to check on the boy, roused him into a groggy, mumbling funk. Good.

On the other side of the summit, over in the westbound shoulder, he found an abandoned Honda. Dead battery but a stick shift. The Honda's tank had taken one bullet. As a convoy thundered by he chewed a stick of gum to make a seal for a piece of radiator hose he'd taken from the Ford, along with the gum.

Back to rouse Sonny. "No, I can't," the kid mumbled, off in his own troubled world.

"You still feel sick?"

The boy wiped his mouth with the back of his hand in answer.

Back at the Ford, he cut off a good length of manifold hose and syphoned gas into one of the empty water bottles. Running back up to the Honda, down to check on Sonny, then back to fill up the water bottle with gas again, Clay was exhausted by the time he figured he had enough gas in the Honda to try to start it and keep going.

Back with Sonny, the boy was throwing up again. They would have to risk an early start. He jogged back to the Honda, ducking when a westbound convoy passed by. The car's front wheels were dug into soft dirt. He changed out the back tire for the spare, leaving one shot up tire. He pushed with all his might, like pushing a wall. He dug under the tires with his hands, trying to free the front wheels from the soft embrace of sand, then tried rocking the car back and forth. Still nothing. He gazed up into the evening sky. The stars weren't out yet, or more likely, had given up on him entirely. "Yaaaagh!" he cried in one last desperate shriek. The car inched backwards, then moved begrudgingly, as its front wheels, one flat, reached the asphalt. He opened the driver's door, corrected the wheel, got the car moving around and backwards, hopped in, straightened the wheel ready to jump start the car. Too slow, too slow, with one tire flat. Now it stopped and he hopped out and started pushing again. Finally, enough speed. He hopped back in, got the stick shift in reverse as the car ga-thunked backwards down the highway. He popped the clutch; the car coughed and died. In the rear view mirror he saw an approaching convoy – not much time. A second try, closer to ignition. A third time and roar, a live car. At the top, he used an access lane to cross over to the eastbound lanes, waited for the imminent convoy to pass by then ga-thunked down to the Ford for a second wheel change. The Ford's tire was too large making for crab-like tracking as he coasted down to Sonny, careful to leave the car slotted for a quick coasting start. Now for the dash to Wendover. If they were caught on the road it was all over.

Chapter 20

Her email was entitled Hi from Boston.

Hello Clay, It's unseasonably chilly here and I find myself thinking back with great wistfulness to our picnic on Angel Island last month – and no not just the weather and the views. I had a weird dream the night before last. Don't worry it wasn't about you – yet somehow it led to you. (I know, being in someone else's dream is creepy. When I was in high school this guy said that he'd had a dream about me and I wanted to scream, Get me out of your lewd head.) But I digress.

All I will say about the dream is that it was about a distant past, and as a result of it I have come up with a story that explains how I feel about you, and how that feeling has changed, even from 3,000 miles away. Isn't it strange that a dream, something that comes so passively, can change one's entire outlook? Before I go into it please, Mr. Rational, don't think I'm saying it's literally true. We're in the world of feelings now. Okay?

To my story. You and I have known each other before, intimately and for a long time. I have nothing specific but let's say we were happily and deeply married from 1882 to 1928. Now our old souls are in new houses. Billions of random transmigrations, or whatever you call them, and by a near-impossible chance our souls have come together again. On one level we're different people destined to go in different directions. On a deeper level, the power of the past is just too much to deny. So we hold back because this wasn't supposed to happen; it's not natural. But on another level it's the most natural thing in the world.

I know what you're thinking: what a nutcase! And, really, what chance is there that Mr. Rational will mesh with Ms. Loony?

I'm writing this because Mom, who is much better thank you, will always have this Sword of Damocles hanging over her. Isn't it ironic that her first stroke, the one in Paris that kept me on the phone when you were at our "interesting people" party, killed anything that wanted to happen between us? And now her Condition is doing it again. The SoD will always be a convenient excuse for ducking out of my life – already I've regressed to a sulky teenager half the time. I guess what I'm doing is pushing back by being brutally honest. Here I am, warts and more warts. I understand now how naïve I was when I told you we could just be friends. No, it can only be something much more than friends – or nothing at all. I see that now.

I'm coming out to SF and will be free the weekend after next. If you have time for me maybe a walk in the redwoods?

Thanks for reading this to the end, and take care, Madeline.

Chapter 21

Dr. Meta Kouri lived in a modest house out in the western fringes of West Wendover. Her dining room was given over to a consulting room, a black Japanese screen – tree boughs bursting with pink blossoms – shielding the entrance to the kitchen. A love seat in black imitation leather, an armchair, and a large table desk were squeezed on top of an oriental carpet.

"Help me to remove his clothes," she said.

Sonny lay on the couch in his underwear, his sunken chest rising and falling erratically, his body like milk against the reddish brown of his face, neck, and arms.

"Sonny, follow my finger," she said as she peered into his eyes with a small light.

"Okay, can you count backwards from one hundred by threes?"

"Couldn't do that... before."

She shared her smile with Clay, a joke being a good sign.

After the doctor had tested many aspects of his arm and leg strength and control, her long thin hands fluttering like birds as the salt and pepper hair fell down from her angular face, she concentrated on his badly lacerated arm. "This is good," she said, "he used this," she held up his arm slightly, "to protect the other parts of his body." She turned to Clay, "Now a few questions for you. You say it has been twenty-four hours since his accident, and little water?"

He looked at the Japanese cherry blossoms on the partition, maybe for inspiration. What could he do? His gas tank plug had failed seven miles short of town. He pushed Sonny, lolling on his, Clay's, bike all that way.

"It's okay, I am not accusing you. I just need to know these things. Dehydration is a concern with a concussion." Her dark eyes met Clay's to show it was more serious than merely a concern.

"What's wrong with a hospital?" Sonny asked, groggily.

Clay shared a long look with the doctor. They had already

explained to Sonny that the hospital's imaging equipment was out of order; that Dr. Kouri had extensive experience in Lebanon and Palestine treating concussions out in the field.

"We must plan for the worst. There's a real risk of swelling. He's the restless kind, I can tell. You'll need to support the head to allow the fluids to drain properly."

"He's not staying here?"

"This is my house, not a hospital." She lowered her voice. "I am a doctor back in my home country, but not here. I am not allowed to practice. Therefore, I am not advising you, I am suggesting." She pulled her gray-streaked hair back from her face, came back to him with her eyes. "People keep coming to me. What can I do?"

"But you were recommended at the hospital!"

"Dr. Rosenburg? Yes? A good man. He calls my practice 'guerilla medicine'. The modern hospital relies very much on their machines. No machines and, well, that's when someone like me, who had not had the benefit of them, has some value."

"We get the difficult cases," Rita Evju told him, nodding towards the bedroom where Sonny, head wrapped in a ice-cooled towel, was lying immobilized by a head brace constructed by her husband Phil – all two-by-fours, foam rubber and large wood screws. "That's 'cause we're okay to take night shifts for round-the-clock monitoring."

She was an elfin lady with short hair that emphasized her small pointed ears, and a wide smile that said, Isn't life an adventure? She exhaled in a where-do-I-start? way. "Good you got the ice."

"Good you knew where I'd find some. How long will Phil be?"

"I don't know. He's over in the Utah section dealing with red tape. You know how that goes."

"The Utah section! You make Wendover sound like Berlin when they had the wall."

"Here's how to understand Wendover. You take two brothers. Big brother has a lot of money and a flashy lifestyle. He lives in a fancy house and employs all sorts of people to do his bidding, as they say. The little brother is poor and religious, lives in a shack, barely getting by. What is the moral here? Damn if I know. Big brother is happy and having a great time. Little bro is all hunched up and poor. It gets so bad that Lil' Bro asks if he can move in with his brother. And guess what? big brother agrees. It's the parents who veto the arrangement." She crossed her legs the other way, gave him an assessing look. "Are you okay with it being so dark? Phil and I like to save our candles for when we really need them."

"You mean like nighttime?"

"Big brother is West Wendover, Nevada. Its success comes – I guess I should say 'came' – from gambling. Little brother is Wendover, Utah. Same town: state line runs smack down the middle. So, Wendover had a campaign to move over to Nevada, but Utah didn't agree." She chuckled. "Why, even if both states agreed, the transfer would have to be approved by the – " she spat the words out, "US Congress." "Let me figure this out," he said. "The hospital in Big Wendover doesn't take out-of-state patients. So the good doctor here covers Little Wendover, even though she lives in Big Wendover. Right?"

"Right. Now Sonny is a Mormon and that should get him a free ticket to the big hospital in SLC. Problem is, Sonny needs to be in the fair state of Utah to qualify. Phil's been a long time haggling over the red tape. Maybe that's a good sign."

"Think I'll go check on the boy," he said.

"How does it feel to be *stabilized*?" The contraption Phil had thrown together, time being of the essence, looked like something out of the Spanish Inquisition.

"Like I'm in Utah," Sonny said.

"You are in Utah. Rubbing up against it anyway."

"Rita's been reading to me. That helps."

"I hope it's not *The Man in the Iron Mask*. It's a good story though."

"Wouldn't matter. I just listen to her voice. The words, well there's a hell of a lot of them."

"Your bike sure is popular," Phil said, finally rolling in. "One day of pedaling like hell and you're in SLC. It's like I'm walking around with a bus ticket out of here hanging out of my back pocket. Don't worry, your bike's okay." He had a bruised forearm, a cut above his right eye, and his walk favored his left side. "They're going to get in touch with next-of-kin," he explained. "If the kin acknowledge him they'll put Sonny on their emergency list for when a space comes up on a truck east. Provided he's picked up in Utah." "Truck east?" Clay said.

"LDS truck. They take care of their state pretty good."

An impossible sound, a high-revving growl, idling just outside. It was the fifth morning in Wendover, and Clay needed all the excitement he could get. He yearned to get back on his bike and pedal some meaning back into his life, and not just his daily run out to the Morgenstern Ranch, a solar array outfit that had enough power to run a freezer for ice. He half ran, half limped out the front door like a prisoner released into the future. His bad knee still ached from the ordeal of getting to Wendover. A motorcycle! The bike sputtered dead. The rider wore black: jeans, boots, leather jacket, helmet, everything. He hung the helmet off his handlebars, shook out his long hair. Black. "I'm looking for Jerry," he called over.

"Jerry?" Clay said.

"Jarome Hargreaves?"

"Oh, Sonny! Sure, I know him."

"All I know is a medical emergency?"

"Concussion's the worst of it. He's bouncing back though. How'd you come to hear about it?"

"Church jungle drums. I got listed as next of kin. I'm his uncle. Tad."

"What about his mother?"

"Can't answer that. I come here to take him to the main hospital in Salt Lake City. Assuming he can hang on for a couple of hours, no stops."

"Why not?"

"USG convoys don't shoot here in Utah, not usually but man, I hear they shoot the shit outta Nevada. Can't afford to take anything for granted. I slipstream LDS trucks. Protection and fuel savings. Kid got a doctor?"

"Yeah, inside, Dr. Meta Kouri."

"How'd Jerry, er Sonny, wind up with a bush doctor?"

"Long story. Short version's the Void and how messed up everything is."

Clay brought him inside. "I'm Uncle Tad, Ma'am. Enchanted," he said, making a show of lifting her hand to a few feet from his lips. "That's what they say in France isn't it? That's as far as my geography goes over there."

"You have not heard of Jerusalem, and Bethlehem?"

"Ma'am I was talking about etiquette knowledge. Here, I brought these." He pulled a baggie full of red pills out of his jacket. "Tylenol. I use them like wampum for trading, but you can have them. They're good for headaches, right?"

"Yes, thank you. You are the one to take my patient to Salt Lake City?"

"If he is in good enough shape for a two-hour ride on a motorcycle. The Tylenol is for you by the way. What I mean is, use them as you see fit; they're not just for Jerry."

"Thank you. You are very resourceful, Tad."

"What now, Doc?"

"Perhaps you could take me on your motorcycle, to see how it will be for Sonny."

"What is it with chicks and bikes," he said to Clay, almost winking.

"Do you have two helmets?"

"You can have mine. We'll have to pad it. Even more for Jerry. I've got a big head."

"Yes, I can see that."

She straddled the seat behind him, intrepidly holding the seat bar behind her, and yelped as Tad roared off. It was ten minutes before that revving growl returned, Dr. Kouri's arms wrapped around Tad's midriff. She swung off, removed the helmet, rearranged her tangled hair.

"I don't know," the doctor said. "He shouldn't ride now, but they have many facilities in Salt Lake City. It is dangerous either way. Who makes the decision?"

"He's a minor," Clay said, "so technically it would be Mr. Next-of-kin here."

"Me? No way," Tad said, "I can't take that kind of responsibility."

"What do you think?" Clay asked Sonny an hour later. "You up to a two-hour ride, maybe in a day or two?" The boy was up and dressed, but sitting quite still on the sofa in the Evju's living room, a catalog version of early colonial.

"Wow, Uncle Tad. I haven't seen him in, like, five years?"

"How's your counting backward from a hundred coming along?"

"Makes me feel like a retard. It's not that I don't know the numbers, I just wander off. You know, bored."

"It's a trick for falling to sleep, like counting sheep."

"I wish I knew what happened – with the fall. One minute, I was sailing on the bike. The next I was sailing without the bike. I can't connect the two."

"Doesn't matter now."

"Does to me. Wasn't it you who told me the main thing about mistakes is learning from them? How can I do that if don't know the mistake in the first place?"

"Looks like your think tank is back to outfoxing me. That's a welcome sign. Kind of."

Sonny shifted his position gently. Maintaining a stiff quiet posture had been a condition of being let out of the stabilizer.

"Think about a motorcycle ride to SLC. You should have seen the good doctor hugging Tad for dear life. I think it's given him ideas."

"Maybe she can cure him too."

"Of what?"

"Mom says he's got a condition she calls permanent adolescence."

"Any woman can fix that in a hurry. Whether it sticks or not is another matter. Okay, seriously, give some thought to the cycle ride. Not today but soon."

"I'm not putting my arms around Tad. And besides it's a trap. If I say I'm good to go then obviously my wits are still scrambled, why else would I want to go to a hospital and be only fifteen miles from home? And if I say I 'no' that means I'm thinking clearly enough to go."

Clay gave a chuckling kind of smile. Sonny was back.

Chapter 22

She came out to his horn dressed like a young wife ready to paint a bathroom. Old jeans, a black Wellesley sweatshirt over white blouse. Sneakers. A fawn windbreaker slung gunslinger style, low around her waist.

"Can you believe it was almost exactly a year ago that you handed me your card at Myshkin's?" she said, settling in her seat.

"Seems a lot longer."

They drove through the city, across the bridge and up Mt. Tamalpais, a playlist of British and Irish folk music he'd downloaded for the occasion playing low in the background. Something about Madeline made him want to be unpredictable.

"Could you turn this one up. Please. It's one of my all-time favorites." Who Knows Where the Time Goes by Fairport Convention. As they wound up the mountain, rising above the fog, the song somehow aligned their moods, serious but carefree.

He took a picture of her standing next to the 'beware of rattlesnakes' sign at the trailhead by the ranger station. She gave him a crumpled chin. *If you can do folk music, I can do rattlesnakes.*

In the wooded ravines, the interplay of the fog's cool and the sun's heat changed with each bend. He led, hiking briskly, and she followed, keeping up but not crowding him. The trail left a final wooded ravine and opened up to a broad bare hill with a wide view of the Pacific, visible in places through the lifting fog. Stinson Beach, their destination, was below, an hour's winding hike down out of the mountains through the trees and ferns.

"Let's just buy something at the store and sit out on the beach," she said when they arrived at the small village.

The silence on the hike down had cast a spell. Sitting on a driftwood log, he looked over at her, and she looked back, smiled.

"Do you think it's down to societal expectations," he said, "this pressure I feel that we should be talking?" That was one of her expressions, societal expectations.

"There will be time for that."

On their climb back up the mountain they took a few minutes on another bare broad hill, lower down, to appreciate the view. The fog had burned off to a gray menace on the horizon. The ocean glittered. The long beach just below them was met by line after line of rollers.

"How's your mother doing?"

"She's okay. For now." A hawk lifted and fell, like a kite, its wings unmoving. Its shadow ran along the hill in front of them. An oil tanker was heading out to sea, an endless sheet of hammered steel. "It's like earthquakes here. Everything's good but it's only a matter of time until the Big One." Her eyes left the sea and went to his. "The answer is I don't know."

"Don't know about what?"

"How much of the Mom story is just an excuse for moving back there. Burying my indecision underneath the noble cause of being there for her. That's what you were really asking, right?"

It was. He didn't try to hide that.

She looked up the mountain. "Well, shall we?"

They started on the long uphill climb back to the Ranger Station. He had put her down as the Jane Austen armchair type, but she showed no sign of flagging as they strained their way up through the ferns and redwoods on either side of the gushing water that flowed down the ravine. In the cool air, the tang of redwood tannin and sea brine merged with a mulch-like fetidness as they hiked, dwarfed by the redwoods.

They rested on top of a boulder, the stream cascading off it so loudly they had to raise their voices. Her neck glowed, strands of her hair were glued to her temples.

"It's so enchanting here," she said. "And serene. The trees, all these big leafy ferns. Thanks for bringing me."

He nodded, thinking how nice it was to sit on this boulder, how peaceful, and how his mind could be empty, as it was after a long bike ride. The last time he'd made this hike, with Gretchen, the sister of one of his MBA friends, it had also been enchanting. Enchanting? They'd talked non-stop, all the way down, all the way through lunch at the café, and most of the way back up again. Gretchen was a corporate lawyer, read the Wall Street Journal, so their conversation ranged over economic and corporate subjects, on and on, effortlessly. Every so often they stopped, as if to come up for air, and purposely admire the view for a long minute before moving on, both more committed to reaching B from A, than breathing in the sweeping vistas. And he got home missing the bike ride he'd foregone to be with her.

Madeline stood up, offered her hand, pulled him up. She took in the redwoods, the light that filtered down among their horizontal branches, keeping his hand in hers for a long moment, her skin cool.

In the stop-and-go traffic getting back across the bridge to San Francisco, he said, "Are you going to have enough friends in Boston?" Her eyes were closed, perhaps concentrating on the Irish number, a fiddle sawing away softly in the background.

"I'll be fine. Are you going to show me your house? I'd like to be able to imagine you moving around in it. How you live."

"I can do that," he said, strangely ambivalent.

They inched up to and beyond the toll booths and he turned right through the Presidio on a straight shot to his house. High up in the Presidio, before the road dips down to Baker Beach, he turned into the scenic pull-out without thinking of taking it. Why did he feel like he was heading into a trap? Something to do with her attitude, looser, yet resolved, the kind of freedom you get once you've made an important decision.

"I get it. You don't have a house. How embarrassing."

"That thing you wrote about old souls."

"Oh that."

"Do you believe it?"

"The problem, Clay, is that you take everything so literally. I was trying to describe something that's the opposite of literal – how I felt."

"And you still *feel* the same?"

She shook her head – either No, or No, I can't believe this. "Yes."

They gazed out at the Marin Headlands across the water. A cargo ship was slipping out to sea. The mountains over the water is where they had been hiking.

"I can't believe this," she said. "I'm going to be gone day after tomorrow. How hard can this be?"

"I'm sorry, Madeline, but I need to understand – you're so different to before. I'm trying to adjust to that."

A medieval ballad was playing low in the background, but the words came out clear: "the only love that she admired lay in the ditch where he was drowned."

"How can you drown in a ditch?" he asked.

"It's about a servant who is killed by a husband for sleeping with his wife."

He started up the car. "Are you sure you're okay with my place?"

She laughed. "Surer than you are."

She was practically throwing herself at him; she'd be gone day after tomorrow. Could it be any easier?

She smiled, a warm, almost maternal one. "Poor Clay. You think you're being...chivalrous? But what you're really being is – I must think of a good word here – tentative? Let me paint you a picture. Two scenes, okay? In the first it's you and me at the harbor. Right over there is your sailboat, and you've invited me out on it for the day. Maybe we will have a good time – work the ropes well together, takes turns at the rudder, hike out as the craft heels over. All that stuff. In fact, maybe we have such an enjoyable time, and we are such a good sailing team, that we go out again next week. And more weeks after that."

She reached around to the back seat for his pack, grabbed the water bottle and after offering it to him, took a sip. "Now for the second scene. We are also at a harbor. Let's say we are in Plymouth in 1650. Before us is a vessel, a much larger one with more masts and huge sails. It is bound for the New World. To board it is an irrevocable decision. It may be that the waves will wash us down. It may be that during the voyage we fight and go our separate ways. But what is certain is that, in the end both of us, together or separately, will be standing in a new world."

"And you are prepared to board this vessel."

"Yes."

She was crazy. Not from Boston but Salem. It was a trap; he should run a mile. Only he didn't want to.

Chapter 23

The farm in Centerville was on a slanted parcel of land in the foothills of the Wasatch Mountains, part of the western side of the Rockies – a small orchard, apples and some pears, a sagging bungalow, with three trailers and two camper shells behind.

"What do you want?" The Patriarch, Eldon Williams, answered the door himself, a big man, early fifties, with a pinched squint as he regarded the blue bike.

"Come to see…Jarome." It had been six days since he'd seen Sonny disappear on the back of Uncle Tad's Indian. He'd stayed in Wendover on Dr. Kouri's advice, his left knee complaining with random jags of sharp pain. Maybe it was the wear and tear of three weeks grinding over all those summits, or the mad running between the woozy Sonny, the Ford and the Honda, or the long walk to Wendover, pushing his bike with Sonny slumped on it. All of the above. He left after five days, reasoning that he could always recuperate in somewhere more interesting than Wendover, spent a night at Uncle Tad's out in the flat salt wastes short of Salt Lake City, another in SLC itself, and now here he was in Centerville.

"He's not seeing visitors."

"He'll see me."

"Has to hear about it first." Williams's large frame, hunched-over as if his suspenders were cinched too tight, blocked the doorway. His flushed face flushed even redder, his lower lip now blubbery. Any second steam would come out his ears. All his anger appeared concentrated in his face, the rest of his body an inert roadblock.

A woman, small with Sonny's reddish hair, was now scrunched up against a back wall, quite possibly to stay out of Williams's reach. Clay stood there, not backing down, letting Williams understand the old ways, one where competing males settled everything through physical predominance.

"Okay you can visit the boy," Williams finally said, nearly spitting out the "boy". "Only one condition. You gotta take him with you."

The woman yelped in pain.

"We been through this Donnelle. Your boy came back here without permission. Therefore, in my heart he's not even here." He turned around to face her, revealing a bruise on the left side of his face, a livid purple. He caught Clay staring at the bruise and said, "I suppose you're going to slug me too? Just like all folks associated with this woman."

"Will you take me to Sonny please," Clay said, addressing Donnelle, "so I can assess whether he's in shape for more riding."

"Fifteen minutes," Williams said to Donnelle, but not to him. Williams shifted his bulk to one side of the door, allowing his wife to slip through. Walking around to the back of the house she glanced back several times, slowing as she did so.

"Tad was here?"

"Uh huh. I told him that violence was not the answer, but he'd already gone and popped Eldon." She stifled a giggle.

An arc of three trailers were placed like an upside-down smile above the bungalow whose front door they had left. He followed her to the right-hand trailer and around it to a camper shell. It could have been the twin of his mother's in Rancho Duro.

Sonny lay resting on the overhead bed. Pillows and blankets were stacked on the gas range. Donnelle came up to her son and stroked his hair which Sonny stoically withstood.

"I'll come back in ten minutes. Can't afford to upset Mr. Williams." She sang the last sentence in an overly merry way.

"How are you feeling?"

"Ready to puke," Sonny said. "Not from any head-knocking this time. Why did I come back here?"

"Looks like Uncle Tad did what I was thinking of doing."

"He'll take it out on Mom. She's the one who'll pay."

"What did the hospital say?"

"It's pretty good but not great. I'm supposed to rest as much as possible and not stress out. Hah. The worst of it is…" he twisted his lips, "that a-hole had Mom and Edenly, she's wife five, in this camper. They're out of favor, assuming they ever were in favor. So where do they sleep when I'm doing all my resting? Right now I share with Edenly, head to toe. She's a thrasher and a talker. Rest!"

A knock on the tin door, a thin strip of a girl with dark blond hair, sharp cheekbones, red-rimmed eyes and a nose she kept wiping with her forearm. Edenly. "Mr. Williams has approved for you to have some food, Mr. Holloway."

Donnelle led him back to the bungalow and to a kitchen table. She searched the cabinets for plates. Knew more about the refrigerator.

Williams came in to supervise from the doorway. "Come here without permission. Can't imagine what Ray's thinking. Boy ups and runs off."

Donnelle set a slab of cold meat loaf before their guest. A glass of lemonade-flavored water.

"When do you plan on heading out?" Williams asked.

"Eldon," Donnelle said, pleading.

"What do you want now?"

"I don't..." Now she stood up straighter. "Angels without knowing it." Four words were all her courage could muster.

"What are you prattling on about?"

Donnelle shrank into herself.

"Speak up. What's this nonsense about angels?"

She flushed scarlet, closed her eyes in concentration. "Do not neglect to show hospitality to strangers, for by this some have entertained angels without knowing it." She swallowed hard. "It's in Hebrews."

Williams, outclassed by the Bible, snorting and scowling, disappeared. Donnelle kept fidgeting and checking the doorway into the main communal room. Clay took a bite of what turned out to be nut loaf. The tastiest meal he'd eaten, maybe in his life, its flavors so intricate and complex after weeks of oatcakes and government goulash.

After revisiting Sonny without asking, Clay went to the main house, trying to locate his knapsack. He could camp in the orchard, visit Sonny one last time in the morning and hightail it.

Williams returned, his face red and sweaty, his lower lip hanging out. He papered it over with a too-quick smile, like a slice of cheese on a sizzling burger.

"You'll sleep here in the main house with me. Now, what's your story, friend?" His 'friend' did not sound all that friendly.

"I'm the opposite of you," Clay said, taking a moment for a silent amen. "I've got one fifth of one wife. She's in Boston, so that's where I'm heading." How cruel, to be presented with this human volcano with five wives and eight sons.

"You appear to be a nice enough fellow. What're you doing helping an underage boy escape from his lawful guardian?"

"I told him to go back when he started following me. But you know, the last teenager I saw who followed orders had a gun pointed at him."

"He was not summoned. You had no business helping him."

"How much do you know about teenagers? About making them do something they don't want to do?"

"Not been a problem for me."

"Right."

They sat in the living room, Clay on a heavy couch with an Indian blanket thrown over it. Williams hunkered down on an equally heavy wood-framed armchair. Maybe he should pull on those suspenders and sling-shot Williams out the door.

"What's it like to have five wives?" Maybe he'd kick him out.

"Friend, don't think I planned this. Nosiree. It's a hard duty. Hard and lonely." Williams took his time, checking to see if he was being mocked. Whatever he found there kept him going. "It's not having five wives. You have a part of each of them, not the whole woman. And most of the time it's the wrong part." He chortled, wallowing in a memory. "I had this farm from my pop. Lived here all my life. And don't you think I went out lookin' for wives. It's just that they're teeming out there like jackrabbits. Some of them are bound to hop my way. They come to me, wanting who knows what. Protection, mainly."

"Protection from what?"

"Life? Three of 'em, the middle three, including Donnelle, been married previous. Married, then abandoned with no experience other than housework. There's always a few who have no folks to fall back on. They hear about this farm, come here asking about work, but in truth what they're after is a home. They cozy up to my first missus and before you know it they've moved in."

"What about the fifth...wife?"

"Well I got talked into two, three and four. Five was pure bonehead. Edenly, wife five, is my first wife's niece. Becca took her in for a time 'cause Gracelee, her sister, had run off again." Williams shook his head. "Yep, number five was a mistake, plain and simple. Lemme tell you a secret 'bout wimmin. I don't mind confessin' that what I'm about to say runs counter to what they tell you in church. But facts are facts." He wiped his red and sweaty brow with the back of his arm. "They get lonely for a man. Some fight it better'n others. I tend to wind up with the quitters."

Towards the middle of this speech two women had entered the room. They waited at a discreet distance for Williams to recognize them. Now, he did.

"Is there anything you'll be needing before we turn in?" the left one said to her husband, her eyes fixed on him. The right one, a half step back from her companion, also had her eyes on Williams, as if trained to do so.

"Nothing tonight. You can go."

The left wife's smile loosened considerably, she uncrossed her arms from her chest. The right wife took the other's hand and they bounced away.

"They sure are attractive."

"Thank you."

Was it showing off, rubbing it in, or just plain disregard that had Williams put his wife-bedding arrangements on display like this? Was he, Clay, genuinely appalled by this multi-wife set-up? Maybe. But most appalling was the way that this pecker head was carrying on his line on an industrial scale. Sure, there's instances in nature where the top stud gets all the action and the other bucks yowl and move around slowly with back legs crossed – but based on alpha male primacy, not this omega-male's sputtering claims.

At night, staring at the ceiling of the small room he'd been allotted, there was a knock on his door, soft, imagined, until it came again.

Edenly. She stood in the doorway, shoulders slumped, rubbing her wet nose with the back of her hand, not looking at him.

"Are you in some kind of trouble?" he asked.

She gave a thin half-smile. "Mr. Williams sent me."

"To me?"

Her smile this time was even smaller.

"I get the impression you don't want to be sent to me."

"Nothing personal," she said in a small high voice.

"You don't want to, right? So, don't."

She just stood there, trying not to rub her nose. "I'm Edenly." She must have forgot she'd been introduced previously out at the camper. Edenly. If from Eden, she'd have to be the snake given her rail thin frame.

"What, does he beat you?"

"Me? No. No, never. Eldon is a good man. He's so much better than me. I am *so* privileged."

He didn't say anything.

"May I...enter?" She stepped tentatively into the room.

"No, leave the door open."

"I can't."

"Come on, what is this?"

She started fiddling with the button joining above her small cleavage.

He went to the door, opened it, stood where she had stood. "I don't know what the hell he thinks he's doing with this."

"Don't, please. Don't swear like that. And don't…*reject* me. Please." She swallowed, a large here-we-go one. Her fear was real enough. "It'll be another of my failures."

"What does he want to happen? It can't be for you and me to be alone together."

"I am a badsinner. Bad. Bad. Bad. I can't help it: I am weak, where he is strong. This is my last chance to redeem myself." She undid the top button of her yellow dress. It had small red roses, the color faded from too many washings.

"How have you sinned?"

She redid the button, and in a small voice she said, "My wifely duties."

"You mean sex?"

"Do we have to talk about it like that?"

"Shall we talk in code?" Here he did a coarse cuckoo whistle.

She smiled despite herself, turned red, embarrassed about being embarrassed, which tipped her into a fit of giggles. "Oh, my God." She brought her hand to the wide O of her mouth – she'd taken the Lord's name in vain. The sins were piling up faster than she could atone for them.

He came back into his room and sat down on his cot. She came and sat next to him. Not close but within reach.

"I don't mind…it." She looked up into his face to assess his shock level.

"What? Fucking?"

She was too intent on her confession to be shocked by his words. "Maybe even a lot more than don't mind."

"Well, that's pretty wicked all right."

She nodded, looked at him with a warming smile.

"I can't take this…nonsense, Edenly. You aren't any sinner. You're probably just about perfect. It's that goat of a husband who's all fucked up. Yes, I said 'fucked up'. Don't the Ten Commandments talk about adultery? The man would be complicit in a great sin. He'd probably punish you for committing it."

"He understands about sin, all right. He says it is difficult but sometimes it is necessary to sin. Like in a war you need to kill. You know, like exterminating circumstances?"

"And what's this circumstance?"

"Life."

"Life?"

"Yes, life." She stood up and started walking the room. "Eldon's got six natural children. You know, not brought in by wives. All sons. Says he's only good for boys." She stopped in front of him. "He wants himself a daughter. Says there's something about him and me that doesn't work, for babies. You see, this is my big chance. Give him a daughter…"

"Probably plans on adding her to his collection of wives."

Once out, the idea blossomed into a completely believable scenario right before their eyes. She gasped, and gasped more deeply, as if he had struck her.

"Wouldn't be his flesh and blood, would it?"

"Not it, she!" Edenly put her hand over her mouth, hugged herself. "It's my last chance."

"Okay, listen, you'll just have to lie. You tell him you, we…you know."

"That would be a sin." She winced. "To lie like that."

"What? And adultery isn't? Double adultery. I'm married too, you know. It's not just you who would be being unfaithful."

"Can we do it together? We can…hold hands at breakfast and…" Her eyes widened, and her mouth became an "o" again. "I know! That's just it. He'll see us like that, holding hands and we wouldn't hafta say anything. He'd understand from that." She bubbled with relief. "That's not even a lie, is it?"

He nodded, as far as he could stomach making such an agreement.

"Breakfast's at seven. I'll come for you before that." She skipped out of the room.

He slipped away at midnight, after rummaging around and finding his knapsack. It was wrong, not saying goodbye to Sonny, but all he'd be doing is witnessing more of the sorry indignity of his compadre's situation.

Coasting down the dirt drive and turning north had the same mixed feeling of liberation and guilt as his Rancho Duro abandonment. He pedaled north, completely free, on his own, the Rockies brushing again his right shoulder.

He camped in an orchard half an hour's pedaling from William's farm. In the mid-morning he cycled free and easy north on 89, his only plan being an anti-plan: not 80. In Salt Lake City word was that interstate had multiple road blocks, hostile locals, and few USG's.

A few hours into his morning ride he came upon a lone woman cyclist, with thin and rounded shoulders, yellow dress billowing. He came up level.

Her eyes were mostly shut, her flushed face full of sweat and tears. Her bike was an old one-speed, the seat too low: she would ruin her knees within a day or two. Probably belonged to one of her step-sons. Stolen. Another sin to thrash around over. All she wore was that dress and flip flops.

"How did he know I was lyin'? How?"

"He kicked you out?"

She didn't answer, too busy maintaining her Determined Stare straight ahead.

"What's your plan?"

"Find you." She glanced over to him, swerved, almost off the road. "He caught me out for lyin'. Says I'm a bad one, a black sheet, says I got the devil in me."

"That would only be true if Williams himself was in you."

"He's hated me a, a long time." In a delayed reaction she shrieked. "How Christian is that, to hate?"

"We never did get along. It's like a seesaw. If I'm up, he hasta be down."

She maintained a good steady pace but it couldn't last. Like a baby awake long past nap time, a big crash would come.

"I need a rest, Edenly," he lied.

He handed her some water and blinked as she drained half the bottle, and wolfed down a slice of bread and a g-bar. My god, he'd traded Sonny for this scrawny needy slip of a girl.

They rode in tandem for a time. They came upon a small army convoy having smokes in the shade of their pulled-over trucks.

"You ever smoked a cigarette, Edenly?" He asked after pulling level with her.

Whether from the food and water, or the distance from her home or both, she started to relax. "Now Mr. Holloway, a girl must have her secrets." Her face, no longer red or teary, held a nice free smile that hinted at a world of possibilities.

They coasted up to the GI's. "You fellas spare a smoke for the lady here?"

"Sure thing," said a gawky GI with protruding eyes. "Where you headed?" he asked Edenly, boxing Clay out of the question with a shoulder.

"North, I guess. I'm running away," she said with such an exuberant amazement and such a delighted smile that all the GI's took their cigarettes out of their mouths and blew smoke up into the air.

Edenly turned down the cigarette but not the private's advances.

Clay, a generation older, listened to their talk for a time, and said to Edenly's suitor, "You take good care of her, okay?" and not looking back swung on his bike and headed north towards Idaho, leaving his companion in the care of the US Government. Once more that liberating yet guilty feeling.

Chapter 24

Madeline walked around his house as if considering a purchase. "You're neater than I thought. Unless you were planning on bringing me back here."

"What would you like to do now," he said, sounding sulky despite his best effort at sunniness.

"I'd like to see your bike."

He led her down the inner stairs to the ground level and to the garage where his blue mountain bike leaned against one of the pillars that supported the middle of the house. A workbench from six owners ago was filled with tools and bike parts. She glanced at the bike, then homed in on a corner full of gardening tools "The man with the rake and the hoe."

"Want to see the garden?"

"Okay."

"Are those vegetables?" she asked, pointing to a bed at the back of the yard.

"Strawberries. They were good until last month when I was away too much."

She surveyed the backyard and he saw it as if with her eyes, the patchy lawn, the wilted shrubs he'd never bothered to learn to take care of, the coarse concrete patio – all so bright and cheap and shabby. In his busy life the living room and bedroom were the places he'd concentrated his money and time on.

In the living room, sipping tea primly, she made the plunge. "Listen," she said, joining him on the sofa, "I'm flying to Boston on Tuesday. The woman you suspect is half-loopy will be out of your hair."

"What you said about the New World and no going back, you believe that?"

"Does it matter?"

"Only if you're right."

"Do you want me to be right?"
"I guess I'd like to find out."

In bed she was unabashed, her body on offer. She seemed to know him already, what he liked, how long, and yet her touch was unpredictable, without a rhythm, as if he was the right lover but her ministrations in the wrong order. He struggled to find a rhythm, wound up surrendering to hers, everything so loose and inevitable and not yet. She bit him, hard then soft and mollifying, acts that provoked his small anger and larger forgiveness. She brought him close and let him cool, playing with that inevitability and let down as if reviewing their entire time together, the halting desires that wanted to flow then didn't. Golden Gate Park, the Manhattans, Angel Island, The Steep Ravine Trail. And then everything was the opposite of halting, unstoppable.

Afterward, tracing lover's loops on her belly, when his mind should have been drifting aimlessly like the droning of a faraway plane, he kept thinking about her old souls story. Now he understood what she meant. This one act was a signature in blood, a contract that could be walked away from but never undone. She must have decided in Boston to come out here and take him down. Now all he wanted was to be taken down again.

Within a week she moved in. A month, and she gave up any thought of a job at Myshkins, started working full time on the volunteer newspaper. She took over the downstairs, the in-law bedroom becoming her office, the yard out the back door her garden. Every time he poked his nose in her door she'd acquired another used item, a large oak desk, a sofa, an oriental rug to cover most of the cheap shag carpet

His non-business hours were hers.

"Okay," he said, when she suggested he donated his season tickets to Boystown, whose Chairman she knew from a petition drive she'd worked on about runaway teenagers. Why not let a volunteer and a boy enjoy a ballgame in seats that would otherwise be vacant?

"You can reclaim any tickets you want."

Between work and Madeline, he had a feeling that wouldn't be all that often.

Chapter 25

He sat at the roadside, admiring the sleek horses in the lush grass, the sharp mountains in the middle distance, outlines of snow on their high shoulders. More green than he'd seen in a month. The ranch house was immaculate, freshly painted, and the long veranda that wrapped around it swept and pristine.

Quickly the door opened to reveal a small, wiry man with crème brulee eyes and an ironic, knowing smirk.

"Friend, I'm not selling anything."

"That include your goodself?"

"What's goin' on, Antoine?" came a woman's voice from within.

"Man at the door."

"Well, show him on into the parlor. He'll want a drink. Include me in that, will you?"

She came to the door, heavyset but not fat, with a sweet sweaty face. She had alert unsettling eyes that regarded him from different angles. He removed his bike shoes and followed her considerable denim-ed derriere into the house.

"I'm Price," she said, examining him as she might a horse. "What's your proposition, friend?"

"Work for grub. My tank's on empty."

"That means you want the food on account. Then you pay me back?"

"Depends on the work."

"Notice anything remarkable 'bout this ranch?"

"No, ma'am. You keep it in excellent shape."

"And that's not remarkable?"

"Utah's a damn tidy state."

"Reason this place's so *tidy's* 'cause I got all the hands I need. Too many, in actual fact. We'll feed you, don't worry. Then we'll see." Somehow that last part sounded ominous. "What work can you do?"

"I used to be pretty good at selling insurance."

"Insurance against what?"

"Everything except what's just happened."

"You have any experience with horses?"

"Most of my riding's been on ones that take quarters."

"Sounds like you started early anyways." After a dubious look, she said, "You any good with women?"

"Haven't met a man yet who doesn't think so."

"Uh huh," she said, pulling her hair back behind her ears. The light in the parlor was rich yet subdued by shutters against the westing sun. "Confidence. Horses and gals, it's the same game for both. Got it?"

"Too bad I didn't meet you twenty years ago."

The next morning the men ate a decent breakfast of eggs, toast and Mormon Tea, an infusion of an indigenous shrub.

Price pointed him to the lower pasture. He may have been full of confidence, but the horses stepped away from any approach, put their heads down to the rich grass. Maybe to hide their snickering. Price slid between the fence rails and came over to him, making a sic-ing noise that got the horses' attention. She walked over to a glistening chestnut stallion, talking nicely, fitted the bridle and walked him over to Clay.

"Let me introduce you to Jump Suitor. Jump's one of my best stallions. Only two problems with him, he's too smart and he's too bashful. You've shown up at the exact right time."

"What do I do?"

"Talk to him. Soft and easy. Man to man."

"I'm not sure the two go together."

"I'll let you in on a little secret: horses don't understand English. Say anything. Sell him some of your insurance. Just keep the tone – "

"Soft and easy. Sounds like a hair product."

"There you go, silky and smooth like yours truly." Price flounced her shoulder length hair, and put her cheek against the horse's muzzle. "Jump's gonna deliver. I can feel it." She handed over the reins. "One last thing. This is a project we're embarking on. The horse needs to identify with you. I need you for a minimum of three work days. Deal?"

He agreed.

"You, friend, are going to deliver. Yesiree, I can feel it."

"Is there a way over those mountains?" He nodded to the east.

"The Wellsvilles? Nope. Those right there have some of the steepest slopes in the lower 48."

All the way to the lunch bell he walked Jump Suitor around, talking to him about his road trip– Rancho Duro, Reno, Sonny, the desert – all in the soft and wondrous tones you use when telling a four-year-old about the Tooth Fairy. The horse's one huge luminous eye peered back at him. Was he taking this in? Probably, he looked doubtful.

"You're good on your own, Jump. The love of a woman is a transient thing. In fact it's double transient since things can go wrong from either side." The eye blinked away a fly. "You're a horse; you know about odds."

They were down by the highway now. A few horses had worked their way down near them, apparently still wary of traffic and noise. There hadn't been one vehicle all morning.

"Met up with Sonny in Lovelock, Nevada. Cycled with him for over four hundred miles. He needed to get back to his Mom in Centerville. You know what? The closer he got to his, the further away I got from mine."

Jump was down in the rich grass near the fence. Once or twice he looked up and around as if thinking, Where's all the traffic?

"But what could I have done? Shoulder Bruce out of the way, set up at Rancho Duro?"

Finally, some road traffic, a man in a Stetson ambling forward on a black quarter horse. He lifted his hat, nodded and kept going after a brief exchange on how pleasant the weather was.

"I've got to be brutally honest with myself here, Jump. How true is my desire to see my quasi-wife again?" The horse swished his tail.

"The thing is, it won't work. I know that. So why am I doing it? Lash myself?" It was getting near to the lunch bell. He started working the horse east toward the ranch house.

"She'll give me a smile that will break my heart – we'll hug, but not kiss, and I'll take in her smell – her hair, her neck. You know what? That right there might be enough to justify the entire trip. But then what?"

Jump looked balefully towards the grass out by the road fence. "How does it work with horses? Say I'm a track star; say I run the 440, one fast lap around the track. Sound familiar? We do it for the glory – that's a fancy way of saying to make the girls clap and the guys cry. Why do you run with such all-out heart? Or is it just that the jockey's whipping you? Us humans have gotta be our own jockeys, Jump."

The bell rang. Clay pretended he knew how to tie a bridle to a fence rail. A buffet was laid out in the kitchen. Bread, thin slices of leftover venison from dinner, jam, baked beans and more Mormon tea.

After lunch Clay led Jump on a full circuit of the pasture. From down by the highway he had a better view of the sharp Wellsville Mountains. Although the lush greenery here was in sharp contrast to the barren deserts of the past three weeks, the Wellsvilles were the same abrupt 3,000-4,000-foot range, which, added to the 4,000-4,500-foot valley floor, created these high snowcapped peaks.

"You're probably a stud, right Jump. It's taken me a long time to get used to being single again. It's been tough. Five weeks after we split up we had one last bite of the cherry. Not forbidden fruit, not even bitter. Just one of those things where you just can't help it. You know about that, don't you?"

Out on the highway a three-truck convoy rumbled north. The GI in the last truck waved. Friendly convoys, that was new. Hard to believe a national tragedy was playing on out there. Why couldn't the country be as unrealistic about the dollar as he was about his wife?

"I'll tell you the question here, the real nut-cutter. Did we create a child? It would be just like the fates to deal two years of nothing and when it's all over, when you're out of chips, deal you a winning hand."

In the evening six hands showered and shaved, climbed into clean jeans and slipped on their best hoe-down shirts. Antoine was cooking tonight, a formal dinner in the dining room.

Price lifted a glass of apple juice flavored water. "I offer up a toast to Mr Hollerway here. He's gonna bring that horse around. I have one of my feelings. Why already Jump's twitching his tail the way he should be."

"Mr. Holloway!"

"You ever worked with horses before, Hay?" In a mild bout of dyslexia one of the hands had taken Clay, mixed in Holloway, and come up with Hay. Either that or he started with "hey" and kept going with it.

"Nope. I usually work with animals smaller than myself."

"Well, you're sure jumping up a few leagues here."

Price said, "We're having this special occasion because of the special occasion I'm anticipating day after tomorrow." She lifted her glass. "To life and horses."

"Life and horses."

After dinner Price and her hands retired to the porch for a smoke. Clay visited the kitchen and chatted with Antoine, the most forthcoming and least monosyllabic of the hands.

"Why's she called Price?"

"She got that name from a town in southeast Utah where she started out as a breeder. Town of Price. As to her real name, if I told you I'd hafta shoot you."

"How come *you* haven't been shot?"

Antoine glanced up from the sauce he was pouring into a jar. "Who says I haven't? That woman…" But he thought better of saying more, and resumed pouring.

With the kitchen cleaned up and the smokes enjoyed, all retired to the parlor. Antoine played piano, rag time and honkytonk, scaled down – slow and easy. Clay relaxed, getting used to being presentable, showered and in clean clothes, thanks to the maid, Juana. He sat there, a boy among men in his cargo shorts.

Price gave Antoine a pained nod and he started out on Hank Williams songs. "Lovesick Blues". "My Heart Would Know". And "Jambalaya", clearly Antoine's theme song. From Louisiana, with a high and whiny tenor, his warble cracked and broke and sometimes didn't amount to much more than a mute strangled rasp. Still, he sang with style, and an echo of homesickness.

"Sire went and died on her," Ruell explained back at the bunkhouse. He was the wildest of the hands. Rode up near the mountains, checking fences and being by himself. The other hands kept out of his way.

"Sire? You mean husband?"

"Yep. That's a lot of woman to take on, that's for darn sure."

Ruell had a dark and dangerous glare, the rangy silent type. This was more words than Clay had heard from him in all his bunkhouse time.

Clay stretched out in the comfort of his bunk, his mind alive from the sheer protein of deer steaks, and wondered if he was being issued a warning.

The next morning Jump Suitor eased away from his approach. Probably tired of his stories. Levon, a gruff, wide-bearded man with soft hands when it came to horses, settled Jump and put the bridle on, scowling. He had better things to do than this minor chore.

"Where's Price?"

"Hafta ask her."

He spent a full day with Jump Suitor, walking and talking. By the end of the day the horse was ignoring him as intently as a long-term partner.

That night the same dinner configuration, the smokes, but no piano. In the kitchen, Antoine said, "She gets this way. Whenever she asks for Hank I know the blues can't be far behind."

In the morning Clay strolled down to the lower pasture and sought out Jump Suitor. He tried out the sic-ing sound. All near horses looked up slowly, looked away much more quickly. But Jump Suitor didn't move away when he approached him. He stood ten feet away, not crowding the horse, letting him get used to the sight of a man in shorts. Nice and easy.

"Who are you going to socialize with when I'm gone, Jump? You're too good a listener for these silent cowboy types. Maybe Antoine can sing to you."

Jump twitched his tail and came to him. Pathetic, it was the best thing that had happened to him in a long time.

"Today we're going to talk about what's happened in our country. Out here you'd hardly know that the USA is in the shitter. Rural spots are pretty darn self-reliant. A hundred and fifty years ago this ranch, the towns around it did fine without trucks or trains."

He patted Jump's barrel and nuzzled his shoulder.

"Am I interrupting anything?" Price said.

"No Ma'am. Just filling him up with my doubts and suspicions."

"You sell him any *in*surance?" She said it as if there was an out-surance.

"He's considering."

She came over and fitted the bridle. He watched with a pang of jealousy; it was his horse, damn it.

"Doubts, huh? Those can be good, forces you to work your way to the positive. You've made progress and that's good because it pretty much has to be today." She stroked the horse's withers as she talked. "Jump's too intelligent. He's like a good man. Hard to find and, when you do, he don't do what you want 'em to."

"What do you want him to do?"

"You'll see."

In soothing tones meant for the horse but words aimed at him, she said, "You, sir, are looking at one of the best handlers in Utah. Get calls all the time. Ol' Jump Suitor here, his line goes way back. Fact, that's how I met Ronan, my second. Not Jump but his line. Ridge Dreamer. Came to this ranch to help with Ridge. He was one fine specimen of a horse. Like Jump, as intelligent as he was bashful. Now, come on."

She led Jump Suitor up to the top of the field, through the gate and over to the stables. Inside, a large room with a sleek butterscotch-colored broodmare pawed the far ground, nearer to them a pommel horse, like in a gym, wider and with no handles. Levon, holding the mare's reins, nodded sagely to Price.

The mare took one look at Jump Suitor and turned away as if in disgust. That got Jump going, neighing and bucking.

"Lead him up to the mount. No, not the mare." She pointed to the pommel. "There."

His eyes met Jump Suitor's one big eye. It seemed to want something from him. Nothing was going to happen until he got it.

"Lead him forward. Forward. Confidence. Now."

Wild and dubious, Jump trained a large eye on his new friend, seeking confirmation. "Good boy." He led him further forward and Jump, prancing and snorting, mounted the fake horse, and wrapped his front legs around the mount, a lover's tender embrace. Now his hindquarters started pumping, pumping, an urgency to deliver the good news that all males understood. His neighing hit a lower register as his eye turned cloudy. He bucked and rocked.

The horse went quiet, sagged, his embrace of the fake mount slipped away and he was on all fours again.

Price came out from Jump's other side holding up a blue sleeve in triumph. "We got the goods."

At Levon's signal, Clay led Jump out of the room for a cleaning up of his not-so-private privates. From Levon's wide smile and Price's whoop, this was a major victory. Not to him, though. It felt wrong, and a betrayal of trust, to have witnessed such elemental helplessness to a flood of hormones. A wild abandoning of everything except for the delivery of the good news.

"Where're you shipping the, the stuff?" he asked.

"Aren't," Levon said. "Not when there's no money, no courier services, no phones to put a sale together. We got lots of stuff and no takers."

"Sounds like high school."

"Just getting Jump used to the drill," he said, after a reflective smile. "Worked on him last season. Nothin' doin'. That horse is smart enough to hold out for the real thing. And even then only Step Lady. 'Course Step's only the best damn dam in the state."

"Why not just let them get on with it?" Even to himself he sounded despondent.

"Real money's in the seed. Easier to ship than a whole horse. Plus horses are like people, they can only be in one place at a time."

Jump put his head down, as if sad to be a whole horse.

"Feels so good to have Jump's AV hanging there with the others," Price said, joining them. "Thank you kindly, Mr. Hollerway."

"AV?"

"Artificial vagina," Price said.

"Kinda like a cross between a condom and a pussy," Levon said.

"We got a whole row of them hanging there like a bunch of scalps," Price said. "You wanna see?"

"No, not really."

"Can't believe it worked," Price said. "Normally we let 'em get a good sniff of the mare to set them off. That's why it had to be today. But Jump, he gets too close to the real thing he'll want the real thing. It sure was close."

Levon said, "He wasn't going to go, then he looked at Hay here."

"Mr Hollerway probably sold him some of his in-surance too."

Price sat with him on the porch while Antoine prepared a goodie bag for the road – his cornbread alone was worth the three-day diversion.

"You have any children?" she asked.

"No. No, I don't."

"Me neither." She gave a long sigh. "A breeder that can't breed. Story of my life. Well, I've got used to it." She read him reading her. "Well, it sounds good." After a quiet spell in which they each made a show of taking in the sunny and temperate day, she said, "You gonna be safe out there? We're cut off here but still we hear tales of cities that're out of control."

"I've cycled through a lot of towns. The smaller and rural places are doing pretty good – which is where I am now. The main danger is the roads. But I'll get there." His finish lacked the conviction he was shooting for. "I'll think about the big cities when I get nearer to them."

"You be careful."

"First step's knowing the fake horse's ass from the real one."

Price gazed out to the west. "There's a front coming in. Don't normally see this by the middle of May. You're gonna run into some rain. Well, come on back, anytime."

He coasted down the dirt track, bouncing alongside the northern border of the lower pasture. Jump was out in the middle, looked up at the motion, stayed up for a time, returned to nibbling the grass. It hit him. Middle of May. May fifteenth, what Madeline called the Ides of May, was their anniversary.

Chapter 26

He pounded north into Idaho, searching for a remote pass over the Rocky Mountains, one not blocked by USG patrols. The highway up from the Cache Valley merged with I-15, the major north/south artery, which in turn became the main street through the town of Pocatello. A cool lawn shaded by tall trees ran along the side of the Idaho State campus. A man stood in the dappled shade, talking to a cluster of younger men seated at his feet. What was this? Education. Here. Now. What could he be saying that commanded such rapt attention?

"And so," mused the lecturer – fifties, short, a gnarly, fuzzy look even though he was clean-shaven and not particularly long-haired – "what do we conclude from that conjunction?".

"That money is a metaphor?"

"Interesting. A metaphor for what?"

"Uh, commerce. Intercourse?" The answerer's voice quivered.

"That is rather circular. The sea is a metaphor for wetness. Now intercourse, if we are talking about the sexual kind, is more interesting. Here is a thought to take away and ponder for next time." He stopped, took Clay in, nodded. "Money is a form of national consciousness; it is the light that illuminates our waking dreams."

"Sir? Who said that?"

"Why, I just did." He worked up a bemused smile. "It's mine, unless I stole it. Gentlemen – till next time"

The young men got up and ambled away in twos and threes, chatting earnestly.

"Where's your toga?" Clay asked. He *was* wearing sandals, though.

"Name's Ewell Blank." He offered his hand, surprisingly coarse. "We got some sharp lads here. All towns do. Nothing more reassuring than kids with a hunger to know. That, brother, needs feeding just as surely as bellies do."

"What about sharp girls?"

"More than welcome, friend, more than welcome."

Blank hefted his knapsack onto his right shoulder. "I got to admit that's one of the many benefits of this Void. None of this political correctness crap. I said girls are welcome. If they attend, fine; if they don't, we don't need a blue-ribbon panel poking their noses into it."

"I didn't see any Native Americans, either."

Blank gave him a "nice try" look.

"Sorry, it's been a long hard ride." He gave Blank a brief outline, ending with his first rest break yesterday at the site of the Bear River Massacre, where US soldiers went berserk, butchering and raping, dashing the heads of Shoshone babies against rocks. The remnants of native Americans ran hidden through this land much like the Humboldt River ghosted parallel to I-80; unless you bothered to take one of the few exits and go looking, you'd never know about it. And Indians ghosted the highway too, by way of the place names of the towns it ran through – Truckee, Tahoe, Winnemucca, Pequop and Pocatello. The Indian massacre story amplified his battle between hope and pragmatism over Madeline. Ever since he'd cycled away from Price he had been praying for an anniversary USGmail from her, while trying to convince himself he wasn't praying. After all what good was any kind of prayer? Hadn't scientists proved that the prayers had no effect on outcomes. Wishful hoping and nothing more. By now hope and despair had been blendered into a pulp that left a cloying and bitter taste in his mouth, like that bowl of mush at Alma Alta.

"What you said about money being part of national consciousness, did you mean that?"

"Working with young minds is not a place for games. I meant it...as a thought exercise. Something that provokes a different point of view."

"That's what the Euro was about, an attempt to create a new consciousness, therefore a new nation?"

Blank took his time to answer, pulling at his chin, a parody of thinking. "I would say that the language of money, how we speak it with our pocket books, is changing. When I was a Professor at Idaho State – hell, maybe I still am – money flowed into my bank account, flowed out again; bills were paid automatically. The rest was plastic paid, even the small stuff. Those few greenbacks in my wallet, Messrs. Hamilton and Jackson, got to be damn lonely. And those gentlemen are our shared past, part of our cultural identity. Now our shared past is a buncha ones and zeroes."

"That's old history, we've got Ronnie and Jack now."

"Celebrities...for our national sitcom."

"Sitcom? You don't believe in the New Dollar?"

"Do you?" Blank didn't wait for an answer. "If you take our former dollar…before the Void there were trillions of them, right? Know what proportion were printed bills and coins? Less than three per cent."

"Where's the rest of them? Where *were* they?"

"Up in the clouds."

They gazed up into the clear blue sky.

"I'm not sure I get your point."

"Just that when you think about the New Dollar and its future…well, the bills are the easy part. Somehow, it's got to go from simple cash transactions to the other ninety-seven per cent, the castles-in-the-air part."

"And it's not even working at the three per cent level," Clay finished for him. "How can you be so…blasé about all this?"

"What choice is there? Sometimes you could swear we're about to work our way out of this mess; other times we appear to be on the verge of anarchy. Mostly though, it's a not unpleasant muddle, a long time-out in a game where we've just about forgotten who's playing." Blank had reverted to lecture mode, standing still, erect, declaiming.

"What'll happen?"

"If history is any guide, a dictator will come along and get folks moving in various unsubtle and forceful ways. Could be our democracy is too entrenched for that solution. Maybe, just maybe, because of that we are poised on the brink of a new way. We'll jet on by, count on that, but for a second it will be exciting."

"New way?"

Blank unhitched his backpack and put it at his feet with a groan, as though toting gold ingots. "Think about it: we have the capacity to direct our evolution, except we have no idea on our destination. Closest we've got is religion, but how do we direct our lives in *this* world? You had the internet and the big cloud, a new consciousness. If we get it back do we have any idea what kind of people that will make us?"

"It will always be about the old virtues and sins."

"Friend. Friend. Do you have any idea what kind of consciousness the Ancient Greeks had? One of the least understood aspects of evolution is change. You change in reaction to your immediate environment. A moth that gets darker to camouflage itself against smoke-darkened cities is not necessarily the best moth that's ever been; it's just the best one for the present circumstances. Our closest approach to perfection may have been the Ancient Greeks. Let me leave you with this: what about the smoke?"

"The smoke?"

Blank smiled. "This is an interesting time. Watch the experiments. Watch the reactions, the way systems are developed. We are adapting to the smoke; but we make the smoke. See?"

Clay took a few steps to retrieve his bike, leaning against a tree.

"Nice bike you got there."

"Any ideas on how I can get across the Rockies? I hear the USG's got all the roads across it blocked off."

Blank whistled. "Best theory I've heard is that the USG have their hands full with the mid-west cities and all of the east. This side's doing better and they want to keep the fun from spreading here. You might get lucky further north, through the Tetons. If you get as far as Idaho Falls, look up Linda Margossian. Ask her about her bank. Now that's interesting."

The message at the Pocatello USGmail center from Susan, back to all caps, said, DID YOU MAKE IT THROUGH THE DESSERT? TELL ME PLEASE. He winced; such a cruel typo. But better news after that. She had succeeded in connecting with Bruce – *Bruce is such an angel*. Now she could do all the Mom monitoring. He sat staring at the screen, trying not to feel so grateful. At least here was a scrap of good news to counter the absence of any word, or USGmail address, from Madeline.

Chapter 27

Steel Umbrella was holding its annual Partner Dinner, an occasion when the company's senior executives along with their partners met at an exclusive restaurant to celebrate and socialize.

"Well, *you're* new." Patricia was mid-fifties, fifteen years younger than her husband, Jack Lenahan, Steel Umbrella's founder, majority owner and Chairman.

"Yes, with Clay it's a new girl every month," Madeline said, hooking Clay with her thin bare arm. She leaned in to Pat: "I've only got two more weeks." He had warned her about Pat, that she was bitter about her husband's infidelities, that she was prone to embarrassing statements and revelations as her way of getting back at him, and that Clay's main purpose at the dinner was to keep Pat on an even keel by enduring her outrageously flirtatious conversation. Why did he put up with it? Well, it got him a seat at the big table with the grown-up executives.

Pat frowned. Was this young thing mocking her?

The fourteen diners stood and mingled over cocktails. Clay introduced Madeline to the important execs, including his boss, Gerard Schrager, Senior Vice President of Sales and Marketing. Jack Lenahan seemed pre-occupied when Clay brought her around. That was fortunate since Jack had all the subtlety of a lounge act when he was interested in a lady.

Finally, the tinkling of fork on wine glass, and all curved in on Jack Lenahan, positioned at the head of the table.

"I think," he said, as if this idea had just occurred to him, "we'll start by putting Ronald here and Stefan there. Then Marika here next to me." He scanned his troops. "Is it Margaret?" he asked, nodding at Madeline. "You will sit here, next to Stefan." A subtle touch, next to Stefan was also next to Jack.

"If it isn't my old pal, Clay," Pat said, next to him.

He risked honesty, for once. "I thought Jack was in a good mood." He looked down at his plate. It was a brutal arrangement, Jack putting young Madeline next to him, then sealing her off with Stefan, the taciturn VP of Risk, and his wife, creating a conversational brick wall. Not only was the Madeline maneuver a raspberry to Pat, he had demoted the CFO and, even worse, Schrager, who would not like Clay having witnessed it. So he sat next to a riled up Pat, and miles away from giving any kind of help to Madeline. How long before she launched one of her anti-capitalist grenades?

Pat too was tracking the Jack part of the Jack and Madeline pairing – all innocent stuff except for the intent and enraptured way Jack's eyes lit up as he nodded to something Madeline was saying. No doubt Pat knew her old goat backwards. Here she sat, forced to witness a reenacting of Jack's previous indiscretions.

After the fourth appetizer had been served – this was a tasting menu – Pat bellowed, "This wine tastes like piss." Several diners near their alcove turned to study her. "Whoever chose this place should be fired!"

Evelyn, the wife of the semi-discredited CFO, rushed over to Pat and inspected her glass. Lucy, Gerard's wife, was close behind, commiserating in calming voices in the hope that Pat would follow their subdued tone. Eventually they succeeded in escorting Pat to the ladies' bathroom.

With Pat gone he was free to try to catch Madeline's attention, but she was busy talking with Jack, her look serious, animated, engaged.

After the entrees, Jack excused himself. Madeline left soon afterwards. The table talk continued at lower pitch. Everyone had one eye on the far corner that led to the bathrooms.

The pair were gone for a long time. Jack emerged and walked slowly back to the table, his face drained. Drained? Before Jack could sit down Pat was on him, gave him an icy glare and a hard slap and stormed out. Shaking his head, Jack pursued her. This happened so quickly that by the time Madeline returned the Lenahans were gone.

After that, despite a few half-hearted laughs and jokes, the dinner failed to get re-energized. Madeline, who had spent a year abroad in Aix-en-Provence, spoke in French with Marika, a Dutch polyglot, the chair between them empty. None of the remaining executives was willing to command the table – a few content to insert comments into the sputtering conversation.

"Jack's quite a nice man," Madeline said in the taxi going back to Clay's. "He says he fights hard for his share, but he respects anyone who does the same for theirs. He even concedes that people like him have unfair advantages."

He gazed at her and smiled, but they weren't touching. Talking about unfair advantages, what about a young woman with her looks? She had to be aware of the stir her little disappearing act had caused. Could it be that she had something to hide? With Jack Lenahan? Surreal.

"Your boss made you pay for the dinner?"

"'Fraid so." Jack usually assigned that task. Without him no one stepped up to the plate. They were all the same level, more or less, all except Clay, so Schrager ordered his subordinate to pay. Would Schrager allow Clay to expense it? If yes and the company paid, that was a tax-deductible expense, best kept away from Madeline. If not, he was out $2,600.

"You were pretty friendly with our fearless leader," he finally said.

"Isn't that what a good little partner is supposed to do? Kiss up to the bossman so that we have enough for a Christmas goose. Dear Clay. I really tried tonight. I wanted to show you I could be the nice corporate wifey if I wanted to."

"I don't want you that way. The whole dinner was a farce. I didn't see that until tonight. I've been too busy playing the game. Look at me up with the corporate gods. Kissing up to the CEO by keeping his wife sweet. Clay Holloway stars in Indispensible. He does what it takes to move on up. Pathetic."

"It's not that bad. I thought Jack was actually rather sweet."

"You are talking about the Hostile Take-over King. He's sweet in the first meeting, when the object is to buy you."

"Here's what I don't get," she said. "It's a man's world, designed by men so of course it plays to your strengths. So why do you men, with all your advantages, still need wives like Lucy Schrager to give you even more? Isn't that excessive?"

"Madeline, I don't want you to be like Lucy Schrager. I don't want to be Gerard Schrager. Okay?" Out the taxi window the fog swirled through the streets as they came up over Nob Hill. A man with a camera was shooting a well-dressed lady, lying in the gutter. San Francisco.

"But Jack's got more dimensions than your boss. And why not befriend him?" she said, meaning Jack.

"What was your shared bathroom break about?"

"Darling, I wanted to get him alone for one reason. He's got an angry-looking mole just here," she said, pulling away from him to point to a spot on the back of her neck. "I made him promise to get it checked tomorrow."

Great, he thought, if she's right this was bad; if she's wrong it's not good either. And if she's right, Pat will be forever convicted of marital neglect.

"He plays a lot of golf," she said, fondly and with a tremolo of worry, as if she was talking about her own father.

Had she really bought his nice guy act? "You're positive about this mole?"

"No. Where's the risk in being careful? Are you saying I shouldn't have said anything?" Madeline was well-informed on most aspects of health, knew the major medicines by their generic names. She had trained in first aid, knew the signs of major illnesses like stroke and heart attack, and after their hikes was worried about Lyme disease and the risks of too much California sun. "Seriously," she said, "what would you have done?"

Handled it via Pat. No point saying that now. And maybe Madeline's instincts were right, as tenuous as Jack's relations with Pat appeared to be.

"Maddy, I just hope you're wrong, that's all."

"He's exactly like my Dad, thinks he's invincible. I had to be sure he'd get it checked out."

"How'd you do that?" he asked, practically wincing.

"I stood there while he left a message on his doctor's answering service. And yes, he showed me the number."

How comical, and dreadful, his girlfriend bossing around his boss's boss. Jack Lenahan, legendary in insurance circles for his ambitious take-overs, two of them hostile, listed in the Forbes Rich List fifteen years ago before one of his companies failed, member of panels at major conferences, called to testify in Washington, meekly showing Madeline the number he was dialing on his cellphone.

After many blocks in silence, holding her to him as he surveyed the fog, now thick and billowing, he said, "Tonight, you witnessed the human face of the evil corporation."

"He admitted there were flaws in the system." She copied Jack's low, gravelly voice now, "if there is a brakeman on this train I haven't seen him." She patted his arm. "I don't delude myself. He says these things because he doesn't take me seriously." She brought her face close to his. "Are you mad at me?"

"No, not at all. You were the star of the evening. I'm proud of you."

"Isn't that the least bit patronizing?"

"For god's sake…" In a delayed reaction, he realized she had been teasing him. And like most of her teasing it came with a little barb in it.

Chapter 28

In Idaho Falls, he had no difficulty tracking down Linda Margossian. Several of his neighbors in the USG line piped up at the mention of her name.

"She's got my house," said a woman holding a little girl by the hand.

"Mine, too," said a thin and bearded man, holding his wife's hand.

"How many houses has she got?"

"I heard about five hundred."

"Bankalinda!" The little girl said.

"Now, hon, why does Bankalinda have our house?"

"Because she's NICE."

"Very good. And nice means we trust her, right?"

While the Mom patted and cooed over her brilliant daughter, the husband behind him explained "Your house has a mortgage. That means the bank owns your house, which means the government does when the bank goes catawampus. Okay?"

Clay nodded.

"So...now the government owns all the houses. However, we are the government, so what we're saying is, this chunk of houses here in Idaho Falls corresponds to our slice of the 'We the people' pizza."

"That's it," said proud Mom. "Why should we – we as in We the People – why should we pay for them to own our houses all over again?"

"What? You just want your house for free?"

"Listen, mister," said the woman at the other end of her husband's hand, "this storm has stripped everything clear. It's not like we have jobs."

"What happens if the USG doesn't agree with that logic?"

"We have more of a chance negotiating behind a block of five hundred homes," the husband said. "And what happens if the USG waves its fairy wand, hits rewind, and says that banks can have the mortgages again? You think those sharks would show gratitude? Why first thing they'd do is say, Why gosh you haven't paid your mortgage for over two years. Out!"

"This town is square behind the program," proud Mom said. "We're tight. No one's gonna play games with us." Certainly not based on that look.

It *was* a tight town, the most motion since Salt Lake City. Plenty of bikes, skateboards, walkers, joggers, horses. Jury-rigged carts, people-propelled, carried supplies to the homebound.

A short ride away he found Linda Margossian sitting on the steps leading up to her porch, her face tracking the sun like a satellite dish fixed on the Yoga Channel. He waited for her to notice him.

She stretched cat-like. Something snapped somewhere in her bony frame. She was youthful in a languid and elongated way, but her hands, neck and the dried-up river deltas of her eye corners said otherwise. If you averaged all that out, maybe forties somewhere.

"I hear you're the richest woman in Idaho Falls."

Her answering smile was rich and creamy. Her brows narrowed. "They'll come for them. All those lovely white sheets will have blood on them."

"Sheets?"

"Pieces of paper. Deeds. All ownership is temporary. That's why I've got them hid."

"What if *I've* come for them?"

"You?" She stood up, a warm smile aimed at him. "No. When they come it will be...not one traveler on a bike."

"Your vision sounds apocalyptic?"

"What can you expect from a system that always asks for more?"

"You are a banker; you should be fine with more."

"This was my daddy's house. He's gone now. It's too big for just one little ol' me. I feel guilty about that. But, you see, I can only ever live alone; I need that peace. People are noisy. Even if they don't say anything they are noisy, their auras are disturbing." She took his hand, her thin fingers on his pulse. "You, however, are so peaceful. How do you do that?"

"Lacka aura."

She gave him a faint smile. "I softened my guilt by taking in art works, kinda a free storage service, but a museum too. The local artists trusted me with their stuff. It all started from there..." Her brows tightened up into a considerable frown. "How do you do it? You are so serene. It's truly remarkable."

"There's a thin line between serenity and exhaustion."

"Exhaustion?" she said, sitting back down on the steps, on one side to make room for him.

"I've cycled from San Francisco."

"You have a long way to go yet. I can hear *that* in your voice."

Yes, a long way. He could feel the Rockies looming to the east. A steep climb to a high summit. Determined patrols blocking his way. Uncertain food supply. Few if any people.

"I have an extra room."

"Thanks, I could use a day to recharge before tackling those little hills to the east of here."

His blue bike may not have been an art work, but it rested in her living room, along with sculptures, pottery, and canvases, while he walked – walked! – around the neighborhood. Such slow progress, such different leg muscles. The afternoon light slanted through the trees in street after street of wood-clad houses. How many of them were owned by Bankalinda?

He returned in the evening, having successfully found the IF USG. So easily negotiated without his bike to worry about. Still the Presidents. The Carter and Elk Reagan, a local version of Irish Stew. IF had a different solution to the Carter problem. No choice you got portions of each.

"I didn't want to intrude too much on your hospitality," he explained when he arrived at Linda's after dinner. She had been a little stiff with him immediately after he accepted her room invitation. Maybe his aura was acting up at last.

"I'm happy to sleep outside," he tried after their few stabs at conversation fell flat.

"No, it's okay." Her eyes sharpened on him. "You'll be fine in the guest room. It's just spooky is all, how there's no noise coming from you," she said in a wistful tone, lonely.

In the morning they sat at her table and sipped their drinks, a concoction he'd watched her put through a strainer twice. It tasted of cactus with hints of yeast and chamomile.

"Now, before you go – you're off on your bike right? – before that, you're gonna help me with the sheets."

There was a galvanized tub in the front yard. She sprinkled soap flakes as if they were gold dust into the water that was building from the hose, water being the one utility you could still count on. They kneaded the sheets together, hers and his. When they were all worked and lying on the grass in kneaded up balls, she said, "Ok, time for you."

She went and sat on the steps, where he'd first found her.

"Come on," he said. "You first. Before I turn the water black. I won't look."

"I don't care. I think it's important for a banker to be seen like this. It's like a statement of principle. Or, transparency."

He did peek at her, just to see how she managed it. She knelt, back to an open view of the street, trellises and shrubs notwithstanding.

"Your turn," she said, briefly hosing herself off before putting on a loose shift.

After he had copied her regime and climbed into a pair of running shorts she had dug up, they rinsed out the sheets and hung them on the line. The tub, the wet grass, the hose, the semi-nakedness – it was like being four again, playing with that girl down the street. What was her name? The same free-wheeling timelessness, the diamonds of water droplets in the sun. *Yes ma'am, I'd bank with you.*

"How do we dry?"

"Slowly. And not yet. There's still the clothes to do."

"I wasn't kidding about turning the water black. We need to refill the tub."

"Soap's running scarce. You're welcome to do a rinse only."

They washed their clothes in the dirty water, rinsed them thoroughly, hung them out, and sat on the front steps. The sun had gone behind clouds and a light breeze brought out tiny bumplets on her thin arms. Her side showed ribs through her wet frock. She hunched her knees up to her chin.

"I wouldn't mind having title to your second bedroom." He chuckled to show he was joking, but serious too.

"If you had that title you'd give it to Bankalinda..." She left it there. "Now one last time, because I still don't believe it. Stay still." She closed her eyes in concentration. She nodded her head vaguely. "I've never...so quiet. So quiet. It's like, like something's been removed. Or, hidden."

Perhaps he should stay another day. He liked the town, felt comfortable with Linda, a woman near to his age who could keep everything so simple, no male/female overtones, undertones, sub-tones, pseudo-tones. But her words came back to him, "you're off on your bike, right?" The tone said, Men, always moving on down the line. Best that he did just that. Leaving wouldn't get any easier tomorrow.

"Be careful out there. Oh, just a minute..." She walked into her house and came back with a small plastic bag of pills. "You'll need these."

"I'm planning on getting high on altitude."

"They're iodine pills. It'll make the water taste awful but you won't get sick."

Iodine pills? If there was one thing he thought he could count on, it was the purity of Rocky Mountain water. Then again, that was based on a beer commercial.

Chapter 29

They could have sat further back, on the bank seats, but Madeline, reading something in his wolfish leer, chose to sit up front in the buttermilk-colored bucket seats, separated by a narrow aisle. The door was shut and the engines were warming up. The pilots, visible up in the cockpit, were going through their final check list.

"Oh, hi Ed." Clay held his phone away for a second. "Listen, I'm just about to get on a plane. Yes, I have thought about it. Uh huh, I can see it would be a challenge. But I'm just not – The Board what? Okay, I'll…let me talk to Madeline about it, okay?"

He slipped the phone back into his pocket.

"You said you were about to get on a plane. That wasn't true."

"It's just weird, that's all, talking about running a non-profit organization from a private jet."

"What about the Board?"

"The Board has accepted my application. You know, the one I haven't submitted? Executive Director of Childlift."

"But if you – "

"Madeline, let's just get this Dubkhadze event out of the way first, okay. Then we can talk."

"You're going to be thinking about it. I just want to get one thing inserted into those thoughts. Don't include me in your reasons for taking it, if that's what you decide to do."

"Got it."

A veteran now of three Georgian orgies, almost a regular, he had been summoned to a personal meeting by Dubkhadze with the curious instruction, "Bring your woman".

His "friendship" with Dubkhadze had never made sense. Yet "friend" is what one of America's richest men had publicly called him, albeit as part of a public humiliation. But taking Madeline to Dubkhadze? No, it couldn't be. Except, how could you turn the man down? Dubkhadze's large premiums were already part of the new budget cycle.

It was only a mild daydream – to be making out in a private jet as it roared towards LA. Anyway, Dubkhadze probably had video cameras watching them. Ever since his first Orgy he had been waiting for the next humiliation. What would the catch be this time? Would Dubkhadze be crude enough to show a shot of a sloppy-grinned Clay with a busty serving wench in his lap?

A blonde, vaguely familiar, stood by a limo parked near the steps down from the jet. She handed a bouquet of red roses to Madeline as Clay visually fitted her with a range of ties from his most recent Georgian Orgy. Certainly, there was something familiar about her.

The limo pulled up in front of a large yet unpretentious clapboard house in Pasadena. Clay and Madeline were led to Dubkhadze, sitting at a white wrought iron table out in an immaculate rear garden. A big-framed woman Madeline's age, sat across from him, her quick jittery eyes met Clay's and ran from them.

"Allow me to present my daughter, Tamara," Dubkhadze said, after Madeline had been introduced. Schooled in Switzerland and summered in Provence, she and Madeline slid easily into French, searching for common friends and locations in the Cote d'Azur.

"Tamara should be practicing her English. She does not often come to Los Angeles," Dubkhadze said, interrupting his general business talk with Clay. The tea came. After it had been poured, and the two women had re-engaged in their conversation, Dubkhadze said, "I had an interesting call the other day. Someone called Gerard Schrager. Phyllis tells me he is Senior Vice President of Sales and Marketing at your company."

"He wants to see you?" Clay guessed.

"I suppose I should be flattered," Dubkhadze said, "to be dealing with a *Senior* Vice President. Tell me, should I keep the appointment?"

"Uh, sure. I mean, yes," he said, sagging. Instead of taking this betrayal like a man he'd shown Dubkhadze his hurt, shown too that he knew nothing about Schrager's plans. Now he sat with a knife in his back, trying, too late, to pretend there was no knife. It had been obvious since that disastrous Partners' Dinner that it was time to leave Steel Umbrella. Now, by waiting too long, he'd allowed Schrager to get in the first shot.

Dubkhadze flashed a smile – almost sympathetic. For the hundredth time he wondered what the great man saw in him.

"I understand your Chairman is quite ill?"

Nicely put, he thought. Schrager was moving out into the open, Jack being otherwise engaged. "Yes, they caught Mr. Lenahan's cancer late. It always happens to the good men." He looked over to Madeline who was talking intently, something about perfumes and a town called Grasse.

Dubkhadze clapped his hands, a little too loudly, bringing the French to a quick stop. "We must go or we'll be late. I have arranged a little concert."

"Is that why you asked for my favorite song?" Madeline said.

Dubkhadze winked at her, then patted Clay on the shoulder. "I think your Mr. Schrager is in for an interesting time."

They arrived late at a Georgian Orthodox Church, walked down the aisle, past the assembled guests, to the front pew. A faint odor of incense gave way to a floral bouquet as they approached the banks of flowers near the altar. Like getting married, Clay thought. To Dubkhadze. As they sat down, a choir of sixteen boys in black slacks and white shirts filed in from a side door, shepherded by a stern-looking matron beating a baton against her ample thigh.

The choir started with hymns, then Georgian songs, then on to Madeline's choice, Ne Me Quitte Pas. How was she to know that her ironic jab at him would be sung by sixteen angel-faced boys, all innocently pleading for a lover to stay and not abandon them despite their many transgressions. The high-pitched plea floated down from the rafters like a blessing from God. Out of the corner of his eye he saw Tamara, cracking a rusty smile.

Dinner was a catered affair back at the house in Pasadena.

"And what is it you do?" Dubkhadze had finally turned to Madeline.

"I write articles for an organization that is campaigning for a fairer distribution of wealth in this country."

"Everyone has their own idea of what fairer means," Dubkhadze said. "Unfortunately for you my idea is to have more for myself."

"Papa, please," Tamara said, softly, almost to herself.

"But this is how we play the game. To win. Always to win. It must be like this." He nodded to Madeline with a complicated smile, a mix of generosity and aggression. "You must have compromised your principles today, a private jet, limos, accepting bread from the enemy..."

"I'm just gathering information. And it's bad manners to take advantage of a host's generosity."

"Your talk of generosity anticipates me. Your campaign is a noble one. And a game is no fun if the other side is losing badly." He raised his voice as if addressing an audience. "I will donate to your cause. You name the organization and the amount. Clay will call Phyllis with the details." He lifted his glass of mineral water and dipped it to Madeline.

"Are you serious about this?" Madeline said, looking to Tamara for support. "What I mean is what can money do when the whole thing is already tied up with a neat bow?"

"You are free to name the amount. Why you could choose a hundred million and buy a state full of congressmen. This is how your system works, does it not?"

"I'm hoping that education will help." Madeline said, without much hope.

"No! No! No! Keep your chin up. Always fight. If you need help you must call me."

The waiter arrived with the wine for the great man to sample. He swirled it once, tasted it. "Much too complex for our simple supper." He waved the waiter, but not the wine, away.

"It is like Madeline here, too complex for her surroundings, for this man here," he said, nodding towards Clay. "This is how it will always be between a man and a woman. We have a saying in Georgia, 'a woman bends like a willow, a man falls like a tree.'"

"I've never heard that one, Papa," Tamara said.

"We also have a long tradition in Georgia," Dubkhadze said, "and that is to lie our heads off."

Walking back to the limo, Dubkhadze gripped Clay's arm as the women went on.

"Madeline is a fine woman, or as we say in Georgia, a fine adversary. I approve. I shall be honored to attend your wedding."

Chapter 30

His dream, his usual one of thwarted transportation, nebulous pursuers, and time running out for unclear reasons, was interrupted by a low booming sound. He shook himself, trying to get his eyes to focus. Where was he? Okay, an early morning, the low sunlight filtering through the pines. He turned his head. A compact lady, late forties, stood staring at him in his bedroll.

"Happy landings."

"Huh?" His folded-up cargo shorts were part of his pillow. Maybe he'd turn his back on her, try for more sleep. She wasn't his wife though.

"This helipad's on private property." She didn't sound all that bothered.

"Helipad? What?"

"George!" A German shepherd sampled the dried-over sweat on his face. "Stop it!"

Still in his sleeping bag, he pulled his clothes on as she worked on a disciplinary challenge with George, her mock stern words more for his benefit than the hound's.

He stood up now. The trees had been cleared away for the concrete pad they were on. Over the trees a steep mountain incline full of pines angled up and up. "Down, George." The damn dog was trying to climb on him, ignoring his master's command. "Named him after my first husband on the theory that I'd finally have a George who followed orders. Huh." She had short brown hair, a regular face – the kind of person you'd need to meet a few times before you started recognizing her on the street.

He surveyed the helipad. Its white bull's-eye contained a looping and intertwined "E" and "R".

"Where am I...Canada?" He still hadn't woken up completely.

"Very funny. This ER is for Elk Ridge. The private property you're on is the Elk Ridge Golf and Country Club." She smiled at his evident confusion. "ER's in Hoback, and Hoback's in Wyoming. I'm like you, a trespasser. It's George here that likes to poke his nose where it doesn't belong. Don't you Georgie?" The hound bounded over to her, nuzzled her crotch.

"Georgie! Please."

"Is there a USG around here?"

"What's that?"

"Government soup kitchen."

"We got no place for socialism here in Wyoming." She broke into a wide smile – a joke, apparently. "I've got some grub I can offer you. And my gutters need cleaning. See we've taken welfare out of the equation?"

"Thanks."

They walked together up a steep road and cut across a field, leaving Elk Ridge property. As they cleared the tops of the lodgepole pines, the view opened out to a sweep of jagged snow-covered peaks, a spectacular vista from northwest to northeast - finally a reward for all that climbing. It had taken three hard days grinding higher and higher out of Idaho Falls, babying his complaining left knee, to reach this view at nearly 6,000 feet. Three one-meal days, just a g-bar for breakfast and lunch. At least water hadn't been a problem – from day two his rest breaks were alongside the Palisades Reservoir followed by the wildly exuberant Snake River.

"That's Garibaldi's place; he'll have a ladder". She pointed to a grandiose lodge-like structure. "I'm Cammie Coletti by the way." When they reached Garibaldi's driveway, she said, "You get the ladder and I'll take your bicycle up to the house. Mine's that one there." She nodded to a large house across the road – all glass which meant all reflected mountains and blue sky. "Oh, and tell Mr. Garibaldi that Louise would appreciate a coupla trout. You think you can handle a ladder and the trout?"

"No problem. Who's Garibaldi, some retired mafia don?"

She smiled. "Have to ask him."

"You sure he's home?"

"Mister, in case you missed the past year, everyone's at home."

Garibaldi's door was answered by a petite blonde in gray sweatpants with UCLA down one leg and a bra-less tank top. She angled a stick-like arm across her chest as she peered up at him. Danger, the moll. And the moll was a doll. He explained the mission.

"Tony?" she hollered into the dark and cavernous house, her small pipes a wavering tremolo. She tapped her sandaled foot, tiny dabs of pink nail polish on each immaculate toe. She gave him a quick nervous smile.

Tony emerged barefooted from the dark in chinos and a burgundy polo shirt, a short medium-framed man, late 30's, with slicked-back black hair and sharp darting eyes.

"Mrs. Coletti needs the ladder again."

Tony looked him over, made a show of doing it, his gaze neutral.

"She also wants two of her trout."

"Brook, you get the trout, I'll handle the ladder. Make it four and we'll have dinner over with Cammie." He nodded at Clay, who nodded back. Yes, he'd inform his new boss of the dinner arrangements.

The Coletti's house was one notch down in size from Garibaldi's. He worked the gutters for several hours with an old dishwashing brush, his stomach growling like an overloaded semi juddering up the Sierras. Cammie brought him cold water as he took a break in the shade.

"He's a nice man. Let's me keep my freezer over at his place," Cammie said.

"Where's he get his electricity?"

"Whatever you do, don't ask him that, okay?"

"A sensitive subject?"

"I'll say it's sensitive. Half the town's on Mr. Garibaldi's case. Maybe more than half."

Clay sat at the dining room table, a new man, after shaving off his six-week beard, and luxuriating in a warm shower with soap – the Coletti house had solar panels – and wearing clean clothes courtesy of Cammie's absent husband Herb: an aloha shirt and chinos. They were as clean as they were comical in their fit. Herb must have been a fireplug of a man.

Cammie had directed him to a view seat, the plate glass opening out to a northern vista of rugged alpine splendor.

"You're going to need lots of luck to get to the other side of these Rockies," Tony said after Clay had sketched his journey and his destination. "Not only have you got your USG patrols, you have your Bolts. They're wild cards, patriots, determined to keep newcomers out of the fair state of Wyoming."

"But I'm already here. And I'm just passing through."

"I'll write you a note," Tony said. "Guess it would help if I lived here myself."

Cammie served trout, potatoes, and early corn, complemented by a chilled bottle of California viognier from a winery Tony part-owned.

The tart fruit of the wine exploded in Clay's mouth and echoed in his brain as he sat in standard dinner format, as if the past eight post-Meltdown months had been a bad dream. When he managed to regain a sense of equilibrium, Tony was still bragging about his winery.

"Do you still own it?" Clay asked.

Tony laughed. "Interesting question. I figure that when this ship rights itself the title deed will count. Meantime, a winery is a winery. Even the Prohibition couldn't stop them."

Brook helped Cammie clear the table, and prepare what Cammie called Indian coffee.

"More?" Tony asked, holding the wine bottle, pouring before getting an answer. As they watched the wine swirl into his glass, Cammie's voice floated out of the kitchen, "Now, you know you're welcome to stay here for however long you want to."

"My wife isn't suited to the Marie Antoinette role."

"I imagine Marie wasn't either, in the end." A load of alcohol hit his brain and the view swam before settling again. "Are we talking about revolution?"

The women returned with coffee, overhearing that final word, revolution.

"There was a bunch of them last night," Brook said, "running their sticks along our gate. It was horrible."

"Like the angry villagers in Frankenstein," Tony said. "Don't you see how interesting this is, hon? Maybe it's the start of a new system, you know, the future."

"Interesting. Interesting. Interesting."

"I paid good money for that fuel, Brook."

"Haven't you heard?" Brook said, her voice quavering. "There's no such thing as 'good money'…anymore."

"The town wants Tony here to donate one of his diesel tanks," Cammie explained. "They're running low."

"Scarce resources…" Clay picked up his wine and stared at it. Nah, this had to be a dream. "Reminds me of one of our big droughts, down in Santa Barbara. Water so scarce you had to wonder what happened if we ran out completely. People not flushing; quick showers with the water off while you soaped up. Gardens dying."

"We're from L.A.," Tony hurried him, "we know the deal."

"Well this town had a rich man with a two-acre lawn. He understood supply and demand, and had no problem paying big money for his big lawn to be watered. But scarcity is scarcity. There's a section at the south end of the supply curve where all bets are off. In the end, we are all in this mess together and there comes a point where you can't sit on the other side of money anymore."

"You sure got a silver tongue," Cammie said.

"Thanks for the lesson, Mr. Economist," Tony raised his wine glass in an ironic salute.

"I think he's sweet." Brook looked across to her hubby to see how much trouble she was in.

Fogged by the wine, Clay turned the screw. "This is my fifth state. I've seen quite a few towns. And yes, some of it isn't pretty. But some of it is.". Winnemucca was a haze. Reno best forgotten, but Idaho Falls, Elko… "It's a neighborhood thing. You pull together street by street and a town has a chance."

"Street by street?" Tony said. "Half the houses here are empty – second homes, or third. What we've got is a patchwork neighborhood. Anyway, what did you do for work, back when things were working?"

Clay gave them a three-sentence bio.

"MBA to charity work. How did that happen?" Tony said.

"My wife. She made me."

"So how does it work? I guess you hit up people like me for money?"

"Once upon a time…"

Brook, still on the previous topic, said, "Tone saw this coming. That kind of foresight deserves to be 'rewarded'".

"Yes, I did." Tony said. "Maybe I should donate my tank to your Childlift boys. That's an awful name by the way." He gazed at his wife, shaking his head faintly. Puffy and restless, she was gazing beyond him out the window. The snow on the peaks was losing definition as the light bled away from the early evening. "How would you get me to do that, to donate my tank container, Mr. Charity?" *Sell me. Try to.*

Clay exhaled sharply through his nose, signaling the difficulty of such a request. There were two types of rich, inherited and self-made. Each of the former was a lump of inert privilege, unchangeable, impervious to outside reasoning. He or she either gave or didn't. The latter, like Tony, had seen the money come in, knew how fickle the money god could be, had probably sailed dangerously close to the wind to get it, and could often be open-minded about donating.

"I've never been able to convince rich folks of anything."

"That doesn't sound very encouraging," Cammie said.

"It's got to be their idea, not mine. Take you, Mr. Garibaldi. You might be surprised to learn that there is a part of you that wants to donate one of those containers. It might even be the largest part of you.

You're just not listening to it."

"Well, this *is* interesting," Cammie said, to laughter.

"You presume to know me pretty darn well for only a few hours," Tony said.

"I admit I'm making a few assumptions." He cast his eyes toward Brook.

"You're saying if I love my wife I should give you my fuel. That, my friend, is close to blackmail."

Clay smiled.

"I hate it, these people who insist they have a right to my money."

"Then you don't understand money."

"Oho," Cammie said.

"Okay, teach me."

"Money has to work; it needs to flow. It's like water in a river. If you have, say, a hundred million in the bank, on-shore, off-shore, that money is worked. It might be yours but it's also mine, in the form of a loan note. And I've taken that loan money and paid it to a company that makes widgets, they've paid their workers, et cetera."

"Most of mine is in property."

"No, it isn't." Brook said.

"The Queen of England owns a river," Cammie said, "the one that flows through London."

"She owns the river but not the water," Clay said. Well, it sounded clever.

"I don't understand," Cammie said, "how this working money flows to you. Your charity I mean."

"I'm not talking about a hard and fast concept, I'm talking about a mentality. It's the opposite of a miser running gold coins through his hands and saying, "mine all mine". The fact is it's the opposite. 97% of US dollars are – were – nothing more than ones and zero in a computer. Not your computer, their computer. Ownership of those one and zeros amounts to so much ink on a monthly statement."

"And the ink started running and we couldn't catch up to it." Cammie said.

Tony said, "Park that to one side for a minute. Diesel is diesel; apart from me, I need it to run Louise's freezer. You see! There's my altruism."

"And I go back to the first thing I said. You want to give the tank away."

Tony shook his head. "You said it before: you're not good at convincing us of anything."

"I'll be gone tomorrow," he said, pausing to underscore the difficulty of his quest. "Usually this kind of conversation takes place over months. I've never compressed it like this before. I'm sorry if it comes over as, I don't know, brusque?"

"And you know your, your patrons better than they know themselves?" Cammie said.

"I never said that."

"But you're saying I want to give away my diesel?" Tony picked up his wine glass, thought better of it, put it back down.

"Let's just say that's true, accept it for now. Okay? How easy would it be to give the town one of those containers after all these weeks, or months, where you've been digging in your heels?"

"I'm not worried about what people think."

Brook started to say something, thought better of it. She sat next to him, hot and frozen.

"You said your wife made you leave your job for a charity?" Cammie said.

"She made me *want* to do that."

"Yes, there is a difference."

"This is blackmail. I'm not buying it." Tony turned to Cammie. "What about you Cammie, are you with *them*, too?"

Cammie laughed nervously. Tony was running her freezer; Brook was her friend.

"So, it's three against one?" Tony said.

"Yes, but not the way you think," Clay said. How strange to be transported back to those days when he was Mr. Childlift, angling for money. Those days were over. Whether Garibaldi donated a drop of fuel or not didn't matter to his charity. The greatest luxury in any job, and a luxury because for one reason or another you can never do it, is to tell your boss, your customer, your colleague what you really think. "I'm not on their side against you. I'm on my side against all of you."

"You are against my poor tearful wife?"

"Absolutely."

Brook started sniffling.

"Okay, you got me." Garibaldi said.

"It's what you said, Tony. She *is* Marie Antoinette. It's the end game and all Brook here wants is to protect her neck. Cammie wants her trout. And you...There's no morality here, no sense that a hospital's need for backup power is more important than a freezerful of trout. To Brook these villagers with their midnight torches are just the unwashed masses that need to go away and leave her in peace." He sat back. How long had he dreamt about doing something like this? Douse his Career Self in gasoline and strike a match.

"How did you know about the hospital?" Cammie murmured. "You just got here."

"There's always a hospital." He put his napkin on the table. "I guess I should go. I apologize for being rude."

"Now wait a minute," Cammie said. "There's room at this table for good old healthy disagreement. Isn't that right Tony?"

They waited for Tony to say something. He sat distracted, thinking. "You take chances my friend. No one talks to my wife like that. You okay, hon?"

"Uh huh." Her eyes widened as her face took on color. She looked at her husband and smiled, basking in this new world, her husband on her side for once. "I see his point. Maybe I have been a tad selfish."

"Come on. Ownership's ownership. What are we supposed to do, give our house away?"

"Tone. When I asked you to give away that tank before, it was because I wanted those people to go away and stop scaring me. Now I'm asking because it's the right thing to do." She met his eyes, her face glowing, the first easy smile she'd shown that evening. "What I'm saying is yes you should definitely do it." She ended with a "so there" look, transformed, no longer just attractive, radiant, alluring.

"That's the way it is, is it? Play one off the other. Turn my wife against me. Thanks a lot Mr. Charity."

"I'm sorry if you feel that way."

"Let me make this clear, my friend. I'm giving this tank away because I love my wife. It has nothing to do with all this crap you've been spouting."

"Understood."

Chapter 31

"I feel like you've hijacked my life," Madeline said. "Before I met you I don't think I ever took a taxi. Now this limo, and to a private jet that is waiting for us? And Tamara practically invited me to spend July in the Cote d'Azur. What's happened to my old, comfortable and messed up life?"

"They'll have a super yacht. You can send me a postcard."

She flashed a I-can't-believe-this look at him, would have put her hands on her hips if she hadn't been sitting down. "Is this what you want? This kind of life? Really?"

"What I want is a stiff drink."

"I saw your pleased smile when I was being grilled by your friend, so proud of me, practically beaming. All I'm trying to do is not embarrass you, and instead you're getting the idea that I might be the right corporate partner after all."

"Madeline, I think I'm going to accept the charity job."

"Seriously?" She turned in her seat, her eyes swimming in a new and choppy sea. "This is what *you* want?"

"A lot has happened today. If I feel the same tomorrow, I'll call Ed Harmon and talk about specifics."

"What about our favorite billionaire?"

"I'd leave him behind if I could. Honestly, I would. But if I take the Childlift job he could be a major donor. That's the way life works, you can never escape."

"If you take the Childlift job," she said, "you must take the donation Mr. D offered me. You can start out a hero."

"Oh no. Dubkhadze donating to your publication is something that needs to happen, if only to prove that the world is an unpredictable place."

"I feel like I've become you," Madeline said, "and you've become me."

"That still makes us different people."

Chapter 32

He cycled out of Jackson, Wyoming accompanied by cyclists, kids on bikes pedaling madly to keep up, joggers and a few riders on horseback – a hero's sending off. Tony Garibaldi had insisted on surrendering his tank to Clay and not to the Teton County authorities, so Clay was forced to oversee a team of men and six horses in extracting the tank container from its awkward position around the side and toward the back of Garibaldi's property. There was one tight turn, the men straining every sinew, the horses less effective in such a tight space where the outcome was in doubt. Finally, the turn accomplished, the horses harnessed, it was a straight run out to the street and a waiting 18-wheeler, which paradoxically needed a few gallons from its load to make the sixteen-mile trip to the county seat at Jackson and the grateful citizens' reception. No speeches, just food, thanks, and a soft bed for the night was how they sold it.

With the big rig idling, Clay and Tony had inspected the premises for damage. That had been one of Tony's two donation conditions, no damage to his property, that and one tank, not both. Garibaldi made a show of examining the path his former tanker had taken. Clay said, "I'll clean up the horseshit in morning." Another line from a b-movie.

"Leave it. We need something to remember you by."

He cycled slowly so the kids could keep up, enjoying the warm pleasant day, the flat valley road with majestic peaks in all directions, and the new weight in his knapsack from an assortment of goodies he'd been given to help him on his journey. A mile out of town the parade fell away and with a wave Clay picked up the pace as he got down to the serious business of covering the sixteen miles back to Hoback.

He took his first rest stop at a campground on the brown and boiling Hoback River. It twisted and charged, almost to the top of the low bank, as it rushed headlong to join the Snake River ten miles to the north. The campground sat at nearly the same level as the water.

Sitting on top of a picnic table to gain a few feet on the river, he knew it would have to be the venison jerky first. His mouth had been puckering and watering for all the miles he'd clocked so far that day. That first chaw, ripping the hide-like jerky with his teeth like a primitive hunter, was everything he had dreamt it would be. Piquant, alive with earthy, meaty taste, each chew drawing out more flavor. He closed his eyes to the cinematic bursts of essence. The urgent spring charge of the river was a muted background to the symphony going on in his mouth. Man, this was living, and he had untold goodies to go. Carob brownies, baklava, who knew what else? The perfect note to start his ascent over the Rockies. With a body charged with jerky protein he could remount his bike and mash out a couple hundred miles over the Rockies and across the downslope of the Great Plains to the Mississippi, all before dinner. Ah, dinner!

What was that? A low "unh", like a big man taking a gut punch. He opened his eyes, quivered his head, the way you do when you see something but don't want to see. A bear. A huge brown bear, twenty feet away, watching him like a mafia protection guy waiting for a store owner to finish with a customer. He ignored an adrenalin rush, one that demanded a mad sprint to safety. Weren't there two kinds of bear in these parts? For one of them the best survival method was to talk quietly and to slowly slink back and away. For the other kind, the opposite, make yourself big, holler, wave your arms around. Either way a shot from his Beretta would be like a slap in the face.

Smokey did an "uh uh uh" grunt that vibrated the forest floor like a passing car blasting rap music. "Take a hike, Smokey!" he said, hitting a halfway point, vocally, between slinking off and making big noise. He tossed a handful of G-bars towards the river. Smokey looked at them, looked at him, didn't move. They regarded each other for a long moment. There was an economy to the bear's strategy, letting his imposing presence do the talking. Such eloquence. Clay heard it, ran his bike around the picnic table, hopped on and pedaled frantically.

In no time that bass grunt was almost in his ear. He tried to shrug off his knapsack, but the bear got it first, its claw grasping the material and pulling him backwards. In a blur, he was free of the pack and wobbling forward, his bike too unstable to remain upright. He lay on the road, his palms re-lacerated. Smokey crouched fifteen feet away, going through his knapsack like a woman looking for her lipstick.

He eased his way up the road, the bear intent on sampling the goodies. An hour later he coasted back to the scene of the crime, and retrieved his mangled and slobber-drenched knapsack. He dangled the wet fabric from his handlebars as he pumped up the grade he'd just sailed down. A safe distance away, he assessed the damage. The knapsack itself was shredded beyond use. His wallet had been partially chewed. He unfolded it. The remaining Kendies had met their 22 November. His driver's license was just about legible. Why had he bothered to bring it? Inside the main cavity his sweater was in shreds, as were his few other clothes.

He stood next to his bike on the empty road, facing a long uphill grind south through the primordial forest toward Pinedale. Or, he could fly downhill, past the now notorious campground and back to Hoback, or on to Jackson. He was too angry to coast. To win all those tasty morsels only to have them swept away after one bite was beyond cruel.

Further south, the land was changing. He left the forests for the flat, sagebrush-dotted expanse that swept all the way to distant snow-capped mountain ranges. These were the high plains at nearly 6600 feet, an 800-foot climb from Hoback. No bears, no food, plenty of iodized Hoback River water. Lost in the middle of the Rockies with no map, no warm clothes save a chewed-up sweater. The smart move would have been Hoback. He was too angry to be smart.

Chapter 33

Childlift shared a floor in a former coffee warehouse with a shipping line that traded into Micronesia. Clay's office looked out over a parking lot, part of the bus terminal complex. He stood at the window watching a bedraggled man pushing his shopping cart up the middle of the street while the one-way traffic calmly looped around him.

Ed Harmon, CEO of Keyway Energy, Board President of Boystown, and former Board Member of Childlift, sat on the sofa. Some months back he had dropped by Steel Umbrella to thank Clay for his ticket donation, and found a young sales hustler with an MBA and an embryonic social conscience. Over several casual phone calls, culminating in the one that reached Clay on Dubkhadze's Lear jet, he had reeled Clay in. His insurance career behind him, Clay was now Executive Director of Childlift, a non-profit whose mission was to expose urban boys to manual skills such as carpentry, woodworking, electrical and mechanical repairs, horticulture, and once a year, the carrot, summer camp up in the Sierras.

"I know you're in a hurry, and that's good. I'm serious, it's good. But come on, you can't fight all battles at once." Harmon shifted his legs and pointed the other immaculately polished loafer at him.

"Look, Ed, I can take most of the bullshit here," Clay said. "Coaxing and flattering the volunteers, recruiting more of them, dealing with messy people problems and complaints. But the Board, why are they so damn passive? What's wrong with a healthy exchange of views? If they don't agree, why can't they meet my eyes and say so? Instead of mumbling and stalling and sending you tiptoeing in... as if the whole subject is like some dire prognosis." His idea about changing Childlift's name was a heresy, apparently. The original founder and funder, J. Muswell Day, a wealthy property developer, had a lifelong interest in boys – several damaging allegations had been quickly muted before quietly disappearing. Over time the snigger factor of "Childlift" had worn off to those familiar with the name, but Clay was still new to it.

"Well, you know the history, it's – "

He turned away from the window. "Ed, I don't care about the name. It would be nice if we could change it, but it was just a discussion point. It was never a *battle*. What I object to, strongly, is the inefficiency. I mean here you are wasting your valuable time over a non-issue. All they had to say was, Forget about it."

"Day's still breathing." Harmon paused to underline his statement of the obvious. "He talks to the Big 3. You need his money. And you need the money from his friends down in Hillsborough. It's a dance, sure it is, but it's a dance for money." The biggest of the Big 3, brought in by Day and still fiercely loyal to him, was the Board President, Max Blair. Once a flamboyant trial lawyer, now throttled by a serious stroke, he retained his intellect, even though it sometimes took him minutes to wrestle an idea into words. At Board meetings that restless wait for a complete sentence seemed to sum up Childlift's stuttering progress.

"Something tells me the dance isn't over."

"You know, one thing about inefficiency, it's more social. You get to hang out longer, get to know folks."

"Great."

Harmon smiled. Even he acknowledged that the Childlift Board was "tired"; an advisory Board that didn't advise, no decision too small to postpone or to appoint a committee to consider it.

"Saturday morning. I'll pick you up, here, around nine. It's time you saw Day again. All his information has been from the Big 3. We need to rebut that."

"And back away from the name change?"

"Yep."

Saturday morning wouldn't be a hardship. Madeline and he were supposed to be going to a crafts fair over in Marin. And it would give him time to sell his big idea to Harmon on the drive down.

"Childlift needs to expand," Clay said as they purred down 280 in Harmon's Jaguar. "Ed, when you sold me on Childlift I told you two years, right? I told you non-profits weren't my career. And you were hoping I'd get caught up in it and stay longer. I want to give you a way in which I'd be prepared to add a year to my commitment."

"Okay."

"You know I have contacts with several major tech firms, right? I've got a couple that are okay with trialing a games program. We send them three boys – my idea is three-on-three mentorships – and the boys see how games are developed, learn a bit about coding. Maybe even advise the company on what they like in games."

"The Board would have to approve it."

"Tell me about it."

Day was a cadaverous man with milky-blue eyes that had the faintest twinkle to them. They sat out on the flagstone terrace as Clay, the MBA, talked property finance, and played up to Day's nostalgia for the old days of development. "That's what's wrong with San Francisco," Clay laughed, as Day nodded and shifted, "all these cheaply built lofts."

"That, son, is exactly what the problem is." Already Clay had learnt that the rich and powerful love being told what they want to hear, the certainty they are right so strong that they are impervious to any self-serving irony. He laid it on and Harman let him run. They moved on to a Childlift status report, sketches of new employees, donation performance, and strategy. Strategy – Clay's eyes lit up, his gestures became grander. The smart play was to keep it tight, stay with issues Day already knew about.

Day was a canny man, could see Clay's passion rising. "That's not going to get Childlift very far down the road."

It was too risky hitting Day with his tech mentoring idea. Day's vision – his condescending and patronizing one many argued – had always been manual training. These things needed to be managed, presented in a formalized way, all the counter-arguments anticipated, the Board already behind it. He needed to stop, it was the professional thing to do, what his position demanded. But he couldn't stop. Avoiding Harmon's eyes, he launched into his tech mentorship plans. "I know it's outside Childlift's remit of crafts, and three-on-three instead of our group format – "

"It certainly is," Day interrupted in a wavering voice. "But I agree entirely. An organization must adapt, sometimes." He turned to Harmon. *Have you marked that?*

Madeline would be glad – another year at Childlift. She supported him in his role, accompanying him on the wine and canapé circuit, double teaming a likely target or working the opposite side of the room, comparing notes, scarfing down a few morsels, fast becoming their standard dinner fare.

"One more year," he said to Madeline later that afternoon. "Then we'll see." Social conscience looked good on a resume, for a year or two. Three at the outside. After that the stain was permanent.

Chapter 34

On the second morning out of Pinedale the dirt kicked up in front of Clay's bike; a moment later the crack of rifle fire. More disturbed dirt, another crack. He stopped, shaded his eyes. Two men stood next to their horses on a rise off to his right two hundred yards away, the morning sun behind them. One of them raised his hat, holding his rifle in the middle at his side as if carrying a pipe. Something annoying about that. He slid on to his horse and came trotting down and over.

Clay put his bike down and, stood legs apart, ready. The high desert here was as open as a chessboard and this was the endgame. After being saved by the hospitality of an old woman in the hamlet of Bondurant, he had pumped and struggled all the way via Pinedale to this area just short of the Continental Divide, first down gravel roads, then double track, severely washboarded in places, and with sandy sinks that gripped the bike's tires into a stranglehold. Who would have thought that this high pass through the Rockies was barren sagebrush-filled desert?

"Morning," the rider said, fifties maybe, with a friendly enough smile and a certain home field confidence.

"Morning, Mr. Bolt." They regarded each other for a long moment. "This is government land I'm riding on, so what's the problem?"

"No problem. Just following USG protocol." He gave a self-satisfied smile.

Clay surveyed the wide and empty desert. How could the USG be doing anything in the middle of nowhere? They weren't doing much in the middle of somewhere. "Okay I give up, what's your protocol?"

"Gotta give trespassers a verbal warning to turn around and get out."

"Then what?"

The rider maneuvered his horse a few steps, unblocking the rising sun. "I'll tell you one thing for nothing. You don't want to find out."

"You'd shoot a fellow citizen?"

"You've had your warning." He tipped his hat and cantered back to his confederate up on the rise.

Now what? He had come 1,300 miles in two months, and the last three days, what with Smokey, hunger, altitude, were up there with the toughest. It was a new land, a desert much like Nevada's only two thousand feet higher, more snow in the distant ranges, and in the looming Wind River Range to the east, then north as he squared toward the Divide, nearer, higher.

No way was he going to let that tin star horseman tell him what to do. He had been careless, not thinking about the sun and what it could hide. Still, those bullets had been real enough, the aim perfect, just in front of him, even accounting for his motion. He maintained his ground out of self-respect, waved and headed west. It was so wide open up here there was nowhere to hide.

That night, having done a wide flanking maneuver on nothing more than g-bars and careful sips of water, he was walking his bike through a stretch of soft dirt. His body ached, his stomach wasn't talking to him anymore – yelling into the night instead. Every fifth step or so he stumbled from not lifting his bike shoe out of the dirt enough. Panic was setting in: only three g-bars and a finger of water remained. He was desperately thirsty. All he could hope for was first light and the Bolts to find and rescue him. It had been folly to loop so wide and try a night run for the Divide on negligible rations.

Now the sound of running water, a light trickle that died out and reappeared in the chill night air. Just when he thought it was gone it came back stronger. It faded away again like bad radio reception. He bundled his heavy weave sweater, a gift from his elderly savior in Bondurant, tighter against the cold.

Now the water sound became a constant burble. A small stream murmured in the moonlight, just off the path. With the looming bulk of the Wind River Range giving him an approximation of north, the stream had to be west-flowing. He refilled his water bottles, broke off pieces of an iodine tablet, shook the bottles for luck.

The night had gone from chill to cold now. On this high plain – nearly 7,000 feet – the stars were so low you could reach out and rearrange them – upgrade your destiny. Now another hallucination. Out in the middle of desolate nowhere a well-maintained stone pedestal with an angled steel plate. *Pacific Springs* read the headline in the light of a waxing half-moon. A lit match told the rest of the story. Here was the first water on the west side of the Continental Divide, here on the Oregon Trail.

His obvious way east was the pioneers' way west, a path of least resistance funneled through this flat pass. From somewhere came music, faint on the night air, more exhalation than breeze. It came and went, but came more often as he walked his bike east. A harmonica. Scraps of melody, then the song itself, a soulful rendition of "Brother, Can You Spare Me a Dime".

He hated that song. At the Comraderie – his name for the band of anti-capitalists that hung out at the Visitacion Valley house – he'd been forced to listen to it, had been taunted with that capitalism-gone-wrong message. Worse, they played the version by Barry MacDuff, Madeline's former flame, the love of her life until he betrayed her. MacDuff added a few spoonfuls of sugar to the opening, "They used to tell me I was building a dream", milking the sentiment, and sailing by the message, idealism betrayed. Out in the night, the cold, black and empty plain complimented the depression era disillusionment of the song. Whoever was working the harmonica understood the song, playing it with controlled hurt and anger, yet giving the melody enough weight to counter those emotions with a wistful optimism.

Down a roll in the plain loomed a series of ghostly structures, their weather-worn boards bleached further by the moonlight. The song drifted up from them, half mocking, half inviting him.

The smart move was to walk on by; he couldn't do that. It was his siren song, aimed at him, calling to him, knowing he was out there. To leave the trail and follow the music was a kind of giving up, yet he turned and walked toward the structures at the bottom of a gentle roll in the land.

A man sat in the doorway of a skeletal one-room building, playing, his face buried under a Powder River Stetson. He was back to the melody, taking his time, not looking up.

Such a quintessential American song, Madeline's Visitacion friends had maintained. Its subtitle should have been "Capitalism on its Knees", or "The Workers Denied". Back then he'd done his homework, fought back. The song, he told them, was based on a Jewish lullaby out of Bialystok, on the eastern reaches of Poland. Here was the real story: impoverished Jewish peasants escaping the racism, the discrimination, the pogroms of Eastern Europe, coming to the bright promise of the New World. Ask them, he said, about capitalism.

"Howdy," the man said, barely looking up.

"Hi. You a Bolt?"

"No sir."

"They're after me."

"I know that."

Wyoming conversations, always terse, over quickly. That let you get back to the wide-open desolation of the desert or, at night, the stars.

The man stood up. He was short, maybe five six. His Stetson put his entire face in shadow. He was in his forties, hair on the long-side but well-trimmed.

"Not much Yankee Doodle Dum now," Clay said, quoting the song.

"It's still there brother, still there." The man finally met his eyes, his head angled so that the moonlight hit his soul patch in a riot of soft bristles.

"I guess you know about my favorite songs."

"Favorite? I don't think so," the man said with certainty. "It's not the song itself, is it? More like the circumstances under which you had to hear it?"

Clay gave his head a rattling shake. He had to be dreaming. All he had to go on was this man and a couple of million stars.

"I'm no hallucination," the man said. "That would be too convenient, wouldn't it?"

"Who are you and what do you want?"

"A man. It's quite some song. Do you know the line that comes after your Yankee Doodle Dum, or Yankee Doodle Dee Dum as some would have it?"

"Half a million boots went slogging through hell."

"Yes, a reference to your first World War. Isn't it interesting that about half a million pioneers trudged by this very spot on their way west to a better life? Why your Mormons with their handcarts were too poor to afford any kind of dray animal. They had to manhandle the carts themselves, husbands yoked to the cart, wife pushing."

Clay propped his bike against the building. If there was a point here he would have to wait for it.

"I love that spirit. People on the move, action, manhandling life in the direction they want and not the ordained one. I have a vision, brother. That vision is that this country can be great again."

"You *are* a hallucination."

"Only in so far as life is one. Now, you asked me what it is I'm after. I will tell you. I need your cooperation. That's it; all I have to say. We will meet again. When the time is right, we will meet again."

"My cooperation, why me?"

"Let's just say that I know you better than you know yourself."

"Bullshit."

"You have the right instincts, the ones I need. Your desire to see your wife again is…well, you don't see too many people cycling across this vast country."

"You know about my wife?"

"I will tell you this much: she's not in Boston anymore."

"What?"

"Questions. Questions. Brother, I know everything about you?"

"That's impossible. And even if you did my conscience is clear."

"Winnemucca?"

He had been dizzy with fatigue before he heard the music. The water from Pacific Springs had cleared his head, though. He drank some more.

"We will meet again," the man said. "When we do there will be more time for discussion. Right now, we need to get you past these Dolts. I mean Bolts. His eyes swept out to the east. "They will be waiting for you on the other side of the pass, out where it meets 287. You got no chance going that way, compadre. You want to take a flanking route, veer north of the Oregon Trail, Crooks Gap Road to Jeffrey City. Then hit Gas Hills Road and Dry Creek. Then Poison Spider Road."

A strong sense of unreality washed over him. Ever since he'd hit Wyoming, dumb phrases had rung out, clichéd lines as if he'd been parachuted into a low budget western. *Waiting on the other side of the pass.* Really.

"If you do run into the Bolts tell them the story of the Oregon Trail. Tell them that, of the half million folks who passed through Wyoming, the only ones that stopped were the ones pushing up the sagebrush."

Did he trust him enough to follow his directions? "These Bolts, they're working with the USG?"

"Up north in the Dakotas there's trouble. A bunch of rebels is trying to take-over one of the fracking operations up there. Your USG is happy to keep everyone away from the operations here in Wyoming. You can see how the Bolts fit in with those plans."

Clay turned his bike around, pointed it east, wanting to be on his way, too weary to go on.

"Now remember, straight across at Jeffrey City. Follow the road 'til after it crosses the Sweetwater. That'll put you on the north side. You and your friends can stare at each other from opposite sides of the river. Oh, and eventually you'll hit the town of Gas Hills. I'd avoid it. They will be searching for you there once you fail to show at the pass."

"I must be delirious. You, sir, are a hallucination. It's the only explanation."

"Merrily, merrily, merrily, merrily, life is but a dream."

The man reached in his satchel, tossed over a paper bag. Inside was a generous slice of pineapple-upside-down cake. Back on the Oregon Trail he polished it off, and sank to his knees in thanks. Being delirious had its advantages.

Chapter 35

Accurate directions from a ghost, he muttered. Yep, the turn-off was right where it should be. He rattled his head around to stay awake, half rode, half-walked as the new double track veered to the northeast. Keep on, keep on, he chanted that mantra. Find cover before the rising sun cast his shadow long, for all to see. Only then could he fall from exhaustion.

The eastern horizon showed a hint of red as he coasted into Jeffrey City. The first abandoned building, locked but with a broken window, was his deliverance. Grimacing at the iodine taste, he drank a good portion of his remaining water, the Sweetwater River not far away – if you believed the Phantom Cowboy. He ate one of his last two G-bars and he lay down, the insistent scrabbling rats something to bother with later.

He slept until midafternoon. Daylight revealed Jeffrey City to be a ghost town. Not a mining or railroad town from the 19th century, but more recent. It resembled an abandoned army base made from glued-together packing crates, sagging and boarded up, their former purpose stenciled high up. Bachelor apartments. Townhouse. Store. Some of the outer crossroads were weed gardens.

Near the highway a truck pulling a trailer purred south on 287 in the right spot to see him. Its engine revved as Clay jumped a curb and cut over between buildings to a parallel street, turned onto a street that said Rattlesnake Dr. A woman at a window was making kitchen sink motions. He knocked on her door. She was a big woman with a ruddy, well-scrubbed face and small arms.

"What're you selling?"

"Selling? Here? Truth be told I'm on the run from Bolts. I sure would appreciate some food and I'll be on my way."

A little girl hung on to her Mama's sweatpants, peaking with large eyes around at him. An older boy, maybe eight, was shooting suction cup darts at a dead TV screen. One of them lost its suction and plopped to the floor.

"Try licking them," Clay said. "Sorry, ma'am, if your husband isn't around…"

"Earl, stop doing that." The boy sloped out the front door, stood with it open, inviting the cold world of the desolate plain to invade. The small room felt like a bright packet of civilization.

She introduced herself as Pauletta, explained that Jeffrey City was an abandoned mining town. She thought uranium, if you straightened out her pronunciation. But what did she know? She been brought up all the way over in Rawlins, seventy miles south.

"Earl, shut that door, would you?" She turned back to Clay, "That desert out there can seep into your bones."

"What happens then?"

"You turn to stone."

"What do you do for food…way out here?"

"Your friends, the ones that're after your hide, drop off supplies comin' and goin' 'tween Lander and Muddy Gap. Not much I can offer you. We'll see."

"What's your husband do, if you don't mind my asking?"

"Hah. What you're really askin' is why we live out in this…place. Well, Taylor's got a full-time job running out on me. Your friends keep promising to run me down to Rawlings, that's where my Mom and Dad are. Never have enough fuel, though."

"Taylor's a Bolt?"

"Would be if he could do one thing for long enough. I'm not counting drinking in that."

Earl came bounding in, two men in his wake.

"Hello," Pauletta said.

"Your boy come and got us, ma'am," the older of the two tipped his hat. He was a lean man, fifties, who tilted to starboard, as if trying to get the world to line up with his angles. His companion was a taller, even leaner man, gawky, a generation younger. "You been harboring a dangerous criminal here?"

"You men and your games," she said, then waved it away. "You boys seen Taylor around anywhere? Taylor Bittinger?"

The Bolts looked at each other, embarrassed. "Up in Lander's what I heard," the young Bolt said. He had a bobbing Adam's apple and protruding eyes.

"Damian, you get his bike stuff," the older man said, "while I go through his pack here."

"Sure thing, Riley."

Riley pulled stuff out of the small sack that Clay had been given at the Pinedale Bart, the lady at the stall sewing two straps to a canvas shopping bag.

Damian came strutting through the door. "You have a permit for this gun?"

"It's in the mail."

Not finding anything, Riley turned his attention to his prisoner. "You were warned good and proper. By ignoring that you forfeited your rights. Do you deny that? That you were warned?"

"It's a free country. I wasn't on private land."

"Free country! What're all the USG roadblocks about then? You were warned; you're trespassing; and you're going to the jail at Muddy G." He turned to Pauletta. "Has this man raped you or anything?" he asked.

"What?" Clay took a step toward Riley, rolled out his shoulders.

"Wouldn't have been rape," Pauletta said.

After an awkward silence, Damian said, "Not sure we got enough gas for MG, not if we are planning on a return trip tonight. And you know 'bout tomorrow."

"Head on home now," Clay said. "I'll be long gone by the time you wake up tomorrow."

Riley gave him a warm, if-only smile, an if-this-were-up-to-me one. "Can't do that. God damned fuel shortage. Pretty darn sad when the USG can't even be bothered about national security."

"Let me get this straight," Clay said. "You don't want me in your region so you're going to arrest me and plump me in jail, thereby making me a full time resident."

"Jailbirds don't count."

"USG pays them a bounty," Pauletta explained

"Pays them with what?"

"Booze, probably," she said, shaking her head darkly.

"Not booze," the young Bolt said, "gas."

Clay readied his Oregon Trail speech. He was planning on a direct steal of that "pushing up the sagebrush" line. Timing, though, was everything. "The USG gives you gas so you can ride around catching people like me? Isn't it obvious that one guy on a bike can't be a fracking terrorist?"

"Whoa. Whoa. Whoa, there friend," Riley said. "How come you know such top secret information."

"Same way you do: it's not much of a secret."

"Where'd you hear about it? One guy on a bike in the middle of nowhere. What? you heard it from a coyote?"

"Heard about it in…Pinedale I think it was."

"They don't know about it in Pinedale," Damian said.

Clay Holloway, the man who knew too much. He needed to say something but all that came to him was speeches. The pushing up the sagebrush one. The America the Great one, hitting on the philosophy, the eloquence and foresight of the double F's, the Founding Fathers. All the soldiers who gave their lives so the country could remain free. Maybe it would make him feel better but it would be wasted on Bolts.

It was getting dark by now. The Bolts repaired outside and argued. Finally, they came back in, Damian slumping, clearly overruled.

"Ma'am I hope you don't mind putting us up for the night. We'll be gone first thing, I can promise you that. Damian, you take the first shift guarding the prisoner."

After all had prepared for bed, they installed Clay in the bathroom, a chair propped against the outward opening door. "Don't worry ma'am, we'll organize a few comfort breaks."

Clay couldn't sleep. What a contrast to the wide-open deserts and high plains, the infinite sweep of stars. Now, to lie in this too-small bathroom in a town so mediocre it couldn't even amount to a ghost town. He tried to doze – he'd slept a good chunk of the morning and afternoon. A half-awake reverie came to him. In Sacramento, Winnemucca, Elko and Pocatello there had been stationary bikes to ensure constant power to the USGMail terminals. What if his head was a TV screen and all this biking did was pump juice to run images? All these shows, episodes of them. The Madeline channel, all reruns. The Bolts, a cops and robbers show. The Road Show, with its Smokey episode, its Linda one. El Rancho Duro, each week a celebrity visitor enters the set to canned applause, followed by manufactured laughter. The problem was that someone else held the remote.

What an ignominious end to his cycling days. The linoleum was buckled off the floor. He could just about stretch out on it if his feet straddled the toilet, but still his head was cocked against the door. He dozed, came to with a searing kink in his neck, unkinked it, dozed some more. He was on his third dozing-unkinking when a "sshh" came from outside his door, floorboards creaked, a door shut lightly.

The bathroom door had an inch of give once he turned the handle. He jiggled the door to get the chair to slide lower, create more of a crack. That worked for another inch before the chair bit and didn't budge. Through the now ajar door he waited, listening: a light snore from the main room, a bed creak in another direction. He got the toilet scrubber, worked it through the gap, laid it on the floor, using two fingers to feel for the chair leg with the scrubber handle, and gently pushed. Nothing. On his third attempt the chair twisted and fell in a mild clatter. An instant later he stood outside the bathroom, wielding the scrubber like a club. A low light from the kitchen revealed the outlines of the room.

From Pauletta's room came a low inquiring drone.

"I'm not done with you cowboy."

Now a weary grunt.

Blood thrumming in his ears he rushed by the young Bolt, snoring on the sofa, boots pointed heavenward, and eased out the front door. He found his bike in the locked truck. He did what he had to with a rock to get at it and was off down the road. In a minute he hit 287. He crossed it and found the double track out to the Sweetwater. The bulging moon gave off just about enough light for avoiding the ruts, holes, and wash outs. As he pedaled, slow, his shoes not clipped in, ready to fall, he thought of all the things he should have done before escaping: return the chair to its wedged position against the door, find his knapsack/second water bottle and his Beretta, let the air out of the truck tires, investigate the horse trailer behind the truck.

His Phantom Cowboy's advice still worked; the brisk charge of the Sweetwater sounded like distant applause. If the Bolts were after him before, smashing that truck window would really get them riled, and so far their truck would be able bounce down the double track faster than he could cycle away. He needed as many night miles as he could manage, out into the middle of wild peopleless country in the dark, with no provisions except for one water bottle. He would have to sweat a good ninety miles to Casper on water and adrenalin.

He stopped on the wooden bridge over the Sweetwater. It finally hit him: it was flowing east. Only yesterday – with no sleep and a missed night his idea of a day was fuzzy – he had sampled the west-flowing creek near Pacific Springs. The pass over the Rockies was such an anonymous high desert tract that the Divide's exact location was down to the reading of river water. The Sweetwater glimmered in the moonlight. With only a sweater he had to keep going to keep warm. Five miles an hour, ten hours a day would get him to Casper in two days.

Chapter 36

They'd been married for close to two years as Clay entered the last year of his self-imposed three-year limit at Childlift. The Board, half-revitalized and more active, approved his move into tech mentoring, which had raised the charity's profile with wealthy tech and private equity people. Donations were up fourfold, and the buzz was bringing in volunteers.

"I can't believe you want to desert Childlift," Eleanor, Madeline's former roommate, said to him. They were back at the house in Visitacion Valley – Deborah got it as part of her divorce settlement – with the Comraderie arrayed on sofas and floor pillows. Or different people, and they were interchangeable. Clay came to the dinners occasionally to keep up appearances. Clearly Madeline been talking to Eleanor about the Problem.

He worked hard at a neutral smile. He wasn't about to discuss this issue with his wife's proxy.

"Maybe you should move to a bigger charity," someone said.

"Hmmm, interesting." Already he had been approached several times by headhunters representing bigger non-profits, but even Ed Harmon said he wasn't long term non-profit material. Too impatient, always on to the next idea before the last one had got out of committee. *Why can't we just agree a plan and do it.* That was his response to committees. This passive operating mode was dulling his competitive edge.

"Just because you're not making an enormous salary," Deborah said.

"I'm tired of all this negativity," he said. "I've worked hard and done a lot of good and all you people can talk about is what I did before and what I will do after."

The assembled anti-capitalists went quiet, as though creating room for their Leader to make one of his pronouncements, one that neatly summarized their views and put the contestant in his place. Only their leader was in Uruguay, or rumors had it, in Canada.

Clay tried to meet Madeline's eyes – this was becoming a nightmare version of Clay Holloway, This Is Your Life.

That afternoon he had been sitting out in South Park with Brad Hogbom, President of X-Urban Inc. Each held their carefully spec'd coffees.

"You'll think about it," Clay said, "joining our Board? I can't tell you how good it would be to have someone like you, someone who can get things done."

"I might not last very long."

"I know." Brad was like him, in a hurry to succeed. Clay smiled, remembering his second pitch to X-Urban, a young company in the first flush of success after one of their video games took off. The CTO, CFO and Brad had looked at each other, nodded, and Brad said, "Let's go for it." No committees, no steering the idea up a backwater so it could die. It was the freedom Clay got riding his bike through Golden Gate Park, through the Avenues to the Presidio, the mad yell of a ride over the Golden Gate Bridge, and all the hard grind and wild coasting up in the Marin Headlands and down to the ocean, his nearly sacred Sunday morning ritual. At least until he met Madeline.

"Clay," Brad said, shifting position on the park bench, "the guys and I have been talking. StreetReady was your idea. A damn good one. It isn't right that we're riding that wave and you're, you're like on the beach watching."

"I had the idea as Executive Director of Childlift, the non-profit organization whose Board you are hopefully about to join."

"I know, I know. Here's the deal. We contribute an agreed portion of the StreetReady profits to Childlift. In return you agree we can advertise that, if we choose to. You've helped us, so we'll help you."

"Okay, let me get back to you," he said with a telegraphed eye roll meant to indicate his Board. Wasn't all revenue positive? But no, there were legal questions, Childlift's non-profit status, and the Board's apparent aversion to anything creative. Besides, he had already pushed the envelope twice since the last meeting. His battles were stacking up faster than the Board could stall on them.

This shouldn't be a huge decision. StreetReady, in which Childlift boys with experience of the projects helped design ghetto-based role-playing video games, had only recently launched. In its first game, Face Down, in which a player has to talk his way out of joining a gang, made a splash with the media. Was this a new trend? A game in which the player had no weapons, one which emphasized quick-thinking and street smarts? Any number of talking heads, columnists and bloggers had weighed in. But so far not many customers.

"Fine. In the meantime, I don't suppose Childlift will turn down any donation X-Urban chooses to make?"

"No, we'll take it. What, may I ask, is the cut you may be basing such donations on?"

"We were thinking fifteen percent. We're projecting a net profit of $150,000. That's over a three-year cycle."

"Twenty percent is a lot easier to calculate."

"Ten percent's even easier. But okay, I'll see what I can do. And we'll see what your Board thinks."

In the evening, he stood at his office window as the light faded and the parking lot across the street slowly lost its cars. It was the wrong time to leave Childlift. StreetReady held that jackpot possibility. Several of the Childlift boys excelled at programming; he wanted to see their potential, all part of his program, fulfilled. And he was becoming more natural with the boys, shooting hoops with some, taking others to the taco joint on Guerrero, trying to like the others, or at least masking any negativity. But if he didn't leave soon chances were he'd never leave. Not that he could come up with a job in the private sector that excited him. All the time, energy and pressure required in his Steel Umbrella job, and the question that came back now was, Why? Money... Make money for them, make money for you. Now, that didn't feel exactly empty – he struggled on his Childlift salary – but it seemed more game than purpose.

"Well, that was fun," he said on the drive back from his This is Your Life session. "I know they're talking about me because you've been talking to them...about me. Can't we leave it between us?"

"It's what you said. It makes me angry, that you don't get any credit for Childlift." At the red light she finally turned to him. "You know what Deborah told me? That I'm bourgeois. Like they've all discussed it and here she is, handing down their verdict."

"That's just Deborah."

"It's like a sin that we live in a whole house."

"I take it," he said, "that you haven't told your friends about your friend Tamara Dubkhadze."

"You. Are bad enough," she said, smiling. "Honey, a change is coming. I can feel it. I don't know why but it scares me, only a little, but it does."

A surge of protectiveness and irritation washed over him. "Is this about me leaving Childlift?"

"It's part of it, but not the main part."

He waited.

"I want you to do what you want to do," she said. "You know that. I mean, who am I to stand there and tell you what you should do?"

"Sweetheart, they're never going to like me. I wear that as a badge of honor."

He parked in the driveway and turned the engine off, but didn't undo his seatbelt. If there was more, better to hear it now, in the car, leave any bad vibes outside the house. She sat stiffly, looking straight ahead at their garage door, shoulders rolled in. "Do you think having a child is bourgeois?"

"What? Bourgeois is just another of their labels. We are who we are. Labels shouldn't affect what we do or think."

She turned half way to him. "You haven't answered my question, about the baby."

That phrase, "the baby", ran like an electric current through him. So this was the trade-off she was hinting at. If we are in fact bourgeois, why not go all out? He could reprise his Big Bad Capitalist self, and she could become the preoccupied mother with the sensible car and new circle of recent moms. He took the keys out of the ignition, hefted them. He didn't want any of it. The corporate job, wifey, and most of all that damn sensible car. He'd rather undergo a ball-ectomy than drive a minivan.

He put his arm around her. She had changed him and now she wanted him to change back? That was okay, they'd work it out, just as before. But it was not just them anymore. Not with the ghost of another being hovering over them.

Chapter 37

Late in the morning he came upon a trailer permanently parked out on a small rise in the high desert plain. An old truck was pointed at it, rusted and on flat tires. Not far away sat a pre-fab house with a newer truck on normal tires.

He walked his bike out over the sagebrush. A man in a black hat and black ponytail sat outside the trailer, whittling on a stick. He said, not looking up, "What I'm doing is not actually whittling; what I'm doing is trying not to cut myself."

He had rounded cheeks in a fat face, and obsidian eyes that matched his hat. "I'm Jim Cochi. You should know that this is Shoshone land."

"Why, is that a problem? One white guy on a bike isn't exactly General Custer." Clay held up his hand to telegraph his fatigue. "I'm sorry friend, that came out all wrong. It's been a long... journey. I'm Clay Holloway."

"No problem. Anyway, Custer? If I remember right, we nailed his hide. You are free to enter here, just as you are free to walk down the street in south Chicago. Whether it's a good decision…"

"You're saying it's dangerous?" Was that possible in this peaceful isolated high desert?

The Shoshone gave him a blank stare. "You'll be wanting food?" Face and invitation bearing no relation to the other.

Clay pulled out a version of his government smile, notched up the humility level several degrees. Jim Cochi didn't show any signs of moving.

"How come you're so far from…everything," Clay asked. Damn, another dumb thing to say. Everyone knew the Indians got the shit land.

"This reservation is a violent place. We hoped the Economic Disaster would be good news for us. No good alcohol anywhere. Even drugs are hard to find. So…less violence. But it's harder here sober.

Imagine you are a teenager, knowing that this is where you'll be living all your days. That is not so easy." He stood up. "I see that you are travelling light." He had a dull sadness about him, the expression of a wife who has given up on her husband but remains married to him.

"I lost my knapsack in Jeffrey City."

"Sounds like a song."

"Yeah. The blues."

"In the old times we Shoshone always travelled light. The only sack we'd be carrying would be our medicine bag."

Clay squinted in inquiry.

"It is a small pouch," Jim Cochi explained, "filled with personal items and talismans that enable us to maintain our harmony with this world and with other, unseen, ones."

"Sounds like my smartphone."

Jim Cochi pointed his knife towards him, then stabbed the table. The knife shuddered as it stood. "Come on in." He gestured towards his trailer.

Books were scattered everywhere, heaped on the floor, in high piles you stepped around and lower ones you stepped over. They were stacked on the oven range, on the dinette table, teetering on window ledges.

As with many encounters the conversation started out with the bike trek. Clay gave an overview with an emphasis on his struggles since hitting the Rockies. "Seriously, these Bolts are driving tens of miles on USG gas when in my home town they're challenged to keep ambulances running."

Jim Cochi prepared lunch in the kitchen alcove. Was that a chicken wing? Instantly any thought of Bolts flitted out the window like a released bumblebee.

"I've heard about your Bolts. You know, I think I was shot at by one. Up on the northern side of the reservation."

While they talked Clay checked out the titles of books on the chipped dinette table. *Consciousness: How Matter Becomes Imagination; The Feeling Of What Happens: Body, Emotion and the Making of Consciousness; The Neurobiology of Consciousness; Zen and the Art of Motorcycle Maintenance. The Catcher in the Rye; The Physics of Consciousness.*

"You've got some pretty heavy books here."

"You laugh. I had to put breezeblocks under the trailer. It's not in the best shape."

"So, this danger. Where should I not go? I'm trying to get to Casper."

"This is the southern edge of the reservation. I'm here because I can go for walks down to the Sweetwater, and away from all this reservation madness."

"If I keep south?"

Jim Cochi gave instructions on how to get to Poison Spider Road. "It runs all the way to Casper, some forty miles."

"You mean this isn't Poison Spider? Damn." After a long pause he said, "who lives in the red house?"

"You'll meet her, that's Granny Toonosay. She'll want to read you. When you meet her, whatever you do, don't let her get you into her bed. She can be tricky that way."

"What? A grandmother?"

"I thought you were going to say, What, an Indian?"

"I've lost track, is it okay to say "Indian" now, or is it still Native American?"

"We prefer Shoshone. This is our once proud nation. "Indian" or "Native American", that's like saying "European" in France, or "Asian" in Japan."

Clay kept quiet. He didn't know much about Indians, apart from the massacres, the raw deals, and the casinos.

"You have been checking out my books – I am writing about Western consciousness and how that compares to ours, so actually it is about our consciousness. Someone like you sees this barren land and thinks, Who could live in such a desolate place. Not so long ago, a few centuries, my people would find endless fascination here. It would have been fully alive, the animal spirits, the wind and its bragging, the clouds that have had commerce with the gods and have just arrived to tell about it. It is a magical existence, free and alive." He paused while they both imagined his vision. "Yes, magical, but not paradise by a long shot. The People suffered sickness, starvation, many early deaths. We depended on limited, manageable wars with our neighbors, enough so our young could prove themselves and the older have a chance for glory, but not enough to risk large losses to either side. It is like a marriage, a delicate balance of hatreds and necessities."

A low light spilled over the linoleum floor when Jim Cochi opened the refrigerator.

"You've got power? Here?"

"Yes, the USG still takes care of us for past sins. One can subsist on the past, but only the future provides real nourishment. I'm afraid even we don't have Cokes any more. Water okay? If you move those books there'll be space for both of us at the table."

Clay stacked books higher on the floor to make room, sat on one side of the small built-in table with bank seats.

"If we are permitted to be simple about our former life, we can call it "being". It is a consciousness I have tried to imagine; but no, we have lost it. That means we have lost the magic. It is ironic. Several of my university friends from Arizona, they have become passionate about Buddhism. They love nothing better than to go on silent retreats where they practice the art of not thinking at all, just being. This is where they learn that thinking wipes out being, just as we have been wiped out. They go for one week, then one month."

Clay struggled to concentrate, most of his neurons were seconded to salivation duty.

"I keep coming back to the same question: could the "thinking" white man live in harmony with the "being" Indian? Probably not. It's like the retreat I mentioned: it has to be off somewhere, separated from the normal world. The two don't mix. Yes, you can argue that a reservation has just such separation. But take these Buddhist retreats, you pay good money to visit them. You drive away in your nice car to go back to your job to get more good money. You see? The retreats are not self-sustaining."

Jim Cochi brought the plates to the table. Those chicken wings, plus potato and three bean salads. Such a miracle of exuberant flavors. He considered a third kind of consciousness – nirvana.

"But even if somehow that worked... the products of your thinking are too seductive. We took Spanish horses, your firearms, no problem. Imagine something as simple as pushing a button to hear music. That button destroys a world. The music no longer "is". Do you see? It is so wrong to own music; it is boxed and no longer free. And yet it is inevitable."

The chicken wings were deep-fried heaven, the potato salad tangy, the bean salad vinegary. All those tastes, sharp as knives, had his eyes tearing up, his salivary glands a burst water main. They didn't settle all that easily in his drum hollow stomach, though.

"So…how do you keep a culture alive when its essence is dead?" Jim Cochi's voice, like his manner, was sad, heavy, considered. "We no longer know how to be; yet our culture is based on that. We live in one world; we live in the other; therefore, we live in no worlds."

After they finished eating it was "time to meet the boss".

"Granny? Look who's swung by with talk of General Custer." The woman who answered the door was surprisingly young, raven black hair, high cheekbones, and an erect manner that established the platform for her penetrating eyes. She was as bewitching as she was intimidating. Her eyes moved hawk-like, as if scanning the brush for movement, a lazy, easy imperiousness about her.

"No talk about dead people."

"Our friend here comes from far away. He has a long way to go…"

"We all do." For the first time she eyed Clay. "Come here."

After he approached her, she glanced at Jim Cochi. "Leave us."

They stood on her small porch, not doing much of anything. He decided to go on the offensive. "Jim says I should be careful not to sleep with you."

"Why, do you want to?"

"I'm married."

"That does not answer my question."

"It does if being married is a true vow." He withered under her intense gaze.

"Jimmy C is a smart man, but only book smart. He does not understand women."

What man does? Nope, levity would no doubt be frowned on – and Granny T had a world class frown.

After an age she came to him, bracketed his face with her thin cool hands. She smelled his neck, below the jawbone near the ear. A feral hunger.

"Haven't washed in a while, ma'am."

"Shhh. No noise."

She put her hand on his forehead, the other on his heart, reversed hands.

"This makes no sense. I have never seen this before. There is a large black space."

"I think that's called ignorance, ma'am."

"What is this ma'am stuff?" She smiled, her first one. Could a smile be so ominous? "It is all black. Know that you are perfectly safe in the blackness." Her sharp eyes played over his face for a long moment. "And then it is too late." Her smile faded. "Now, I must think." She hummed quietly to a hee-muh-hay-yuh rhythm, took his right hand. "Men. They are usually so simple." Her eyes drilled into him with even greater intensity. "It is like entering a three-room house. Two of the rooms are anger and self-doubt. Only the size changes. The third room is the only interesting one. Yours…the door is locked."

"How do you know that if all is blackness?"

"Quiet! I am talking in simple words to describe something that is not simple."

"What is in this third room?"

"Easiest to call it destiny. Again, I am being simple."

He waited for more. When the silence stretched out too long to bear, he said, "Maybe because I'm not from your tribe?"

"Sshh! I am thinking."

Only her fierce glare kept him on the porch. Finally, after long minutes, she said, "You must send a message to me. One year from now. Tell me what happened."

"What do mean, 'what happened'?"

"This three-room house I talk about. Someone has been in it. I have never seen this. Never."

He didn't want to leave her yet, even though a minute before that's all he could think of doing. "I met a spirit man up at the Divide. He had strange powers. It might have been him."

"Tell me about this man."

He did, an honest recounting of the facts.

"He will be back."

"That's what he said." When Granny T didn't answer, he added, "What do I do?"

"The spirits have chosen you. It is not possible to be unchosen. You will have a hard way. Very hard. I wish you luck."

Her dismissal brooked no argument. As much as he wanted to ask her more, another part of him craved ignorance.

He walked back to the trailer, shaking his head for Jim Cochi's benefit. Granny T stood on her small porch, staring their way, a statue.

"What happened?"

"Nothing good."

Jim Cochi walked over to talk to Granny T. A long conversation followed, with lots of unreadable gestures. Jim perhaps pleading, Granny T adamant. Or maybe Jim was trying to leave and Granny T was not letting him. They disappeared inside. Jim emerged eventually with a paper bag.

"You must go. Your *new friend* gives you this food. I have written my USGmail and put it inside. Granny asks that you send us a mail in a year or so. Let us know what happened."

"What happened?"

"She says that something big, something impossible, is in your future. Greatness. Shame. Everything."

"Unh," Clay said, like a combination of an "um" and a gut punch.

"I have known Granny all my life. I have never heard her admit she doesn't understand." He stared at Clay as if this was the first time he'd seen him. "Do you know what she told me? That you scare her." He regarded Clay with calm inert eyes. "Granny scared? Next the USG will give us back our native lands." He held out the paper bag. "I'm sorry, she has asked me to get you away from her quickly. I've never seen her like this."

"She's just not used to reading people outside her tribe, that's all."

"Yes, that must be it."

"Did she predict this current mess? The Void?"

"She tries to keep our Shoshone hearts pure. This means staying away from all the complexity of your world. As I said before, 'being'."

"But it's a world that…you have no choice but to be part of."

"True. Granny T is a leader. She must do this by example. She is not liked, because she talks without fear. Often, her news is not good news. She lives out here on the edge of the reservation to keep her heart pure. Also because she is not liked."

"That's a tough assignment."

"She is working on a new ghost dance."

"What's that?"

"There was a time, about 1890, when the People were in despair. We had been pulled off the table the way a dealer removes with a paddle the losing hands; we were discarded, and shuffled and dealt to forlorn places like this one; we had played with pureness in our hearts but the dealer pulls cards from the bottom of the deck. Who knows? Maybe the cards would have been against us anyway. By then, 1890, only a miracle could have restored to us our essence, our magic. We were adrift like in a boat without oars. We floated passively."

"How does this dance solve your problems?"

"The dance fights dissolution with purity of spirit. It restores the world to an earlier time, before all the modern distractions. Once again we can live in the old-young Indian world."

"Did it work?" It was such a stupid thing to say that they laughed at the same time.

"In the 1890's your government outlawed the Ghost Dance. Maybe they believed in it more than we did. We danced because the music was in us; we were shot down for our trouble. One of the last massacres."

"What's it like?"

"Similar to our War Dance. The warriors are in the center, showing their fighting spirit, their grace, power and agility. They are surrounded by non-warriors and women, yelling and shrieking encouragement. It is important to everyone, warriors and watchers, that the fighters succeed. It is the most important thing in the world."

Chapter 38

It was a year now that the Holloways had been trying for a child. Madeline had no obvious medical cause for infertility, while his potency had been assessed and pronounced acceptable, although on the low side of the range. It was just a matter of time.

"How did it go?" he asked. Madeline had just returned from a Visitacion evening.

"Same as always. Oh, we all talked with Jorge by the internet. And you'll never guess – he's got a family down there? A wife and kids? None of us even knew."

"It doesn't exactly fit with his industrial scale womanizing here."

She laughed. "That's how we found out. We were talking about why I can't get pregnant. Naturally they all think it's you. I said it could just as easily be me. I won't go into the experiment that Jorge proposed. He gave his two daughters as evidence. You know Jorge, he wasn't serious, not unless I was."

"Maddy, this is all too private to be discussed like that."

"You don't think I know that? It's not as if I brought it up. Not when I'm starting to panic. Anyway, you were right: I should have never told Eleanor." She put her hand on his shoulder, he was reading in his favorite chair. "Back in the beginning it was such good news, that we were trying, I had to tell someone. Now all it does is add to the pressure."

"We'll get there." He was tired of running through the bullet points he had assembled, over-bright encouragement, unsubstantiated optimism, and quasi-religious fatalism meant to make her relax, take a broader view. "Hey, here's an idea. Dump them, Eleanor, Jorge, all of them, and there'll be no pressure."

"And no friends."

StreetReady's first game *Face Down* was slow in its build to X-Urban's projected sales. The company nevertheless made a few small donations to confirm their informal deal. In any case, the program's main purpose was to give the Childlift boys some exposure to a real company with a product they could identify with. In return for sitting through a presentation on writing code, the boys could test beta versions of new products, eat donuts in the conference room, and sit in on brainstorming sessions on ideas for future games.

"To what do I owe this honor?" Clay asked, after offering his couch to the President of the San Francisco Board of Supervisors.

"Clay, I'll spare the preliminaries, mainly because you're a spare-the-preliminaries guy." She paused, letting that settle. "A few of us have been watching you. You know what we see? We see a man who works a room like he's running for office, hobnobs with the power brokers like he's running for office, makes speeches like he's running for office. And you know what we said to ourselves? Maybe he should run for office. We're thinking Board of Supervisors. If you agree I can just about assure you of success. Don't answer now. Think about it. Call me if you decide to take it further."

"I do all that because it's my job."

"Politics is a job too. A hard one."

"Listen, I – "

"Think about it. That's all we ask."

Politics? They had to be joking. Why, he couldn't even say which party he supported. How had he gotten caught up in an extreme version of the Peter Principle, not merely rising to his level of incompetence, but switching careers in pursuit of that? All he wanted was go back to the private sector – if only he could come up with an area that interested him.

"You look like you've seen a ghost," Madeline said.

"Tough day." It wasn't safe to tell her about the Approach. She would tell Eleanor and it would become another aspect of him up for discussion by those snarky anti-capitalists. In any case, absolutely no way was he going to go around kissing babies, donning yarmulkes, making more promises than a company trying to stave off insolvency.

Once Madeline would have been all over that ghost look. "What happened, honey? What's wrong? Tell me." And there was a time before that when he would have come home beaming, ready to laugh over it. She would have seen sides of it he didn't, generous interpretations all about him, how good he was, how proud she was of him. They would have speculated, the scenarios ever wilder, Holloway for Senator, Holloway for President.

Now Madeline's front page only had room for one headline. Read all about it, Barren Couple Struggles On. It was sad, the way she turned away, went back to her highlighter and textbook. (She was taking classes in Behavioral Health). Sad too, that that didn't bother him as much as it once would have.

Chapter 39

"That's okay, that's all right, come on boys let's fight, fight, fight!"

The chant woke him up to a slanting light, cooler, wrong-angled. His stomach was full of gnawing, scrabbling rats. He unglued his eyes, de-crusted them with the back of his hand, stood up, stretched to uncramp his calves and unknot his back. What was this phrase "ghost dance" that was echoing dully in his head? He focused on a large and empty grandstand across the football field, in front of which three cheerleaders were yelling and stepping and kicking.

He had reached Casper, Wyoming, in mid-evening, arriving like a corpse carried by waves and deposited on the beach. The long wind out along Poison Spider Road, the dust, the heat, the slow going in places, had been so arduous he toyed with finding one of those eponymous spiders and ending it all.

"That's okay, that's all right, come on boys let's fight, fight, fight!"

Cheerleaders. Practicing on the track lanes between the stands and the field. Maybe he'd died and woken up in a new world where the schools were open. This fresh day – when was the last time he had seen passion for a cause? – stirred something in him, something too nebulous to be called hope. He climbed into the steel bleachers on his side of the football field – he had slept in the soft unmown grass in front of them – and watched the three girls going low and coming up with pom poms shaking. Jumping. Ever since Pinedale on the other side of the Divide he had been engaged in a desperate battle of survival and forward motion. Scraps of memories played to him. A man on a horse trotting out of the eastern sun. The low burble of the stream just west of the Divide. The dull crash of rock into truck window. An Indian woman's fierce stare. The never-ending grind on Poison Spider Road, the most willpower he'd summoned forth in his life.

And yes, he'd skipped over the meeting at the Divide with the Phantom Cowboy. Let that stew for a day or two, come back to it.

Maybe it would go away in the meantime. Yeah right. The things you purposely skip over have a way of skipping right on back.

"That's okay (step and kick), that's all right (step and kick), come on boys (low crouch), let's fight (rising with pompoms flourishing), fight (rising, flourishing), fight (jump)."

It wasn't much past sunrise. Weeds were growing in the red track lanes; the unmown grass hid any gridiron markings. What were these girls doing? More importantly, with schools obviously closed, who were they rooting for? He could ride over and ask them. But no, he was varnished with nine coats of dried, dust-encrusted sweat, and a two-week beard – that long since the surreal dinner at Cammie Coletti's.

He found the North Platte River, then a park along it, washed as best he could, including his clothes as he stood in them, and lay out in the sun, drying. It was pleasant, peaceful on this day in early June. But he couldn't laze for long. He was starving.

He sat on a sagging dark blue sofa in the classroom, holding the hand of a tomboyish teenage girl who couldn't talk. Above the blackboard opposite them, a line of stern hirsute presidents got up to Andrew Johnson before running out of space. At the Johnson end was a multicolored map of the United States. As a nine-year old boy, he would stare at a similar map on his bedroom wall, trying to move from California to the East Coast by hopping on as few contiguous states as possible.

Two middle-aged carers sat in folding chairs opposite them. One held a newborn boy, his face with that fierce pucker of intense sleep. The other, Lorena, said, "Everyone's calling him Jesse. I just called him that 'cause I had to call him something. The little mother here can change it as soon as she can talk."

Jesse was handed back to Lorena, who offered him to Clay.

"Come on, Lorena, I'm biking through here. It's not like I can put him in my basket and change him on freeway shoulders."

"Just hold him. We get so few fathers in here."

The Big Crèche was a USG-run baby support center run out of a former junior high school. The activity was muted: mothers in need of supplies, or support; a few abandoned or problematic babies like Jesse. In a month, however, the country would be marking the nine-month anniversary of the Meltdown. Candle light, poverty, and dwindling prophylactic supplies: the crèche would soon be full to bursting with newborns.

"I'm no father," he said, holding a teenage girl's hand.

"Yes, I can see that," Lorena said, smiling at him. As a newcomer at the Casper USG he'd been aggressively jostled by three sunburnt farm boys. It was starting to get ugly so he diverted to the Big Crèche, where men were welcome to the cafeteria as long as they had a female sponsor. Somehow the blond tomboy had homed in on him as he stood behind the cordon that separated the Crèche from the outside world.

He pulled his hand out of its paternal role, but the hand of his teenage charge twisted snake-like before striking and finding its quarry again. She was a thin blond. Her fine hair fell from a central part, pink at its roots. Her thin arm was folded tightly in front of her as if cold on this warm and pleasant day. Something bad had happened to her, so bad that it scattered all her words.

The other carer had left by now. "Please, just *hold* him for a sec," Lorena said, "while I talk to your friend here." Then, while trying to connect with the girl she said, "Just walk him around a little. That should settle him." And give us some privacy.

After a few minutes Lorena approached him, holding the girl's hand. "She's not the mother, at least that's what she answers to my yes/no questions. We'll be right back."

He wanted to object but Lorena's solemnness reminded him that something bad was in the background of the girl's story. Then, watching the pair retreat, it was too late.

Jesse was squirming. His red face twisted into a big yawn. His eyes slid open and he stared at Clay, checking him out. *So, you're the guy I've got stuck with. First abandoned, and now this.*

"Yep, little guy, you deserve better than me."

It was dark out. All he knew of the Crèche was the cafeteria and this former classroom. He headed down the dim hallway, carrying Jesse like a halfback would a football. Any second the baby would be bawling. It got darker this way, less strips lit overhead. He retraced his steps. Now the first cries. The kid had a good pair of lungs.

"Bear with me. Just a few minutes, okay. I'm working on the problem, believe me."

Jesse looked up to him, as if deciding whether this holder deserved a reprieve. Who would have thought a newborn mass of protoplasm was capable of considering him?

He opened a door to the outside, somewhere in this jumble of buildings there was the business part of baby caring. Was it okay for a baby this young to be outside? Down a partially lit hallway of a second building he heard voices behind a door that said Principal on it. That would be his fallback. The hallway had more working lights down the far end. Faintly the sound of a crying baby drifted from behind a door.

The warm evening was just starting to cool. He took the open door out the other end of the hallway and found another door that led into the gym. In the dimmed light there were eight cots, and two women patting babies against their shoulders. He ran to the first carer.

"He, he needs stuff done to him."

"Why, if it isn't little Jesse." She stooped, a baby still pinned to her shoulder, gave Jesse the sniff test. "Probably hungry. Never seen one eat like him. He's gonna be a bruiser. Here." She took Jesse after handing the baby girl to Clay, and went to the corner where a refrigerator and an electric plate were running off a small generator.

"Can I put her in her cot?" he said, when she returned with Jesse sucking mightily on his bottle.

"Babies need the human touch. A lot of it. This one, she just hates being by herself. Even when she's sleeping."

"It was Lorena who…" he wanted to say checked him out, but this wasn't a library. "Had him before me."

"Yes, I know. Jesse can't feed himself, so just bear with me."

He held the little girl, who kept working her lips as if chewing, a little smacking sound there. He needed to leave. Already he'd been here for eight hours, two meals, and two babies.

"I see you found the Crèche," Lorena said with relief as she approached him. "Took longer than I thought. Obviously." She accepted the little girl from him. "Now there, there, there," she said settling the baby. "Your girlfriend, the one back there," she tossed her head behind her. "She's Jesse's aunt, if you can believe that. The mother…" she shook her head.

"No wonder she couldn't talk."

"Carried Jesse four miles until she could find help."

"Where is she now?"

"Her name's Cyndi. She wrote it down. Wrote all the other stuff, too. Emergency services is dealing with it. She'll want to say good-bye to you," Lorena said, somehow divining his thoughts about cutting out quickly.

"Okay. I'll go see her. That one," he said nodding to the girl Lorena was holding, "she wants to be held all the time."

"Makes you wonder doesn't it, if they can tell the future."

Cycling out of Casper was like cycling out of all towns he'd visited, only amplified. The limitless freedom, the open road like an open question. The loneliness of another solo trip. He'd stayed too long at the

Crèche, but he didn't regret it. When was the last time someone needed him like Cyndi did?

The next morning, after an hour of riding, it dawned on him what was missing. When was the last time there had been no mountains hemming in his world? All the way to Casper there had been California's Coastal Range, then the Sierras. As for Nevada, its endless desert threaded around 300 accordion pleat mountain ranges, culminating in the East Humboldt range. There may have been a time on the Utah flats when he couldn't see the Humboldts retreating or the Wasatchs advancing: he was too busy surviving to notice. And finally there had been the Rockies. Mountains and flats, ancient lake beds. Daysful of desert. All the way from California he had been aware of the next looming challenge, even while he suffered through the existing one. Now, entering the Great Plains was like stepping out onto a bare stage.

Chapter 40

They walked along the cliff tops, out where the upper left of the thumb of San Francisco curves toward the Golden Gate Bridge at the top, and the ocean funnels into the bay. The lapping waves of the gray-green sea, and the brown and rolling hills of Marin across the narrowing water, usually calmed Madeline down, created some perspective. And Madeline needed a lot of that. Two years without a baby made for a doomed aura. One of them was defective; it wasn't going to happen.

"Clay…"

"Did it help, being away?" She had stayed at Eleanor's a few times before, but only for a night, not three, and always saying where she was going.

"I don't know. How can you love someone when you don't like yourself very much?"

He slowed his pace, even as he wanted to move quickly. What chance did he have? Eleanor with her fish-not-needing-a-bicycle stance on men, her baggy tiger stripe pants, loud and clashing tops, combat boots, and an eyebrow stud that added a certain quizzical air to a frown otherwise so glumly certain. She was bound to poison his wife against him. He took Madeline's hand just to see how she accepted it. A jolt ran through him. Three nights away - maybe she hadn't been with Eleanor? Barry. Her ex, the folk-singer, artist, the guy who probably threw pottery when he wasn't meditating at sunset. He was her true soul mate, except for the cheating. Clay had never met the man who had hurt her so badly. He'd seen his picture though, on one of Madeline's CD's, The World of Barry MacDuff. There was his mug, the soft beard, straight, beaver-like teeth, green eyes the color of pond slime.

What could he say that he hadn't said dozens of times? Suggesting that she unwind, that she take on a broader perspective – there were millions suffering far worse conditions – that they think about alternatives like adoption or IVF, were hollow by now. "I missed you."

"I saw you in the paper. With the same woman."

"Madeline?"

No answer.

"You're accusing me of having an affair with Mariel Hunter Dorfmann?" MHD was one of his main patrons, the fabulously wealthy wife of private equity maven Henry Dorfmann. Hang around MHD long enough and you were certain to appear in the society pages.

"I don't know, you're handsome. I know I haven't been…there for you." Except when her cycle came around and the klaxons sounded. Their uncontestable sensual delight had become a perfunctory performance, a science project. Madeline with her thermometer, ultimate positions, her latest readings, theories, vitamins, diets, visualizations, breathings.

"That's ridiculous."

"Of course it's ridiculous. But you know what? You want to hear a lesson I've finally learned? Life is ridiculous. I'm ridiculous. So maybe you are ridiculous too."

This was her clique all over. The neat labels that explained everything. Corporations are evil. Government is the answer. Life is ridiculous. Here she was, walking next to him, more slowly than usual, but he could not come up with a way of making her his again. There had to be a way. He just needed to think harder, work harder. He had never failed like this before, and failed in such an undefined way.

"Okay you've used up your "ridiculous" quota. Why don't you try "complicated" or "messy"? They're also nice adjectives that don't explain a thing."

"You know if you did, I'm not sure I'd blame you."

"But I haven't. And won't." Really? There had been evenings, at receptions, waiting on the tram platform, walking to an appointment in an early evening alive with possibilities, when if the right woman had presented herself…But she hadn't. Maybe, compared to Madeline, she didn't exist. Maybe he was a straight up moral guy.

"I have a confession." She let that hang for an agonizing time. "The group thinks, well they think they won't see you again. That we've split up, actually. I've never said that in so many words but I didn't…I let them believe it."

"Because soon it will be true?"

"Because they're my friends and I need them. I know they can be maddening. Even I can see that. But they mean well. They want a better world, just like I do. Maybe even we do."

"A better world, sure."

They finished their walk at a coffee place out by the ocean, driftwood, surfboards and espressos.

"What's the latest at Childlift?"

"The latest is I'm still there."

Childlift was thriving. He had won a major battle to establish a small fund for promising boys. In hitting up the wealthy, he had learned along the way that individual stories have the most impact and immediacy. Why talk to a patron of the symphony about urban boys needing to learn a craft, when he could trot out the story of a promising violinist who needed lessons because his drug addict mother spent all the money on her habit?

The tech mentoring program was also flying. A group of his boys had showed a flair for programming, attending a bi-weekly session at X-Urban to review current efforts. StreetReady's two games had, in Brad Hogbom's phrase, "washed their faces", which meant broke even, and X-Urban had donated a total of $20,000 to Childlift. Hogbom had even joined the Childlift Board, and often talked about Clay coming over to the private sector. "Maybe we should switch jobs," Clay had wryly suggested.

Madeline took a sip of her skinny half-caf latte. "Do you ever wonder about your career, what it would have been like if you hadn't met me? How far up the ladder you'd be by now?"

"Not really no. What purpose would that serve?"

"Sweetheart. Everybody *wonders*. Just like everybody dreams. You don't say *what purpose does it serve* about *dreaming*." She repeated his words an octave too low, to match his voice. There was an element in her tone of trying to cheer him up, even as she lightly mocked him.

"I've stayed with Childlift because of what we're going through. I want to us to be together. What went wrong, that's what I *wonder* about."

"What went wrong is me. We've been dealt a hand. It's not like the end of the world that we can't have children. I keep telling myself that, over and over. You know what's weird? I believe it, I really do. It's not the end of the world. Not at all. But that's just logic."

"Yes, logic and not feelings," he said, the husband dully repeating his wife's overfamiliar argument.

She sighed, "I know what you think about me. That I skip from project to project, cause to cause, so why can't I abandon my baby cause like I've done all the others. That's what you think, right?"

"Not really," he said, lying.

"Do you remember when I talked about us having two old souls? I still think that – that ever since we met something powerful has wanted to flow, something still does. Deep down, on the old soul level, we have always worked, and always will. But there's a new power now that wants to flow. The two old souls that weren't supposed to meet need a child. Do you see? Do you see how the power that brought us together is now tearing us apart? What wants to flow is parenthood."

Right on cue a little boy, chasing another boy, bumped into their table. She took Clay's hand, gave him a pained smile. Life and its cruelty. "Clay. I still want you. I still love you. It's just that I have no idea how to conquer this old soul's insistence. And please, don't go all logical on the old souls stuff. I'm not saying there is such a thing; I'm just saying it's the best way I can think of to explain how I feel." She tried to meet his eyes, fix his misery with a smile. It couldn't work if he wasn't looking. Wouldn't work if he was. "I'm determined to fight this, truly I am. My instinct is that I need to figure this out by myself. Alone. Maybe for perspective. To concentrate without distractions." She patted his hand. "And you have always been such a sweet distraction."

Chapter 41

A dirt road, framed by ripening wheat stalks on each side, made a long curve, and straightened out to reveal the top of a steel silo and the edge of a red barn. Closer in, a low-slung house spread out in the shade of a line of trees. Around the side of the barn he found a trim lady with brassy hair and a befuddled look, as if she had wandered into the wrong play, out feeding the chickens. She was wearing a silky dress and shoes with medium heels.

"I'll take care of the hens, if you're late for the ball."

She came over. "Gotta dress up occasionally. I got a better chance of these chickens appreciating that." She handed him the feed bucket. "You hungry?"

He nodded. Truth be told, he had been eyeing the chicken feed.

He sat on the porch, the shady part with a view of the front steps, and put his aching back against the wall, so weary that all his mind could summon up were two words. *So, Nebraska.*

A gentle tap-tap on the sole of his bike shoe jerked him out of a doze. The farmer, thin and knobby – Adam's apple, chin, elbows – with Modigliani eyes, blue like the pale vault of a scorching humid day. "Name's Tye."

"Nice farm you got here," he said, guessing.

"We got ourselves a hundred and twenty acres. Too big for one man, too small for the USG to take an active interest. They drop off a few barrels of diesel and say, you're on your own, pal."

They ate formally in the dining room. Tye's wife, Myrna, had changed into overalls and a checked shirt, unbuttoned to the bib and showing a string of pearls. Clay forced himself to match their glacial eating pace. Not that he was staring or anything, but from the loose bulge at her bib sides, she appeared to be untethered. Tye kept his eyes on some unseen furrow as the conversation meandered through Clay's journey. The RV's in a circle. Jump Suitor. His encounter with a grizzly.

Myrna asked the standard question, his destination and why. He gave her his standard line about a wife stranded on the other coast.

"Madeline, huh?" Tye said. "You must be real fond of her."

"Do you think you'll make your way through all the looting and violence we keep hearing about?" Myrna said, beaming with vicarious excitement.

"It's not that bad," he said, "at least so far. Yes, there's a redistribution of wealth, in that there's no wealth right now, only title, if you can hold that down."

"Well, nothing's changed much here," Tye said.

"No radio. I miss that," Myrna added. "I'm not counting the government station. It's all talk of the sunshine to come. That and radio plays from England."

They put him up in what they called the bunkhouse, more of an in-law apartment. His first bed since Jackson, back when he was hero for a day. No inevitable rock in the ball of his hip. No waking up feeling like his skeleton had been taken apart and re-assembled with a few parts missing. It was so comfortable he couldn't get to sleep. Like a city-dweller unused to the absence of emergency sirens. Or, in his case, a desperate battler coming down from wild mountain challenges to the normality of the flatlands. And what could be more normal than a farm in Nebraska? Honest toil under a vast sky. Eggs from chickens; milk from cows; food taken care of, roof over your head? Here he lay well and truly past the Rockies, beyond its longest shadow. The Phantom Cowboy, and his shadow, though. Surely a mountain apparition, like Yeti, Twisted Face, Bigfoot, Skookums. Leave the mountains and you escape their dominion. And anyway the details were sparing: a dark night, an unlikely song, a character shadowed in the moonlight. A million indifferent stars.

He lay in his comfortable bed, pulling his blankets, as if normality itself, up to his chin. How easy to place all memory of the Phantom Cowboy in a box marked "hallucination" and cart that box off to the attic. Easy? Since when had 'easy' been part of his vocabulary? He knew in his bones this wasn't over, that the Phantom Cowboy would revisit him as promised. The annoying man with his sharp eyes and bad timing waited for him down the road, just as Granny T's apocalyptic forecast of greatness and shame did. Like getting over the Rockies, forward meant danger, impossible encounters, challenges to his idea of himself. How delicious it would be to give up on his mission, sink into this farm life, just as he sank into the sweet lethargy of this bed. But like sleep itself, any escape was temporary.

In the morning Tye showed him around the farm. Half the acreage was planted with winter wheat, a hardy crop, Tye explained, planted in late summer and harvested nearly a year later, the dormant spell in the winter delaying its maturity. The other half lay fallow. While Tye applied the remains of last year's insecticide to the wheat crop (he was fighting the first signs of Russian wheat aphids), Clay set about tilling the fallow field as part of a weed control program. They traded tractor time.

Even Clay could see the amount of work was piling up faster than the two of them could handle it.

"Now, you promised us two days," Myrna said, reminding him of their deal. "My man needs a break, before he collapses from exhaustion."

"Country needs feeding," Tye said.

That night he had a dream, a wild chase through the fields. Pursued by a tractor, he ran in a low crouch to stay hidden in the wheat stalks. Sometime during the pursuit, the tractor became a front-end loader, with its iron jaw swinging wildly as it hopped and bounced, tilted and lunged toward him. The tractor whined ever nearer. He turned this way, feinted that, the sound never faded. A wild image now: Tye driving, Myrna up on the claw like a sailor in a forecastle searching for the whale. They would pursue him with the mad obsession of Ahab through this ocean of wheat. Wheat without limit. He could thrash his way through three states and wind up back where he started. Wheat without end; work without end.

The second day they built up a rhythm, Clay working the fallow field, pulling up some of the larger weeds, spading over the others. At the bottom of the field a line of green trees traced what was probably a creek. He never got down that far.

That night Myrna served up another roast chicken. His eyes swam with tears of ecstasy with each flavorful bite of the tender flesh. And yet he wondered which of Myrna's brood had been sacrificed. They'd all been so grateful for the seed he'd scattered. And...had it been delicate Myrna who had wrung its neck?

"Thanks for all your help," Tye said in a bronchial rasp.

"Don't suppose we could convince you to stay over for longer," Myrna said, not managing to meet his eye. "You've been a godsend to Tye. Who knows? maybe the USG will get around to releasing Tye Jr. and Chet." Both their sons were in the Marines, had been cleared to come back and work on the farm, subject to paperwork from a government that had run out of paper.

In the morning Clay bounced out of his billet. It was a perfect June day. His legs were rested. He was ready to knock off at least fifty miles over the mountainless Nebraska plain.

At breakfast Myrna served up scrambled eggs on toast, and retreated to various kitchen doings, not joining them as previously. Tye ate oblivious.

He got his things together in the bunkhouse, rolled the heavy items in the blankets he'd secured in Chadron, Nebraska, put his few clothes in the kid's pack, one with cartoon characters that just about fit him, put on his bike shoes, and carrying his bedroll and pack, took them over to the porch. Time to retrieve his bike, stored around the back.

It was propped against the back wall, mangled beyond any possible use.

"Didn't even know she could drive a tractor," Tye said, walking Clay out to the road.

"She's fighting for her man, I get that," Clay said. "What made her think I'd hang around after something like that." He fought back his anger, determined not to give Myrna the pleasure of witnessing his wrath, which, no matter how powerful, was not going to un-crunch his bike.

"It's a long way to the next town. She doesn't understand that you don't know that."

"How far are we talking about?"

"Twenty mile or so."

"You sure it's okay to tromp off in TJ's boots?" Clay had his bedroll in a bear hug as he walked, thinking, This isn't going to work over any distance.

"By the time TJ and Chet get back I reckon we'll all be going around barefoot. Anyways, it's the least we can do."

They didn't say anything more until they reached the road. "Here we are, Crazy Horse Memorial Highway. Good luck getting to your wife."

And good luck stuck with yours, he thought but didn't say.

Chapter 42

The temperature was starting to build toward another day bordering on hot when his replacement bike, a one-speed built for ten-year-olds, collapsed. The seat post, raised too high, had sheared off. He walked the seatless bike down the road and propped it against the first signpost. He felt guilty about abandoning it. An elderly couple, a four-hour walk from Tye's farm, had spared him a few eggs and threw in that bike, once ridden by their son, Lester, who had been killed in Iraq.

The road sign held a badge with US 20 East on it. Here he was on foot in the middle of one the world's great landmasses. Throughout his sojourn, each pedal pump asked the question: where to and why? Now he was down to foot falls. Straining up the western side of the Rockies he had dreamt about the Great Plains on the other side, conveniently tilted so as to spill him down to the Mississippi. He could roll off a hundred miles in a day, maybe more, the topography on his side for once. Now here he was, walking in heavy boots. At this rate he'd be crawling into Boston. If he ever got that far.

An old Cadillac purred by, not slowing, and in a delayed reaction pulled over with a jerk and waited for him to catch up.

"You need a lift?"

"In more ways than one." The driver, an old lady, wore her Sunday finest which meant it was probably Sunday. "I'm afraid I've been on the road for some time, more showered on than showered."

"Well you're not sitting in the back if that's what you're angling for. I'm not your darn chauffeur."

She peered over the steering wheel, her white-gloved hands clutching it like parrot talons a perch. She had a bright red smear of a mouth. A string of pearls sat high on her liver-spotted breastbone.

"That's an unusual name, Neelee," he said after he'd hopped in and they'd traded names.

"There's a small town in Antelope County of the name." She spelt it: Neligh.

"You're on your way to church?"

"Yes I am. The Good Lord saw to it that I had a full tank of gas just before he pulled the toilet handle on this country. Psssuuh." She laughed, a certain wild freedom to it.

"What happens when you run out of gas?"

"Probably just shoot myself."

"You got ammo!"

She punched him on the arm, her bony knuckles found bone. Ouch. "Where are you riding to?"

"Boston. My wife's there. Well, she might still be there and she might still be my wife."

"Why that's mighty gallant of you." She looked him over. The car started drifting off the road.

"Uh. Ma'am..."

She yanked it back the other way. "Mighty gallant."

"It might not be as noble as it sounds."

"Cut out on you, did she? A woman can tell these things. Believe it or not inside this bag of bones beats the heart of 69-year-old." Her smile had a twinkle to it. "My first left me too. I couldn't go after him though."

"Why not?"

"Because he upped and died on me. Friday night. We were watching the God channel. He slumped over and that was that. Didn't notice for a time. Sometimes there's a thin line between resting temporary versus permanent. The Good Lord chose to give him a tumor in his brain. Not much else growing up there. Truly it was a testing time."

"What would you have done if he *had* cut out on you. Let's say he went off to Chicago because he needed his own space?"

"Owen? His own space? That man had the bulk of a small planet. He didn't need space; he took up space."

The dead straight road whizzed by, all those anonymous wheat stalks, shooting up four feet at the sun like a million kids wanting a treat. "I'm sorry if this is nosey, ma'am, but how did you keep believing in the Good Lord's mercy...after that?"

"Preacher helped me through it. A good man, a patient man."

"I'd like to meet him. Maybe he – "

"Preacher Lowestoff's been called in by his boss. I tell ya it's getting to be like the party's in the other room."

"Well then, could you at least tell me the gist of his words. Lately I've been struggling with the concept of the Good Lord's mercy."

"Words?" She beat her white-gloved fist lightly on the steering wheel. "There are many kinds of comfort in this world."

"You mean you and the preacher?"

"Oh Lordy, when a preacher tells you to get down on your knees…" She waved a thin arm at him, reprised that wild free laugh, then frowned. "That's what folks in this town think, anyway. To the extent that they exercise their noggins at all." She slowed down. "Now if you go around talking about me and the preacher…"

"Listen ma'am. Why don't you and I recite the Lord's prayer as you complete the final miles of your journey." Anything to stay in the car.

"You saying I'm about to croak?"

"I'm saying I can see a steeple on the horizon." He couldn't, but figured his eyesight was better than hers.

"How do you plan on winning her back?"

"Rely on my natural charm."

"Charm, huh. The thing with a woman is timing. You be there for when she's ready, but let her control the moment and the angle."

"What?"

Neligh laughed with a contained abandon. "You know what I find attractive about you?" She left that for a moment. "Fact that I'll never see you again. Why, hell's bells, I can tell you anything and it won't matter."

He watched the town of Valentine hove into sight.

"Here's what I'm gonna do. I'm gonna drive to the other side of town and out a mile beyond. You're gonna promise you'll keep on headin' east, away from town." She hit the accelerator. "You know too much."

Now the outskirts of the town, the same buildings as in any outskirts. Strip malls, tire dealerships, burger joints, used car lots. Anywhere, USA. And Anywhere, USA was closed for business.

"Being seen with a young man's bound to bring back old memories. Done that for me. I'll tell you when to be slouching. Got it?"

"If you say so."

"What we were talking about, me and the preacher, that's ancient history. Heck, I'm ancient history. Reverend Thorndike's been here coming on thirty years. Now, his wife is made of sterner stuff than Preacher Lowestoff's. That woman put a shotgun barrel in her mouth and dispersed her brains all over Cherry County."

"You blame yourself?"

"How's a Preacher to know about sin unless he experiments a little? From the edges, like peering into a chasm. Ok, now down."

He slouched, the town's main street a reflected smear on the inside of the windshield.

"Aren't they gonna wonder where you're going?"

"Let 'em. A woman needs some mystery about her."

He kept quiet in the safety of the well. "Stay like that." The car came to a stop. "Gosh darn it. Sit up quick! Pretend you were looking for something."

She rolled down her window.

"Got a new boyfriend, eh Neligh?" A man's voice.

He entered the clapboard church, trying to let his companion lead. All that did was slow their procession down the aisle. From the packed pews the women stared; the men looked down and chuckled. So this is what it's come to, he could hear them thinking, picking up homeless men – this one dirty and in cargo shorts. He was shuffling forward so slowly that Mrs. Litton, the lady on crutches whom Neligh had been prevailed upon to take to church, was catching up to them.

He followed Neligh into an empty pew near the front. The preacher stood in the area between the congregation and the altar, his hands clasped behind his back, watching his flock file in, nodding here and there.

"There's some spaces up front," the Reverend called out, before he turned and approached the pulpit. Nobody came to share their pew, an appropriate homonym for his state.

"Let us pray."

The congregation stood. The Reverend, a stooped man with vigorous eyebrows and an Adam's apple that emphasized the tremolo in his high tenor, said his prayer; they sat. The Reverend talked about what it meant to be a good Christian in these trying times. Like a war, it was those who banded together in common purpose who survived. Clay's thoughts drifted. Could it have really been more than twenty years since he'd been in church? The Episcopalian church in Seattle had lost him easily and early. If children know one thing, it's when something's not fair. Church was a rigged game, one in which you'd lost before you started. Even at nine, he did not like to lose.

Exiting the church, there was no avoiding the Reverend Thorndike. He stood receiving his parishioners as they filed out into a fine Nebraska morning, a private word for each of them.

The Reverend beamed at Clay. "You are new in town? We don't see that anymore."

"He's just passing on through," Neligh said.

"Has there ever been a more appropriate time to talk about moneychangers in the temple?"

"I don't know," Clay said, leaving it there. But the Reverend wanted to hear his opinion, a real show of how open-minded he was, so Clay started. "Didn't Christ counsel his followers to sell all their possessions and give the money to the poor? But to sell your worldly goods to make yourself more perfect means you are knowingly making the buyer less perfect. And if everyone – "

"Come on," Neligh tugged him away with surprising force. "This isn't the time for philosophy; there's others waiting behind us." They joined the other parishioners on the bright green lawn in front of the church. Neligh seemed determined not to make a quick exit, even though she was a woman apart from the rest of the congregation. "Those boots of yours look like they're good for a thousand miles," she finally said, fishing her car keys out of her handbag.

"Yep," he said, "and that will just about get me half way."

Chapter 43

Five weeks before the Meltdown, the last time he had set eyes on Madeline. She had been living with Eleanor for a month, and now she was sitting in his favorite chair. Normally she collected her mail and personal items when he was at work. Not difficult since he was there all the time now.

"Did Mrs. Dorfmann ever back your girls' campaign?" Her "Mrs. Dorfmann" as opposed to his "MHD" emphasized age, marital status, an ironic respect for a patroness who could deliver a ballroom full of tables at five hundred a seat.

"We're still talking." He hadn't even asked MHD yet. Childlift had come under increasing pressure from their tech sponsors to add girls to the mentoring program. It was only fair: even he couldn't come up with any reasonable counter. Childlift would either have to accept girls or bring in a separate non-profit, one with which they would have to work so closely that it made more sense to develop their own program. MHD knew what was coming; he had prepared her for his next Big Idea. His Board, however, was dithering. This was too far from Childlift's charter, from Day's original vision. Day and his stooped-over associates contributed 18% of the funding. Clay Holloway is empire building, they whined. It's all about his ego, his career, and not what is best for Childlift.

Damn Board. Were they giving him any credit for *Call of Beauty*? The third StreetReady game had gone viral and sales were huge. Out of nowhere X-Urban sent a check for $90,000. Even if you halved their projections, big money was on the way.

"Are you still planning on leaving?" She knew he stayed because of her, because he wanted to salvage their marriage. Maybe her real question was, Have you given up on "us" yet?

"I have no plans." He couldn't bring himself to look over to her. "How about you?" Everything between them had been effortless once. "What's new?"

"That's what I wanted to talk to you about." Her eyes softened and she crumpled her chin. "I'm thinking of moving. Well, to Boston."

"Boston." He swallowed a rising tide of stomach acid, certain that her "thinking of moving" was merely her way of softening the blow; or her way of torturing him with hope.

"I know. I know. I've had time to mull it over. You, you've just been hit with this. It's what I said before, I need to get back to being someone I even like. So maybe going back to where things worked will help." She laughed inwardly. "To the extent they ever did work. I've changed. You've changed me. I'm not saying that's bad, I'm not saying that at all. I don't know, I don't understand how I've become the person I've become. I don't even get along with Eleanor that well anymore. It's like half the time I see her the way you would. I'm rambling. It's because I really don't have an explanation. You know what? I'm tired of having to explain. I know this sounds crazy. I'm not the woman who is your wife, but I want to become that woman again. I'd like to wear your ring. Still. But I know it's not fair to play you along like that. I would understand if you said enough's enough."

Boston, he kept repeating to himself. He sat on the sofa, not his usual spot, unable to move – or talk. He couldn't come up with anything to say; her declaration had taken his words away.

"While you're figuring out the right swear words, I'll just pop down the hall for some things. Okay?" She waited for an answer, then gave up.

He found her sitting on the bed. "What's wrong?"

"There's so much stuff here…still. I'd forgotten. Is it okay – "

"Sure, leave what you want."

She stood up from the bed. "Boston's not an answer, I know that. But it's a…I don't know…direction?"

"It won't be once you're there."

"I'm not asking you to understand. And please, this is hard for me, too."

Those caramel eyes came to him, seemed to understand for the first time his pain. She put a hand on his shoulder, a touch and not a claim. The tentative start of a different conversation, easy, fluid, physical. Just like that they were kissing, cool, considered kisses that showed no sign of slowing down. They kept going on a low flame, as if they were walking, holding hands, around the familiar empty rooms of a fond old house. These two other beings, the two who had always got on so effortlessly, who had caused these new selves to fuse and to spark and finally to explode, also needed to say goodbye, and in the most intimate way possible.

Chapter 44

Stiff, aching, dirty, and bikeless, he arose from his rough camp at the edge of a wheat field. He had been walking for two days, never certain when the next town would be randomly plunked down for his convenience. One thing for sure: the slower you travel the less you think about your destination. Boston had retreated to a theoretical concept as he trudged by the endless wheat fields of Nebraska.

Ten big rigs were pulled over on the shoulder a few hundred yards to the east. Eight men were lined up in the early morning sun, standing at attention, their gray tee-shirts announcing "US Army" in small black letters.

"Men, your orders are clear." The sergeant berating them was a big man, big ears, erect yet with padding in the belly area. "Minton, what are your orders?"

"Clear, sir."

Clay approached, close enough to watch from a respectable distance.

"Trujillo, what are our orders?"

"Stop any private car, biker, or pedestrian on the highway using a reasonable amount of force. Sir."

"A reasonable amount of force. Johnson, is nothing reasonable?"

"That would, uh, depend, sir."

"Depend? What kind of pussy ass answer is that?"

Two of the men stifled giggles. One of them swatted at the other when the Sergeant wasn't watching.

"Next time we pass someone I want to see some action. IS THAT CLEAR?"

"Yes sir, Sergeant, sir."

"Trujillo, what are your orders as relating to private citizens walking down the highway?"

"To use reasonable derisory force, sir."

"McNear, what does that mean, 'reasonable derisory force'?"

"Don't know, sir. Flip them off? Sir."

"Trujillo?"

"It means, sir, we should mock their sorry plight to let them know they shouldn't be out on a highway. Sir."

"And how did we go about letting this gennelman over there know how sorry his plight is?

Eight pairs of eyes swiveled toward Clay. No one said anything.

"Minton!"

"As far as I can recollect, sir, we didn't pass no one, sir."

"And how far is it, Minton, that you can recollect?"

"Pretty far, sir." Minton exchanged brief glances with his fellow sufferers. "We didn't pass him."

"Minton, I draw your attention to the fact that the gennelman in question is standing right over there."

"Yes sir, he is. Sir"

"And what direction is that relative to us, Evans?"

"Uh, west sir?"

"West is correct. What does that imply, Johnson?"

"That we passed him?"

"Passed him, sir!"

As the Sergeant walked the line, turned and walked back, they nudged and kicked one another when his back was to them. Finally, the Sarge called "at ease" and walked over to Clay. He wore uncrisp khakis, "Staff" on the nametape above the left pocket. "What can we do for you, sir?"

"Reasonable derisory force?"

The Sarge smiled. "You're not supposed to know that."

"Know that? Hell, I've been *derided* from California to here. Another thousand miles and it might mess with my self-confidence."

"You're not supposed to know it, policy-wise."

"So is that what the girls up in the cabs are for? RDF?"

"I've trained my men," the Sarge snarled, "I've trained them hard. No riders. Ever. There's too many rigs out there. Not enough me's to train these jerk offs." A weight settled in his voice and on his shoulders. "Anyways, tell me what you're doing sleeping out in a wheat field?"

"It was night; all the inns were full..."

"Well, gotta get movin'. Don't know how far east you had in mind but y'all welcome to ride to Chi-town with us."

Clay did a fish-out-water imitation. "East? You'll take me east?" After trotting back to his camp to scavenge for items of use in Chicago and beyond, he followed the Sarge back to the trucks.

"I'll have to arrest you. Chain you up and all."

"You have eight armed men – and you need to chain me?"

"I have eight armed jerk-offs." The Sarge scratched his head. "Or does that make it sixteen?" He gave a rueful version of his stern smile. "C'mon men, let's get this parade to Chi-town."

The big rig had a pair of large bucket seats, one for the civilian driver and one for the private riding shotgun. Clay sat on the bed behind, hunched forward to converse with Trujillo.

"Sarge said something about chaining me up" he yelled over the diesel.

Trujillo laughed. "Just his so-called sense of humor."

"Has anyone ever tried to hijack you?"

"We're new. But no. It would take quite an operation. USG's more worried about protecting the diesel is what I hear." Trujillo picked up his rifle, poked at the gut of the driver, a lean, older gent with a Fu Manchu moustache and a belt buckle that bit into his belly. "Here's your hijacker. We don't trust Shearer here. He takes off and is treated like a hero in any town he pulls up in."

"Let us drivers have the guns," Shearer said. "We'd scare off any hijackers easier than these fuck-ups."

Clay gazed out at the flat Nebraska counties blurring by. The first half an hour it was a miracle; after that the endless wheat couldn't go by fast enough.

"This is a two-day training run for these boys, Idaho to Chicago," Shearer said. "Twenty tons of potatoes."

"You do longer runs?"

"Did. Got tired of those hauls out to the Coast. Things I've seen. And I'm not talking out the window."

An indecent smile spread over Trujillo's face.

They rolled on in silence, the low whine of the truck engine hypnotizing.

"How soon before you go off and ride around the country, protecting valuable commerce?"

"Doing that now," Trujillo said. "Larsen tells us this is the Sarge's last mission. USG's given up on training. Sarge tells Larsen everything. So… after Chicago the world's our oyster, and you know what they say about them?"

At the next rest break, the semis pulled over, the Sarge, who had been in the lead truck, came back to join Clay and Trujillo. "I'd better ride tail truck now. Holloway, you wanna bring up the rear with me? I could use some adult company."

Clay gave him a crisp salute.

"Not bad, Holloway. Don't need to hit yourself, though."

The trail truck. Last mission. Something didn't feel quite right. But what would he know about army drills and dynamics? Besides the amount of real estate they were whizzing past was dizzyingly spectacular.

A private called Wolfram was driving the rear 18-wheeler solo. Two of the civilian drivers had skipped out, a common problem.

"I heard the USG is giving up on training?" Clay yelled to the Sarge from his perch on the sleeper bed behind the big rig's bucket seats.

"I can't say that's wrong. I'm more of a den mother than a tyrant. Why hell, Larsen cried the first time I cussed him out. Some of the others…" He ran out of steam. "Private Wolfram, you haven't heard any of this."

Wolfram tightened his grip on the wheel. "Any of what, Sir?" After a moment he said, "Sarge? Why've we got a rider when we're not supposed to?"

"This man is under arrest. Your orders are to shoot him if he tries to escape."

"What's the charge? Did you interrogate him?"

The Sarge closed his eyes. "Are you questioning me, private?"

The private changed down a gear, though the road remained flat and straight

"Wolfram, you're wasting precious fuel. Upshift now, that's an order."

A tiny smile worked on Wolfram's lips. He shifted out of gear and let the truck coast, slower and slower.

"Wolfram, what in the hell are you doing?"

"Saving fuel." The truck coasted to a stop. "See, maximum fuel efficiency." He turned off the engine.

"Wolfram, let's just get to Chicago. Five hours and it will be finished."

Wolfram grinned as he turned the engine back on and chased the nine trucks ahead, which had slowed down, allowing them to catch up.

After endless wheat, the Sarge yelled back, "You ever fly a jet in formation, Holloway?"

"Can't say that I have, Sir."

"You ever drink alcohol?"

"Absolutely."

"We're talking delayed reaction here. In a jet you give it a burst to keep on the wingman's tail. Experience tells you there's a delay so you gotta approximate what is needed and hold back on any more and sure enough, after a delay, the jet inches forward to where it needs to be. A rookie with no training would say, uh oh, it's not moving and give it more. He'd be into the wingman's wing. See where I'm going with this?"

"Delayed reaction?"

"Experience."

"Okay."

"These boys don't know shit. Hell, I was no different at that age. They're not gonna listen to the voice of experience but they will listen to the crack of the ol' whip." He crawled back and sat next to Clay on the sleeper bed. "I still can't believe it, the most powerful nation on earth, a country that's been that way ever since I learned to walk, reduced to this." He held a revolver, stroked his cheek with the barrel. "Our country, Holloway, is like a plane with too much weight, going faster and faster but it can't get to wheels-up."

"You toss some weight, right?"

The Sarge shook his head. "You ever served, Holloway? You ever put your life on the line for your country?"

"No, I haven't."

"Well, lemme tell you, it's a hell of a lot easier fixin' to die for something noble and good. When I served over in A-stan that's how I thought of it. A bright white cross in a green field under a blue sky. Your basic funeral colors. Do you think a country's like a person, once it's lost its reputation it will never get it back?"

"I'm prepared to see the USA as exceptional."

"You ever been under fire, Holloway?"

"Been shot at. Can't say how intent they were to nail me."

"Bullets have a mind of their own." He emptied the bullets from his gun, hefted them, as if at a craps table, down to one last throw, reloaded and snapped the magazine into the gun.

"Sergeant. I wish you wouldn't wave that thing around."

He emptied the magazine again. "That better?"

He nodded.

The Sarge put the barrel up to his eyeball. "Pretty dark in there."

Blam.

The Sarge slumped forward, his blood and brains sprayed all over the sleeper bed. Wolfram started honking madly. Mayday. Mayday. He had reflexively slowed down and already lagged the others. Clay's face, hair and right shoulder were dripping. The wet seeped through his shirt. He swiped with his forearm at goop trailing down his cheek, then lunged for the passenger seat, got the window down and let loose.

"Just pull the damn thing over!" The front nine semi's disappeared over a fold in the highway.

They buried Sarge out in the corn fields of Iowa, the better to keep his name unsullied by suicide, and to escape the crippling bureaucracy of being debriefed on a death. The men were in a hurry to be free agents on the next convoys out of Chicago.

They dug with calm fury using tire irons, hands and metal bowls until McNear, a farm boy, assured them that Sarge would be resting below the reach of any tractor claw. The grave ready, it was somehow understood that it fell to Clay, as the Sarge's confessor, and possible provoker, to say a few last words.

"I can't do it," Clay said. "I've known the man for a few hours. I haven't even got a shirt on."

"Well, we're all okay with it," Trujillo said.

He stepped up to the lip of the grave, threw his blood-stained shirt so it covered what was left of Sarge's head. "Today we honor the service and the life of a fine American, a true hero, a man of his times who has tragically run out of time. I've only known Sarge for a few hours. When I was asked to say these words I thought, I'm the exact wrong guy to do that. But you know what? If in a few hours a man can impress me as completely as Sarge has, well that really tells us the kind of man he was. A man ever concerned about the army, his country, and what was happening to both of them. In the career of a brave man, it was truly a final act of bravery to say, I can't bear to see my country like this. Sarge, you rightly criticized my poor civilian attempt at a salute, but I tell you what, I'm going to do it again. We all are. Gentlemen, let us give a final salute to a fine soldier, a concerned citizen and true leader of men. Sarge, may you rest in everlasting peace."

The men milled around the grave, all reluctant to cast the first fistful of dirt on the body down below and to the blood-stained, brain-globuled shirt partly covering it. For a split second all went dark, some inner malfunction, Clay's vision gone. When the colors returned, when they stopped swimming and formed into hard lines and shapes he tossed his fistful down into the grave. It sounded like the first drops of rain, which picked up as others tossed their dirt. The rain stopped and all was quiet.

"Where's Larsen goin'?" McNear asked as the men trampled down the moist earth with their combat boots. Larsen walked spectrally out into the depths of the cornfield, his shoulders twitching.

"Let him be," Trujillo said.

The men helped Clay clean up the suicide cab, all diving in and ducking back out to retch before going in again.

"Someone needs to go get Larsen," Wolfram said.

"He was the Sarge's special project," McNear said.

"It was comin' to an end," Johnson said, "one way or the other."

Larsen was nowhere in sight. The spuds were needed in Chicago. Trujillo stepped forward. "Men, Larsen's run off. Just like the Sarge. We straight on that?" The mumbles sounded vaguely affirmative. "I said, Are we straight on that?" The men gave a sharper answer, still in need of work. Now Trujillo turned. "Mr. Holloway, sir, we have good news for you. You are no longer under arrest." Trujillo smiled ruefully; Clay would not be coming with them to undermine his embryonic leadership.

Long after the big rigs had faded to a dot on the far horizon, after they winked out of view completely, he stood on the highway near the burial site. How did he get to Iowa? Only this morning he had woken up in the middle of Nebraska, facing a two-hundred-mile walk just to leave the state at Sioux City. Unless he hadn't woken up at all, and this was all a feverish dream in which he'd been tornadoed Wizard of Oz style to a new state or State.

He glanced over to the many boot prints of the tamped-down dirt where the Sarge had been laid to rest. If only he could rewind those easy truck miles, start over on foot, and miss out on the Sarge and his end. What had Granny T predicted? *Something big, something impossible. Greatness. Shame. Everything.* Was that starting? This impossible future she'd foretold?

But Granny T, despite her fearful visage, was merely a reporter of the future, not its agent. The Phantom Cowboy had hinted at a plan, knew telling details about Madeline, said he would visit again. He was the one to watch out for. It was all so frustratingly passive, as if he stood, like a pin on a skittle board, waiting for the mechanical tornado to twist by and knock him down.

In the ice water plunge at the Sarge's end he had forgotten about the scant personal effects he had managed to collect since escaping the Bolts at Jeffrey City. They were in the trail truck, heading to Chicago. He needed some basics, including a shirt on his back. That meant walking to the nearest town, Waterloo, the one the convoy had breezed through when the Sarge was talking about dying for his country.

There were no markers out in this anonymous stretch of endless corn fields, no obvious way of mentally marking the burial spot. Trudging westward, half-clothed, he counted his paces to the first notable highway sign – one of those badges with "20 West" on them. He counted the US 20 badges until he hit Eagle Lake, just south of the highway. He was running before he had time to think about running, stripping as he neared the lake. Once under the warm water he rubbed his head and hair with the vigor of Lady MacBeth. He floated weightless, neatly escaped from a world with too much weight. The whole Sarge episode screamed out there, up there. But down here it was a silent scream. While the strong Iowa sunshine filtered down into the water, he floated and floated, face down as if he didn't need to breathe any longer.

"Nice day for a swim." The woman was standing with a little girl, just by his pathetic pile of belongings

"Needed to clean up."

"I figured you were in emergency mode. I'm Reverend Holly if there's anything about your emergency you want to talk about." She nodded, and led the little girl away.

He kneaded and wrung out his clothes, all four pieces, put underwear and shorts on wet, and walked barefoot along the lake, dangling his boots and drying socks.

He found the Reverend Holly at a picnic bench up on a rise. The girl stood down by the lake, kicking at the shallow water.

"Is your emergency over with?"

"More like taking a break."

"Ah, one of those." Reverend Holly smiled. "Here, take this," she insisted, placing a towel over his already red shoulders.

"Are you heading back to Waterloo?" he asked.

"Sure am," she smiled, glancing at the girl still kicking at the water. "You're welcome to join us, if you're not in a hurry. I'm letting Crystal there call the pace."

He sat at the foodless picnic table and scanned the warm pleasant lake, a light breeze working in his almost dry hair and beard, his stomach growling. He took his cue from the Reverend: this was the girl's story. His could come later.

"The poor child lost her mom, not six weeks ago." She smiled, a small wearisome one. "You know we take a lot of pride at how well our town is coping with this Void. But there's not much we can do about a shortage of medicine."

"A friend of mine said this Void is like getting the wind knocked out of you. Everything's normal and okay, but you just can't get started with a breath."

"Sounds like some kind of poet."

"Hadn't thought of him like that."

They sat in comfortable silence for a while. "I'll go down and see if she's ready to head back."

"Don't hurry on my account. By the way is your town named after the battle? Waterloo?"

"Best we can tell it was a random choice from a book. But a lot of folks associate us with that battle. I like to take the glass-half-full view. After all Waterloo *was* a famous victory."

Chapter 45

Clay sat in the conference room at Trilby, Cornwall and Blair, Childlift's legal advisers. Ten days had passed since Madeline relocated. He took in the fine walnut veneer of the endless oval table, the buttery leather swivel seats, the view out to the bay. All he could think of was the hit to his budget.

"We need to go over this again," the lead lawyer Tremont Wheeler said. Wheeler was assessing possible violations of Childlift's non-profit status. Two other lawyers, Alexei Connors and Trisha Hashimoto, were working on the defense of a lawsuit against Childlift.

"I've already gone over this twice. What are you trying to do, catch me out? I'm not on trial, damn it."

"Not yet, anyway," Wheeler said. "We're going over it because *in my experience* that can trigger memories, sometimes just the littlest detail. Like last time when you remembered that you negotiated the percent from fifteen to twenty. I can only successfully defend you if I know the worst. We can build up from that."

"But I'm – "

"If the IRS or the Feds choose to prosecute, if they allege you made a verbal contract with Hogbom..."

"I told him I needed to run it by my Board. We didn't shake on it. Doesn't our government have better things to do with their time?"

"It's great politics," Connors said. "People are so pissed off about Booty Call. You know, give the people what they want." Call of Beauty, the third StreetReady game, had been a major departure for X-Urban. In it a teenage girl must use her street smarts to dodge six bros intent on initiating her. The player wins if she gets out of the room. Call of Beauty may have been a slow burn with gamesters, but it was an instant hit with the media. The girl player angle; the implied rape controversy. A second visit to the entire StreetReady vision of real world street smarts, no weapons. And there was the programmer, LaMichael, a tall and skinny black kid with MalcolmX glasses and a world class scowl.

The kind of success story the country liked to congratulate itself over. Up from the projects, obvious programming talent. Call of Beauty was his baby, and he'd had the balls to negotiate a separate deal with X-Urban. As one none-too-subtle columnist had it, "this young man has single-handedly shown an entire city of struggling brothers the genius of the American way, how hard work and the capitalist impulse can be more rewarding than drug dealing."

As the PR fed into the sales and Call of Beauty rocketed up the charts, two girls came forward, claiming in a press conference that many of the responses in Booty Call, as everyone was now calling it, were their own words, used in fear, in real life, when trying to fight off their initiations. With their contingency fee lawyers standing behind them, they announced they were cooperating with the DA, and they were suing X-Urban, Childlift and LaMichael himself for the psychological trauma of being plagiarized in such a brutal fashion. The DA had not yet charged LaMichael with rape, but with the entire country outraged at having been conned, charges were inevitable.

"What teenager uses words like psychological trauma?" Clay said.

"Well-coached ones," Hashimoto said. "We want to hear about your conversation with X-Urban because there's the delicate question of who LaMichael's employer was, X-Urban or Childlift. Or can we argue that he was an independent contractor?"

"X-Urban is in deep. We need to get you as far away from them as possible," Connors added.

"Christ, what a mess…"

Given the Childlift imbroglio he should have cancelled his meeting with Mariel Hunter Dorfmann to discuss her becoming the Board President of a sister charity for girls. Then again, she should have cancelled it, too.

She sat where she always sat when they met, at the head of the table in the small conference room at the offices of the Dorfmann Family Trust.

"You know about our push to include girls in our tech mentoring program. It would help if I could say you are behind it."

"How far behind it?" If this was a joke, it was her first ever. Usually she was so buttoned up and proper. She waved her joke away as if it were a bad smell. "Clay, I don't want to talk about charity things now. Things need to settle. Both of us know that." She squared up to him, shoulders lifting. "How much do you know about investing?"

"Buy quality, hold on to it no matter what. Like marriage." He glanced at his wedding ring, Madeline three weeks gone in Boston.

"I suppose I didn't mean investing, I meant money in general." She was the epitome of the stolid, immaculately dressed and coiffed power patroness – but just sometimes, at a certain angle, she appeared younger, less polished to a dull sheen, a college girl playing a middle-aged part.

She glanced at the door. "Henry is talking about moving." She swallowed. "To Switzerland. I think Henry would call that limiting his downside. He sees dark clouds. Black clouds." She folded her hands together and rested them on the mahogany table in front of her. "Have you heard anything?"

He wasn't in her husband's league, didn't even play the same game. She knew that. But wait a minute, he knew someone even bigger than Henry Dorfmann.

"I've got someone I could call."

"Don't bother. It's just nice to talk. You know how it is, someone like me saying something like this could be considered irresponsible. Not you, I trust you."

"I don't mind making a call. Asking discreetly. What have you heard, rather than have you heard dot dot dot."

"I'm not moving anywhere. I am an American." She chuckled. "I know, so's Henry. But you know what it's like with rich people, they're above nationality. It's like their passport is issued by the Republic of Filthy Rich. Honored everywhere."

He didn't need to call Dubkhadze on Mariel Hunter Dorfmann's account. Still, he had to wonder, would Dubkhadze take his call? It had been over a year since Clay had talked to him. Missing the last Georgian Orgy might have sealed his doom. Phyllis in LA put him on hold. Now Dubkhadze was on the line like a long-lost friend.

"What's that crackling sound?" Clay asked. "Have I got you at a good time?"

"It's a fire. I'm burning my piles of money. You can tell Madeline I have converted to her philosophy."

"I'm sure she'd like that."

Dubkhadze was another passport holder from the Republic of Filthy Rich, a recently minted US citizen who still talked about the US in the second and third person. *You* Americans. Guess what *they've* done now.

Now Clay heard singing, the strumming of a stringed instrument, more high pitched and clattery than a guitar. "It must be an enormous fire."

"It is cold up in the mountains."

"I hear it will soon be cold everywhere."

Dubkhadze laughed. What had Madeline once said, coming back from a black-tie fundraiser? The rich don't need to laugh. "You must come and visit with me. I am here in the old country. Always you will be welcome. In a few months we will have you singing Suliko in *our* language."

"I'm afraid I'm pure Californian."

"Pure? My dear chap, you may be a Californian, but even further back you are Caucasian. This means from the Caucasus, where I am now standing."

That Sunday he attended the ballgame as the guest of one of the banks that sponsored Childlift; a second-tier bank taking him to a low-profile game. What did they think about the future of the economy? He listened to them talk about cycles, and bubbles, and consumer confidence – a prepared script, all kneejerk optimism. Business over with, it was pleasant to sit up in the corporate box and look down on the immaculate green field, hot-dog gobbling families, the rainbow coalition of ethnicities, preferences, and proclivities. If he leaned far enough out of the luxury box window he could hear the ironic shouts of encouragement. The Giants were out of the race. The game didn't matter. And soon baseball wouldn't matter. There would be no play-offs this year.

Chapter 46

It was flat, straight and hot as he pedaled east. US20 was as empty as the now-unplugged information superhighway, not one convoy in the last two hours. That left an eerie, incomplete feeling that, combined with the events of yesterday, left him in a sullen, reflective mood. A tailwind pushed him along, kicking up dirt on the highway's shoulders, as if fate was hurrying him past the Sarge's grave. No, he decided, if I don't look I can still believe it was a dream.

He had found the bike, a brittle-tired woman's three-speed through the Church Bake Sale in Waterloo. Tables full of sugary goodies. You made your purchases with Good News scrip – slips of paper that had verses from the Bible on them. He had stood there dizzy with choice.

"What are you going to do with all these?" he asked an elderly lady, nodding to the bowlful of scrip behind her wares, fruit tarts.

"I just hand them around. The Good News is for passing on. Here." She gave him a dainty fistful of slips. 'Whatever you do,' he read from the top one, 'work at it with all your heart, as working for the Lord, not for men. Col 3:23'.

Yeah, cut out the middle man. And which book was Col? He shouldn't be so jaded. It was nice here, friendly, functioning. People willing to pitch in and help. When he told his Good News vendor about his need for a bike, she got right on it. One of her vendor friends had a bike she was willing to lend.

"Lend?"

"That means lend it on."

As he pedaled east he kept an eye on the wobbling front tire. He'd be lucky to make the Mississippi. Could he smell the river from here? Sense its looming presence? Tomorrow he would be standing on the bridge that took US20 over the river watching its mile-wide bulk flow by as if the nation's juices going down the drain.

His too-small bike forced a regimen of forty minutes of pedaling, five off for stretching and knee bends and general de-stressing of his ligaments. At the same time he could check on the tires. He was just getting off his bike, having given up on finding any shade on this flat and wide open road, when there on the eastern horizon a shape moved out of the heat lake floating above the roadbed. During his stretches and bends he kept pointed at the mirage: now it began to swim into resolution as a vehicle, emerging out of the heat lake, growing, leaving the water behind. After all the empty hours on the road, it had the feel of a grand and lone entrance.

The vehicle swam into view. A '57 Chevy, high-profiled, aquamarine with white roof and fin trim. It pulled up in front of him, heading against the non-existent traffic on the wrong side of the highway, corn stalks wedged in its front bumper.

The driver waited behind the glare off the windshield as Clay walked his bike over. The window rolled down in uneven jerks to reveal a man in his forties, his dirty blond hair swept back to expose a pale and bony forehead. Soul patch like a blond and upside-down version of Hitler's mustache. Light blue eyes, like Tye's, except these had ground glass in them. The harmonica player from the Continental Divide.

"Ola," he said, his bristly soul patch jabbing out from his chin.

"Uh, hi." The car was cherry, dusty but otherwise right off the showroom floor.

"Howdy," the man said, with the air of taking it from the top. "Of course, Iowa. How silly of me. I must pay more attention. We have met, that's what's important. I have come a long way for that."

"I didn't know these babies came with air con," Clay said, annoyed that the car was still running, like an open refrigerator, like a bonfire of twenty dollar bills, back when they were worth something.

"How rude of me, mocking your fuel-starved country." He shut off the engine, came back to him with a "that's settled" smile.

"Where are you from to have come a long way to see me?"

"A penetrating question. I like those."

Clay folded his arms across his chest.

"I like questions, the more the murkier. Don't you think it's rather unfair to be put in a game without being told the rules?"

"Uh, look, friend – "

"Or the game, or who you are playing?"

He wore a heavy tan corduroy jacket over a crisp checked shirt buttoned to his neck. If the car had air con before, the turned-off engine and the rolled down window had swamped that. Yet he seemed comfortable – and unconcerned about any approaching convoy.

"Who are you?"

"As I said before, a man. A man who has your best interests at heart."

Clay stood before him, arms still crossed, bike leaning against him, not knowing what to say. "Aha, silence. Don't you think that silence between people is really just another question?"

"Look, friend, I best be making my way to Dubuque."

"No."

"No?"

"No should never be a question. It is the absence of questions. This is why I oppose all no's."

"But you just said no. You started it."

"True enough. You forced my hand. You, sir, are a worthy opponent. But what am I saying? Calling you an opponent. We are on the same side. I've rushed over here because you have reached the great river more quickly than I planned. It is quite important that you do not cross it. That is why I have come for you."

"You've... come for me?" Clay closed his eyes tight in the hope that the man would not be there when he opened them.

"I said we'd meet again, did I not? You, sir, are dealing with a man of his word."

"Who are you?"

"Ah, a question, a palpable question. Thank you."

"It only counts if you don't answer it."

"You, friend, are a quick study. A worthy addition to our side."

"How are you going to stop me going to Dubuque? It may not be much of a country, but last time I checked it was still free. Kind of."

"Oh that. You know I really do hate answers. I will make an exception in this case, to my worthy comrade." He opened the door and got out. He was clad in mid-calf suede boots, the kind a Renaissance minstrel might wear. "You have a wife. You're going to Boston to find her. You want to know if she is... okay. You are taking great risks to answer that question." He kicked at the dirt, overplaying his reluctance to bring up such a sensitive subject. The rhythm of the man's conversation, his gestures, his accents, were all approximations.

"Is she by herself? There?"

"Straight to the heart of the matter. I like your style, sir." He frowned, his timing late. "Is your wife a mom? Are you a dad? That's what has you pedaling day after day, yes?"

He slumped, wishing he'd been able to hold back on signaling such defeat. "Do you know the answer?"

"The answer is ...well, let's say yes, yes I do know the answer."

"But you're not going to tell me, right? So why don't we leave it there and I can go on my way."

"Do you really expect a full explanation to flutter to your feet like an autumn leaf? And besides, is it not worth any number of ordeals to see your wife again?" He fired up his baby blue eyes. "Are you saying you would cheat, take a short cut, to put conditions on what has up to now been a pure and noble quest?"

Clay slumped again. "You'd better tell me what it is you're after."

"That's the spirit. I need your help. It will take a lot of hard work, that's all."

"That's it?" In his halting progress through these farmland states he had tried to block out his midnight meeting at the Divide, and Granny T's fearful reading. It had been reduced to a background trepidation, like a bass guitar rumbling from a separate room. But now he was in that room, and there was something familiar about it, a sense of finality, as when the light has a certain alien quality just before a life-changing event – a quality the gut reacts to first, fluttering while the mind catches up. "What do I get in return for my hard work?"

"A child."

A flash of ice water passed through him. "A child?" he said, just to confirm he could still talk. "There must be a catch."

"It's simple. You work for me – I estimate two years plus/minus – and in return I will bring your child to you."

"*My* child?"

"Yes, your child. It is the only way you are guaranteed to see her."

"Are you out of your mind? Madeline would have contacted me. Definitely."

"I hate long explanations." He brushed his hair back from his ashen forehead. "Know then that when you die there are no Pearly Gates. From what I've managed to piece together from the souls I've worked with, at death one becomes part of the great universal ho-hum." He managed a small yawn. "I'm sure it's all quite nice. One is all atingle from morning 'til night. At my place we don't do any humming. We stick with the individual. We let each person bang his own drum, for that, friend, is one definition of humanity, with all its doubts, inadequacies, fears. I hardly need tell you that to be human is to experience rough with smooth, light with dark. Compared to the blinding light and great ho-hum we are probably the black sheep of this two-sheep set up. We're little different from a well-run little country, say Finland with better weather. With me so far?"

Clay blinked repeatedly, trying to focus.

"Have some water. Squirt your face. Don't worry, I have more in the car."

Clay sat on the Chevy's back seat, his legs swiveled out the open door, his feet on the hard roadbed, his body bent forward to escape the heat in the car. They were facing the wrong way in the middle of a highway and it was the least of his worries. He tried to clear his vision, shaking his head. Sat and waited for his eyes to work again. Finally, he got up, a tad unsteady on his feet.

"Ready?"

"Not really, but let's have it."

"What did I just say about death?"

"No to the pearly gates. Yes, to a daughter."

"One last piece and that'll be it, I promise. Know then that every sexact..." – he ran the two words together as if hopping over hot stones – "... with every sexact the universe splits in two. If you pay close enough attention you may even feel it." He massaged his chin. "In one world there is a pregnancy; in the other not. You are a dad, sir, many times over."

"Wait a minute. Every time?" What about that waitress way back when? And that time in Vegas. The countless times with Madeline? "But if they are in different universes, or worlds, or whatever?"

"Here's the complicated part. Let's take that last night..."

"What last night?"

"Your wife is sitting on the bed. Then standing. Then, uh, lying."

"You were there! My god."

"Your God? Maybe He stayed. I am discreet. You can't imagine what That Act looks like from my viewpoint. Can you remember when you were a boy, the first time you found out about it, how gross it was? Multiply that by a hundred. So, no, I'm not going to sit around listening to every smack, slurp, suck, grunt, smooch, slap, burp and fart. Every baby, baby..."

"Okay. Okay."

"My point is that that Last Time may have resulted in a pregnancy here; or Elsewhere. You can take the risk that it happened here and blow me off, or you can be assured of seeing your daughter, one way or the other. You see the nicety here?"

"Daughter?"

"That last time was a daughter."

"What about all the others? Between Maddy and me we must have... my God, is this all true?"

"I do wish you'd leave God out of this. For reasons I'd rather not talk about it is usually easiest – more satisfactory – to go for the most recent conception. Especially in your case."

"Assuming she's not in this world?"

"That's right."

"What do you mean about *my case*?"

"Well, it's not like the second most recent time was the day before."

Clay twisted his lips into a victim's smile. "What is this hard work you'd have me do in…wherever?"

"I've chosen New Mexico. It's complicated. It's risky. If I told you, it might scare you off."

"But you know about Boston, our last night. So, you must know how this, this hard work in New Mexico turns out."

"I don't know the future. The past is my specialty."

"If that were true you wouldn't be parked in the oncoming lane of a highway."

The stranger hooded his eyes in thought, or in approximation of that. "Nearest eastbound convoy is…" He gazed at the near infinite corn rows for inspiration. "Twenty seven point three miles away, travelling at 62 mph. Let's see, 60 mph is a mile a minute which would mean twenty-seven minutes, a little faster so let's say twenty-six minutes."

"What am I supposed to do, sign in blood?" He squared up to his provocateur, his vision clearing. "All for a bullshit promise of some impossible child…" He checked himself before he got carried away. Who knew what powers this strange man had? "What do I call you? Mephistopheles? Beelzebub? Satan?"

"Very good, four questions. So compactly done. Thank you. My good friends call me Luce."

"What do I call you?"

"I have chosen you. I can be relentless if I need to be. You can't imagine how annoying it is to deal with someone who knows every last thing about you."

"Why me? There must be a million more qualified people. Some of them probably live in New Mexico already."

Luce approximated a smile. "I could say that I work in mysterious ways, but that tag line's been taken. In any case 'mysterious' is just a shortened way of saying that existence is constructed in a way that you cannot conceive – sorry, imagine. I've already told you too much. Let's just say that you, sir, have the right impulses and instincts for our mission."

"So, it's true about my soul? That I must sign in blood for it."

"No. You could help me because it is your duty. Our project, by the way, is to get this country back on its feet."

Clay closed his eyes for a long moment. It had been too much before, now his country wheeled in. All this time, ever since Luce had mentioned a child, he had been assessing every aspect of the scene for intimations of reality, that this was not a dream. The scene had scant detail: an empty highway, a flat plain full of endless corn stalks, a blue sky, whitened by heat. Nevertheless, he could move his head, direct his eyes to that section of corn stalks fluttering in the light breeze, to that lone puff of a cloud, the shape of Virginia, drifting east, now down to those strange boots the man wore. Yes, he was actively taking in the scene and not just receiving it.

Luce jumped up on the trunk, nimble as a cat, sat just behind the rear window. He knocked his boots together. "It's the one thing I've never figured out. The feet part. So uncomfortable."

"What if I help you in New Mexico and we just see how it goes?" Clay tried.

"You may not be surprised to learn that I've had conversations like this before. Theoretically, you should be one of the easy ones. But then hypocrisy gets in the way. Every time. It is *so* annoying. November 12, four years ago." Such a brusque segue, the date jammed up against the previous sentence.

"So?"

"That's the last time you blew off any belief in immortality. You said, 'how can anybody believe all this religious garbage. You die and that's it. Goodbye world; hello worms."

The "hello worms" part sounded familiar, certainly like something he'd say. "Okay, I get your point: if I don't believe in an afterlife why would I worry about a deal with you?"

"So much nicer when it's phrased as a question. Thank you."

"So, you're calling me on my beliefs? Nobody can know any of this stuff for certain. Why can't you just bring my, my child to me without the soul part?"

"Wiggle, wiggle, just like your worms." Luce kicked his legs back and forth like a little boy. "Even if I could do that..." He swallowed hard, and set off in a high declamatory voice, "Is not a child worth great risks, great sacrifices? Are you saying you would qualify under what circumstances you'd deign to see you own flesh and blood?"

"I can't take this," he said, loudly. "You're just throwing all this stuff at me. My alleged child. My soul. My country. Speaking of my country, you're the Devil, right? But you're recruiting me to help get our country out of its current mess? Why here? Why now? Where were you during the world wars, the Great Depression?"

"Your earth has eight billion people. I would settle for a planet with a few million. What I cannot accept is none. Your nuclear weapons have changed the balance here. I am forced to protect my livelihood. Your country, your nation needs to be the leader of the free world again."

"No, I can't do it. Your sexact story is ridiculous."

"Hmmm, it's too bad your internet is down and your libraries closed. You could look up Dr. Hugh Everett's Many Worlds theory. It explains how matter can be in two places at the same time. The famous cat is both alive and dead – alive in one world, dead in another. It's a theory accepted by 57.2 per cent of all PhD-level physicists."

"Making love is hardly splitting atoms."

Luce hopped down from the car, hitting lightly, yet wincing at the contact. "Now," he said, leading him around to the back of his car, "let's seal this deal." He opened the trunk.

Clay took a step back. His blue bike lay there. Yes, his with its two different-colored water bottle holders, the place on the left fork that had been scraped raw from his plunge down the coastal hills, a lifetime ago now. He knew: if he took the bike, that was as good as a handshake, as blood on paper, as a soul bargained for. Did he have a soul? He hadn't devoted two neurons to that notion and yet, now, risking it was the most important decision of his life.

"I've got a headache."

"No, you don't."

"Okay, here's what I can agree to. I'll sign. I'd prefer it if it didn't have to be in blood. You'll have me at your place."

Luce arched his brows, the left one higher.

"But I can't agree to the child part. Not yet. I need to understand the impact on the child, what this means from her standpoint. That means I must talk to you about that part, later, talk about it in good faith."

"Perfect. A laudable concern. The child will be optional."

Clay pulled his bike out of the trunk, underneath it his bike shoes, and set about re-attaching the front wheel.

"Welcome to the fight. This time I know your country will be great again."

"New Mexico," he said, just to say something.

Luce nodded, light angling off his soul patch.

He got on the bike and slowly circled the Chevy, trying New

Mexico on for size, getting used to south and west after two months of north and east. "Why here? You could have intercepted me the first time. At least Wyoming is directly north of New Mexico?"

Luce inhaled deeply, the kind you take when you are savoring great natural beauty. "Have you ever been in the exact middle of an immense field of corn?" He stretched his arms wide. "You can't imagine the power there."

Chapter 47

Clay flew west down the straight and level highway on his trusty blue bike – or some version of it. How quickly he was back at Eagle Lake, scene of the washing in the water. He turned to the lake and followed the dirt path along its southern shore, the one the Reverend Holly had led him down on the way back to her parsonage. Yes, he wanted to see her again. Maybe she would smell the Devil on him, and confirm his awful bargain. He followed the path by the water, through open areas, crossed a road, and ended at a major road. He remembered the ranch style house opposite, a right here would take him under US20 and straight to the modest little parsonage that lay half a mile down a wide, flat and leafy road. Anywhere, USA.

The note on the parsonage door said the Reverend Holly was out on calls. How refreshing, to find someone with such purpose. He sat on one of two hard chairs placed on the concrete slab before the front door, and examined his blue bike, propped against the clapboard house. Where had he left reality behind? Sonny had been real, the ride up through Utah and into Idaho seemed fairly normal. Idaho Falls might have been the last solid anchor, except for Linda Margossian's amazement at his serenity. He was not a serene individual. After Idaho Falls his route up to the Divide seemed more or less defensible. And somewhere up at the top of the Rockies it had all come loose. The harmonica-playing version of Luce, Granny T, Neligh, the Sarge. Luce again.

"Why Mr. Holloway, this is unexpected. I had you closing in on Chicago by now. Come on in."

"Thanks." Something so wholesome and unassuming about her, her presence the kind of unconditional comfort you got from your mother when you were five.

As she fixed a drink at her countertop she said, "Is that right, your third time in Waterloo? Well, good things happen in threes."

"The Father, Son, and Holy Spirit?"

She rewarded his bible skills with a considerable smile. Her voice dropped in pitch. "You've had the Visit haven't you?"

"The...what?"

"Oh, don't bother to deny it. I know the look. It is so overwhelmingly good, such an honor and privilege – and so scary. That's what people don't understand, how scary it is. To have something, something in which you've strived mightily to believe, confirmed so, so physically. And I'm talking about believers. I can only imagine how it must be for someone like you."

"Me...who?" he squeaked.

"The jaded west coast hipster." She flashed an understanding and compassionate smile as she set a pastel-colored drink before him.

"I, I guess I've been through a lot. Recently."

"I know. Why me? What have I, a poor everyday sinner, done to be chosen like this? What does He see in me? Sound familiar?"

He mumbled something.

"There's any number of Christian narratives, but let's take the Prophet Mohammed for some balance. He was one of the most powerful and influential men who has ever lived. Now why did his God choose an illiterate businessman with no formalized religion? You know how Mohammed described his visitation? 'It felt like my soul had been torn away from me'."

"Not all businessmen are illiterate."

"The point I'm trying to get to is that it takes time to reconcile yourself to a world where shades from another one can come calling. That's perfectly normal."

He took a sip, held his glass as if considering. "What do you make of the devil?"

"You know what? I don't get too hung up on the literal stuff. True religion is about the heart and the spirit. Certainly, there is evil in the world. You can say it's due to a malicious agent like the devil, or to random impulses within us all. Which one it is doesn't matter that much." She gave him her Bake Sale smile: everything good, simple, wholesome. "The devil is part of us. A part that makes it difficult for us to live in harmony. You know, discordant."

They were quiet for a time. Finally, the Reverend got up from the kitchen table, collected the glasses and took them to the sink. She said, coming back to him, "You, sir, appear to be a sensible man. You have a strong moral compass, right? Follow your heart as long as it does not lead you across the line that separates good from evil. Focus on the good news that's been delivered to you. It's okay to feel honored. Think of your soul as a cold hearth that has now been lighted. Use that light to make this world a better place."

"A better place," he muttered to himself. "It would make more sense if I had been visited by the Devil..."

"Give yourself time. It is my experience that He appears in a form that the one who is visited can understand."

As they'd been talking various congregation members had been poking their heads in the Reverend's door, arriving for choir practice. The organ's booming tones rumbled through the parsonage walls and vibrated the glasses in the kitchen cupboard.

Outside, on the parsonage steps, the choir's high and heavenly notes cascaded down the scale like manna from above. The great, universal hum. What had he done?

PART TWO

Chapter 1

Holding his five-year-old daughter's hand, Sonny Hargreaves walked up the garden path to the modest house, like it was the first time at a new daycare place. They had driven up to Idaho Falls from Centerville, their visit there cut short by Sonny's animosity towards his stepfather.

The doorbell set off a tolling of chimes, echoing in what sounded like a cool dark chamber. It was hot out of the truck's air con. A slim, languid woman in her fifties answered the door. Sonny laughed, high-pitched and too fast. "Guess you won't know who we are."

She smiled, an evenly spreading show of stubby teeth and pink gums. "Anniversary people?"

"We're hoping you're Linda Margossian."

She nodded.

"Anniversary people?" Sonny said, letting go of Opal's hand. Still in need of her father's protection, she grabbed it again.

"The Anniversary Special by that big media lady? I should remember her name, she came out and interviewed me. Anyway, people keep knocking on my door to remind me."

"They wanted me on that show," Sonny said, "pestered me something fierce. Mentioned her name like she was the pope or something. I told them what's my business stays that way."

"You're smarter than I was." Her eyes and her smile went wide. "Why you must be Sonny. Don't know your last name."

"Hargreaves."

"And you must be Sonny's daughter," she said, stooping down to meet the girl face-to-face.

Opal tightened her grip on his hand, and turned her face into the leg of his jeans.

It was cooler in the house. Linda brought them drinks. Opal twisted her mouth after taking a sip. "Thank you very much," she said, her politeness lessons overcoming her distaste for the drink. Her look at Sonny all but stuck out her tongue. "Who's that?" she said, pointing.

"That's a sculpture. It's a kind of statue," Sonny said.

"Where are her arms?"

"It's called art, Opie. We'll talk about it later, okay."

"Centerville," Linda said, after Sonny told her where they'd come from. "Clay Holloway came by here just a few days after he parted ways with you."

"The parting of the ways," Sonny said, half to himself. "Opie, it's fine to look, just don't touch anything, okay."

"But I've got arms, daddy."

"Parting of the ways – Oregon Trail had a place that's called that," Sonny said. "A fork in the trail. Some headed on to Oregon, others headed south to California. Only, me? I got stuck in quicksand on the main trail. Did Mr. Holloway have a skinny young woman with him. Red eyes, runny nose, always tearing up?"

"No. He was by himself. Heading out for the Tetons by himself. You know, I really can't tell you much about him. He dropped by because he wanted to know about Bankalinda – you may have seen a few signs around town?" She explained the theory of communal ownership, and how that ownership evolved into a modern-day bank when the True Dollar took hold. "Apart from that we didn't talk much. I think about ninety-five percent of his brain was working on how to get across the Rockies. This place was like a base camp for his ascent."

"That's interesting. We all thought he'd run off with wife number five."

"That's a lot of wives. Are there more?"

"Not as of yesterday. No point in going into it. You can imagine how screwed up it is." He twisted his mouth in disgust. "Opal, please." She was running around the armless sculpture.

"Sun's moved around enough to sit out on the porch by now. Maybe Opal would like to run through the sprinklers?"

Opal ran to her Daddy at that suggestion.

When they'd relocated, she said, "So, your reason for calling is the usual, to find out where Clay Holloway disappeared to?"

"Not exactly, no." He sat in a wicker chair on the porch, holding Opal's hand. "My wife, well, I guess it sounds pretty corny but she was the best thing that ever happened to me. Louise come into my life and started with all sorts of questions I didn't know the answers to – questions I should have known the answers to. I've spent a lot of the past ten years working on those answers." He took a sip of apple juice – its tartness explained Opal's twisted mouth. "This is nice but, would it be possible to sugar up Opie's drink?"

"How about some honey from my very own bees?" she asked Opal. To Sonny, "There's a tub round the side. If you fill it with water, I'll bring a few floating things. Would you like that, Opal, a boat in the water? Just down there, close to your dad." She pointed down the concrete path.

"Now where were we?" she asked, once the tub was filled and she was sitting in the matching wicker chair next to Sonny's. Opal stood by the old galvanized tub, frowning down at the plastic boat floating in the water, sipping her new drink.

"I was makin' a speech 'bout my life by way of explaining why we are here. Don't worry, there's not much left. Mr. Holloway sure was good helping to get me home and I appreciated it and all, but in all the hassle and shouting of being back with my step-dad and his wives and all the kids… Anyhow, Louise couldn't believe I'd spent three weeks with Mr. Holloway, that he'd done all that he had done for me, and here I was not giving a, a fig for what happened to him. Not even bothering to learn what he got up to in La Purisima before he disappeared. Here's a national figure, she said, who tried to control the country's currency, and who sounds like an entirely different man to the one you described, and you're not curious about that contradiction?"

"Daddy, can I go in the water?"

"Sure, Opie." He took a sip of the juice. "So… Louise passed about seven months ago. School's out, so we drove out to Centerville – we're in Victorville about an hour northeast of LA – but that didn't go too well. So we extended our road trip." He ran his hand through his reddish brown hair.

"Too many wives?"

"Nah, it's the one husband that's the problem. It's not worth going in to." He studied the floor, did another finger combing, then said, "I won't let Opal sit in that man's lap. That's all. My Mom understands that, except she'll do anything he tells her to. Got tired of policing my little girl."

"Opal seems to be handling things pretty well."

"Nights are the worst with no Momma to put her to bed. Momma could calm her down. All I do is get her excited. Me? Mr. Excitement." He shook his head.

"I'm sorry about your wife."

"Thanks." He exhaled in one reflective burst and said, "I cursed the Good Lord when he took her. But then again I cursed him when Louise got pregnant."

Linda tucked her legs under her and made a point of watching Opal splashing around in the water, still in her jeans and tee shirt.

"Lots of folks come to you looking for what happened to CH?"

"After the anniversary special. Not so much now. I shouldn't complain, most of them are friendly enough, and a lot are interesting. You'll never guess who dropped by last summer."

"Daddy, the boat won't swim anymore."

"Boats float, Opie. Pour the water out of it." He showed Linda his open palms.

"His daughter," Linda said.

"No kidding. How's that even possible?"

"She must have been conceived while he was still in San Francisco – with Madeline. You've heard about her?"

"Sure," Sonny said. "She was the star he pointed his bike at."

"Paige, that's the daughter, was born that first summer of the Void. That makes her twenty-one now. And no question, she is his daughter."

"Did he know?"

"He didn't when I saw him. I guess it's possible that Madeline told him, eventually. She told Paige all right. One thing I can say for certain is that the two have never met – or talked. As of last summer anyway."

"She knocked on your door hoping to find her old man?"

"I guess so."

"That trail's pretty darn cold?"

"Sometimes it's the trying that's most important. Keeps you pointed in the right direction. All she had to go on was this Crook of the Century nonsense. She'd just driven up from New Mexico. Hey, you know what? She stopped off at your farm. On the way up here."

"I didn't hear that. How did she know about me?"

Linda smiled. "Everyone knows about you, even before the special. You've heard about Clay's book, *The Coin Age*? He mentions you in it, his cycling partner across the Great Basin Desert. It's only a few words in the introduction, but two of the words are Sonny and Centerville. With those clues all she had to do was ask at the church."

"Daddy, I'm wet."

"I'll get a towel," Linda said. "I'm afraid I don't have a dryer, unless you count the sun."

"No problem, we've got clothes in the truck. Should I do anything with the water?"

"Leave it for now."

After Opal had been dried off and changed, she wanted to see the woman with no arms again. Now she wanted a snack.

"What Opie wants is my attention. What did Paige say 'bout visiting the farm. In Utah?"

— 238 —

"Not much. I got the impression it was a short visit."

They watched Opal, back to playing at the tub, getting wet again.

"No surprise there," he said, watching Opal and shaking his head. "I'd heard about Mr. Holloway's book. Just didn't know I was in it."

A boy rode his bike down the street, tilting it back so the front wheel was in the air. Opal started up the steps to her Dad, stopped and looked back.

"He sent me a parcel, Clay did. Well, to himself, care of me. I never opened it. I gave it to Paige."

"What was in it?"

She shrugged. "Papers and documents would be my guess. Who knows? Maybe she's decided not to open it."

"Why wouldn't she?"

"Last I heard, he's not officially dead. I hope you have another change of clothes."

"There's always her pjs."

"She sent me a Christmas card, Paige. The usual nice talk. She would have mentioned if she'd found anything important, don't you think?"

"Yeah."

"She doesn't like taking her clothes off, does she?" Linda said, watching Opal.

He shrugged. "She's unsettled." After a pause he said, "If you were Paige?"

"I'd open it. But you know how it is, there are parts of a parent's history you'd rather not know about."

Opal came up and put her head in Sonny's lap, kicking her foot on the porch floor. "Guess we'd better be moving along," Sonny said. "Opie, do you need the bathroom before we go?"

"Why doesn't she have any arms?" Opal cried.

Linda stood up. "Maybe she has them behind her back. Like this." She put her arms behind her so they disappeared.

Opal's eyes danced over Linda's armless torso. Her face brightened and she walked around towards Linda's back. Linda turned away from her.

"No fair."

"Opie, it's a statue not a real person. The artist only wants to show certain things. It's art not a real person."

Sonny nodded to Linda and went inside and moved the sculpture into a bedroom off a small hallway. "Now it's your turn Opie. Bathroom, please."

Opal came back screaming. "She's gone! She's gone! No arms, and now no nothing."

"I always make it worse," Sonny said to Linda. "No matter how hard I think first."

"Maybe it's good to get it all out. Do you want to help us water the vegetables, Opal?"

"No."

"Is it all right if we use the water in the tub to help my vegetables grow? Would you like to see my big red juicy tomatoes?"

"Tomato is a fruit," Opal said.

"Is it really?"

Sonny rolled his eyes and nodded yes at the same time. The burden of having an intelligent child who remembers everything.

Chapter 2

I arrived in La Purisima, New Mexico ready for a change. I was at one of those watershed points when your life gets ahead of you, and some unknowable force is pulling you into the future. I'm not a person who likes being pulled anywhere. Besides, it was the past I wanted to know about.

Walking around La Purisima – its name is from its main church, La Iglesia de La Purísima Concepción de la Santísima Virgen María – I couldn't believe this is where Clay Holloway came to develop his new money. How on earth did he know that this town of 10,000 could form the basis of a nation-conquering currency? What an elaborate hoax that such a small and foreign-looking place, with its adobe walls embellished with poles, ladders, flags, would be the cockpit of the True Dollar.

The accommodation I'd booked was perfect, a smartened up shack the owner called the Goathouse, a modest room with a perfunctory kitchen along one wall. A table with two chairs, a double bed, and a dresser, were all that interrupted the unblinking whiteness of the plaster walls. I plunked down on the bed and focused on the parallel poles that held up the ceiling. No, after four days of pointing my car down the road I needed to move, so I walked around town, finding my bearings. Windows full of art works, postcards, locally-made salsas, pestos, honeys, breads, cheeses. Hard and cracked chilis draped in bunches like local flags on a limp day.

I gravitated to a small sun-dappled plaza, full of trees, low walls like an incomplete maze, plaques, benches. Along one side, a line of stores under a walkway held up by posts. It was too prettied up for gunslingers, but that's what it reminded me of.

The next morning, I drove out to the Mas Grande commune, south of town, right where the goateed guy working the espresso machine – handsome, cold – said it would be. From the road where I parked, the wall appeared dirty, dirt that turned out, on closer inspection, to be graffiti: "Headquarters, World Domination International." "Just say no to Secks appeal." "Evil is the root of all money." "Free Clay Holloway." "Insert Seck in slot and pull the lever – flush."

Behind the wall was a small house with a noticeboard in front of it headed Mas Grande Commune: "This house was the main (bullet hole) meetings and (knife gouge) from where the (ripped out section)."

I bounced and weaved down the dirt track next to the house, as directed by Mr. Espresso. My poor car. I'd already had to buy my nine-year-old Avenger two new tires in Missouri, and a cheapo temporary muffler fix in Wichita. I slowed down and nursed it deeper down the increasingly bumpy dirt track.

A man sat out in front of what looked like two packing crates glued together. He was playing a guitar, his eyes tracking the car and not the frets.

"Howdy," he said, not breaking his musical stride, a slowed down bluegrass number. "I'm Hal."

"Hi, I'm Paige," I said, getting used to a world that didn't jump around in all directions. "Is Mas Grande – "

"Closed down thirteen years ago. Couldn't handle the fame – or the opposite I guess you'd call it. These rabbit hutches still work," he threw his head toward the box behind him, "as what you could call affordable housing." He was sixties with a long gray ponytail, ruddy pock-marked face and pig-like eyes. "You write your name up on the wall?"

"Not my scene."

He chuckled. "So I can tell you a little secret. They whitewash it every spring."

"Who's they?"

"Why the whitewashers of course. Every state's got 'em."

"The greenhouses are gone?"

"No ma'am, they're closer to the river – 'bout a ten-minute walk."

"You've lived here a long time?"

He stood up. "Guess you're one of the curious ones. I'll just put this away and walk you around. If that's what you want."

"If it's not too much trouble."

"Trouble? None of that here now."

I followed his loping stride toward the river, whose faint rush came and went in the still air. The dirt road was so uneven now that it was easier to go single file. The cloudless sky, high and vast, was a deep blue. Hal walked with his hands clasped behind his back like a philosopher.

"If you don't mind my saying so, you aren't the usual tourist we get down here."

"What kind is that?"

Hal stopped and turned to address me. "Conspiracy buffs. Folks that are working backward from a story they've dreamed up that makes more sense than the official one."

"Conspiracies? Really?"

"When you don't understand the whys and wherefores of an event why not blame it on the USG? Some have it that Holloway was a USG agent all along; others that he did the Seck part himself and now the USG's got him locked up somewhere. Supermax is just up the road in Colorado. How else could someone go missing the way he has?"

He set off once more down the road.

"You knew Mr. Holloway."

"Yes I did. I lived here when he arrived. Didn't see him go, but then again no one did."

"What was he like?"

"Like? What's anyone like?" He held that for a moment. "He was different. Driven. Came here on a mission. He come in, took over, raised MG to the sky, raised it even higher conspiring with those San Fran folks, and then when we were really flying we looked around and there was no one in the cockpit. The man was gone. And we were all like, thanks a lot."

"You really think the USG's holding him."

"No, I'm just repeating what others are saying. Some others. This country has what? 320 million citizens? All of them know about Holloway, what he looks like. It's just a convenient way of explaining where he could have got to. The world is a complicated place; people want simple explanations. If there isn't one, they have to go out and make one up."

Now the rush of the river formed the background to our talk. A steep wall of black rock, part of a gorge the river flowed through, appeared as we came over a small rise.

"There's his hacienda, right there." He pointed to another crude box-like structure, similar to his. "He liked to stay down with the HPs. He called them his engine room. What he based his currency on. He was a man apart."

"HPs?"

"Hydroponics. The greenhouses you mentioned earlier. We had four of them, where plants grow in water filled with nutrients. You can see the roof of one of them just over there." He pointed to the south.

"Does anyone live there now?" I said, walking toward the small hut.

"No, too remote. Nowadays everyone wants to drive to their front door." He motioned me to stand back from the door. "Opens out 'cause they're so cozy."

The door complained loudly as he swung it open. One room, maybe twelve by fifteen. A single mattress on a plywood sheet up on single breezeblocks. A large table and chair. Shelves made of planks sitting on more breezeblocks. A window facing the river, a smaller one opposite. Curtains stiff with dust hung from both.

"Holler wasn't the last to live here. It hasn't changed much though," he said. "We called him Holler. Had to have been here. He was a soft-spoken man, but within that soft speech I guess he was hollering a lot of the time. For us Grandees the sun was something to lightly close your eyes to and groove on the colors floating behind your lids. To Holler, the sun was a key element in photosynthesis."

Resuming our walk toward the river, he said, "I suppose you'll want to see one of the HPs."

I followed him off the dirt road, or what had been a dirt road a decade ago, toward the roof he'd pointed out earlier. "The HP's are close to the river for the water. Haven't been used for years as you'll see."

We stood before a dilapidated glass and aluminum structure. About half the glass was missing. Weeds were growing out of the joins were the sidewalls met the floor. Hal rolled out his hand. "Welcome to HP3."

"Engine room 3?"

"That's one way of putting it."

"I guess we can't go in?"

"Not for another dozen years, 'til all the glass falls out." He lifted the door to open it and I poked my head in. Long rows of raised beds with plumbing overhead, and along the floor. Empty, humid.

"That musty smell is from our flower-growing time. After MG fell apart, a core of us persisted here. The generator broke down same year Miss Sally passed. We had no money for a new one. So, we switched to flowers, grown the old-fashioned way with soil and with water from the river. Worked for a while."

"It seems crazy that this falling-down structure is a key to a national currency." I shut the HP3 door. "What are you chuckling about?"

"Holler lecturing, it's just come back to me. A religion starts, he said, by a prophet having a vision, then selling that vision eyeball to eyeball. That's the only way people will believe in something radically new. Paper money is the same. His Seck would need to start locally, and sold eyeball to eyeball." He looked down, shaking his head. "How did he figure out this stuff?"

We stood staring at HP3 for a long time. I don't think either of us was really looking at it.

"All this is part of a 500-acre parcel called the Flying W Ranch," Hal said, his arm doing a long arc around us. We were walking toward the river again. "Back in the day it was owned by one of Elpy's most powerful ladies, Miss Sally Werner. Why did Miss Sally pay for these greenhouses? Holler could tell you. He got on with her, spent a lot of time up at her ranch house. For sure she had the money, 'cept she was tighter than a – well, never mind what she was tighter than. She liked to promote Elpy and its businesses, just not with her money."

"The greenhouses came in before Mr. Holloway arrived?"

"Yes ma'am. By about two years. Another explanation is that Miss Sally could see the future. Come the Void she had her steady stream of produce – that's what we paid her with for her investment – and she had a hundred Grandees ready to protect her interests."

"If this is the Rio Grande," I said, when we finally reached the river, "that must be Mexico?" I pointed to the opposite bank. The river coursed by, a sparkling blue against the steep brown hills opposite, a sharp black rock face to the north, and, where we stood, an open rock-strewn area, the only reasonably flat land on view. Above this rugged scene an implacable blue ache of a sky, a western sky as I was learning. To call it cloudless would be admitting to the possibility of clouds.

"Two hundred years ago you would have been right. The river's got to flow another coupla hundred miles before it touches on Mexico."

There was something hypnotizing about the fast-running blue water, so clearly from another, alpine, world, and not this arid rocky one. We sat on separate upended logs placed as seats for river watching. "Those conspiracy theories you mentioned – do you buy the official story? Clay Holloway, national conman?"

"I had a ring side seat." He looked off to the south for an answer. "No, Holler wasn't any villain. But as I said before it's a complicated story. If you're like everyone else – wanting simple – you'll be disappointed."

"I'm here because…" I wanted to tell him that Clay Holloway was my father. I couldn't. Mom had drilled into me from when I was eleven that I must keep quiet about him. Kids can be cruel, was how she put it. In any case, out here I would learn a lot more by keeping my relationship with Clay Holloway out of the way. "I'm here with an open mind."

"Fair enough. There are many things about him that are hard to explain. How he showed up, for example. He came charging into town as if he knew exactly where to go and what needed to be done. I mean, how? And his departure was hard to figure out too. He does his big deal with San Francisco with his mysterious Mr. Sottovoce, and when the merged currencies took off and all of sudden Elpie was like the center of the universe, puff, a smoke bomb. When it clears the maestro is gone, never to be heard from again. Don't get me wrong, I understand why he had to get out, and make way for the new bosses. I even kinda understand why he didn't say good-bye. Still, he could have trusted us with his secret. We worked hard for him. Very hard."

"You could say you worked hard for the country."

"And it's the country's story now," he said. "They're the winners so they get to write the history. That means Ol' Holler has to be the loser. USG couldn't risk him going around giving interviews and taking credit."

"Wait a minute, you're sounding like a conspiracy guy now."

He shrugged. "I'm just trying to give you the different points of view. And I'm not going to invent stuff to make the story any simpler."

To bolster my dwindling travel fund, I got a job waitressing at a café three blocks from the plaza. If I was careful I could break even after room and board, the latter being two meals at the café on the five days I worked there.

"Yep, I knew Clay Holloway. Never slept with him, though," Stacey was a fellow waitress. After the lunch wind-down, I took to joining her in the alley behind the café. That first greedy inhale on her cigarette seemed almost indecent. She was up in her forties, beaten down, blonde hair chopped more than cut at the neck, bangs up top similar. I always picture her with dumpsters in the background.

"What?"

"Sex, honey. You ought to try it. At Mas Grande it was change partners. He didn't go in for that kind of thing. Made us feel uncomfortable."

"You watched him hatch his plan to take over the country? You saw all that happen?"

"It drives me crazy, so I don't think about it," she said, taking a long drag. "Clay Holloway as Mr. Evil." After a moment's pause she blew smoke out her nose in one long and even stream. "And these!" Reaching into her apron she pulled out some tip money. "True Dollars! What crap! If they were true you wouldn't have to say that would you? It's like, like those communist countries that had "democratic" in their names. Or restaurants that say they're *world famous*." She took another drag with her ample, twisted lips. "Clay worked his ass off; now he's a cross between Hitler and a hedge fund manager. Give me a break."

She took a last hit, scrunched the butt with a comfortable waitressing shoe. "You know what, hon? I've been to enough political speeches to know that when people want to believe something, well, small things like facts, logic, common sense don't slow them down all that much. They'll overlook the obvious in their stampede to believe what they want to believe."

"You sound like the voice of experience."

"You can't fight it. The people have decided to believe this crock. The Great American Come-back. The True Dollar triumphs over all. You've read Clay's book I take it. Well, you're one of the precious few. Most of the first run is toilet paper by now." She picked a fleck of tobacco off her lip, flicked it. "What I'd like to do is go back to the old Mas Grande, back when we were a self-sufficient commune, back to the simple days of back-stabbing bureaucracy and meaningless partner-swapping. If only we could move it to some island, somewhere protected from these national delusions, lies and self-serving egomaniacs."

"So...Clay Holloway was a good man?"

"Sweetheart, I'd tell you he was a Great American if that didn't put him in the same corral as a whole bunch of self-promoting posers, bucking and broncing when the cameras are on them."

I met all sorts of interesting people in Purie – I prefer that nickname to Elpy – and if college wasn't calling who knows how long I might have stayed. Judge Newton, one of the café's best customers, was a wily old man with slow knowing eyes, blotches on his bald head and a weary smile that said, Oh well. One lunch time, after all the orders had been delivered, we got to talking.

"You knew Miss Sally?"

"Yes. She and I go way back to when I was a boy caught trespassing on her ranch. She was a tough woman, fierce in protecting her interests, the kind you didn't want to make an enemy of, that's for sure. But once you were allowed into her hacienda she was pleasant, and funny. And loyal, she'd stand by you, no question."

"She was loyal to Clay Holloway?"

"That's right. That was Holloway's big advantage. Miss Sally didn't get on with the former commune leader, the one Holloway deposed – or so they say." The Judge took a sip of his tepid coffee.

"Let me fill that up for you."

He waved that away. "I didn't know Sally well until later. If you wanted to get her going just mention Holloway and the raw deal he got. Only time I've heard her curse."

"She could have used her power to change that, that perception."

"No, not Sally," the judge said. "She sat in her fortress cursing the world in a hundred ways. Everything outside her 500 acres was always going to the dogs."

"Nobody I've talked to here seems to believe in Mr. Holloway's bad rep. Yet it persists."

He shrugged. "The story's been distilled into a myth. The nation has its self-image to consider. And that self-image took a major hit with the Void. Believe me, it was a close-run thing. If you examine the details two things hit you. First, the brilliance of what Holloway did. The way he built up the Seck and then incrementally brought the USG back into the picture. You had to have been here. Two years of sound and fury from Washington, people suffering through privation and terrible winters. How could you ever restore faith in the machinery of government? And yet he did it."

"And the second?"

"Second is that there are too many things that are – I don't know whether to call them mysteries or miracles. I imagine history is full of incidents where blind luck was a factor, and over a few millennia there will be a couple of times when we've flipped ten heads in a row. You know, blind luck on a large scale. That may have been the Holloway story."

"And this myth has no room for Holloway as a national hero?"

"Maybe one day. But myths are difficult to shift."

"You don't sound hopeful."

"Take me," the judge said, playing with his cold cup of coffee. "I knew Holloway. Not well, but I knew him. Seemed like a decent enough fellow. Sitting here nearly twenty years later what do I think of him? Generally positive, but all the unexplained stuff gets in the way of any kind of warm glow. It's like he's standing over there and you want to go over and thank him for all he's done, except there's this swamp in the way. So the best you can do is wave from the distance."

I had never been an outdoors type, not an active one. But months of hiking, rafting, and bike riding put a glow on my face and suffused me with well-being. Different places make you want different things and if I had to come up with one word to sum up La Purisima it would be "less". A beer sitting with my back against the sun-warmed adobe wall of the Goathouse as the evening took hold was better than any number of Manhattan dinners. This was the life, simple, easy. I had planned to stay for a month; I tore myself away after four, missing out on the Fall term at UMass. I can always return to La Purisima, I told myself. Maybe I even believed it.

Chapter 3

"Jerry?" Uncle Tad said, answering the door, and rubbing his eyes, sleepy, even though it was one in the afternoon. "What are you doing here?"

"Stopping by – on my way from here to there."

"There being where?"

"Wendover."

"What are you? Sixteen?"

"Closer to seventeen," Sonny said.

"Uh huh." Tad stood in the doorway, considering, or waking up, or both. "Running away from home. And to Wendover? That's like two acts of desperation right there."

"Maybe."

He motioned the boy in, combing his sleep-disturbed hair with his fingers. "Do you drink coffee? I sure as hell need some."

Sonny sat stiffly on the incongruous sofa, the kind with skirts hiding the gap between its base and the floor.

"Hey, I'm not saying as I blame you," Tad said. "Your step-pa is a first class...well I don't have to tell you what he is."

"Comes a time when you have to face up to the facts. I always thought when I was old enough I could take Mom away from that ratbag."

"What happened?"

"Had a talk with her. Tried on the idea of how nice it would be to do what she wanted, not having to ask for permission all the time. I reckon she knew what I was getting at." Sonny shook his head. "Oh she said, I don't think Mr. Williams would allow me to leave the farm." In a falsetto he said, "He is so much wiser than I'll ever be." Back to his normal voice, one that still squeaked occasionally. "I didn't know what to do first, puke or get out."

"Sounds like you hit adulthood without a chute."

"I always thought she was faking it, that some part of her was anyway. That I just needed to get old enough to escort her off the premises, so to speak. But, no, she seems happy – no that's not the right word, resolved? – to act as servant to that man."

"Listen bud, I'll let you in on a little secret. Out here in the adult world? Everyone's faking it."

"How are you faking it?" Uncle Tad had always been so free, so pleasure-driven. Beer. Cycles. Women. Food and sleep slotted in, as and when.

"You remember my ex Nadine? I'm pretending I don't miss her. Don't get me wrong, there's a ton of stuff connected to her I don't miss at all. You see the problem is you gotta live with that shit 24/7. The good stuff? That's like lines of coke spread randomly…uh oh." He raised his hand in oath-taking mode. "That's in the past now."

"Your place looks a lot tidier than last time."

"That's what running out of beer does to you," he said, slowly shaking his head. "That home brew stuff…Tell you what I've come to realize: it wasn't about drinking beer; it was about popping those tops, like some alcohol-run clock that marked my progress through the day."

"Still ridin' your Chief?"

"Yep. Old Chief and I been running south at night. Just got back this morning in actual fact."

"South, huh?"

"Don't usually do night runs anymore. The highway to the south is opening up. There's big noise down there and it's comin' this way. Forking west out of New Mexico and up this side of the Rockies. Let me show you something." He stood up from his armchair, reached into his jeans pocket and pulled out a coin, cupped it in his hand as if a dying bird. "Here's the tree side. See? And check out this lady." Flipping it over he held it nearer to Sonny to show an Indian woman whose fierce glare challenged the viewer to dare take issue with her or the coin she represented. "You know how one of our early flags said, Don't tread on me? This Indian lady is on the same page. I love it. I LOVE it! No Latin shit. No religious shit neither. Just a thousand-yard stare. It's what the message of any country should be. Do *not* fuck with us. We're tight."

"What do you mean 'country'?"

"Secks are taking over in New Mexico."

Sonny took the coin. It was heavier than normal coins, larger, its rim slightly rough and its reeded edge more pronounced, like micro teeth of a gear.

"Seck for Sequoia, the tree on the coin. I tell you, it's reached the point where everything's flipped. In one finger-snap. People have gone from frowning at the Indian lady and saying what the hell's this? To saying, 'I want that. I want as many of those as possible.'" He made a fist and shook it in a vague right-on way. "Sound familiar? Sound like the country we used to live in?"

"So why are you making these runs?"

"Good question. I heard the rumor and I had to go, like there was a new star and it was my destiny to follow it. I got there, saw the coin and just flat-ass loved it. And because they got a working currency down there they got a lot more stuff than here. I bring some of it back to trade." He grabbed the coin, tossed it up and snatched it greedily out of the air. "These first coins will be collectors' items one day."

After Sonny cleaned up in the bathroom from his five-hour bike ride, Tad said, "What's in Wendover?"

"You remember Dr. Kouri?"

"'Course I remember her. Tried to nail her, didn't I? Never dated an Arab lady before."

"You? Dr. Kouri?"

"Why not? Let me give you some advice – now that you're an adult. If ever you're interested in a lady, any lady, always let her know. Every damn time. It is your obligation to help keep the planet spinning along. Nothing too obvious, you gotta treat them like delicate little birds that might fly away unless all your moves are slow and smooth. Got it?"

"Yes sir, except for the planet part."

"Never, ever, call me sir. Makes me feel about…well as old as I am, but let that pass. My point is that I did a number on the good doc. Enough for her to know I was interested. Enough for her to be flattered. But easy enough for her to wave it away with a laugh. Good healthy flirting. You never know where it can lead."

"What if I don't see any women I'm interested in?"

"You need to get out more. As they say, plenty a fish in the sea. Not too many fish in Wendover, though. Anyhow you haven't said why you're going there. Auditioning for a new Ma?"

"There's lots of people I need to thank. Without Dr. Kouri, the Evjus, all the other folks…and there's you."

"After you say thanks, you're going to be standing there saying, Oh shit, I'm in Wendover."

"There's a ranch there. They work with solar panels. They had enough power to make the ice that kept my head from swelling too much." Sonny stood up and started pacing around. "Ever since I heard about that ranch, about them experimenting, I've been restless, wanting to go there. Show up and volunteer. I want to learn everything about solar."

"Okay. I can get you there in less than two hours. That's the fast part. Slow part is waitin' on some corn juice. Dude owes me three gallons."

"What on I-80? Is that safe?"

"It's changing fast. Each time I've gone down to New Mexico the roads have been safer, more open. Down there the convoy guards leave drivers, bikers, cyclists, even peds, alone. Don't ask me how but they have more gas down there. That's starting to happen here. Big time. It's like, like what? The sky getting lighter before the sun actually shows its ass. And the sun's the Seck."

"The fuel for the Chief – "

"Don't worry, he'll pay. Always has."

While they waited three days for fuel, Sonny helped put new siding on the western, the windward side of Tad's small home, the materials borrowed from an abandoned house down the rough gravel road out into the salt wastes. On one of his breaks he rode his bike a couple of miles out to I-80 to watch the convoys go by. He hadn't had much problem coming the forty-five miles from Centerville on non-highway roads, and put that down to Utah and its efficiency. Standing well off the shoulder the first convoy ignored him, all eight GI guards staring stonily forward. Closer in, the next convoy ignored him too. Pedaling slowly along the Interstate, he could hear the next convoy bearing down on him, louder and louder. Three weeks of experience on this highway demanded he pull over and play it safe. He gritted his teeth and pedaled on, hunching his shoulders in expectation of a loud horn as the first 18-wheeler snorted just behind him. But there was no horn. When it drew level the semi was half over in the next lane, giving him a wide berth, the seven other big rigs following suit. He pumped his bike with a wild sense of freedom. To be valued as a human being! Not just some tin can on a fence for target practice. And all the way back to Tad's – his exuberance had taken him miles down the highway – he couldn't get that Indian lady's visage out of his head.

"We're gonna take Wendover on Plan A," Tad said, just back with three gallons of fuel in his tank. "That means a mosquito ride in the daytime."

"What's that?"

"You'll see."

Once on I-80 Tad cruised westward at about 80 mph. Within

twenty minutes the end truck in an eight-rig convoy came into view. Tad gunned it, ninety, one hundred, one ten, then braked sharply in the last truck's shade, and set about slipstreaming it at sixty-five.

"Blind spot," he yelled, his voice fighting the noise of the grinding truck, the howling Chief, and all the wind.

"Damn it," Tad yelled after forty minutes. Or maybe Sonny read those words into his head shake. The rear doors they'd been staring at above the Kansas license plate were slowing down. "I hate that fucking thing," he added, at thirty.

"What?"

"Hang on."

They shot out of the shadows just as the 18-wheelers were coming to a stop and roared past the trucks, ten miles per hour faster per truck. At the head of the convoy the lead driver pushed his door open as they growled by at ninety. Tad veered the bike to the fast lane, back to the slow lane, weaving until out of rifle range, and settled in at sixty-five.

"What's this thing the trucks stopped for, the one you hate so much," Sonny asked, when they pulled in at Dr. Kouri's house

"You didn't see it?"

"See what?"

"Well, you didn't miss much, that's for damn sure. Out in the middle of nowhere, in the middle of the salt flats they got a, a what? A statue? A structure? It's a big cement tower with balls hanging down from the top. Folks pull over because they think they're hallucinating. Whoever designed the thing, he's the one on acid. It's called the Tree of Life."

"Doesn't sound worth hating."

"Nah, you're right. The state does one wild thing and they have to set it way off by itself. Never mind."

"Aren't you comin' in?" Sonny asked.

"Nah, got some other folks to call on here. Please give the Doc my warmest."

Dr. Meta Kouri came out onto her small cement porch, the Chief's growl calling to her. Tad shook Sonny's hand, a business-like shake, then saluted towards Dr. Kouri and thundered down the road.

"Really, he likes you," Sonny said to her as the bike's roar faded away.

"Yes, I know."

Chapter 4

I'd had an epiphany in New Mexico, one of several: my major in Business Studies was more an anti-Mom, pro-Dad statement than an expression of my real interests and passions. I spent three months, starting in late October, in Amherst getting ready for my debut as an English Major. Each morning I arrived at the UMass library by ten. I had my favorite cubby hole on the eighth floor where I'd spend most of my time until lunch working on Dad's story. The parcel Linda Margossian had given me contained five notebooks, mainly Dad's retrospective notes about his bike trip, a little bit about his marriage and a few random thoughts, phrases and ideas. The parcel was postmarked Fort Collins in Colorado and franked exactly three years from the announcement of the Big Jump, the Seck's merger with the San Francisco-based currency, the Condo.

At first I struggled to decipher his forceful scrawl, slowly transcribing the result in my computer pad. After lunch I'd go over literary criticism books, covering novels on next quarter's syllabus. I spent the nights feeding that literary criticism hopper with new novels.

I met Steve in the library. He was drumming his fingers on the table top as he read. I asked him to stop, a little too harshly. After that we couldn't study near each other but we had lunch together on those days he came to the library. He was handsome, dark hair and deep set eyes over which fluttered eyelashes of almost effeminate delicacy and length. We liked each other. My relations with previous boyfriends had been like polite conversations in the foyer; Steve was down in the cellar, working on the furnace. Only, Steve had just broken up with a long-term girlfriend, Lisa, and needed time to get over it. He made it clear to me: he wasn't ready to follow through on what wanted to flow between us. And me? Half the time going further with Steve felt like an abandonment of Dad. And holding back made our relations less complicated, if not frustrating.

One week Steve didn't appear at my cubbyhole. I didn't even have his number. During that week I finished Dad's notebooks. Transcribing them made me feel that I was getting to know him, building up my allegiance to him, to the point where on some days I wanted to stand up in the Student Union, where I had lunch, and yell, "I am Clay Holloway's daughter."

Teasing out the meaning in his handwriting, it was as if Dad grew before my eyes, even as I shrank. "Two old souls, married in a previous life" the writing said – there were even details of their last night together. And I was the product of these two old souls on that night. Too much information, from too many angles.

And there was Luce. Not only the fact of him, but his talk of sexacts and daughters in different worlds. Half the time I wondered whether I was the daughter of a late 19th century couple who combined one last time to create me, real in their world, transient in this one. Naturally I wouldn't be allowed to meet my own father; that would complete a circuit that lit a light that would take me out of this shadow world. If only I could get back to 1900 or whenever, or find a new world with a better story, one that respected me and my future.

I must have been desperate because I called Mom, who was staying in a villa in Martinique with her new husband, Adrian – Adrian Cassel, the bigshot scriptwriter and film director. I couldn't tell Mom about the notebooks. Never mind any promises from her, she'd still tell Cassel. He'd either want to turn Dad's story into a film, or tip off five eminent history professors who would come running to pore over the notebooks. It was all too private, and even if I got by that there was the Luce bombshell to consider. It was too great a national secret to keep to myself; I couldn't see how I could share it though, not even with Steve.

"How'd you find out where I lived?" Steve said, poking his dishevelled head around the door, open about a foot to keep the cold out.

"You don't want to see me?"

"I think you know the answer to that," he said, his eyes softening as they met mine.

"You're glad to see me. I'm that way with you. Isn't that good? Shouldn't that be enough?"

"If I was a junkie and you were a dealer ...?"

I glanced at those lashes. "Can I come in for a minute?" I stood on the porch of the sagging house, protected from the light snow, but not from a cold that seeped through every possible defense.

He opened the door wider and swept me in with an exaggeratedly courtly arm.

"I've come because you're the only person I can talk to," I said. "That's not something to throw away lightly."

"You need to talk?"

"That's right, I've come here to dump on you," I said, trying on a light smile.

"You must be cold. Did you walk here? I'll make something hot."

The house was only marginally warmer than outside. Its other residents were off for Christmas, and it was heated just enough to keep the pipes from freezing. He scrounged around in the large kitchen, found a jar of instant coffee. "Is it about those notebooks?" he asked, putting water in the kettle. He had seen them on the library table.

"Not now, I need to warm up first." I was shivering. One quick call to Adrian Cassel's New York travel agent and I could have been on the next flight to shirtsleeves and sunglasses.

Getting into bed may well have started as a survival technique. His single bed took up most of the floor in a closet-sized room, stacks of books all around. Lots of pillows. The only place to work was in or on the bed.

Even under the covers, feet like blocks of ice, it was a challenge to warm up. Steve rubbed my feet, my hands, no sense of rush for the prize. I relaxed under his practiced care, floated. He stayed up top, running a light hand up and down my back as his lips went exploring. His hot, moist breath, the nibbles, little bites, the soft pulls on the lobe, now a few bass grunts. I turned my head away, he got the message, enough with the ear. He was in the flow, eyes lightly closed, his rhythm, his varying caresses, his destinations and the little dances he performed there. He came back to the ear, more breathing and bass grunts there. I had been so close to being lost in the moment, but that was gone. I wanted to snap, "I'm me! Not her."

Not that there weren't enough nice things happening.

Finally, he got the ear message. The show had drifted south anyway, into another dance with Lisa: his caresses and kisses finely calibrated to her breasts, not mine.

Hard at work, digging for the prize, he called out terse endearments – sweet something or other, baby something else, and something about sugar and a candyman. Sink! Forgive! I told myself. No, forgive first, then sink! But a small part of me listened for what next semi-dirty thing came out of his mouth, those shared lover's names. As the ghost in this ménage a trois I wanted it to be worse: filthy, cruel.

"So..." he said, up on one elbow, "Hi."

"Hi."

"Are you okay?" he said. Steve remains the most empathetic man I've ever been with.

"I'm fine," I said, wondering for the twentieth time about Luce's sexact story. Our lovemaking, even with an ex-girlfriend butting in, had been in a different league to all my previous episodes and escapades. With Steve, once we got past Lisa, it would be natural, almost predestined. So I believed – or hoped. And yet, all this shared, determined and frenzied effort, it only seemed reasonable it would result in something more than transient nerve tingling.

"What are you thinking about?"

"Babies." I broke out laughing. His look just then.

"You shouldn't joke about things like that."

"I wasn't joking," I said. "But don't worry, I'm not brooding or anything."

"It's a sensitive subject, that what we've just done could create another being who one day will be selling life insurance policies, and…well, you know."

"Life insurance? She could be a great scientist or poet."

"I'm going with the odds." He sounded bitter.

I had come for comfort, human warmth, the sympathies of a man who bothered to wonder about my side of things. And I got it. So why did I leave feeling worse? I'd barged in on Steve's world only to lose out to a ghost, the ghost of girlfriend past. What did that say about the shadow world I was struggling to emerge from?

Chapter 5

Manleigh, Chelsea and Louise were driving from Colorado to California – Chelsea to start her second year at the University of San Francisco; Manleigh to start her first, and take a part time shot at a modelling career. They would drop Louise off in Sacramento for a bus north to Corvalis, where she was starting a Marine Biology degree at Oregon State. They were in their early twenties, their education stalled by the Void. Universities, just getting back to something resembling normal, were pragmatic toward a generation that had missed blocks of school. Admission was solely based on a dumbed-down SAT and a personal essay.

Two years after the True Dollar supplanted the Secondo – the merged Seck/Condo currency – commerce still had its rough edges. Only a few chain stores and fewer gas stations took credit cards. Cash was king, but even if you were lucky enough to have a nice wad of True Dollars there was often not much to buy. Scarce items from overseas, especially shoes, medicines, and anything that plugged into a socket were snapped up from the delivery trucks. More importantly for the three travelers, gas supply was spotty. At a station flying a green flag you pulled in, even if you still had half a tank. Crossing the Great Basin Desert could mean waiting at strategic stops like Wendover, Elko, Winnemucca or Reno until the next tanker truck pulled into town.

"Lulu, are you sure about this ranch?" Manleigh asked.

"C'mon it sounds interesting," Louise said. "I'm betting if we learn to sail and triple up on a room we can swing it."

"I don't get it," the third girl, Chelsea, said. "We can't sail until tomorrow, so we're going do what? Drive to the Bay Area tomorrow night? Ten hours? We'll wind up in a ravine somewhere."

Manleigh, turned off the freeway to look for gas. "I say if there's gas here we take that as a sign and go for it, to the ranch that is." They'd done one previous road trip, much shorter, to Yellowstone. Manleigh and Chelsea proved more than capable of doubling up – and not with each other. Louise slept in the car.

They had no problem finding gas in Wendover but was it ever expensive. They bought enough to get them to Winnemucca, in case Elko was short.

"I bet that Ranch will bait and switch us," Chelsea said. "They say it's reduced rates but there will be a catch. There has to be a catch."

"Baited and switched, how painful is that?" Manleigh said, in her role as the outrageous one.

The Morgenstern Ranch was up on a bluff overlooking the salt flats. "The winds are blowing up good in the afternoons," Kevin the substitute front desk clerk said, answering Louise's question about rate reductions. "So you ladies learn to sail in the morning and the afternoon winds kick up as forecast you can probably reduce our room charge by a lot."

"What's a lot?"

"Best might be thirty percent, but don't take that to the bank."

Manleigh proceeded to discuss the rate that would be reduced. "We're only poor college girls."

After the business side of checking in was finished, Chelsea said, "Why can't we learn to sail now?"

"Great idea, Chelse," Manleigh said, putting her tanned arm on the reception counter and leaning in with a flirty smile.

"It says here," Louise said, reading from a brochure, "you reserve the right to assign the craft. What if we get one that has a deflated tire, or bad windings in its alternator?"

"Yeah, we need to generate all the electricity we possibly can," Chelsea said, finally warming to the spirit of the enterprise.

"All our craft are well-maintained, ma'am. Is it all three of you?" Kevin said, picking up the phone. "I'll see what I can do. You'll have to be quick, it's only two hours 'til sundown."

After he'd helped them with their luggage, he took them down to the docks where the Sun Sieve II was being readied. The girls hopped on board. Their pilot, Tim, looked up into the sky. "I hope you ladies are fast learners. We haven't got much time." His eyes met Manleigh's, moved away quickly. "Sonny, are we set?"

Sonny nodded, untied the line and pushed the craft away from the dock as Tim worked the ropes, deputizing Manleigh to take the helm. The wind grabbed the sail and they were off with a jerk. "We make power two ways," Tim shouted over the noise from the sail and the growling purr of the four tires. "The sail is embedded with solar material just like your normal solar panel. And the tires generate electricity as they turn."

"What's the ratio," Louise asked.

"Depends on the speed, sun angle, all sorts of variables. And the sails soak up the sun when the craft is docked. That's why our mast folds down so we can work the angles." He took the helm now and set a tighter line, the windward tires lifting off the salt flats. "But much more from the tires."

"Do we get any credit for this ride?" Manleigh asked.

"That's not my decision ma'am."

"But you can put in a good word? For us?"

Tim turned to Sonny, who was trimming the sail.

"You're probably pretty darn good at making your own case, ma'am," Sonny said.

The craft shot east toward the blinding light off the salt crystals, both windward tires four feet off the flats, the passengers and Sonny hiked out on the raised side as counterweights.

"It's too bad we're so petite and slim," Chelsea shouted, ostensibly to Louise and Manleigh.

Wind direction, the angles of attack, the no-go zone, what to do if in trouble – Tim and Sonny rushed through the standard intro course. The craft hummed and roared out to the east, further and further away. Finally, they looped around and Sonny explained how to work back against the wind.

"Tomorrow, when you're in one of the small craft," Sonny said, "you gotta pay careful attention to how far downwind you go. You see that pole over there with the red flag? That's the last chance saloon. You get this far, you turn back, no question. Okay?"

"What if we flip the thing?" Louise said.

"That's hard to do in the smaller craft. You'll be in leathers and a helmet. If it happens relax and roll with it."

"Can't we take this one?" Manleigh asked. "Faster means more power doesn't it? We need to sell back as much juice as possible."

"Takes a week to get certified on these babies," Tim said.

When they got back to the dock Chelsea said, "How much did we earn?"

"I can make a rough calculation. Give me a minute," Tim said. "Sonny will have a more accurate measure once he hooks up and off-loads from the batteries."

"What's wrong with him?" Manleigh asked Sonny as he hooked up the power cable to the Sun Sieve II.

"He's married. It would be good if you ladies respected that."

"Are you trying to say we're not," Louise, standing with Manleigh, said.

"I'm just explaining things, okay. From Tim's side. That's all."

After Manleigh drifted off, Louise said, "That was a little harsh."

"I'm not good at being subtle." He half-met her eyes. "Neither is your friend over there."

"Moving right along," Louise said, peering at the meter above the power socket the cable fitted into, "how do you decide the tire size and craft dimensions in relation to the sail area? And mast height? Are there equations that optimize that?"

"We do most of our optimizing right out here on the salt flats – as far as I know. There's an aeronautical engineer in Seattle we talk to – sometimes."

"But that's inefficient, isn't it? Building different sizes, trying on bigger tires, then smaller ones. There will come a point where it doesn't make any sense to build a bigger craft. Right?"

Sonny was about to speak when Louise put her hand on his arm. "And please, it's Louise, not ma'am. Okay?"

"I'll do some asking and try to have an answer before you leave. It's tomorrow, isn't it?"

"Yep, in the evening." Manleigh and Chelsea were standing on the wooden walkway that led back to Morgenstern Ranch's hotel, calling her to leave. "Oh, one last question. I'm skipping over the others by the way. What happened to Sun Sieve I?"

"Guess we needed your equations." He gave her a shy smile. "Louise."

"It's not right," Sonny told Louise the next morning as he helped her set up her craft. "That poor mother. Stuck behind with her baby while the husband goes after…your friend."

"Do you think I'm happy about it. Chelsea and I stuck in the bar for hours while Manleigh commandeers our room," Louise said. "Being hit up left and right by eco-schmucks too cheap to buy us a drink. And what about you? Why don't you do something about it?" Louise grabbed the halyard and prepared to hoist the sail. "Sorry, I'm a bit of a grouch this morning."

"Me? She's your friend."

"Believe me, Chelsea and I have covered the woman's angle. It's time to sail closer to the wind."

"Closer to what wind?"

"Tell Romeo what a rat he is. It's not like he can complain about it."

No way was he going to poke his nose in someone's personal affairs. Except this woman standing next to him had him contemplating just that. "Uh, if you ladies care to stay another night, on us, we were wondering if you'd be interested in trying our new trail. You and Chelsea – and Manleigh, if she can still walk." When Louise didn't say anything right away he added, just as she started to talk, "we, uh, will have you ready to roll west by noon. Maybe even earlier."

"Who's we?"

"It's the bath tub hike," he said, focused on his speech. "It's all about this area 15,000 years ago, when it was a huge lake."

"You didn't say who 'we' is. But sure, if the others are okay with another night. Well, if Chelsea is."

"We want to see what kind of appetite our guests might have for a hike like this. It will be interesting, but you have to be in good shape. It's either two or six miles depending on whether we do the loop trail or not."

"Are there others?"

"Seven so far. I'm kind of nervous to be speaking in front of so many people. It would be – good to have you along."

She smiled at him.

The group of ten hiked up the arduous 800-foot ascent of the bathtub rings in the early morning before the heat took hold. Sonny, who had ranged all over these mountains, had devised a six-mile loop trail that showed many of the ancient lake's secrets.

"Here we have the Bonneville ring" he started. "The whole set up was like a bath tub. The lake level couldn't go any higher than this ring because there was an overflow, in this case a pass up in Idaho. About 12,000 years ago something snapped up at that pass and three hundred feet of this huge lake charged through the lowered pass and out through Idaho, then Oregon and Washington. You saw the ring down below, that's from after the huge flood, when the lake was at the lower level."

"Isn't that about the time the first Indians arrived?" A fiftyish, professorial man asked.

"Yes sir, I believe that's right. There's some thought that others got to the Americas before that. I certainly haven't been able to find any evidence of Indians up at the Bonneville level."

Four of the hikers and Karen from the Ranch's admin department, hiked straight back down from the summit. Sonny with Louise, the Professor, and a young couple continued on the loop trail.

"This here is rattlesnake alley," Sonny said. "Let's see what we got." He used a pole to probe among loose rocks, levered up a large slab, then he stooped down and came up holding a twisting rattler by its head. "Poor little guy. He's not fully grown yet – about a year old."

"How do you know it's a he?" Louise asked.

"I'm guessing. The tail looks longer. To really find out you need two people, one to hold the head so it doesn't strike, the other to examine the tail area. Any volunteers."

"No way," said the young woman, taking her boyfriend's hand.

Now a first rattle. All the hikers except Louise stepped back, then back further.

"There's a nice view from just over there," Sonny called, pointing with his snake-free arm.

"What do you do with him now?" Louise asked, when she was alone with Sonny.

"Put him under Manleigh's pillow."

"I guess you must have had words with Romeo. Was she ever fuming."

"She knows it was me?"

"I can't think of any other reason she'd call you a…never mind what she called you. Anyway, you did the right thing." She cocked her hips the other way. "I'm proud of you."

Sonny put the snake down, securing its head with the pole until he was out of range. "Sure as hell ruined *his* morning."

"We're thinking of a mountain bike trail up and along and down these ledges." Sonny told the group after Louise and he had rejoined it at the scenic overlook. "Those steps you see were made by the wave action of the lake when it was at different levels." Out to the east the strengthening light jumped and dazzled and blinded over the salt flats. The dim outline of the Wasatch range, the western margin of the Rocky Mountains, was lost in the glare. It was his idea, modifying bikes so they generated electricity on their downward run. It fit with the Morgenstern Ranch theme and now that Louise had filled his head with thoughts of equations there must be a way to calculate the net energy produced.

"It looks exactly like our lakes when we have a bad drought," the boyfriend said.

They trekked down to what had been a beach 12,000 years ago. "Talk about climate change," the professor said. "All this happened before cars and greenhouse gases and all that. Isn't that staring your eco-ranch in the face? That all this solar stuff won't make any difference in the long run?"

"Why burn a finite resource and pollute our planet when the sun can do all that from 93 million miles away?" Sonny said. "Clean and efficient is our motto."

The professor, if that's what he was, wanted his say. "Still, isn't my point valid? With the wide-scale natural changes we see right here before us, whatever man does is almost irrelevant."

"I'd have to disagree," Sonny said, shifting on his feet. "Yes, 15,000 years ago we would be standing here looking out at a vast lake, and yes, over the course of thousands of years that water shrank and shrank, until now it's a puddle on the bathroom floor called the Great Salt Lake. But that process happened over thousands of years; global warming threatens the next fifty to a hundred."

"I want to see some of these fossils you promised us," Louise butted in. "You fellas can solve the world's problems back at the ranch."

The fossil field was down the loop trail, a vast pile of shale. Sonny squatted down by a stack of shale slabs and showed them how to use a rock pick to split open a slab, like wedging open a fused book in the hope of finding a pressed flower – in this case fossils.

"Here we go," he said, hammering at a block of shale with his pick. "See this critter here?" he said after several attempts, pointing to an oval-shaped fossil with a pronounced spine and leaf-like lines perpendicular to it. "This critter died and sank into the bottom of an ancient sea, then more sediment came on top of him until he was crushed and preserved. See how the layer I've just pried open is moist? This water has been trapped in here like this for up to 500 million years. That's how old this trilobite is."

"And mankind has had, maybe, 6,000 years of civilization," Louise said.

Sonny was walking past the administration building when Kevin came out and waved Sonny over. "Your friend's been abandoned," Kevin said.

"Huh, what friend?" Sonny said, in a hurry to get back to his main job, out at the solar crafts.

Kevin pulled a card out of his shirt pocket and read, "Ms. Louise Wilder."

"Wilder?" He stood there scratching the back of his neck. "You mean the others have cut out?"

"You'll tell her?"

"The empty room will tell her."

Kevin shook his head. "Some friends, huh?"

She took a long time answering the door, her hair wet from a shower. She wore cream shorts and an apricot polo shirt.

"I'm supposed to come over and tell you what you already know," he said.

"It's just so childish," she said, retreating into the room, bumping the backs of her bare legs against the extra cot.

He stood in the doorway, not knowing whether to slink away or not. "I got money – cash – if you need it," he said. "To get to wherever it is you need to go. You can pay me back whenever."

"Sonny?"

"Uh huh."

"I think there's a snake under my pillow."

Chapter 6

They speak French in Martinique which is why Adrian Cassel rented a villa there, Villa Tortuga, forgoing his usual spot in Antigua. Not that it was a vacation. He spent the early mornings into lunch working on his new screenplay. Mom and I made a point of going out shortly after a breakfast of coffee, fruit and the fresh croissants that Emile the driver brought up from town. Emile took us on local excursions to the parks, the interior, the shops, the harbor, before dropping us at the Grand Marche, the local food market, where we would pretend to haggle with the vendors over their local produce. We bought enough for a light lunch, usually fish, vegetables, a sensible dessert, and lots of fruit for that day and the next morning. Adrian was a creature of habit. We had to be back by 1:30. He'd insist on cooking the fish – like everything else about the man, he was an expert, explaining about oil, pan heat, and flesh temperature. After lunch Adrian spent about five hours on the phone. On those afternoons when Mom and I stayed at the villa, lounging on the terrace by the pool, his animated conversations drifted endlessly out the open window of the room he'd requisitioned as his study. Was that pleading "Ivan" that floated out his window Ivan Grieg, the hottest actor in Hollywood?

He had a startling bark of a laugh that took some getting used to. At 8 pm Emile took us into town to eat at one of the four or five restaurants where the Cassels were already well known, and well taken care of.

On my first day I lounged by the pool soaking up the novelty of warm weather, trying to read. Amherst with its snow-buried streets felt a world away, as did Steve. Still, I thought of him, of how selfish I'd been to demand his physical attention when he wanted to be left alone. I was still adjusting too to a mother so comfortable and assured in this expensive villa, down from her luxury co-op in New York. Her one nod to her former anti-capitalist self was to forgo the cook – which sent the Cassels into town so other chefs could cook for them instead. And on top of that there was Adrian, his celebrity, his energy, his intense focus, which sometimes fell on me.

In our car, Mom liked to sit up front with Emile. They'd chat away in French, Mom translating tidbits. "Emile says the new boutique on Rue Victor Hugo is all the rage."

Maybe the fancy boutique comment was a set up. Mom with a platinum credit card! "Let me buy you a nice dress. Something in tune with this weather." And in tune with the restaurants I had been overwhelmingly underdressed for.

"Isn't it strange to have all this money?" I said, over lunch at a restaurant more downscale than Adrian's usual choices. For some reason Mom had left him up at the villa for the day. "Your own villa. A huge apartment in Manhattan. What would they say at your old bookshop?"

"They know about it."

I waited her out.

"Honey, did I ever tell you how I met Adrian? It was at a reception at his apartment. Where we live now. Wine and chitchat. Famous people. Rich people. I had no idea that's where I'd wind up when I volunteered"

"Was that the teen mother one?"

"No. A famine relief drive in East Africa. Another one. Adrian was offering dinner for four with himself as the prize." She chuckled. "Typical Adrian – and he'd cook it, of course. Not that he was alone, other famous people were offering themselves as prizes in one way or another. TV people, sports, that kind of thing. I guess what I'm saying is you can be rich and still do good works."

I took a sip of the white wine and winced in disappointment. With Mom it was house wine. I had already become used to Adrian's discriminating choices.

"I was hypnotized, watching Adrian work the room. A light touch and then on. Another and another. Always leaving the last party with a laugh. And then he did the light touch on me."

"And he didn't move on?"

"No, he did. But he came back." She saw something in my eyes. "Yes, I know, what does the great Adrian Cassel see in me? Well, let me tell you, a woman knows a seduction act when it oozes in like a warm fog. And you know what? It probably started that way. Adrian likes a challenge. I suspect he put so much work into winning me that he thought, I may as well keep her."

"Well, that sure sounds enlightened."

"Oh bah. Men and women can be equally good as lawyers, engineers, criminals, what have you. I guess by 'good' I mean the same. But they are entirely different when it comes to romance."

I must have winced.

"Paige, Adrian backs a lot of worthwhile projects. I help with that. Yes, we have money, but that money makes more money so we can do more of these things."

"How much do you think about Dad?" I asked, reddening.

She searched for something in my face, avoiding my eyes. "Oh, I don't know. Bits and scraps are always popping up. Emotions, scenes, phrases. Things I should have done, but didn't. Said, but didn't. A panel of judges would probably conclude that I was cruel to him. Or maybe it was life and I was life's main agent. You are right to be on his side. I don't begrudge you that at all."

"There must be sides?"

Mom laughed, not quite naturally. "You're right, there shouldn't be."

"You never talk about him. Even before you met Cassel you never talked about Dad."

"There are many things about your father I feel guilty about. It's only human nature to avoid that kind of thing."

"How hard did you try to contact Dad…about me?"

"Paige, please, I'm with Adrian now."

It was a warm, near tropical, early afternoon as we sat out on a deck overlooking the boats in the harbor. Over by the pier a group of tourists were waiting to board a fishing boat. All I'd ever had was Mom. Growing up we shared a room at her friend's house in Providence. And I can't fault Mom: she attended all my school productions and sports events, showed up for the teacher conferences, took an interest in my educational progress. What was missing? If I got C's instead of A's she would come up with one of her summary closes: well you tried your best. I am her daughter; but I've never been her cause.

"You're here a month now," I said, "but next year it will be two, and pretty soon you'll be living here."

"We have work to do, Paige. But you're right it is lovely here – to the point where it doesn't quite seem fair. I guess you've heard about the ice storm you're escaping?"

I hadn't.

"I tell myself that there's always a catch." She flicked her eyes to me, testing my reaction. "Did you know that in 1902 Martinique's former capital was buried in a volcanic eruption? Two minutes and, bang, wiped off the map, along with all 30,000 inhabitants."

We moved our salads around with our forks. Grabbing the privileged life with both hands, I asked the hovering waiter for a better glass of wine. "Does it bother you that Dad was heading for you? That he probably would have made it if he didn't turn around in Iowa?"

"I've thought about it. He didn't, though, and I take comfort from the fact that he did a lot of good out in New Mexico. I don't know how much you've read about those times, but it was the cities where all the real trouble was. Chicago was out of control. Most of the Rust Belt. Boston wasn't so easy either, I can tell you. The last part of his trip would have been the most dangerous. By far. There you have it, my cop out, what I tell myself to make me feel better."

"What do you think happened to him?" My heart raced; I'd never had this kind of talk with Mom before. Usually she dodged any direct questions.

She shrugged. "The man who was single-minded enough to ride across the country, I know that man. But turning around, no. New Mexico, yes, I can see that quite clearly; it's him all over. But disappearing after that. No. Essential character never changes that much. Your father was never a quitter, or someone to do a cynical deal, like with the USG."

"There's people who say he's being held somewhere."

"No. I'd feel that. I really think I would."

"If you had to guess? What do your feelings say?"

"He seems so far away." She swallowed. "But..." She swallowed again. "There's no sadness connected to that. Distant yet positive. Are these feelings, really? Or just wishful thinking disguised as feelings? That's the question."

"You mean he's not dead?"

She twisted her mouth and started crying, softly, sort intakes of breath in sync with her twitching shoulders. "I hope not," she got out between sniffles.

I sat there playing with my wine glass while she composed herself.

"I lost your father, and now..." she couldn't continue.

"Adrian?" He was the same energetic polymath I'd seen the few times I'd stayed chez Cassel in New York. But he wasn't the same sparklingly dinner host, a weariness I put down to the exertion of creating a screenplay. And Mom, now that I thought about it, had had a heightened protectiveness of him.

"He insists on finishing his wretched screenplay before he starts on chemo. He has a conference call with his doctors." She glanced at her watch, the inexpensive one she wore when out and about. "Just about now."

On the plane back to arctic Amherst I stared out the window at the cold sun and wondered, Do I carry the Luce story within me in the same way as Adrian carries his disease? Something you must conquer within yourself, or fall to it? Something that cannot be shared – except for the pain. In Martinique I kept thinking about Steve; now that the landing gear had grinded down for Boston my thoughts were of that sunny island, and one nagging question: had Adrian's illness cut off my one candid talk with Mom, or had it enabled it in the first place?

Chapter 7

Sonny and Opal lived in an anonymous bungalow in Victorville, California, on the margins of the Mojave Desert, yet only a little over two hours from the Pacific Ocean, a sensible compromise between a solar energy tech and a marine biologist. It had been eight years since Louise had perished in a diving accident off Mazatlán in Mexico. At the time Sonny didn't care for explanations. She was gone and that was 99.9 per cent of the story. Opal, at five, was too young to disagree, and now, at thirteen, knew better than to probe at that scar.

"Dad, we need to talk." Opal said, standing in the kitchen. "I'll put some coffee on."

"Okay…"

"Remember how you told me that Mom couldn't understand why you weren't more interested in Clay Holloway?"

"I knew I shouldn't have told you that." Sometimes it seemed as if Opal had come along to take up where her mother left off.

"Well, you did. The point is I decided to make him my project, for history. The problem is the more research I do the more lost I get. It's really fascinating. A frustrating kind of fascinating. And you knew him! How amazing is that?"

"What can I do?"

"I've put together some clips. Could you watch them. Please. You knew this man; I didn't."

When the coffee was ready, he abandoned the installation specs he had been studying at the kitchen table – the five huge arrays out in the desert that he oversaw kept him busy at home as well as at work – and took his coffee to the living room.

"This guy worked with Mr. Holloway a company called Steel Umbrella," Opal said, as the talking head – older guy in a smart suit with no tie – started talking: "Back then Clay Holloway was The Man, a real corporate animal. Star sales dude, closer extraordinaire. The sky was the limit for someone like that. And then he bailed."

"And this one is Ed Harmon, dad. He's the man who recruited Mr. Holloway to his Childlift job."

"Yes, he was driven," Ed was saying. "He was a businessman who was impatient, wanted to get things done. But he had a heart. Mark that if you will. You *can* be a businessman and have a heart."

Now the video jumped to the hyper-sharp image of a modern clip. A man and a woman in their fifties, shifting awkwardly. The woman said, "He came to Mas Grande on a mission and that was to convert our sleepy commune into a capitalist oasis. Success. Success. Success. That's all that mattered to him."

There were other clips. Tony Garibaldi calling him a do-good socialist; Linda Margossian calling him blessed; then a middle-aged woman, sobbing. "No one would listen to me. No one. But he did. He came to the crèche like a savior, took me by the hand and made certain my interests were represented. He was a good man." And finally, the Reverend Holly describing him as a spiritual seeker.

"Finally, Dad, let me read you a passage from a book called *The Pathology of Success*. 'Clay Holloway was an atheist; a spiritual seeker; a socialist; a ruthless capitalist. According to others, he was a detached stranger; an empathetic carer; a talented businessman. A man intent on his mission. A lost soul. A man who passed on by; a man who stopped and helped. In the end Clay Holloway is everyman and no man.'"

Opal bunched her thin hands into small fists and grrred theatrically. "I need to do this. But what's the theme?"

"Where do I come in?"

"You *knew* him. He can't be all these things."

"Does a person have to be the same thing all the time? Maybe you're saying he's an imperfect man, you know – human. I'd hate to think of someone writing my biography. What a scary thought." He took a sip of coffee. "Is that it?"

"No, you haven't done anything yet. I need your help."

"What have you got so far?"

"That he was more than one man. The guy on the bike was only claiming to be him, and the guy in New Mexico was different from the first two. There's no common witness. That's where you come in."

"Opie, it's not – "

"I don't believe that; it's just all I've been able to think up."

"What does your teacher say?"

"Ms. Treadwell thinks her job is to help me get an A. Of course I'll get an A. That's not the point. I want to know."

"What about he's a great American?"

"Dad, that's too corny."

"But it would be going against the flow, a contrary position. That's your specialty, isn't it?"

"It's an idea." Her voice trailed away. "Now Dad?"

"Uh huh."

"You know I've been messaging with Paige?" She met his eyes, readying him. "I want to go to Washington. D.C.? She's going to be there with her class, like, on a field trip. The kids are all my age. It's all set up. There are only a few snags. One of them is something called parental consent." She came and sat on the arm of the sofa next to him

He smiled to himself. What chance did he have against one of his daughter's charm offensives?

"I'd like you to come with me. It'll be your chance to finally meet Paige. She really wants to meet you." Her eyes narrowed, just like her mother. "And when was the last time you had a vacation?"

"All set up, huh?" She *was* like her mother. You picked your battles, ceding territory to consolidate for the grand offensive – the one that never quite seemed worth the effort.

"I've booked a hotel near the dorms where the class will be staying. Twin beds so we can share a room. It won't cost that much. And I'll pay my way. And I can do some research on my history paper."

Sonny took a sip of coffee. His slow deliberate ways his one meager way of pushing back.

"I've blocked out the dates on your planner. You only have three meetings you'll have to move."

He got up, hugged his daughter. Truth was, as long as she came to him he was fine with her winning.

Chapter 8

There's a new teacher at our Junior High. Andrej Malinowski is an Americanized Ukrainian from Odessa. He is my height with corn stalk blond hair that seems charged with electricity, a nose whose bulb resembles a sack of old clothes and shoes, and the careful manner of a chess player. Those students who hit my English class after one of his math or science ones sit down with a melodramatic grown, a painful reminder of how far I've come in selling out. Half my class can barely articulate a thought, let alone string together a coherent argument. In a truer world, Andrej's temporarily, I would send my failing students to remedial classes, or hold them back, or at the very least, mess with their self-esteem by giving them the grade they deserve.

The first day of a new class: how you start is how you continue. Friendly but no nonsense. Establish authority before all else. They'll push the line, and you push them back across it. I learned this from Mr. Heller the school's star disciplinarian. I worry that my first-day-of-new-class mode carries over to non-school encounters. Not in any direct and obvious way, but something unconscious, a hint of steel in my eyes, a controlling impulse implicit in my questions. Maybe that's why I haven't had an intimate connection with a man since Steve.

Andrej has an MSc in Physics. He wants to do original work, and to do that, he says, he must work outside the "intellectual straitjacket" of the university. The poor man thinks he'll have plenty of time and energy to do physics once his day of subjugating cocky, know-it-all thirteen-year-olds is done, not to mention grading and the demands of his wife and two sons. I want to befriend him, not only because he hasn't meshed with the other staff yet, but so I can ask him about Many Worlds, Luce's scientific justification of his sexact story. I've researched the basics, but I want to hear a living breathing scientist talk about near infinite parallel universes that are exact copies of this one, except for one minor variation.

I've been sitting on Dad's notebooks for eight years. In a jumbled syllogism, I believe in Dad; Dad believes in Luce (why else turn around in Iowa); therefore, I should believe in Luce. And, when regarded from certain angles, I do. If the Devil is confusion, seductive reasoning, mental discord: bingo. Using science for specious reasoning, that too. But come on, this is the twenty-first century; we know so much we've dismissed God, and with him his archrival. Sure, there's evil in the world – you only have to read the news – but who thinks of the devil as its agent? We have arrived at a point where it's all about contested explanations and little about wonderment. To get in touch with the latter I'd love to fly out to Iowa and talk with the Reverend Holly. She died three years ago, though.

In the staff room I make a point of sitting at Andrej's table. Friendly but cool and professional is what I'm shooting for. Don't ask me how I know this, but I am the subject of gossip. Spinster is too Victorian a word, but at twenty-eight that's what I'm considered. And no wonder – they are thinking – too aloof, dismissive, demanding, impatient. I'm the type of bottled-up school marm a guy sees and thinks, I know exactly what she needs to loosen her up, which in turn attracts the guys who want to do just that, which in turn plays to my alleged aloofness and distance.

What I like most about Andrej is his open-minded, considered approach to a question. You could ask him if it's true the White House is made from sugar cubes, and he wouldn't snap back with a "ridiculous". He'd think about it, talk about the structural integrity of sugar at various levels of compactness and temperature; cite reasons why it wasn't possible – rain, foundation damp, whatever – devise a few possible tests, and then give his level-headed response.

When I'm next to Andrej I can't help but hear the sarcasm in the "mind if I join you's" and the "I'm not interrupting anything, am I's". Andrej is either oblivious or doesn't care. He's not the type to talk about the weather or school politics. Physics, though, and he can talk animatedly for hours. His passion for his subject is not his passion for me – but only I seem to know this.

You would think it would register with our tablemates, our talk, Andrej's lecture, about the preposterous quantum world of objects existing in two places, Schrodinger's cat, the potential of quantum computers. Who knows? maybe they see it as cover.

Early October. I suspect someone's had a word with Andrej. He's cooler now. That's fine. We uncross our paths, keep our eyes in other directions. That's what you do when you have something to hide, though. There's no way to win. Enter the staff room and, if Andrej is already there, where could I sit that didn't make some kind of statement? All his talk about parallel worlds made me wonder whether the real world was the one that existed in the teachers' imagination, and not this limited one with just me, and to some extent, Andrej.

I don't want to exaggerate. Our alleged affair was not the all-consuming talk of the school, just a minor undercurrent that surfaced when Andrej and I were in the same room. But then in November a fresh storm got the rumor mill turning. Marina had to go back to Odessa to be with her mother whose impending operation grew more dramatic with each telling. (A direct question to Andrej confirmed it to be a mastectomy). Every night the school turned up at Andrej's house, unfolded deck chairs on the sidewalk, and waited for my inevitable arrival, checking their watches every so often. That's what it felt like.

We met at the café across from my gym on a Saturday morning, the start of his second weekend as a single dad. The stress and frustration showed. It took him an hour of calling, he told me, to arrange for Nick and Ivan to play over at friends' houses so he could attend a "Saturday morning seminar".

"Thank you. For inviting me. I love them," he said of his children, "but it is certainly possible to have too much of a good thing." We had the inside of the café to ourselves. All the other patrons were at outside tables enjoying the unseasonably warm day.

"You look like you could use a triple something, cappuccino?" I said, getting up to make it clear I was paying for his lesson. The sun, angling in, showed his stubble.

The caffeine perked him up. I started with the cat.

"In science," he said, "we have two worlds, the very big, this world around us, and the very small, the atomic world. Each has its own set of very successful theories and equations. But the two worlds do not talk to each other very well. What Schrödinger does with his cat is connect the two worlds. He makes the life of the cat in the big world depend on a crazy quantum event in the small one. In this way the craziness is transferred up into our world to emphasize the craziness of the small world."

"That's a lot of crazies. This is the observer thing right?"

"Correct. The original theory from Copenhagen said that a particle is a cloud of probability and the act of observing it forced the cloud to become an actual particle, matter. Now, there are many interpretations."

"Including Many Worlds."

"Yes."

"And what do you think of Many Worlds?"

"Me? It is at once simpler and more mind-boggling. Can you call that an improvement? I don't know."

I prodded him for more.

"Copenhagen doesn't talk about where the other cat goes, the one not in the box. Just somewhere else."

"Cat heaven?"

"You send a live cat there? This is a fifty percent chance. Many Worlds sends it to a parallel universe."

The middle part of our talk was full of arcane phrases and concepts. Decoherence. The Quantum State of a Macroscopic Object. Preferred Basis. And my favorite, the Decomposition of the Universe. It was my one chance to get the full story, uninterrupted, observerless. Or so I hoped. I didn't understand much of it, but Andrej's seriousness sold me on the possibility of its truth.

"So, let me get this branching off idea straight," I said. "It takes an act, a conscious decision, to trigger it? I decide to go for a second coffee and the world where I have just one coffee is suddenly infinitely far away or in a new universe? What I mean is it takes an act, the act of deciding?"

"Decoherence – this is our term for your branching – is controversial. It's all controversial. It makes more sense to talk about probability. If something is probable then it will happen, the question is where. Let's say there is a small part of you that is thinking of ordering another coffee. There is a wavefunction that wraps you up, this place, me, the world and creates a new universe in which you go up to the counter. It is not so much a decision as it is a consequence of the probability curves. This is if you believe Many Worlds."

"What about the consequences of an act? You decide to drive to the lake and are involved in a crash where others are injured. Or here's an extreme example," I say, pretending to have just thought of it. "You sleep with someone. You don't have a child, but that doesn't mean it couldn't have happened. There's no entirely foolproof method of stopping that. What I'm saying is that in all these collapsing of wavefunctions a child will result somewhere, off in another world. And if this child was the result of a union in say 1712, he or she will have many generations of progeny – all off somewhere else. Is this possible?"

"If you accept the Many World theory then I would say yes, it is possible. Why are you so interested – "

"Nothing personal," I butted in. "It's just the weirdest part, that's all, beings created here, but not existing here."

"I wouldn't worry about it. You're still young." Did he mean that as a joke? His stubbly face was flushed from his ardent lecture, his summoning up of his passion, his sharing of it. He pulled up now, the way a married man should, a surfacing to the world around us, a world that expected this and denied that.

We were at the point – Andrej might call it an inflexion point – where our world could branch off in various directions. Should I share my passion with him? Dad's story and his encounter with Luce? I had been holding it inside me for so long. There were times, shopping at the supermarket, say, where I had an intense desire to approach a stranger and tell all. Why a stranger when I could tell Andrej? He had the exact right non-judgmental attitude. The right scientific background. It would be such a release to get this outside of me, this secret that was clogging up my life. I'm sure part of my reason for requesting this surreptitious meeting was to do just that. But poised right now, Andrej waiting for me, for my next question, I couldn't do it.

Instead, I said, "I read somewhere that your theory says there are millions of copies of each of us scattered around the universe."

"This is not Many Worlds, it is simply mathematics. Take a deck of cards and imagine that you are four queens and an ace. This hand will be dealt many times over the years. Ah, you say, you are much more than these five cards. This is obvious. The universe, however, is impossibly large. It is so large it allows for repeating of infinitely more complicated hands. It is merely the probability supported by huge space and the relatively small numbers of atoms in it."

"Andre, you say this so matter-of-factly. How can you be so indifferent to a world where there are millions of Andrej's buzzing around?"

"There is possibility, probability, and actuality."

"Meaning?"

"The closest Andrej is fantastically far away; there is no way of connecting to him. Ever. He may as well be character in a novel."

Chapter 9

"Man, oh man," Sonny said. "I can't believe it." I stood back with Opal, shaking my head. It had been a two-woman effort to drag him here. "It's his, all right. One yellow, one silver bottle holder, same banged up fork. I spent three weeks following this bike."

"See, Paige was right, about coming here," Opal said, even though she had been the prime instigator, all part of her Clay Holloway project.

"It's all shined up," Sonny said, still staring at the bike, "unlike its rider."

There were twenty-seven eighth-graders, three teachers and three parent chaperones in our Junior High's pilgrimage to the nation's capital. It was a full-time job keeping the kids in line, focused, disciplined and off their phones, as we ran from this monument to that museum, our schedule so wildly optimistic it acted more like a teaser for a fuller visit than any kind of learning experience. Opal, staying at a nearby hotel with her father, was also my responsibility.

The trouble began on day two. Our jostling, cocky band of students had one problem kid, Briony, whose parents were in the middle of a bitter divorce. When Opal was starting to get along a little too well with the class leader, Jake, one of Briony's friends called her a slut. Then Briony said, "What do you expect from someone who sleeps with her father?"

I didn't see, but certainly heard, the resulting slap. Almost immediately Opal turned herself in to me.

"I know I shouldn't have done that, but I had to. Anyway, I'll just spend the rest of my time here with my Dad." She was a thin, short girl with red strands in her auburn hair, a sharp nose and sharper eyes that could drill you, bringing on a self-aware smile. Her eyes dug into mine for a microsecond then found the floor.

"Now, I'm sure we can patch things up," one of the parent chaperones said. "I know your feelings were hurt, but – "

"I don't care about me," Opal said. "But nobody says things like that about my Dad. If she says one more thing, anything bad about him, I will skin her alive."

All the slap did was bring Opal closer to Jake, who intervened on her behalf then wrapped her in his protective cloak. Jake was almost too good to be true, top of his class in all subjects, including my English one, good at sports, got along with all cliques in his friendly yet distanced way. On the bus the two sat together, talking non-stop, Jake always on the outside. On the last day they disappeared, arriving back to the cafeteria for dinner with an excuse just about plausible enough for Jake, as class valedictorian, to be let off with a shrug.

"It looks like you've succeeded where so many girls have failed," I said to Opal.

"Jake just wants to get to my Dad. He's crazy about solar power. He's angling for an internship this summer."

"Jeez, g-bars," Sonny had said, when we had first arrived at the Smithsonian. A pyramid of them took up one third of a glass box in the first display case on the Great Recovery. "Does that ever bring back memories. I must of ate a hundred of those suckers if I ate one." Opal and I had talked Sonny into spending part of our last day here. The rest of the school were on the long bus ride back to Rhode Island.

Food coupons; a government-issue heater; diaries; loops of interviews with a cross section of the country. Triumph over adversity was the theme. How the citizens pulled together, and shared for the common good. Plenty of talking heads: doctors on the challenges of running a hospital; social workers on tending to the infirm, bedridden and troubled; men talking about their escort duty on the great truck convoys, of what an honor it was to keep a great nation fed.

High up on top of a middle display case stood that blue bike. It was almost comical how Sonny stared at it, left for other displays, only to come back to it. Again and again. The previous day he had gaped at the Wright Brothers plane and the Spirit of St. Louis suspended from the ceiling at the Air and Space Museum. Now this.

"Why are there only men in that line?" Opal wanted to know as she stood in front of the display case covering the rise of the Condo. Receipt stubs, the unit of trade in San Francisco, had been tossed like confetti throughout the case that contained pictures of citizens engaged in commerce

The San Francisco Condo Depository issued receipts like the ones shown for items of value that could be redeemed at will, the label said. *The receipts became a unit of trade giving us the Condo.*

"I think it's because it's the gay district," I said.

A banner hanging above the display read: Seck + Condo = True Dollar. Under that, in smaller letters: trust + value = our Future. The story, as presented, was that the Seck and the Condo generated spontaneously out of the rich soil of the nation, growing tall and great so that their branches intertwined, an organic process, natural, inevitable.

On the wall behind the display case hung a large photograph of the SF Mint, sitting up on its rocky pedestal. During the Void it had become the self-styled San Francisco Condo Depository. A line of parked cars with sagging tires climbed the rise in front of it.

"What is it?" Opal asked – I think I must have gasped.

"See that car right there, that's a '57 Chevy." I'd done my research. And it was the same aquamarine with white roof and tail trim as described in the notebooks.

"What does that mean?"

"Oh… It's just a car I heard about a long time ago."

"Cars didn't move around back then, did they?"

"That's right. My father came across this one in Iowa. Moving." I shuddered. "It's spooky."

"Do you know whose car it is, or something?"

"I have a name. A first name." The world was rotating, wheeling. Any second the walls would lift like theater scenery and I'd be standing on a bare stage. Luce, real?

"I bet Dad's still gazing at that bike. I'll just go get him."

I went with her. Sonny was standing in a large group encircling a guide who was just wrapping up on the New Mexico section. She motioned for a security guard to join them. "I happen to have in my hand one of the first Seck coins. But don't run off with it, or I'll be in big trouble."

"How much is it worth?" an Asian lady asked.

"I've heard about ten thousand True D's," the guide said. She was a roly-poly middle aged lady with chipmunk-like cheek pouches and a prairie dog way of holding her head up, as if searching for stragglers or new recruits. Her name tag said Anita.

"But that's only paper money," a man joked.

We followed the tour to the San Francisco section. Anita briefly outlined the rise of the Condo, and handed around receipts that had been issued for goods on deposit.

"Is it true that the Condo started out based on condoms?" a man asked.

"Yes, we believe that is the case, although soon other items of value were accepted."

"How can something that is being *used* all the time work like that? What if the currency was based on potato chips?" He asked, his laugh a high-pitched tremolo.

"As I said, that's probably why the Condo moved on to other items. And remember we're talking about the receipts and not the items themselves."

I cornered Anita as the tour was winding up. "I don't understand the San Francisco part," I started. "I've read Mr. Holloway's book. Who is this mystery man, Sottovoce? How did they connect? How did they figure out they could merge the two currencies?"

Anita's eyes sharpened on me, as if sizing up an adversary. "Here's our challenge: how do you cover an event where the two principals…well, one has disappeared, and the other is impossible." A married couple lingered behind with me. On my question the woman nestled up against her husband. "The man Mr. Holloway calls Sottovoce *is* impossible. To do all he did, all Mr. Holloway alleges he did, there's no way he wouldn't be known out in San Fran. And the level of communication required between Sottovoce and Holloway… with the emergency phone lines available, well this Sottovoce would be well known at the USG phone exchanges. We've checked that: nothing." Anita frowned. "And yet, it had to have happened. Mr. Holloway's side stacks up as he described it. Clearly, he must have been involved in the merger of the currencies. So it is impossible that there was *no* Sottovoce."

"So it's better to ignore it and not point it out as a mystery?" Sonny asked.

Anita swept her hand around the museum. "We'd need a whole other room to go into it in the depth such a mystery deserves."

"And we already have the Holloway mystery. Where he disappeared to?" said the husband.

"Yes, you're probably right," Anita said. "One mystery is enough to be getting on with."

"But you didn't talk about Mr. Holloway," Opal said. "About all you did was put his book on top of a pile of other books."

"Well, I'll be sure to make your opinions known to the museum curators. I don't personally have a say in any of this."

We headed over to the Vietnam Memorial, a short walk away. Sonny's great uncle on Donnelle's side had his name on the wall. One of 58,000. It was a brisk spring day, a trifle too cool for shirtsleeves. I let them go on ahead, and watched. Father and daughter seemed so natural and comfortable together as they bent down, searching at the lower part of a section of an endless array of sections. Here was a daughter who had a father all to herself. Yes, she'd paid and paid dearly, but that shouldn't matter in the world of emotions. I should have been jealous. But I wasn't.

Everything in D.C. is so drenched in the bright light of communal dreams, American dreamlight. It felt as if we were walking around a scene stamped on a coin. We sat on the grass just short of Lincoln. Opal stood a little way off talking on her phone. To Jake.

"I'd kind of forgotten about that bike ride," Sonny said. "What I mean is the real stuff like g-bars and Secks and the whole thing really."

"And the people," I said, "like Nora and Beatrice."

"Yeah, I'd forgotten about them too." he said, but left it there.

I didn't answer. Come on Sonny, react. Engage.

"That's what was in his parcel. Diaries, right." He was looking off toward Lincoln.

I told him everything. Not just the facts but also me, my doubts and fears. My anger with the fates for keeping me away from my father. My gnawing feelings of incompleteness, a shadow person in a shadow world.

He took my story with such blank disregard I might have been telling it to the salt flats.

"I believe in my father, so I have to believe his notebooks. Sonny, you knew him; I didn't. He doesn't seem the kind to make stuff up. And you've heard from Anita so you understand how the fact of Luce answers most of the San Francisco mysteries. It all points to the truth. When I first read about Luce I thought, too much sun. He's gone temporarily delirious. And, yes, that could explain Dad's 180 in Iowa. It doesn't explain the Luce-as-Sottovoce part. That's much later."

"Okay, so it's true."

"And that doesn't astonish you?"

"Don't know that it does. If what you say is right, that most scientists believe there are millions of copies of you and me out there, I reckon we could sneak the devil in and hardly notice it."

He seemed so unfazed. That unblinking desert acceptance. Opal, off the phone, caught my eye and came over.

We walked to our last sight-seeing stop. The White House. See if our heads fit between the fence rails. Opal's phone rang and she fell back a bit. "Don't worry, he'll be okay with it," I heard her say. She fell further behind, her voice softening.

"You're just mad you didn't get to meet your Pa," Sonny said. "Everything else is mental..." His right hand barrel-rolled into insignificance.

"That would make sense except for one thing. Dad bought the story. It's what turned him away from me." Turned him away from Me so he could meet another me? Is there any better sign of the devil's work? "What do you think about Luce? Really, truly. Tell me."

"He gets in the way of everything, doesn't he? Messes it up. Sounds like the devil to me."

"There's the country?"

"Guess I was talking about you personally. If I understand your story right, the country thing was in his own interest. You know, not out of any sense of doing good."

I looked out to Lincoln, inert in his memorial a few hundred yards away. A flash from a conversation with Andrej came to me. Could the universe really be full of other Lincolns. Lincolns as plentiful as pennies? Pennies scattered like stars in the heavens.

"Mr. H said something once," Sonny said. "At the heart of any system is an essential wildness, is what he said. I see that in the turbulence off wind turbine blades. Deep down, it's all wild."

We said our goodbyes at their hotel. The shuttle to the airport was idling outside. Sonny gave me a sideways hug, patted my back twice to some internal rhythm. He picked up their bags and headed to the van in that loping walk of his. Opal hung back a moment. "Come out and visit. Promise?"

I nodded, one of those things you mean at the time.

At a café near Union Station I scrawled down ideas, impressions, theories and suspicions in my notebook. I had an hour before taking the train to New York to visit Mom, five years a widow. I felt drained of all bitterness and regret. In my notes, thinking while writing, I decided that there is another truer world that's somehow folded in this one. A world of emotional truths, not logical ones. In this other world the sole reason the Void happened was to keep Dad away from me. And the reason that he didn't make it to Boston is that I didn't summon him with all my will. And the reason I don't have a boyfriend is that I'm married to Steve. And the reason I'm so calm is that for some ineffable reason Sonny is my true confessor. And the reason I'm not jealous of Opal is that there is something pure and generous that blocks that. And to condense all these words into one line: all these previous pages are my story and no else's.

As I said, the world of feelings.

The train crept north like confederate pickets probing for the Union army. "We can get to the moon all right," an ageing businessman at my table of four griped, "but practically a century later is it too much to get to New York in under four hours?" Our foursome plus the foursome at the table across the aisle became our stage set.

"They still handing out those things," a young guy said, grinning at the business cards the businessman was shuffling through. Then he returned to his wiring diagram. Tech guy.

A man across the aisle said, "My all-phone says it's a suicide, up the line by Chester."

The younger man next to him, said, not taking his eyes off his large screen all-phone, "I can see the stopped train. Don't see any signs of an emergency."

"Is your sat view in real time?" Tech guy said, glancing up from his spec.

"You're hoping for some carnage. It's sick," Mr. Sat View's girlfriend said.

"Sure is," Sat View said, ignoring her. "No ambulances, no paramedics. Front of the train is clear as I look down on it."

"Well if it is a suicide I can't imagine being so selfish, holding up so many people," said a woman diagonally across from me in a smart lavender suit.

"First one of us to die can look him up and give him what for," the businessman said. "All this satellite view stuff is a grand diversion. You can see the three cups in real time, still you have no idea which one the ball is under."

"I like that; it's almost profound." The man sitting next to me wore a sharp blue suit and a salmon tie. He put his folder to one side and cast a glance at my book. *The Coin Age.* "If you are into disasters," he said to me, his sharp eyes flicking to my book, then softening as an assured smile spread over his tan face, "perhaps I can buy you a drink in the bar car?" His smile ended in faux humility.

"Don't do it lady."

"You won't get within a hundred feet of that bar now."

"Hey the train is moving. The one up in Chester is moving."

"Disaster?" I said, shaking my head and frowning at Mr. Smooth next to me. I held up my book as if selling laundry detergent. "This right here is the greatest success story in American history."

Also by Jeffrey M. Anderson

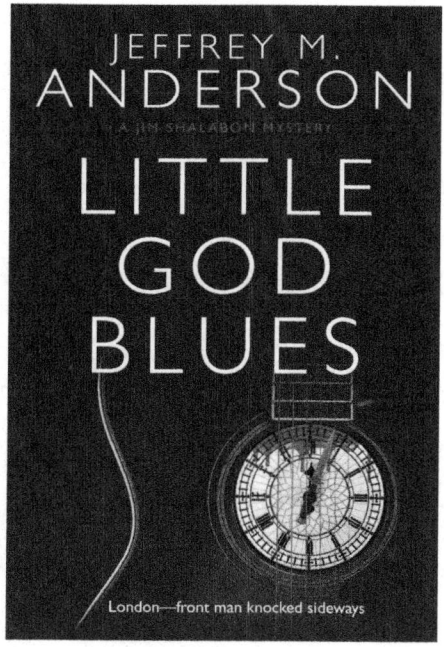

LITTLE GOD BLUES

In this first installment of the Jim Shalabon series Jim travels to London to visit the alley where his best friend and former bandmate fell dead of an overdose. Several aspects of that death don't add up and reluctantly Jim puts down his guitar to take up an amateur sleuthing gig. With a style and technique he makes up as he goes along, he works his way deep into the mystery, holding his own against dismissive London cops and society lights with secrets to hide. In solving his case he learns more than he ever expected about his dead friend, and himself—and inherits the case of the missing Englishwoman, the subject of Black Widow Blues.

For updated information please refer to
www.jeffreymanderson.com

¶ IKEN press
www.ikenpress.com

Also by Jeffrey M. Anderson

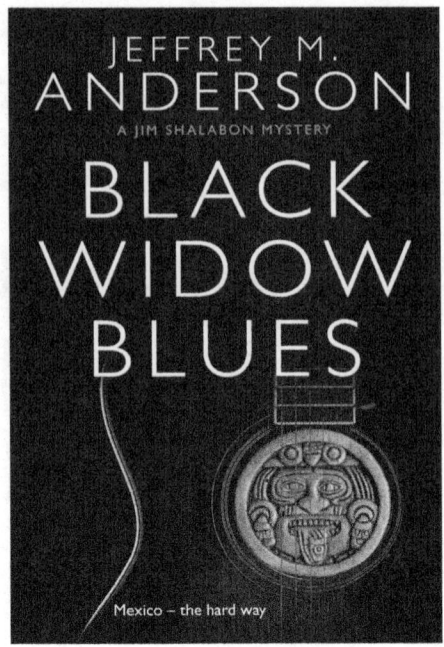

BLACK WIDOW BLUES

In this sequel Jim Shalabon travels to Mexico in search of Claudia Steyning, the one part of his London case still unresolved at the end of Little God Blues. The clues from Mexico City, where Claudia was last seen, are dire: a corpse, cocaine and dark hints of drug enforcers with guns. Jim attempts to probe the edges of the treacherous swamp that is Narcoland. But Mexico with its passions, corruption and violence scoffs at such a careful approach, and soon the threads of the case threaten to drag him out into the black water.

For updated information please refer to
www.jeffreymanderson.com

¶ IKEN press
www.ikenpress.com

Also by Jeffrey M. Anderson

LOS SUEÑOS BLUES (coming soon)

In this third installment of the Shalabon series Jim is living in Los Angeles. No sooner does he move there with his Greek girlfriend than he is visited by one of Hollywood's most alluring actresses—who is murdered three days later. Her visit leaves enough unanswered questions to entangle Jim in a murder investigation, one that sends him back to an enigmatic disappearance from fifteen years earlier.

For updated information please refer to
www.jeffreymanderson.com

¶ IKEN press
www.ikenpress.com

Printed in Dunstable, United Kingdom